NEVER GET OFF THE TRAIN

VINCE CRAIG

Never Get Off The Train

Copyright © 2024, Vince Craig.

First published 2024.

Published by Harvest Publishing for Larkspur Press
Melbourne, Victoria, Australia.
Email: harvestpublishing@houseofjt.com.au.
Phone: + 61 3 9079 6955
Publisher URL: https://harvestpublishing.com.au

Layout and Typesetting: The Good Black Sheep

Never Get Off The Train By Vince Craig
Printed Edition Paperback ISBN 978-0-6454431-3-4
Digital Edition ISBN 978-0-6454431-4-1

Tales from the War in Ukraine
Parts One & Two

'Slava Ukraini, heroiam Slava!!'

'Glory to Ukraine, Glory to the Heroes!!

'Let me not then die ingloriously and without a struggle but let me first do some great thing that shall be told among men hereafter.'

Homer, The Iliad

This book is dedicated to all the brave volunteers who have travelled to Ukraine, since the war's inception, from wherever their home may be, with valiant hearts and a dogged resolve to take up the good fight against an evil that is absolute and unrelenting.

Foreword

This novel is a semi-fictional account of the war in Ukraine, during the early months of the conflict in March, April, June, July, and August 2022. In all honesty, ninety-nine percent of the people and events that are depicted *are* based on real encounters! Although it may sound fantastic, the stories surrounding these occurrences *did* happen! The attitudes of many of the Ukrainians *are* genuine, as I witnessed! The descriptions of the craziness and abstract behaviour of some of the principal foreign and Ukrainian characters *is* authentic! The utilisation of any form of literary license resided in the creative need to thread the 'reality' of all my experiences into an engaging, yet faithful storyline. The names and some of the places have been altered to protect many of the Ukrainians and foreign volunteers still fighting for the Ukrainian homeland as well as for OPSEC (operational security) reasons. It is also for the protection of the gallant volunteers who returned home.

The sole intention of this book is to illustrate untold aspects of the fight against Russian tyranny through the eyes of a volunteer who travelled from distant Australia to a country at war, thousands of kilometres away in Europe. I have endeavored to truthfully describe the people I came into contact with, the opinions I discovered and

a remarkable side of the war that certainly wasn't being articulated in the mainstream media narrative. For this, I make no apologies for any outlandish comments or positive or negative scenarios that have been vividly presented as this was *my* Ukrainian war experience – *warts and all!* No doubt, discerning and thoughtful academics will eventually compose lengthy treatises on the *Russo-Ukrainian War,* but I hope this novel will also assist with the construction of a complete and therefore, 'total history' of the bloody clash between Russia and Ukraine and, if nothing else, provide the reader with a uniquely informative and compelling insight into such a bloody and senseless conflict!

Vince Craig

Acknowledgments

Firstly, I would like to thank my beloved Elizabeth for her critical input and unflinching support, not only on this work but in my first novel, *Truth be Told.*

In addition, I wish to acknowledge two other 'strong women' in my life, who are no longer with me, my mother Dulcie, and Vivien, my wife of thirty years. I am certain they would be immensely proud of my writing as they, over many decades, guided and championed me to this destination in my life. Words fail to express my admiration and appreciation!

Finally, a great deal of thanks must go to my publishers. A special mention belongs to Jenani and Samy Therone of *Harvest Publishing* who have dedicated themselves to unearthing stories from the nation's many veterans, which adds a significant, yet vital, narrative to the Australian literary landscape. They have been here, beside me, from the outset, with encouragement and advice, offering many critical insights into the 'writing process,' which has kept me on the 'true path' to creativity and self-discovery. Thank you!

The Author

Vince Craig is a pseudonym. He is a former *Special Forces* soldier who spent over 15 years with the Australian Army and has worked with the American *Green Beret* and *Rangers*, *U.S. Navy Seals* and British *SAS*. Besides his two stints in Ukraine, Vince spent time in Iraq as a *Private Military Contractor*. Along with the military, Vince has over 20 years volunteer experience with numerous emergency services groups and has acted as a mentor on programs attempting to help 'at risk' children.

Vince is also a former academic who has instructed students at college and university level and now enjoys music and fitness training in his retirement and currently resides in rural Victoria.

Part One

THE LONG, LONG JOURNEY...

'It is in the darkest of times that honour and courage and service shine brightly. So let us make this pledge together, you and I... that we shall always hold true to our ways, our laws, and our traditions. Then centuries yet unborn will look back on us and see, not our darkest times, but our most glorious.'

Dave Duncan

Chapter One:

WELL...THIS IS A FINE MESS

'Today is the day I'm gonna die,' thought Nathan Philips. He hadn't been 'roughed up', physically restrained, or coerced to remain motionless, but the two burly and imposing Ukrainians who stood, menacingly over him in the dappled, half-lit space, made it clear he had *zero room to manoeuvre...*

Never a man to quit, but this time, he thought, with sad resignation, *'This must be the end...'.* The wooden and stained slatted bench that he lay upon was heated to a cruel intensity that made it painfully uncomfortable and intolerable for him to lie face down, and he wriggled, twitched, and fidgeted in a vain hope to solicit some comfort; a smidgen of joyful respite from the unbearable agony. The taller and stockier of the two men slowly advanced toward Nathan purposefully with what looked like a large bushy stick in his bulky right hand - *which resembled the size of a small melon*, and he flung the obscure, floral object into a bucket of foul-smelling liquid for a few seconds. He then proceeded to flick the pungent fluid, repeatedly and nastily at Nathan's muscular frame, then came a repetition of aggressive slapping to the body with the bushy object. The sensation was like nothing he had ever experienced, and he assumed this is what the *cat o nine tails* had to feel like!! It felt like small barbs of fire or microscopic demons danced joyfully upon his sweating back with every malicious, prejudicial strike! The tall man, aggressively dispensing the punishment then decided to traverse the entire length of Nathan's naked form, including the balls and arches of his bare feet, *which was particularly excruciating...* As tough and supremely fit as Nathan was for a man in his early fifties, it was impossible for him not to emit small pitiful yelps, like some whimpering defenceless puppy. The treatment was viciously cruel and unrelenting. At times, his lonesome cries were much louder and agonisingly intense... *Argh*! *Owww*! *Fuuuck...* such was the anguish and torment! This was nothing like the intense resistance to interrogation training he had endured in the *Special Air Service*, as part of selection... nothing like it at all!! It was *much, much worse...*

The second man slinked forward, calmly, creepily, and quietly out of the darkness of the small space and hurled a large steel bucket of icy water over Nathan and the bench, which was still dripping profusely from sweat and the previous drenching. The piercing cold made Nathan gasp and his body *recoiled and wrenched in spasm*...more than once. The concept surrounding this punishment was simple but callously effective. Repeat the cooling process every so often, thus building in the mind of the subject the anticipation and fear for the escalation of further heat, whipping, drenching and prolonged abuse... For the men inflicting the misery, it was genius! *Pure maniacal genius!*

The larger thickly set man then doused the bushy stick and re-commenced the vigorous spanking of Nathan's lean and muscular torso. Nathan's acute cries of anguish became more *frequent*, *louder*, and *extreme*... The 'whipping man' was fiendishly methodical and worked his way up and down Nathan's tortured body; the soft flesh of his vulnerable buttocks receiving special attention...

More screaming followed...

Nathan was ordered to turn onto his back, and after another thorough dousing of iced water, the flagellating process started all over again. He wasn't sure how long he could endure this treatment or what other punishment his tormentors had in mind, but he was just praying, *begging for it to end!* When it felt like the unrelenting torture and strain had lasted an *eon*, and he could endure no more, the second Ukrainian leisurely bent down and leant within a millimetre of Nathan's ear. He breathed heavily but whispered slowly in a thick, deep, Slavic accent 'Okay Nathan, this will do... I have something else, *something even more special for you...*' A long, five second pause followed... 'God almighty, what else can they do to me!' thought Nathan, innately terrified at the prospect of *more* distress... *more* torture! Then, in a bright and upbeat voice - *the man had suddenly dispensed with the sinister tone* - he coolly and chirpily announced: *'Time for a shower and to drink some cold, frothy beer and to eat some salty snacks!'*

This was the 'sweet', glorious reprieve that Nathan had been so desperate to hear, from the moment he ventured into the large, wooden steam bath. Sure, he was accustomed to sauna and loved the cleansing, refreshing ritual, but Ukrainian *Banya* isn't for the faint-hearted and to some, it must closely resemble the torture regime at *Abu Ghraib*, the infamous Iraqi prison!! For Nathan, the searing heat was hotter than he could withstand, and he felt as though his eyes were literally melting... at most other times, *he could hardly get his breath*! He imagined he was dissolving, like the 'Wicked Witch of the West' in the magical *Wizard of Oz,* or the sinister Nazis in the concluding scenes in *Raiders of the Lost Ark*.... when the *Ark of the Covenant* imposed its supernatural authority and pitilessly obliterated the 'bad guys'. But now, it was time for respite, and all the sweating men walked sluggishly out into the *ante* room, where cold showers were waiting for them. Within seconds, loud and boisterous gasps from the men could be heard outside as the cascading icy water drenched and showered their sweaty, naked bodies. It was at this precise moment Nathan wearily reflected... *'sheesh, what a man has to do to win the trust of these guys!'*

The men quickly dried themselves and donned clean, fluffy white robes or threw a large towel around their frames and walked gingerly out into the plain, but sunlit, waiting room. Large bags of salty chips and plastic litre bottles of Ukrainian lager adorned the top of a scarred wooden table that had seen better days. The tough Ukrainian men started pouring icy cold, frothy beer into sizeable clear plastic cups and began 'educating' Nathan about the 'joy' of *Banya*, an ancient and fundamental tradition of their culture. As Denis, the 'ice bucket man,' confessed to Nathan, with a touch of smug, nationalistic pride, 'We only gave you 20% *Banya*, but *I* have experienced *Banya* where peasants, workers, old people and even priests, grunt loud, deep, and often to exorcise their pain and to remain in the sauna'. He began to speak louder and infinitely prouder... 'It is important for Ukrainian men to show their strength and endurance... *like the mighty Zaporizhian Cossacks!*'

At times, the experience had been quite pleasurable and invigorating, with Nathan joking like some pasty English grammar schoolboy to the Ukrainians, 'Please Sir, may I have another' as they struck his supple body with the robust bush made of fresh oak leaves. Nathan had only been 'in-country' for a short time but already knew how 'hard' and fiercely determined the Ukrainians were. They weren't *easy* beats...they never *have* been he mused. 'Heaven help the Russians - *these boys are as tough as Krupp steel!*' While the men continued laughing and chatting in their native tongue, always loudly and gregariously, with other roguish friends who had been waiting for them, Nathan embraced a few long, satisfying gulps of the refreshing beer. His thoughts meandered to the start of this magnificent and bizarre adventure... almost three months ago and it had all begun with what seemed an innocent phone call....

He took another deep swallow and amid his enjoyment of the cold alcohol, his mind flashed back to the present, and he promised himself he would *'never go full Banya'*...ever again!

Chapter Two:

A FRIEND IN NEED...

It was early afternoon at Nathan's cosy and warm cabin on the bush block, just after midday lunch in fact, when his mobile phone rang. Unaccustomed to receiving many phone calls, he was somewhat startled, but let the ringtone of *You'll Never walk Alone* play to its conclusion, as he always did. He made it a point *never* to respond to annoying, unsolicited messages. Eternally busy, Nathan was *always* engrossed in whatever he had a passion for. This time it was re-stringing one of his favourite guitars – the *Fender Telecaster*, with lighter gauge strings. Six months and two seasons had passed since the matter with the *Agency*... The business with 'Madison Baker,' the 'Carlton Crew,' and the 'Creswick Drug Runners' had violently and suddenly concluded. Outside of some obligatory sniffing by Federal detectives, the file had been officially closed. A major drug deal and government agency investigation had collided; gone horribly wrong and resulted in mayhem and multiple homicides. Well, that was the 'official' version! For Nathan, there were no regrets – *his conscience was clear.* Lives had been taken but this violence had been conducted in the *Benthamite* philosophy of what was necessary for the 'greater good'. A young girl now knew the facts about her father, evil people had been dispensed with and the 'truth' was in the public domain. But *that was another story...*

Now, it was early autumn, and the bush block was looking resplendent with the late blossoming of native flora - It had been a miserably damp and wet summer. *'Damn you La Nina,'* Nathan would frequently cuss as he cherished Australia's long, hot summers and fondly remember how his beautiful mother would ferry him and his two siblings to the beach or to the local swimming baths on the very hot days. He paused to briefly reminisce with a tinge of melancholy, '...how the years had gone by, *so quickly...*' and he recollected how someone, a long time back, told him that 'Grief is the price of love...' But this legendary, soft felt saying didn't do much to comfort him of his lost loves, or shield his sensitive psyche from the frequent, jabbing bouts of depression.

But today *was a good day* for a change, as he surveyed his acreage from the cabin's windows. If nothing else, the sporadic wet weather had yielded a glistening and enduring sheen upon the isolated property. Golden wattles, which dotted the usually rugged bush landscape, exploded with a brilliance of gilded colour here and there. Vibrantly plumed parakeets, corellas and galahs danced, somewhat cheekily, amongst the various native trees, bushes, and ground covers... at times providing a mighty cacophony of intense screeching but still a familiar and unique Australian chorus. 'Life' out on the block was pleasant and simple, but honest, and there were always plenty of chores and improvements to do. Sometimes Nathan would say, in his usual deprecating manner, that it felt like *'he was polishing a turd'*, but he was content with his uncomplicated, affordable surroundings, and his peaceful lifestyle. Anyway, the block acted as therapy; keeping him industrious and occupied... mostly from 'things' he didn't need to, care to, or shouldn't, think about...

Amid his musings, Nathan had just fed "Moochee", his beloved but aging 'moggie'. He had been happily snacking on a double chocolate muffin, with a flat white coffee in an old black British Army field cup steamed on his dining table close to hand. His brow was furrowed, and he looked bemused and slightly irate at his mobile phone for a few seconds; as if in a mini trance. He was trying to figure out who owned the 'damned' telephone number. Nathan maintained the pause while his mind ticked over... *the phone continued to ring...* He vaguely recognized the digits, and then the significance of the simple combination of numbers came to him. It read like a lost relic, *from long, long ago...* Finally, he answered the phone with a curious, questioning but simple tone of 'hello...?' A woman's voice blurted out, very friendly and loudly, 'Hi Nathan, its

Kathy, how are you?', followed rapidly by a quieter, more beseeching plea of '*I desperately need your help...*' Well, this was a blast from the past...an old girlfriend ringing him up! Kathy was once his sweetheart, he thought the 'love of his life', from his early army days. But he hadn't seen or heard from her or her husband, Steve 'Dutchy' Holland, for five or six years now...

It really goes without saying that life is just a constant procession of encounters, both good and bad, long, and short, and this relationship from the past was no different. The Christmas cards from these once close friends had been regular.... until they became irregular. Kathy and Nathan had dated when he was a strapping young soldier in the battalion in Townsville, North Queensland. Steve had been his best mate and, to others, a lovable rogue. There had been some 'fire' between Nathan and his beauty, Kathy. She had quickly fallen for his rugged, 'Stathamesque' looks, but when the fire extinguished and they split as a couple, it was Nathan who had introduced her to Steve and *their* love blossomed. They married and had some kids; the eldest boy being named after their dear friend, but everyone called him Nate, just as a point of difference. Nathan had followed his 'calling' to *Special Forces* but stayed in touch. Years later, the men would work together as 'Private Military Contractors' (PMCs) in Iraq as Australian Embassy Security in Kabul, and after that, as private security detail in Victoria. Both men shared similar interests, such as sport and fitness training, and a love of rock music and playing guitar. They would frequently busk together in the damp and graffiti coated laneways of Melbourne, and both were accomplished musicians. Sadly, for whatever reason, they had lost touch. For Nathan, those fun filled, carefree times now seemed like a world away...

'Hey Kathy...' Nathan continued, and shot gunning a multi-response reply, asked 'How are you, what's up, and what can I do for you?' Kathy's soft, sparkling opening tone quickly changed to a serious and worried pitch. In haste, she described how things hadn't been that great in her relationship with Steve for some time, years in fact. To say their marriage was 'strained' was an understatement. Nathan spotted the quivering quality in her voice, and could sense it was awkward and painful for her to articulate her sadness... but she bravely went on... Steve had grown continuously restless since leaving the army and finishing his private security stints. Semi-retirement, the middle-age blues, and post-traumatic stress issues had waged war on Steve's self-worth, and he would often fly into bouts of anger, depression, and 'hard drinking.' His physicality was not like it was as a young man; something he struggled to come to grips with. Her husband had reluctantly visited plenty of 'know it all psychiatrists' as he called them. He had performed the usual run-around with 'DVA' (Department of Veterans Affairs), but the jumping through bureaucratic hoops had deteriorated his state-of-mind. It had not come as a surprise to any Australian veteran when the Federal government announced a Royal Commission into the DVA and Veteran Suicide. Like the ongoing veteran suicides in America (around twenty-two deaths a day!), many Australian veterans had been committing suicide at an alarming rate - courageous soldiers don't make remarkable 'paper shufflers' or 'cleaners' and require positive outlets for their unique talents. For the most part, they don't need to fight a war with DVA and battle unnecessary paperwork either! Someday the government and community will come to realise this, but at what cost? Or, as Nathan constantly pondered, was it closer to the truth that politicians, bureaucrats, and dare he thought, most of the public, don't really care?

'Hell, they've got 'Anzac Day' to strut around like heroes, what else do they want?!'

When Kathy imagined that things couldn't get any worse, the horrific news broke - announcing a Russian military invasion of Ukraine! Steve had been glued to the television news and was captivated by the rapid incursion, especially the atrocities that were committed at Bucha, just on the northwestern outskirts of Kyiv, the capital. Initially, Steve felt obliged but then became compelled, in fact possessed, to do something to assist the Ukrainians defend their country from their Soviet aggressors. He believed, like so many other former military people around the world, that the war was like a 'calling', some kind of righteous crusade... As Nathan would later find out, when he spoke to a plethora of Westerners in Ukraine, many men and women felt it was a 'time to step up,' in much the same way volunteers across the globe had responded to Franco's Spanish Fascists in the 1936 civil war. As Steve would angrily bark at Kathy, 'A man's got a skill set that's worth two cents in this country, *but I am sure it is priceless in Ukraine!* It's all well and good sending these people *Bushmaster* vehicles, bombs, and rockets *but what they need is expertise!* Blind Freddy can see *they don't know what they're doing!'*. Fired up with rage, Steve began ringing the Ukrainian Embassy in Canberra incessantly to offer help, as well as scanning government forums and other pro-Ukraine websites online. He quickly tapped into an Australian social media site that offered advice from former military members who were making the hazardous trek to Eastern Europe. So, armed with a 'sliver of information' and a 'barrow full' of intent, Steve made the startling announcement that he was heading to Ukraine to join the newly formed *International Legion of Territorial Defence.*

The mentioning of this new unit had Nathan intrigued... He had heard some extreme and bizarre things about this new international formation. Essentially, it sounded like a band of 'rag tag' glory guys gagging at the bit to fight the Russians. The news services were filled of images of young *and* old men, British, American, and European, all eager to get at the Russian military. This bold initiative was a stroke of political genius by President Zelensky to involve ex-military from the world's nations to support Ukraine and, by association, involve the host nations of these men. It certainly would give Putin something to think about... As far as it went militarily, the plan wasn't conducive to creating an effective and competent fighting force; too many competing elements - fitness issues, different age groups, a plethora of diverse languages and varied military experience and training regimes. Apparently, there were some professional and committed soldiers within this outfit, but also a lot of military 'wannabes' or unfit, aging veterans - you know the type - really unfit guys who had been living a cushy life for the last twenty years, and now trying to test their manhood on the greatest and most dangerous stage of all! Nathan stopped and thought of the absurdity of the situation... *'Damn, what were these guys thinking...? Duh, time for a major reality check!'* This was no limited 'bush' war in Africa, or counter-insurgency war in the Middle East being sniped at by sweaty insurgents from some rocky outcrop; but a 'full-on,' 'knock down,' 'winner takes all' conflict with tank battles, artillery duels and aerial dogfights across European boundaries!

To make matters worse, it was rumored that command and control in the 'new' foreign *Legion* had been extremely slack. Nathan had heard reputable stories that stipulated that if anyone changed their inclination to fight with this international force, largely because they were 'tourist warriors,' they would have their passports confiscated and threatened with execution. Another popular narrative circulating was about soldiers being sent to the 'front' to fight with one AK 74 rifle magazine with only ten rounds of 5.45mm ammunition!! Not surprisingly, the world media was quick to pick up on these horror stories, and variants of the same vile theme. One American ex-marine declared he had seen more combat in two weeks in Ukraine than during a twelve-month deployment in Afghanistan, and was quitting, shell-shocked! Former Legionnaires had vented their frustration and resentment of their volunteer service on *YouTube*, denoting the whole experience 'as a fucking trap', and warning others not to enlist! Forever the historian and romantic, a vision suddenly appeared in Nathan's mind's eye... of swarthy, *Kepi Blanc* wearing French Foreign Legionnaires loitering around Marseille bars, Algerian markets, or *Rick's Café Americain* in *Casablanca*, smoking *Gauloises* or casually sipping *Pernod* in a smokey Arab café. Unfortunately for the young and old men 'gagging at the bit' to enlist in the *Legion*, their fanciful and unrealistic beliefs were as *quixotic, far-fetched*, and as ridiculous as Nathan's *faux* French stereotype!

Nevertheless, this was the course of action Steve decided to embark upon and his cataclysmic decision came as a massive shock, a *real jolt* to Kathy. She accepted that she couldn't steer him away from this course, no matter how ludicrous and dangerous it was. Before she knew it, Steve had dusted off his old combat boots, gathered some of his old, tatty army gear, and bought a cheap one-way flight to Warsaw, offered his glib goodbyes, and flew out of safe and sunny Brisbane! Kathy could see her husband was driven, and there was nothing she could say or do to prevent him from leaving... In his haste to leave, Steve did promise he would only be gone for a month or two but would keep in constant contact. He declared that he needed to do this to lay the many demons from his earlier service to rest; *'one last hurrah'* he would confidently say. Kathy could grudgingly see the merit, albeit misguided, in that whimsical belief. Nathan paused and briefly thought this over... How many times has this scenario been played out? How many men have inflicted this cruel pain upon their loved ones, guided by non-sensical fantasies of fortune and glory? Nathan sure as hell knew he was hearing a few of his own home truths in Kathy's pathetic tale...

Well, that was Steve's zany plan, and Kathy hadn't heard from him for two weeks. So much for the promise of constant contact! Now the real frustration began.... any attempt to glean information as to his whereabouts from the Ukrainian government, the military or police was fruitless. The 'Cyrillic' language is a *killer* to understand by most people from the West, and Kathy could never seem to talk to anyone in authority who had a competent grasp of the English vernacular. Kathy revealed that she was starting to feel like *she was losing her mind*, such was the anguish and worry, and the only dependable person she could turn to was Nathan. After hearing the pain in her voice long enough, Nathan said, 'Okay,' in a calming, somewhat matter-of-fact voice, 'Don't worry, *the bloody dope has probably lost his mobile phone.* He always does stupid things like that, we all know this, nothing to worry about...' To downplay the seriousness of the situation was Nathan's subtle way of trying to lighten her torment, even if it was just 'BS'. 'Right, just text me all the information you have - all his contact details, anyone he was travelling with, any places he was going to visit and, most importantly, a recent photo. Don't worry, I will get onto this ASAP.' As the conversation was closing, Nathan made a pledge in a determined but light-hearted tone in the hope it would alleviate at least some of the strain Kathy was experiencing, 'I promise you, cross my heart and hope to die, *I will do my best to try and find him.* Leave this to me and I will be in contact in a day or so.' Nathan's voice softened further, 'By the way Kath, it was great to hear from you again, *even in these circumstances...*'

Deep down, he wasn't offering any false promises as he was acutely aware of the deadly situation in Eastern Europe and any search over there, for a lone Aussie, wasn't going to be a walk-in-the-park! At the same time, a part of him was curious why he had been contacted by Kathy. Sure, he was her old boyfriend, but she knew a great many of Steve's ex-military colleagues were better prepared for this role, financially and physically. Now, with drier eyes and sounding so much more relieved, Kathy offered a heartfelt thanks, a simple goodbye, and hung up. For a slightly confused but somewhat excited Nathan, it was time to make another large mug of plunger coffee and to start formulating some serious plans, and to let other trusted friends into this complicated and dangerous situation.

Chapter Three:

UKRAINE – PLAN 'A'

As Nathan slowly sipped his deliciously hot brew, without really noticing he was drinking his coffee, *like he always did...*he began to devise a loose but incisive strategy on how to make the long and arduous journey to war-torn Ukraine. 'Damn,' he thought, with some irritation, 'I have only travelled to Liverpool, on occasion, to watch my beloved 'Reds' play and this is the closest I ever got to Europe... *never mind Eastern Europe!!*' All he knew was the English language rapidly disintegrates into the ether the further east you go. Likewise, the hospitality, or *so he had been told...* Without a shadow of a doubt, the mindset is uniquely different; decades of brutal and unrelenting Soviet domination will do that to a country and its people! Like stock car veterans, they pilot tiny, boxy vehicles on the other side of the road. Customs, traditions and particularly the opulent food are like nothing he will have ever encountered. 'Oh, wonderful,' Nathan groaned, rolling his eyes at the prospect of gastrointestinal illness and cultural isolation, 'I'll get crook on the goulash, and nobody will understand a bloody word I say!' He had only started to become accustomed to the annoyance of gastric reflux in his later years; an annoying condition he had inherited from his mother's genes. On the bright side, the money exchange rate was in his favour. At least that was one tiny, bobbing boat of positivity on a surging sea of negatives! What was more significant, however, was that the only contacts he could rely upon resided in the West and his funds were excruciatingly sparse these days.

For a moment he stood immobile, with his brew mug in hand, and pensively stared out of his cabin window at a feeble baby crow; a tiny chick with its first new grey feathers that was screeching incessantly and loudly for its mama, a fat juicy worm, or a lost companion and he pondered that he could barely afford a train trip to Melbourne... *let alone a plane ticket to Ukraine*, plus living expenses! His mind wandered fancifully... He thought briefly, how in some abstract way he would be akin to Joseph Conrad's Charles Marlow, the intrepid British explorer in Africa in the popular Victorian novella *Heart of Darkness*. However, instead of some daring adventurer journeying to the interior of 'darkest' Africa, he imagined venturing to 'dark' and 'medieval' Europe. And like Marlow, Nathan wasn't sure what he would find or *if he would return*... Suddenly, his phone pinged, and Nathan was quickly shaken back to reality. He was now privy to all the pertinent information Kathy had forwarded him on Steve and his grand Ukrainian frolic! As much as he despised his mobile phone, the texting, scams, and inane social media, it did come in handy sometimes... 'Well,' thought Nathan, 'if I don't get my hands on some money, I won't be going anywhere... fast!' He then pressed the speed dial on his smartphone to call his best mate, Uncle Phil, *building owner, night club proprietor, motorcycle gang confidant* and *entrepreneur.* Nathan really didn't want to 'hit him up' for any money or favours, especially after the drama they experienced just a few months back with the *Agency*, the gangsters or drug runners, but he couldn't think of any other way to acquire a plane ticket or enough funds to initiate and sustain what could well become a lengthy search.

Phil's phone rang three times before his old friend answered. A long, drawn out 'Mate.......' was always the usual response followed by a laconic '......how's it going?' Nathan began by going into great detail concerning his historical friendship with Kathy and Steve, and the predicament they were now in. Phil had heard of Steve when he and Nathan reminisced over their old army days, especially when they served in infantry battalions of the *Royal Australian Regiment.* After chatting and circling around the issue for some time, Nathan finally cut to the chase, and announced that he needed some rapid funding to get an old comrade out of serious trouble. 'Sure, not a problem' was Phil's jovial response *but it was to be on one condition...* Phil would be going along with Nathan to act as his backup and in return, he would cover all the expenses.

As far as Phil was concerned, there was no debating the point that he was accompanying. Since the bloody gunfight outside his Melbourne apartment and the intense dramas connected to the *Agency,* Phil had decided to resurrect himself. He had embarked upon a fitness regime and was exercising with great intensity daily; he had even resumed his martial arts training. Remarkably, he now carefully considered what he ate and drank, and was ensuring he was getting enough rest – no more late-night parties or binge drinking sessions! The realisation dawned on him that if he didn't start looking after himself, he was not long for this world, and the only thing that would save him was to markedly improve his physical condition! Not exactly a 'renaissance man', but he was attempting to improve his general existence, sanity, and physical well-being, if only in small increments. In a sense, he was now as fit and dangerous as Nathan and the two men would make a formidable couple if anyone or any group decided to take them on.

Initially, Nathan thought this wasn't a particularly good suggestion as he didn't want to see Phil hurt or killed, but after his initial concerns and hesitation he cordially thanked Phil and told him that this was, in fact, a sensible idea; among other things, they would spend time together, like they did in the good old days. Phil offered to arrange the flights and they would probably fly out as soon as possible; in a day or so. Nathan would travel down to Melbourne and rendezvous at the airport, giving the old friends at least one day to prepare. This was all they needed... With this newfound purpose and excitement, Phil was now as 'chirpy as a canary on steroids' as he made his goodbyes. Nathan was buoyed by the fact that he and his best mate would be working together again, to help find a dear friend, and former soldier. *But neither man was kidding himself....* It was a perilous and unpredictable part of the world they were travelling to. They both knew the dangers but were supremely confident in their abilities, intuition, and experience in tight situations.

'Okay, so that's the money side of it,' Nathan thought. 'Now I need to contact someone who can help us big time when we land in Europe. There would be little time to *dilly-dally* as the situation required them to hit the ground hard and keep running; 'high speed and low drag,' as they would say in the army. It was painfully obvious that people don't go to Ukraine or any other war zone unless they have a bloody good reason to!' They were going to need a plausible cover story, continued physical assistance and reliable communication links along the way if they were ever going to have the remotest chance of succeeding. Nathan scrolled down the list of useful contacts in his smartphone until he came, with some dread, to the name – 'Marcus Hayden.' Marcus had been, to use Nathan's terminology, 'a stooge, a tool' for the *Agency* and the government, and had been dishonest with Caroline, his long-time friend. Fortunately, those issues had been resolved and he had remained in contact with Caroline and Marcus after their whirlwind marriage. While he didn't completely trust the man, Nathan remained genial with him for the sake of his friendship with Caroline. As had always been the case, if Nathan acquired a hatred for someone or something, *it was enduring*.... Caroline had sold her coffee van business to rest in anticipation of the birth of twin boys, while Marcus had decided to utilise his connections in the security field, and work as a high-end consultant to *Forbes 500* businesses and foreign government security agencies. Leaving the *Agency* was the best thing he could have done. Financially, they were doing extremely well, and the couple couldn't be happier or more in love.

Nathan sent Marcus a cordial greeting, quickly followed by a brief text outline of the proposed operation, making special mention that time was of the essence – if Marcus could, and was willing to help, a rapid response would be appreciated! Time to make another coffee and to keep thinking... *keep this plan ticking over...* The slight drizzle that had been softly caressing Nathan's block now began to pour, and big drops they were, landing loudly on the cabin's tin roof. Before he knew it, the downpour ended abruptly, and the sun began to shine brightly like a glowing, golden umbrella above the lofty native trees. Another one of those rejuvenating rainfalls that kept his plants thriving around the cabin's perimeter. For a moment or two, he fossicked for a sweet biscuit in his pantry and threw some fresh cat biscuits in a ceramic bowl for Moochee. His phone 'pinged' softly and the response from

Marcus was 'Ring you in five.'

The kettle had just boiled to a whistle, and Nathan was finishing a second dark chocolate digestive, while pouring another mug of coffee when his phone rang. He picked it up expecting it to be Marcus. 'Hi Nathan' came the cheery response. 'How are you?' asked the familiar female voice. Nathan responded that he was doing okay without going into too much detail, and asked Caroline how motherhood was treating her, and how she was coping with the twins. What a shock to her system that must have been; single for years then suddenly married and mother to not one, but two babies! He made no inquiry into how Marcus was... After the quick chat, Caroline handed the phone to Marcus and the two men got straight to the essence of the call. Nathan was forthright and disclosed what the crux of the operation was but mentioned that he was completely out of his depth concerning this part of the world and that he had zero local contacts. Marcus confirmed that this would not be a problem as he knew 'people' across Europe from his previous life. He would be able to arrange an interpreter, or two, to assist Nathan and Phil, and possibly some transport along the way. He could also guarantee regular and accurate *Intel* briefs, so that they could keep up with what they were doing but more importantly, the bigger 'game' at hand, specifically the war.

Of concern to Marcus was Phil and Nathan getting out of Australia, particularly carrying any select military equipment, such as plate carriers, web belts and pouches.

Marcus was candid and suggested Nathan leave this type of equipment, behind and purchase necessary equipment in Poland or Ukraine. Gear is generally cheaper in Eastern Europe, and there would be enough floating around, in reputable stores like *M-Tac* in Ukraine, or easily obtainable on the black market. Nathan was impressed with the suggestion and was glad there would be a buyer's marketplace on offer. Unlike America and other nations, Australia has a very restrictive and adolescent policy concerning the possession of body armour, particularly in relation to carrying it overseas, even for personal protection. Marcus knew of guys having their plates confiscated before departure, as well as being interrogated by federal authorities before departing Australia to that part of the world. No point in attracting unnecessary attention...

A second and significant consideration was the 'cover story' to satisfy Australian and overseas officials. Marcus recommended they utilise their previous military history; it would be futile to try and conceal it as it would be easily found in the 'system'. Better to focus on the first aid and medical side of their service. Moreover, it would be useful to emphasise their ages; being on the wrong side of fifty – *'Damn, we're too old to be playing soldiers again or fighting Russians!'* - may help satisfy those with badges and suspicious minds. Humanitarian assistance doesn't set off any alarm bells and is the flavour of the month on the Polish/Ukrainian border. People with these types of invaluable skills were streaming to in from all over the globe; *Egyptian Red Crescent* and *Médecins Sans Frontières* were two of the first humanitarian organisations on the ground in support of Ukrainian refugees. For Nathan this 'screen' would be simple. Besides his background as a patrol medic, he boasted decades of experience, knowledge, skills, and documents with emergency service organisations, especially the *Volunteer Coast Guard, St. John Ambulance* and *St. Andrew's First Aid Australia*. He could easily and without trouble verify his lifesaving and emergency services credentials. Nathan could also arrange similar documentation for Phil, backdating his memberships and upgrading his skillset. Although loosely connected to the *Cossacks Motorcycle Club*, Phil had never been charged with a crime, nor was ever a 'person of interest.' So, there shouldn't be any detailed inquiries or serious questions posed by border and customs officials at Melbourne airport. Marcus also commented he would start making phone calls to confidants, to arrange the interpreters and the other issues he thought needed attention, such as enlistment in an army of a foreign nation. Nathan was bemused by this, but Marcus was just trying to cover all the bases. Steve could be in serious trouble with the Australian government on his return; particularly if he were connected to the ultra-national, right-wing *Azov* group. With most of the details now agreed, both men expressed a curt 'goodbye' and hung up. Nathan wasn't warming to Marcus, *not by a long shot*, but appreciated his professional courtesy and the fact they didn't despise one another anymore.

'Well, that call went well,' thought Nathan, and he continued to interrogate his thoughts on what had been discussed. He decided to ring Phil and give him a quick brief on the latest information and what was additionally vital for their impending trip. Phil had been busy; he had already booked the one-way flights and he relayed the details and departure times to Nathan. No sense selecting a return flight until they knew what the situation was on the ground. For the present, all they knew was that they were flying out tomorrow afternoon. Both men possessed current passports, had recently been tested as *Covid* free and held all the required evidence of *Covid* vaccination certificates, so all that was needed now was for them to pack and rendezvous at Melbourne's Tullamarine airport the next day. That, and on a personal note, they had to quickly attend to pressing logistical issues, such as Nathan finding a minder for Moochee and sorting out Phil's credentials and Phil needed to organise access to funds and arrange some accommodation for their arrival in Europe. The packing could be done overnight. There would be plenty of time for sleep on the flight, and time to discuss tactics and strategy on the arduous journey ahead. Phil was excited to be part of the operation. If nothing else, the 'adventure' would take him away from the on-going marital problems he had been experiencing over the last few months. Phil wanted to talk on and on about the trip as the anticipation was palpable, but when Nathan thought the moment was right, he interrupted him, warmly wishing goodnight, and suggesting they both continue with their preparations, as the clock was ticking.

By now, the daylight was leaving, and the cabin had become chilly. Even though it was early autumn and the sun's diminishing rays bore little warmth. The pre-prepared fire was lit, and Nathan flopped down wearily in his trusty, worn leather armchair for a brief, but deserved rest; like *Danny Glover* in the *Lethal Weapon* movies, he was convinced he was also getting 'too damn old for this shit'. But he owed it to Steve, and Kathy, to at least try, make a bold attempt to find him. As Moochee chased fat grasshoppers outside, like she was still a kitten, Nathan ruminated over the scant details of the plan; carefully ticking off point after point in his mind.

Following on from his earlier conversation with Marcus, it had now been confirmed that arrangements had been made for Nathan to connect with two American operatives who would provide private personal security to Nathan and Phil and assist them to the border at Medyka, where a great deal of the Ukrainian refugees were transiting through. Brilliant idea, thought Nathan, 'we could always do with extra expertise and 'muscle'! Who knows what we will find or come up against?' It wasn't only the war Nathan was concerned with, but Eastern Europe had the unenviable reputation of being a *petri dish* for gangsters, human traffickers, terrorism, drug barons and illegal immigration. At least at Medyka they would discover a multitude of volunteer opportunities with the countless humanitarian organisations operating there, and this would build additional layers upon their cover story, especially with newly acquired foreign documentation. The idea of assisting the throng of refugees touched Nathan and, for a man with such a lengthy volunteer experience, he considered this would be an added bonus of their expedition in to the unknown... Now, with these thoughts firmly tucked away, he soon realised his packing wasn't going to do itself and he thrust himself forward, with some vigour, out of the clutches of his warm chair, and started looking for his worn but trusty rucksack. He thought, with a slight annoyance at how the day had flown and he was now into the late evening, 'time to get cracking and packing...'

Chapter Four:

ONTO EUROPE AND THE UNKNOWN...

It was around two in the morning and now surprisingly frosty by the time Nathan had finally sorted his kit. The first icy tentacles of winter were now creeping out, slowly but surely across the land, and he knew it was going to be a bleak and unfriendly winter, as it had been the year before and the one before that. *How he had shivered...* The small but intense fire had long burnt out with the flickering coals now emitting more fumes than heat; the cabin now smelling a might smokey. All the perfunctory items, such as sturdy clothing, wet weather gear, warm socks, toiletries, and other personal essentials, and smart phone cables were assembled a lot quicker than he anticipated. Nathan had always been clever, swift, and thorough when putting his gear together; another life skill from his army service. As his main luggage, an ordinary civilian 90-litre olive coloured rucksack, would be checked in, he decided to pack a small round bladed knife, much in the design of a skinner's blade as he believed he needed something to protect himself once he landed. 'For God's sake,' he thought, he was heading off to a war zone and needed *some* protection. He had flown on many airlines before with his 'tactical pen', essentially a tough, aluminum writing implement that could be used as a gouging and glass breaking gadget, and he carried this as it never raised any suspicion. Along with a local paper and chewing gum, he would also purchase at the airport gift store a thick and sturdy magazine that could be rolled tight and rigid, into a potent baton. In his main luggage he also packed his trusty grab bag and included items he thought would come in handy, such as small personal alarms, cable ties, duct tape, shemagh scarf and para chord; other essential items would be purchased upon arrival. He glanced at his watch and was alarmed at the time. *'Damn,'* he announced, as he turned toward Moochee, *'I better get off to bed before it's a new day.'*

Almost before he knew it, his phone alarm rang... loudly; like it always does when you're sleep deprived. Nathan dragged himself up from under his bedding and out from his intense slumber. The *Toyota Coaster* shuttle bus that had quickly ferried him to the airport from rural Victoria had been punctual and the journey was without incident. Nathan leaned close to the tinted window, which was smeared in light condensation and wiped it off with the back of his gloved hand. He peered out with evaluative interest at people and the vagaries of life while, at the same time, creating various good and bad scenarios in his head of the coming trip to Europe. A plan *A*, *B*, and *C* for most situations... It was always hard to change old, and trusted military habits. Phil, who was wearing jeans, *Skecher* boots and a sturdy, three quarter black denim jacket, was patiently waiting just outside the bustling International Terminal; his casual smile quickly transformed into a large grin when he saw his best friend arrive. Nathan could see his mate was bubbling with excitement and he didn't want to say or suggest anything that may dampen his enthusiasm. Yet, Nathan knew they were heading towards danger... *That was a given.... The facts were in plain view...* This was the first major war on the European continent since *World War Two*, between two incredibly determined adversaries; brave, resilient Ukrainians fighting for their homeland, and a 'madman' attempting to etch his name into Russian history as a victorious, celebrated leader by exerting his influence, militarily, in Europe and who knows elsewhere... Regardless of the outcome, Nathan was supremely confident they would achieve the goal they had established and that, simply, was to locate an old mate, *a brother-in-arms,* alive or dead...

To his credit, Phil had purchased quality airline tickets and the men waited, quietly, in the *Business Class* lounge before departure. Nathan phoned Kathy and presented her with a brief schedule of the trip, informing her of only what she needed to know. Kathy sounded infinitely better than the other day and again, thanked Nathan for his diligence and trustworthiness before she hung up. Some snacks and beverages were consumed while they sat, and the two old friends chatted about common interests, such as motorbikes, fast cars and, for Phil - *fast women.* Phil gushed with excitement, 'Do you think we will have time to meet some of those Ukrainian beauties? I've heard Ukraine and Russia have some of the most stunning women in the world.' The only thing Nathan had to do with Russian women was his memory of them as flashy, conniving prostitutes who solicited all the major hotels in Dubai when he was working as a PMC in Iraq. The alluring women knew the contractors were cashed up, and cognisant these men were keen for a 'wild night' as they were rotating out of the Middle East on their way home. 'Mate,' said Nathan, slightly raising his voice, just a touch irritated and with a stern look at his friend, *'Let's keep our eyes on the ball and remember why we are going to chuffing Europe!* If time permits, I don't have a problem with you getting your end away, but the job comes first. *This won't be a freakin' holiday...'* A silent, weighty pause ensued and then Phil slowly nodded his head, obligingly in agreement, but Nathan could see Phil's thoughts were elsewhere... He would need to keep a close eye on his old friend, *on so many levels...*

The call came soon enough for the men to board the *Airbus* and being *Business Class* travellers, they were admitted before the bulk of the passengers. They took their seats and lightly grasped the icy cool, crystal flute of complimentary French champagne from the attractive female steward. Before the men knew it, the safety brief was presented, the plane taxied and was airborne. At cruising height, the seatbelt light was extinguished, and the stewards began their work in earnest, shuffling and fluffing about, preparing drinks and other mandatory refreshments. As it was a late evening flight, Nathan lowered his wide recliner, placed on his eye mask, inserted his ear plugs, and prepared to go to sleep; he would eat later. This was day one of a mighty adventure and he knew he would need all the cherished rest he could get...

Chapter Five:

DESTINATION WARSAW...

Nathan had managed to sleep soundly for a solid six hours and woke around five am the next day, feeling exceptionally rested and spritely. The sleek plane landed at Dubai airport a few hours later and, after all the customary and annoying security checks - taking off belts, removing shoes, presenting laptops, the men had occupied a leather three-seater couch in the luxurious *Business Class* lounge, which gleamed with glitzy, faux gold panelling along its endless walls. In turns they used the showers, ate a satisfying meal, and drank multiple cups of strong, sweet coffee. They took in the sight of the interesting and seemingly endless procession of multi-cultural, multi-denominational passengers from all the nations of the world. After three hours of 'killing time', they boarded their next flight, the one would take them to Poland. Realizing it would be some time before he had the chance again, Nathan watched a couple of the latest movies and was grateful he wasn't travelling economy. *He hated using the bathrooms...* It always amazed him how every restroom on any plane in economy class was trashed not long after the plane had taken off. 'Geez,' he thought, 'what's wrong with people, are they freakin' animals or something?!'

Suddenly, the *Airbus* bounced violently and there was some small, residual turbulence for a few minutes, but that didn't bother Nathan. Terrified gasps and muffled screams could be heard as the plane jolted about a couple more times. In these situations, he would remember standing rigid on the cold steel ramp of a military *C-130 Hercules*; the stalwart, multi-use, transport plane flying nap-of-the-earth, in the pitch-black darkness of night, bumping violently up and down, low over terrain as he steeled himself to exit the aircraft into the black void and gushing tail winds. During these exercises, some of his colleagues would be vomiting, and to be honest, he couldn't wait to parachute from the plane. Heaven forbid, he didn't want to 'spew in sympathy' like some of the other men...not a good way to enhance one's reputation as a member of a Free Fall Troop! But those events were far behind him, now just insignificant specks of memory, or faded neurological sparks in *the vast catacombs of his mind...* Today he was flying in supreme comfort for a change and *knew* they would arrive in Warsaw in great shape because of it. The plan was to stay at the *Holiday Inn* and then rendezvous with the contact that Marcus was sourcing for them.

Overall, the trip had passed very smoothly, and had been unbelievably comfortable. Now, the last leg of their journey seemed to take an excruciatingly long time; maybe the expectation of getting into the 'thick of it' made the latter part of the trip long and slow. Who knows? Funny how time, space and expectations play tricks on the mind... Anyway, it wasn't too long before their plane touched down in Poland and the two slightly weary men were proceeding through Polish customs.

Nathan had gazed through the window on the airliner's approach to landing and had only viewed fields ladened with crops and lush green belts of countryside. It became quickly evident there was no comparison here with the terrain *or* the customs situation in Australia, where it looked like anyone 'off the street' worked behind the security barricades and officers frequently and unprofessionally called you 'mate' as you arrived. At this airport there appeared to be an abundance of young, fit, eager, and heavily armed customs officers patrolling everywhere that Nathan and Phil gazed. There was around 50/50 male and female officers, and they were so effortlessly attractive they all could have modelled for Polish Cosmo! As Nathan took in the spectacle, he muttered, *'Well, that's a turn up, you certainly wouldn't see this in Australia, that's for sure...'*

As they ambled through the terminal, Nathan turned casually to Phil and reminded him, 'Be sure to say that you're here to provide humanitarian first aid for the refugees on the border and, later, for some tourism as you've never been to 'warm and exciting' Poland, who knows, *a history trip to Krakow, Auschwitz and Birkenau could be on the cards...*' Phil nodded in agreement and the men shuffled forward to the customs booth with their passports obligingly and compliantly open in hand. The perfect tourists... Both men, in their wild imagination, expected a curt demand of 'Papers!' to be issued by the customs officers. But this firm request never came, and they handed over their official documents to stern Polish faces who scrutinised the passports and its various stamped pages and back at the two men, a number of times. They were asked a few routine questions, like 'purpose of visit', 'duration of stay' and 'are you carrying prohibited items?' As it so happened, several international flights had landed concurrently, and it was clear that the authorities were attempting to accelerate the examination process early in the day. As luck would have it, Nathan was saddled with a 'customs dragon' who sported a look that could only be described as 'resting bitch face'.

After a lengthy and extremely thorough examination of his passport, the female customs officer offered a last expressionless glance at Nathan and remarked flatly and loudly in a crude monotone of English, *'Velcome to Poland and enjoy your stay.'* Nathan acknowledged the finality of this painful scrutiny with a quick nod and a closed mouth smile, and walked quickly past the tiny security booth through to where Phil was already waiting.

Together again, the two men trotted downstairs, without delay, to the crowded and somewhat noisy luggage carousel area, picked up their meagre belongings and caught a *Skoda* taxi outside. Minutes later, the driver glided past the university precinct of the city and Nathan could visualise the pre-modern beauty that had now been blended with newer buildings, creating a hotch-potch, architectural abortion of 'old' and 'new' designs. As he glanced through the taxi window, he wasn't impressed with what he saw, and he thought the city was suffering with a post-modern identity crisis!

There were old decrepit buildings of various European architectural influences that dated back to the turn of the nineteenth century, and long before, while some *baroque* façades still sported bullet marks as a reminder of the cruel German occupation of the city during *World War Two*. As part of their preparation, Nathan had exchanged some Australian dollars for euros at Melbourne Airport and thought this a safer bet than to change from currency to currency in multiple countries. They would purchase some Ukrainian hryvnias once in Ukraine and could sparingly use their credit cards. The taxi arrived at the *Holiday Inn* within thirty minutes and the men were promptly checked into their rooms, which felt fresh, clean, and obliging.

While all this had been going on, Marcus had sent Nathan a short but succinct text, already knowing they had arrived in Europe. An interpreter, plus security operatives would be waiting for them at the Warsaw train station around eight the next morning. Nathan expected a bit more information in the communique, but 'short and sweet' was probably all they needed right now. Nothing else for it but to shower, refresh their bodies and souls, and to orientate themselves to their surroundings. The men planned to go for a long, slow walk to iron out any physical stiffness and to resist an early night so their biological clocks could tune into the local Eastern European time; there was a seven-hour time distance and Australia was in front, at least in a chronological sense... The weather was surprisingly cool and the breeze piercing at times, as it had been a long, frosty winter in the northern hemisphere. The cheerful concierge had remarked that spring had been incredibly late, and many of the trees lining the streets and parks hadn't budded yet. Still, the men were keen to walk, talk and later, have a beer or two at their hotel.

As they wandered the streets of Warsaw, Phil was taken back by the dour faces of many of the city's inhabitants. He thought about how, even in Melbourne, most people seemed to look happy or at least content, and would offer some form of greeting or brief salutation. He passed this social observation on to Nathan. 'Well,' pronounced Nathan, in a somewhat professorial tone, 'I suppose if you live in a country that's stone miserably cold three-quarters of the year, you spend your life striving to eke out an existence and live in fear as your country has been a perpetual gateway for invaders since time immemorial, *you wouldn't look so delighted either'*. Although Australia wasn't the 'lucky country' that it used to be, both men were glad they lived on the other side of the world. While modern aircraft had closed the gap between Australia, Europe, and Asia, there still existed a 'tyranny of distance' that afforded relative isolation, safety, and for some, 'blissful ignorance' to the world's numerous problems.

As relaxed as the men were, Nathan had secreted his modest knife to a position where he could access it easily, if need be. He also paused frequently and randomly to utilise shop windows as *de-facto* mirrors, to observe and survey the streetscape, behind and around him. The centre of the path was adopted by the wary men as it avoided the unseen danger that could lurk in dark alleyways or the vulnerability of hugging the curb and becoming an easy target for a 'seize and throw', into a darkened vehicle.

It was common knowledge that Westerners were prime targets for 'snatch squads.' This was more so in Ukraine, where unbelievably, Ukrainians had handed over their own countrymen and women to the Russian government and spy agencies. For some, it was the lure of money but for others, it was the mixture of a Russian/ Ukrainian heritage, where the Russian bonds were more profoundly cherished and secure than the national ties of their biological homeland. *Nathan wasn't taking any chances...* After an hour or so, Nathan turned to Phil and plainly said, *'Fuck this,* let's go back to the hotel, *I'm gagging for a cold beer'*. Phil didn't have to respond as 'yes' was written all over his cold, blueish face, but he just quickly nodded, all the same. They walked a further twenty metres upon old, wet, blue stone pavers, turned right at the next corner and headed back to the *Holiday Inn*. A few cold beverages awaited them. Nathan thought this was probably enough for their first day in Europe. He knew, without doubt, the tempo would increase, markedly, as of tomorrow...

Chapter Six

THE TRAIN TO MEDYKA

The next morning came quickly. *Too quickly, in fact...* Last night's beers, merry conversations, long, luxurious shower, and sleep was now a blur... It was an early start, again, and Nathan momentarily thought of how many 'bloody early starts' he had endured in his life. 'Damn... *there had been so many...*' In Phil's case, he needed some noisy cajoling to extricate him from his soft, toasty bed and inspire him to be upwardly mobile. Being his own boss for some time had made Phil a little too casual for Nathan's liking. Both men quickly packed, surveyed the room for any missed personal items and then made their way downstairs to the breakfast area. It was well lit, spacious, and inviting with its clean and modern décor and intoxicating aromas...

A few people, mostly business types, judging by their dresses and suits, were moving from one gleaming serving tray to another and selecting plain or chocolate croissant, Danish pastries, or cold meats for their continental breakfast. A long queue had formed at the automatic coffee machine, which was working non-stop. Piped music was being played softly and several foreign languages could be heard above the breakfast commotion. The only other clamour was from the serious American female reporter discussing the current war events on CNN and commenting upon how many European nations were 'flip-flopping' in their support of Ukraine. Nathan kept 'security skimming' the room while talking to Phil about the plan for their meeting with the interpreter and security operatives. Nathan indicated he would initially contact these people and if he deemed the situation safe, he would gesture for Phil to join the group. No point in both men walking into a trap! Nathan was following two of his old adages - 'never trust anyone', and 'if you want a job done properly, do it your bloody self!'. He hadn't picked these people; he didn't know them, and they would have to prove their worth before he offered them his allegiance.

With a light but delicious meal eaten, it was now time to check out and walk the easy fifteen-minute journey to the train station. The concierge passed on brief travel instructions and Nathan warmly thanked him for their pleasant stay. A slightly grey and cloudy morning greeted them, and they didn't need to be told the temperature was in single figures Celsius! Head down and 'arse up' was the call for speed and warmth and the men moved quickly and purposefully along the flat and even walkway to the central railway station, which was divided in two lanes, one for pedestrians and the other for cyclists. The transportation edifice appeared before they knew it - very new, large, glass lit and mightily imposing, like a majestic bull elephant on the vast, flat African savannah. Inside, a throng of people were walking about or lined up for tickets at the one or two ticket windows that were open, even though there were a dozen windows available!

Newly arrived but dishevelled and anxious Ukrainian refugees were studying their surroundings, conversing with aid workers. At a separate counter, young and enthusiastic Polish boy scouts were translating Polish into English and other languages for travellers and refugees alike. The two men took in the sad and worried expressions of the evacuees and could see tired and desperate people clutching their children and meagre possessions; people who wondered how they would respond to being homeless or standing in the few clothes they possessed. Still, in the midst of this collective human calamity, the dirty, lined and tear streamed faces of the adults gave Phil and Nathan some hope... They could identify resilience in the eyes and attitude of these people to keep moving forward and to just survive if nothing else for the foreseeable future. No mega plans or proclamations but simple survival as human beings, *having to just put one foot in front of the other...* Both men didn't need to say a word but deeply respected these people who were trying to latch onto a grain of dignity at this sad juncture in their troubled lives.

In the ongoing process of people shuffling by, Phil positioned himself under the cement archway of the stairs in a spot where he could easily scan upwards, while Nathan made his way upstairs to the *McDonalds* restaurant, the designated meeting place. Phil shuffled quickly from foot to foot in an attempt to warm himself as the concrete floor was annoyingly cold. 'What is it with me, *McDonald's* restaurants, and secret meetings', Nathan wondered to himself, as he selected a bolted down seat that was the closest to the entrance and clearly visible to the roving transit police who were patrolling on the upper level. *Any protection would suffice in this situation...* Exactly two minutes later, three plainly dressed men walked into the busy restaurant and sat down in a booth by the window. A powerfully built man of around six feet five and over 260 pounds, sporting a bright red biker beard, but who looked remarkably like the towering giant that was 'Opie' out of *Sons of Anarchy*, gazed across the booth and nodded slowly to Nathan. Nathan promptly and casually walked over and sat down. Another man, on the left side of 'red beard' who was sporting a greyish beard and 'man bun' and reminiscent of an older version of John Cena, the *WWE Champion*, also nodded casually at Nathan. It was a lightly built Ukrainian man in his late thirties, or perhaps early forties, with shaven hair and a face resembling the actor, Jeremy Renner, who caught Nathan's eye. He wore faded jeans, white *Adidas* trainers and a sturdy navy-blue jacket. The Ukrainian spoke first, in fluent English, but with a slight hint of an accent.

'Hello, my name is Sascha. Marcus has asked me to be your interpreter and guide' he said. In a Texas drawl that surprised Nathan, it was 'red beard' who introduced himself as Bill and 'grey beard' as Garen. Both men could pass for heavyweight fighters or pro-wrestlers and certainly looked like nothing physical could trouble them. They were confident in a relaxed, professional way that appealed to Nathan, and he suspected their background was high-end military or Government security. Although imposing, both men were instantly likeable. Garen was wearing a large black and white *Texas EMT* patch on the right sleeve of his tan work shirt, and this was his 'cover story.' He had served as a combat medic and paramedic over the last thirty years and on various deployments and could easily pass any scrutiny. Bill supposedly worked for a Scandinavian firm that championed his stance to provide humanitarian support to the refugees fleeing the war, and that was his storyline... Nathan assumed he was the 'weapons and tactics' man. Bill complemented the 'biker' façade by sporting several aggressive looking tattoos; guns, women, and demons – the usual 'tough guy' motifs. He had worked for the DEA (Drug Enforcement Agency) as a deep cover operative into drug and gun running by biker gangs and the tattoos were his reminders; they could also be judged as his 'badges of honour', such was his success as an operative. Sascha spoke again, 'the train is leaving in 15 minutes on the lower platform. We will head down there in a minute or so, and you and your nervous friend under the stairway can follow... loosely behind us. Here are two tickets.' Sascha wasn't as simple as he looked, and Nathan could tell that what this man lacked in physicality he made up in brains and cunning. He was one of those guys you could bank on to gauge a situation in an instant. 'Well done, Marcus', Nathan thought, extremely impressed... 'I think I like this guy already'.

Nathan quickly left the table and made his way to Phil, who was diligently scanning each and every way into the station, like Schwarzenegger's robotic *Terminator* character, except that Phil was slightly obvious, but effective, nonetheless. The plan was quickly relayed, and the men waited until he could view Sascha, and his colleagues moving casually down the concrete stairs towards the platform. They followed, *taking their time...* The cold and uninviting platform was saturated with people and their belongings - suitcases, bags, and even small animals. Although the war was just over the border and cities like Lviv had been blasted by cruise missiles, and the Russian Army was heading westward, life still went on in this country as per normal; like it had done in so in any other war... *Life must go on...* A great many of the passengers would disembark along the line or change at larger stations such as Tarnow for other trains. In another minute or so, the somewhat dated train and its carriages arrived noisily and unhurriedly down the tracks, bringing with it a mighty gush of frigid air until it eventually came to a weighty stop at the congested platform. As people swiftly boarded, the train's engine huffed and puffed in *staccato*, like a stressed asthmatic desiring a *Ventolin* hit. Nathan waited until Sascha and his two companions boarded the train and located a seat, and then they nonchalantly boarded and joined them. They were looking at an all-day train ride, so the men would talk during the long journey. Nathan presumed that he and Phil would be fully immersed in the 'goings on' of the war in Ukraine by the time they reached the border. A loud roar from the train's whistle soon followed and the train slowly chugged and puffed its way out of the station.

As it so happened, the train wasn't as crammed as they thought it would be. People had been dismounting consistently and the men had occupied a compartment in the carriage that reminded Nathan of *Harry Potter's* Victorianesque cubicle on the *Hogwarts train*. A male, middle-aged train conductor in a smart, dark blue railway uniform came and punched their tickets (which was printed in an unintelligible script), and he didn't seem to care they were all sharing a space that none of the men should have been in! During the journey, the group had been making small talk, feeling each other out and talking about the sort of 'operations' they had been on in their pasts. Nathan knew Marcus would have sourced 'solid' operators and he felt confident in the abilities and the potential of the two large Americans and their new, Ukrainian friend.

It was Sascha who first spoke about Steve Holland, with the little information he had. 'My sources tell me that your friend made inquiries at the Ukrainian embassy when he arrived. Apparently, he didn't have much luck there, but was told by Polish volunteers at a 'Lion's Club' tent nearby that he needed to head to Medyka on the border, and this is where he could find a recruiting tent for the *International Legion for Territorial Defence*. As this is the route most used by Westerners, this is where we are heading. Although it will be difficult, I plan to talk to the recruiters there and to reach out to my other contacts to obtain more credible information. Some type of gratuity for their time will do the trick... But I must warn you, everyone is suspicious of Russian agents. There have been executions at night in the streets and being a Westerner won't save you if you are suspected. Also, you must understand the war has slowed and complicated the lines of communication.' Sascha continued, 'you must be aware that there have been over four million refugees heading back and forward from Medyka, countless humanitarian volunteers, church officials, Polish military, authorities from nearly every embassy, spies, hustlers, musicians, and every type of security operative from all over the world, passing through here and the other checkpoints on the border. The best and the worst of humanity!' Sascha emphasised his next sentences in an elevated but sincere voice. *'The chance that someone will remember your friend is extremely remote...*

The chance that we will find your friend alive, even more improbable.' Sascha looked straight at Nathan and could see his short speech wasn't what Nathan wanted to hear, but he continued, 'but I will do my absolute best to help you. I give you my word on that.' Nathan had only known this man for a few scant hours but could tell Sacha would be true to his honest declaration. He had always been a good and reliable judge of character and he was certain of Sascha's sincerity.

A few pleasant hours soon passed, and it wasn't long before the train was pulling into Tarnow, ten minutes by Nathan's calculation. This would be their stop for a connecting train to the nearest station and city to the border town of Medyka, and the congested border crossing. The men stirred and began to collect their things and moved, as a collective, to the narrow hallway outside their compartment. Within a minute, the train slowed noticeably and came crawling into the station. There were many Polish people standing in the hallway looking out of the windows and the scenery that appeared before them. A few seconds later, the train halted at the platform. In a strong but polite southern American accent, Bill 'begged his pardon' and politely asked for the passengers to move aside or alight from the carriage, so the men could get off. Believing he was misunderstood, Bill repeated his request. Again, *nothing happened... No one moved... No one said a thing... Absolutely nothing occurred!!* Bill may have been the Pope or the Secretary General of the United

Nations for all the good it did him as the passengers completely ignored his pleas for them to move, quickly out of the way! The train was still stationary, and Nathan and his colleagues had to get off this train - *now!* The men looked at each other, with a tinge of panic, and decided to move rapidly down to the far end of the carriage, in a desperate attempt to exit via that door. However, before they had a chance to do so, the platform conductor blew his whistle and the train chugged off, quickly picking up the pace. The men looked at each other completely stunned! The ticket collector then entered their carriage hallway again and was checking tickets. Nathan was fortunate to explain the situation in broken English to the conductor who informed them they would have to get off at the next station, catch the next train two stops back from Tarnow, and then re-board another train in 90 minutes that would re-connect with Tarnow. To say that Nathan wasn't impressed was an understatement! He cursed under his breath with the occasional '*fucking dumb Europeans*' and '*lousy give up merchants*' that was clearly intelligible to the other men and anyone else listening.

A slight air of deflation briefly descended upon the group but before too long they were waiting on the platform at the small station where they would wait for the Tarnow train. Funnily enough, two British passengers, a father and daughter, had also missed the opportunity to alight from the train and were now waiting with Nathan and his colleagues. The two courageous Brits had travelled from Grimsby on the northeast coast of England with the intention to sponsor a refugee woman and her daughter but had decided to travel to Medyka in an attempt to expedite the matter - as always, bureaucracy had thrown challenging and bothersome obstacles at them. It was their hope they would gather the two refugees at the border and safely deliver them to their home and a more tranquil existence. Nathan could see by the look on the faces of his new colleagues they all thought the Brits to be a real 'gutsy' pair to set out on this course of action. The strangers, now united by circumstance, had become a unique group, and began chatting as if they were old friends. There was nothing really for it but to travel together and assist one other. For Nathan, he could see the benefits of a mutual association with these people as it provided more credence to their 'cover story' of being humanitarian aid workers, *and there was always strength in numbers...*

As it turned out, the English pair were exceptionally good company and Nathan had a common ally in Mike, the father, as he also dearly supported *Liverpool Football Club.* Before too long, the train arrived and soon bustled them to the small but grand-looking Tarnow station, where they managed to disembark this time without any concern. Their tickets had to be altered at the station master's office as all the timings had changed but this wasn't a problem. 'Don't worry,' shouted the plump female station master, *'I will get you on your train...'* By now, the annoying delay had taken them into the early evening. The coolness of the day had transitioned into the coldness of the evening and made to feel even chillier as the diminutive streetlights attempted to pierce the night's blackness. For the most part, it was a feeble endeavour. Condensation began to extend its icy and unfriendly reach to metal and plastic and to drip, incessantly, from the station awnings; water vapor from breathing made it look like everyone was smoking. The next train arrived in thirty minutes and the group soon located their compartment, which was empty but surprisingly toasty. This train was of an even older variety and very noisy and dirty, unlike the semi-antiquated trains they had travelled on during the day. Nathan, Phil, or anyone else for that matter wasn't caring, as each passenger seized a space in the compartment and decided to attempt sleep. It would still be another hour or so before they arrived at Prezemsyl, and it would be getting extremely late in the evening. As far as their plans went, they would arrive and board one of the shuttle buses that crisscrossed between the station and the border and hope to locate some accommodation for the night; even a marquee tent would suffice.

As Nathan could hear members of the group lightly snoring and closely snuggled into their seats, he could not but help remember Sascha's remarks about the likelihood of finding Steve alive. Nathan hoped he wasn't going to be too late, but so far the news of the fighting in the front and the situation of the war left him with no illusions... This was no small-scale affair, people were dying in their droves, by the thousands, especially the military. Russian armoured convoys had been caught defenceless on highways and obliterated, leaving the twisted hulks of once formidable T 90 tanks now rusting and useless alongside lush hedgerows or major Ukrainian arterial highways; the only influential force the tanks now provided was that of a stark reminder of where many a Russian mother's son had his young life snubbed out. Chechen soldiers and *Wagner Group* mercenaries had been thrust forward by Russia and had been decimated. Numerous drones had been employed to locate Ukrainian military who were subsequently attacked with profound effect by Russian mortars and artillery. As he contemplated, quietly, and now with his eyes lightly shut, he was also angry with Steve and wondered how he had made such a poor and heartless decision. 'Damn you, Steve. I know I have gone on these 'crazy rides' too, but I don't have anyone at home anymore waiting and worrying about me, *like you do!*' If by some miracle, he did locate Steve, his old friend and army buddy, alive, he was in for a real ticking off! Nathan tried to concentrate but he too was fatigued and slowly succumbed to the convivial warmth of the cocoon like carriage, and the robust snoring of his new companions only seemed to solicit an invitation to sleep. Nathan was more tired than he realised. He was out before he knew it...

Chapter Seven:

ON THE BORDER...

It was the sharp and inconsistent jolting that first woke Nathan... He performed a quick one-eighty degrees scan with his groggy head and blurry eyes and soon ascertained that it was just the aging train coming to a violent stop at Prezemsyl, the last station before the border. He quickly rubbed his eyes, with some force, and kneaded his shaven head vigorously with both hands, back and forth. Other members of the group were also physically shaking themselves out of their stupor and looking about, either sleepy and half-interested, or yawning, wiping gungy eyes, or scratching unsteady heads. It was Sascha who reminded the group this was their final destination in Poland and not to leave anything behind. He also suggested that everyone be careful with their money and other valuables as pickpockets and criminals were known to frequent the area. It was Phil who said what most were thinking... 'Great... bad enough that there's a war on. *I now have to watch out for some low life trying to steal my wallet!*'

The war and crime in and around Ukraine was no

different than any other conflict in the long, bloodied history of humanity. Already stories had circulated that weapons, with serial numbers removed, were being sold by Ukrainian military officers to Belarussians. Politicians were being bought off by businesses, while military commanders were fudging the numbers of their units to receive more government funding. Also, some of society's more influential people were actively avoiding the 'front', the 'meat grinder,' as people were attempting to secure a safe ride in all this struggle. Local celebrities, popular bloggers, and wealthy individuals were creating their own 'foundations' or heading up organisations or military units that weren't going anywhere near the fighting, especially some of the Territorial Defence formations in Kyiv. Some of the units that had gone to the 'front' had received 'bloody noses' and were now sourcing Foreign Military Advisers (FMAs) to raise the military competency of their units. To the uninitiated, it looked like they were championing the cause but, for many of these war 'entrepreneurs', it was a means of securing survivability or an opportunity to score political points, gaining the popular vote - down the track, or *to make bucket loads of filthy cash!* For a great many Ukrainians, life went on as normal... During one of their chats on the train, Sascha had informed Nathan about the British member of the *Legion* who had organised a 'go fund me' page to raise money back home to pay for the prostitutes he was entertaining in Kyiv. Apparently, this 'gentleman' had a favourite 'lady of the night', and he could only keep her off the 'game' if he was the only one to pay for her services. A despicable act, but like many other of his *Legion* compatriots, he was still probably owed thousands of hryvnias for his service.

It also became obvious to many Westerners that not all Ukrainians were as honest as Sascha. It was common knowledge that a lot of illegal merchandise was making its way into Ukraine from Poland and Sascha had caught sight of weapons, body armour and other military essentials that were concealed under first aid supplies being ferried into Ukraine on vehicles stamped with the Red Cross. Of course, this wasn't the legitimate *International Red Cross* organisation. Just about anyone who drove a *Ford Transit* van, coming back and forth across the border, displayed a red cross facsimile painted or conveniently stuck on the side in red electrical tape. Large, stuck on signs citing 'humanitarian aid' were also hurriedly and popularly plastered over trade vehicles. Of all the international aid that had been gathered for Ukraine, Sascha had visited large warehouses, such as a massive, private brick complex in Lviv where first aid supplies, hygiene products, military equipment, plate carriers, food and other vital items were just sitting idle, piled high upon high. *'Talk about a cluster fuck!'* said Phil, loudly, using an old and well-used military expression. 'It seems like so many people connected with this war are rowing their own boat, yet the smaller Ukraine army are still giving the Russians a pasting. *Imagine what they could do if this country really got its shit together?'*

Having become a tight-knit group, the weary band of friends, old and new, rapidly made their way outside where there were supposed to be shuttle buses taking desperate people from or back to the border. The late-night air was extremely crisp, the road was wet, and anyone who had gotten off the train had been picked up, long ago... At a glance, it looked like the town was completely deserted, still and deathly quiet. *Not even a mangy cat to be seen!* It soon dawned on the group there were no shuttle buses going anywhere, let alone to Medyka!! Nathan approached the solitary taxi that still had a light on and politely asked if they could be ferried to the border. The driver did not comment, but grunted, wound up the window, drove twenty metres, braked, and turned off the engine. Nathan looked at the group bemused and posed the obvious question, 'I suppose that means he isn't' going anywhere?' The group were dumbfounded by this petulant display and started exploring options on how to get to the border. To their surprise, suddenly a mid-sized man in a dark crimson puff jacket appeared out of the shadows and was heading fast by foot to the station. Phil called out to the traveller, 'Hey mate, do you know how to get to Medyka from here?' 'Mr. Hurry' stopped instantly in his tracks and turned toward Phil and Nathan - *'Kiwis*?' *'Aussies!'* remarked the two Australians, in loud, proud voices! The man began to talk with a frustrated tone, 'If you're hoping to get to Medyka tonight, forget it! All the vehicles stopped running an hour ago. I'm hoping to catch the last train to Krakow and *to get the hell out of here!*' Garen inquired, 'Have you been into Ukraine, Lviv or Kyiv?' 'Yes,' replied the man who now sounded more like he had a slight Scots accent. 'Yeah, I've been to Lviv all right. *What a fucking rock show! The city is getting rocketed nightly, air-raid sirens are going off, yet the people carry on as if it were a Christmas market, or some bullshit like that.*' As the man relayed his experiences, he was getting further agitated, moving about, and frenetically waving his arms in complete frustration, and his Scots accent grew thicker... 'I tried assisting refugees with travel, temporary shelter and so forth but take your pick - mistrust, incompetence, bureaucracy, or a combination of all three. *Nothing happens or moves quickly in Ukraine.*' Having concluded his lengthy list of grievances, the frustrated man dived into his large jacket pocket and produced two thousand Ukrainian hryvnias and basically threw the money at the group. 'Here, take this,' as the money floated earthward like confetti, 'I hope you do better with it than me. *I'm off back to Britain where I will be more useful writing letters to my local Member of Parliament than wasting my time here!*' And on that claim, he turned and dashed off to the train station and the ticket office. In an instant, he was gone as quickly as he had appeared! Again, the group stood around bemused at this display...

'Okay,' said Sascha in a cool, calculating tone, 'It looks like we either find some accommodation and, *good luck with that at this time of the night,* or walk to the border and sleep in the tentage that is to be found there.' The British father and daughter pair opted for walking as they were in a hurry to assist the refugees they were sponsoring. The two Americans nodded, indicating their eagerness to march onwards. Phil looked at Nathan and said, 'Well, I'm up for it.' With the group decision being made in the affirmative, some quick adjustments were made to their rucksacks, socks pulled up and boots tightened before the group set off. Phil asked Mike, who was navigating with his phone's GPS, how far they had to go. 'Oh, not that far, bit of a doddle really', laying on the British charm, 'only sixteen kilometres.' Phil stood perplexed, as the gravity of those words sunk in. He hadn't been on a decent route march since his army days, and it was a good job he had taken up fitness training again. *Is that all? Why not push for Kyiv while we're at it!* he jokingly replied. Nathan smiled as he could hear his mate mumble and grumble to himself as he threw his pack on, *'And I wanted to come on this trip?!'*

In no time, the group was 'smashing out' a rather brisk pace with Mike and his daughter navigating, followed by Nathan and Phil, with Bill, Sascha and Garen covering their rear, single file, as per military formation. A few 'street kids' passed them riding BMX type bikes but didn't even take the time to routinely examine this eclectic band of strangers. As the minutes flew by, the night became increasingly frostier as the group hiked along the freezing pavement. As luck would have it, they weren't marching into a raging head wind or snowstorm. They had marched twenty minutes and as the varied group negotiated a steep road and bridge, they were met on the other side with the familiar 'golden arches' of a *McDonalds* restaurant. The surreal image was not lost on the group with most people commenting this was the last thing they imagined coming across at this time of night and whereabouts! Nathan stopped, examined the visage, closed his eyes, shook his head, and commented with some jest, *'Hello again, old friend!'* Nevertheless, a quick consensus meant this would be an ideal location for a brief stop and refreshment before they continued. Who knows what they will find at the border or when their next decent meal would be? It was here that Nathan suggested to Sascha and the two Americans that they turn off their personal locaters on their phones. There had been various stories circulating that the Russian military and spy agencies were aggressive in their tracking of Westerners in Ukraine. Of course, there are a lot of crazy and random stories that always circulate in a war zone but why take the chance?

In a short while, most probably thirty minutes, the group finished their 'brews and burgers', threw on their weighty rucksacks, and headed purposefully, but laboriously toward the border. Again, Mike was performing navigation and the group fell back into the same formation as before. It wasn't long before the course took them off the main road and they skirted around houses in a small village. In the semi-darkness, an ensemble of dogs began barking and it seemed as though every house in the quaint village possessed canine security. A few lights went on in a random house or two, but the group trudged on their merry way without interference; no cars or humans to be seen and, occasionally, there would be halts so the rear guys could catch up. Garen had decided to carry his full EMT kit, which made the going for him slow and gruelling. It was obvious that speed wasn't his forte and his giant frame was struggling under the weight of his load.

After four hours, and at around one a.m., it was painfully evident the group needed to break for the night as the trek had descended to a snail's pace. Nathan looked around for a small wooden barn or inviting tin roofed lean-to, but nothing was to be seen... They walked for five minutes and then another ten... and five more minutes after that. Then, as they trudged through another pintsized village, he discovered a small grove of densely configured pine trees, shielded, on one side, by a six-foot-high stone wall, adjacent to the village. Without hesitation, Nathan suggested they stop, '*This will do for the night! I think we've all slept in worse places than this...*' It didn't look like rain, but it was the clearest of nights and Nathan knew there would be heavy dew in the morning. No point starting the mission with wet sleeping bags and dampened spirits! The generously thick canopy of the trees and sturdy wall would provide some rudimentary protection from the elements, and the ground was much drier here as a result of the abundance of pine nettles. Within moments, sleeping bags were hastily rolled out upon dry sleeping mats, all the men passed on any spare bivvy bags or poncho liners to Mike and his daughter, as they only had what they stood in. Such was the tiredness that no-one spoke and the night's quiet descended upon them. Within minutes, the group had sought shelter and were now tucked into the warmth of their dry and inviting bedding. The last thing on Nathan's dreamy mind before he crashed out was the thought of how this was day one and they still weren't at the border!

Chapter Eight:

RUDE AWAKENINGS...

It was early and barely light, around 05:30 in the morning, when Nathan slowly woke. He had slept soundly, but in fits, and now had to remind himself of his location. It all seemed so bizarre that he had crashed out in his sleeping bag, late last night in a copse by a road in wintry Poland, and for a second, and a brief one at that, he imagined he was dozing in his comfy bed back at the bush block. Nathan thrust his head half out of his sleeping bag, in much the same way a meerkat cautiously emerges from out of its desert hole, and slowly peered about, looking all around for a few seconds. The morning was fresh, but still, and the area was noticeably quiet. It hadn't been long after they put their heads down for the night when Mike woke Nathan and informed him that the two Brits were pushing on to the border. They had been bitterly cold and decided to move on; the temperature had dropped considerably and there was a light, dewy mist enveloping the village that added to the chill. After being briefed, Nathan had, for the most part, slept deeply and only loosely heard Bill and Garen lightly snoring during the night.

He peeped around again and there wasn't any movement or noise from the remaining party. 'Time for breakfast', Nathan thought, so he wriggled his way out of his sleeping bag and fossicked around inside a small dry bag for a few seconds, just inside his rucksack... *Voila! Food!* He opened a sizeable jar of cold baked beans that had been purchased at a mini market while they had been waiting for the train to Tarnow, and a thick crusty bread roll complemented the meal. He reminisced at how difficult it had been, not being able to converse in Polish, and he very nearly bought some cans of sauerkraut or some obscure Polish delicacy. He pondered how easy it is for the simplest of life's basic functions to become exceedingly difficult in a foreign country! As he ate, sitting on his rucksack, the day was becoming lighter by the minute, and he was contented... As the morning developed, vehicles were starting to pass by their location, which was just adjacent to the main village road. As the daylight began to take hold, and the *ad hoc* campsite was on full display, it wasn't long before drivers and passengers began to flash the 'stink eye' in his direction and, as he surveyed their rough camp, Nathan thought they certainly resembled 'wandering gypsies' or people who were 'down and out.'

Nevertheless, Nathan got on with finishing his

delicious beans and crusty roll, when a small, muddied looking police sedan shuddered to a halt, on the road that was slightly elevated above the sleepy travellers, about ten metres away. The officer on the passenger side, who wore a dark blue padded jacket with a fur collar, tucked up high by his ears, in a feeble attempt to harness some warmth, gestured for Nathan to come to him. As Nathan approached, the side window was methodically wound down. A not too happy man looked at Nathan and said, flatly, *'Passports?'* Nathan passed over his passport and climbed back down the bank from the road to wake the sleeping men. Upon Nathan's loud calls, Bill and Phil woke almost immediately but Garen was in a 'dead man's sleep,' -- *he was out cold!!* Nathan shook the large man ferociously and in a few seconds two startled eyes opened and looked at him, almost blank and in a state of trance. Again, Nathan attempted to coax the Texan in a loud voice - *'Garen, the flipping cops are here, and they want to see your bloody passport!'* Still, Garen could not comprehend... Nathan continued with the verbal barrage and physical shaking but now with a great deal more intensity... Finally, Garen emerged from his stupor, quickly appreciated the urgency, and produced his American passport.

After receiving all the documents from Nathan, the police officer wound up the window, much to the dismay of the travellers. 'God, I hope they aren't going to confiscate the passports,' thought Nathan. But the officer wanted to examine the documents in the cabin, by the heater.

After three to four minutes, the window was wound down once again, and the officer asked why the men were there. Nathan declared that they were humanitarian workers on their way to the border, and they had to stop as one of their group members fell ill, late last night. *A slight stretching of the truth but it wasn't a complete lie...* The passports were promptly handed back, the window wound up, and the police car trundled off without further inquiry. Not a single word needed to be said as the police visit became the catalyst for unbridled action! The men dashed about frantically, quickly dressed, and packed away their pieces of equipment. 'Well, nothing like an early morning police visit to inject some impetus into the occasion,' reflected Nathan.

In less than five minutes, the campsite was clear, and the men were off down the road again hiking the few remaining kilometres to the border. This time Bill was navigating and soon they found themselves on a newly made double highway that was heading in the right direction. Without warning, another small police car, most probably a *Lada 2110* this time, pulled up by the men and demanded passports, yet again. '*Man,*' thought Nathan, '*This shit is getting stale!*' At least the police officers this time looked friendly, inspected the documents, offered their thanks, said a cheery goodbye, and drove off. The men still had a couple of kilometres to go, but Garen managed to flag down a taxi, and a big SUV one at that. Bodies and bags were piled into the large vehicle, and they were soon deposited at the entrance of the refugee area within minutes. After all the dramas of the last two days, *they finally reached their destination!* A sense of relief now descended over the weary men. The trip to the border had been gruelling, with many challenges, to say the least, and it was at this point that Nathan imagined the tough and nuggetty 'Ant Middleton' from the *SAS Australia* and UK television program to appear, and congratulate them in a rolling, Cockney accent – *'Well done lads, you've made it this far in selection, orright?'* But he quickly dismissed such fanciful imaginings and scanned around the ubiquitous sea of unique people and distinctive tentage. The men stood motionless, gazing, stupefied at their new environment, like a child does at the wonderous glitz and glamour of a country fair or a circus big top; *they were totally and utterly stunned!*

The amazing spectacle that Nathan saw before him was like nothing he had even seen or could have imagined! On either side of a three- to four-metre-wide paved avenue that meandered uphill to the immigration buildings, and past the significant and sizeable security fencing on the Polish side of the border, there was a myriad of coloured marquees that dispensed all types of international cuisine, clothing, first aid and medicine, animal supplies, and even wood fired pizza. Jewish doctors – big and small, male, and female as well as cheerful Spanish aid workers, Sikhs and Jehovah Witnesses all occupied the tight spaces along and either side of the pavement and were there dispensing a brand of humanitarianism, in their own, unique, secular way. Besides the 'professionals', brightly dressed clowns tossed coloured balls into the fresh air and dispensed wrapped chocolates to small, excited children, clutched by tired, anxious parents. A young Gaelic-looking man wearing white impresario clothes played pop hits and the classics from a beat up black grand piano he had trucked in from somewhere in Western Europe - thought to be Paris. A lay preacher from Germany was blessing all and anyone he could get his hands on. At the same time, Polish police, Polish military and even a frocked Cardinal waltzed up and down the wet, cluttered, dirty avenue, scrutinizing and sanctifying the refugees that streamed into Poland from the east. Yet, in the midst of all this, many refugees were now heading back to Ukraine with newly acquired provisions. Depending on the media's reporting of the ebb and flow of the war, these poor souls decided to take their chances and return home.

Nathan had expected to see an orderly and well-run camp, with 'a place for everything and everything in its place'; his military experience demanded it!! Yet here, on the one hand, as far as he could see, lay a mighty uplifting spectacle of volunteer dedication and, along with it, the delicate, but determined clinging to existence by hordes of refugees; both worthy exemplars of the immensity of the human spirit! On the other hand, this shameful exhibition of refugee damnation also demonstrated the black, evil emptiness that can also fester in the human soul, this time perpetrated by the Russian Federation. He muttered under his breath, *'What a 'freaking circus...'* In Nathan's mind, these words formed the only relevant assessment he could declare to adequately describe what lay, pitifully, distinctively, and annoyingly before him.

While the men were gradually taking all this in, it was Sascha, glued to his smartphone for some time, who turned to the waiting group, which continued to stand in mute awe of this mighty procession, this supreme pandemonium, and its scintillating atmosphere of humanitarian *carnivale*. 'My Ukrainian military contact says he needs some more time to try and locate your friend; places he visited and stayed at, and people he met -- *you know the drill*. He suggested we stay here for a few days and help out; join one of the humanitarian groups, and this will give you more "street cred" if you need to go into Ukraine. Less suspicious for the *SBU* (Ukrainian Secret Police). He will have the information for us soon. Don't you worry.' Sascha's comments were disappointing... Lolling about for snippets of tales of adventures from the 'front' wasn't what Nathan wanted to hear but he realised this was the gruelling process they would have to follow, like it or not. Garen volunteered to locate the *Polish Red Cross* and offer his services there. Bill looked at the closest tent; an enormous, 'Barnum and Bailey' circus big top facsimile, total white in design, and belonging to the *United Sikhs* from England - he would chase them up to see what was on offer. Sascha would locate some accommodation and

Nathan and Phil would check out the food, showers, and transport situation. They would rendezvous back at this spot in exactly one hour.

Without a further word having to be said, the men dispersed and set about their tasks. Nathan and Phil must have wandered up and down the people-choked and dirty avenue of 'humanitarian attractions' at least two or three times. As Phil remarked, 'this place looks like Nimbin on a good day.' The reference to Australia's 'alternative lifestyle capital,' was not lost on Nathan but he replied, disparagingly, 'I'm not into hippies.' The avenue was probably five hundred metres in length until it stopped at a security checkpoint and people slowly stirred themselves forward in groups to the immigration buildings. In what seemed like no time, the hour was nearly up, so Nathan waited patiently for the other men to arrive at the arranged spot. It was Bill who arrived first, followed by Sascha and then Garen, who was trying not to be late by walking fast to the group meeting area. Bill had secured volunteer work for the men at the large, white, Sikh marquee. It was being utilised as a respite facility for women and children traumatised by the war, and it was off limits to men. As Bill stated, 'Apparently, this area is rife with human traffickers and paedophiles, who promise free transport and accommodation anywhere in Europe for the refugees. Our job will be to provide security for the women and kids; anyone suspicious is passed onto the police. It will be long days, but we will have some time off and can work in shifts, as we like. They have also offered to feed us.' In a more sombre tone, he informed the men that police had intercepted a van of refugees who were being taken to Germany, to a warehouse where they would be the unwitting participants in a 'snuff' movie. Sex, gore and then murder of the participants was the usual cinematic premise. Bill was disgusted and said, *'Can you fucking believe that - a snuff movie, in this day and age?'* It was easy for paedophiles and human traffickers to create a cheap sign and peddle the story that a ride was awaiting refugees, free to any destination in Europe, as they pretended to help the needy. *That was the cruel enticement... That was the hook...* People were so desperate to be free and to survive, but the scum of humanity preyed upon those innate desires. The men, although hardened by tough military lives, were visibly shocked, appalled by Bill's story.

Nathan then informed his colleagues that showers were only available at a small hostel on the other side of the road at the low end of the avenue. This is where the buses ferried the refugees to a waiting area for processing back in Prezemsyl and other sites throughout Poland. The showers had to be paid for. There was also a small supermarket nearby that was doing a roaring trade and 'World Central Kitchens' was on site providing free catering to all volunteers. There were other small kitchens too in the locale, and the men could take their pick from Indian dahl, pizza, or anything else on offer. Garen had waited over an hour for the head of the local *Red Cross* team to arrive, only for the manager to tell him in no uncertain terms to *'Leave, immediately...'* It seemed many of the humanitarian organisations were in competition with each other and did not champion outside interference or specialised intervention. This attitude seemed bizarre in a time of such infinite crisis, but bureaucrats and politicos here had built their own 'kingdoms' and did not want to share their 'toys.' Sascha then spoke in a reluctant tone, 'Do you want the good news or the bad news?' After a round of inquiring looks, and no takers, he continued... 'Good news is I have found accommodation, bad news it is camping in tents.' The weather was still very wintry and would be for some time. It would be hard living, but all the men had experience in these situations and knew how to pace themselves and how to afford each other 'personal' space. Apparently, the tents were on the other side of the avenue, over a small dodgy wire mesh fence that had to be climbed, and located in part of a muddied car park, half full of vehicles. There had been a number of French humanitarian volunteers who had owned this camping equipment, but they decided to help somewhere else, and had left everything behind. Upon seeing the trashed site, Phil spoke out aloud, *'Damn, this place looks like the beaches at Dunkirk in 1940... what with all this abandoned gear!'* Amazingly, there were camping tents, deck chairs, a large fire pit and even several electric heaters that had been discarded. Phil and Sascha chose a bright yellow two-man tent on flat ground, while Bill, Garen and Nathan had no alternative but to put their gear into the larger, blue and red three-man tent that resided on a small rise. It certainly was a far cry from 'glamping', but at least the tentage and accommodation didn't cost them a cent and they would only be here for a short time. *Hopefully*... On a sadder note, no one had seen the two Brits from Grimsby that had briefly travelled with the group earlier. Though few words were spoken, it was evident that all the men hoped that they had rescued their refugees and made it out of this debacle. It was now late in the day, and time to prepare for the wintry evening. *Tomorrow would be a day like no other...*

Chapter Nine:

JUST ANOTHER DAY IN SUNNY POLAND...

Again, coffee and croissant was the breakfast fare... Outside of Garen rolling about, extremely restless during the night, sleeping on an angle, and occasionally 'tap dancing' on Nathan's groin with his massive size eleven feet, it was an uneventful evening! Bill, Garen and Nathan would commence the first security shift at the *United Sikhs* refugee tent, and they would be relieved by Phil and Sascha later in the day. It had started to drizzle, oh, so lightly, which further lowered the mood, and the sight of cold and sodden refugees, heartbreakingly clutching their few possessions, wincing from the rain, hit home to the men and they thought tenderly of their loved ones and how truly lucky they were... Unlike the refugees, Nathan and his colleagues were there out of choice, not desperation... This is the eternal problem with Europe mused Nathan, there have *always* been armies raging back and forth during history and the collateral damage connected to this warfare cast its net far and wide, mostly with the women and children... 'No way could I, or would I, ever buy a house or want to reside here permanently.' As the men took up their security stations outside the tent, they spent a great deal of their time trying to remain warm and dry, shuffling their cold feet, rubbing their frozen hands, and sheltering under the small, adjacent marquees where clothing was being offered to any refugee that passed by. The miserable rain, although slight, continued, unabated... They chatted and laughed about their past military service, and the similarities between the armies of different nations, or just gazed at the visual spectacle of displaced people toiling and plodding past them.

The function of the enormous, white tent was simple, it only housed displaced women and children from all over Ukraine. A male refugee, who had to sleep elsewhere because of the 'female only' stipulation, had arrived at the border with his wife and small child. This small troupe had trudged all the way from the north of Ukraine, near the border with Belarus, hundreds of kilometres away!! Not to worry, a bed was soon found for the man in a humanitarian tent, close by. There was even a 'cat lady', the stereotypical elderly woman who had ferried at least a dozen felines and their cages out of her besieged country. *The smell of these animals was incredibly vile... The incessant, noisy meowing nearly as offensive and annoying...* But empathetic aid workers understood the intrinsic meaning and value of the 'tabbies' to the woman, and kept themselves busy, disregarding any and all forms of umbrage credited to the cats. Most probably, they were her only belongings and 'family' left in this world...

Regardless of all this public theatre, Nathan and his friends were there, doing their bit, but this didn't mean they couldn't have some fun... While sitting on a bench outside the tent, one afternoon, Phil started lightly singing an old tune from the 1990s - 'What if God was one of us,' the only big hit by American chanteuse, Joan Osbourne, and it soon became the group's theme song, even though Phil's repetitive choruses and off-key singing made it highly irritating, especially to Garen, who would just look at him, tiredly, with squinted eyes! Nevertheless, the 'black' humour, pop songs and funny anecdotes helped pass the time and aided in the bonding of the group, now entrenched in a peculiar, if not bizarre environment of Ukrainian evacuees and their unique problems.

It was at this time when Nathan bumped into an old friend of his, a Kiwi named Mickey Johnson who came walking, calm as you like, down the avenue of tents. This chance meeting didn't surprise Nathan as he had once met several friends that he hadn't seen for years on the famed *Kokoda Track - of all places*, and was always running into colleagues and old mates in the most peculiar places... Mickey was ex-Kiwi SAS and had conducted a tracking course for the Australian SAS down in the south of Western Australia, way back in the late 1980s. He wasn't a tall or broad man but was a mad keen rugby union player and had the fighting heart of Mike Tyson. Nathan couldn't believe his eyes and the two men shook hands and spoke as if it had only been yesterday; this frequently happens with ex-military. *Very direct and straight to the point, no fuss or bullshit.* Mickey was in Ukraine to pass on his expertise, like so many others, and when informed of Steve Holland and his MIA status, he gladly volunteered to tag along and help as best as he could. Mickey possessed a buoyant and infectious personality and was soon welcomed by the rest of the men. He had managed to locate a one-man tent that wasn't too far from Nathan's bivouac.

Along with the unrelenting swarm of bedraggled refugees, eager volunteers and numerous authorities, there were other noteworthy and suspicious people 'ghosting' in and out of the teeming evacuee area. Alongside the world's media, there were the 'wannabe' heroes, wearing old military style uniforms, even some from the era of the 1990s Operation Desert Storm, who were taking selfie documentaries and commenting on how dangerous it was 'To be in the war'. *'Oh, the horror,'* they lamented... strutting about as if they were combat veterans and the subject matter experts on this 'new' war. Nathan and his friends viewed these people with utter disdain – what poseurs, what fakes! Back home, these 'valour cheats' would have been torn to shreds, verbally and physically, but here was not the time nor the place.

In addition to these fraudsters, there were a large number of security and aid officials from many of the Western nations, checking out how things were being done and where they thought they could best help. Some individuals were a lot more obvious than others... The more standout operatives were those, particularly Americans, wearing brand new 5.11 tactical clothing and operator caps, trying not to look conspicuous but coming off as 'spooks' from any number of intelligence/security services. Some of the most ultra-obvious types were the Australian Embassy people with 'Official Diplomat' emblazoned on their *hi-vis* jackets, who came for a quick inspection and most probably a day off from the mundane day-to-day goings on at the *Aussie* embassy in Warsaw. Phil, Nathan, and Mickey looked at the 'soft' Australian officials and just shook their heads in disbelief with a 'Yeah, what a fat load of good they'll do', being on the forefront of their minds.

Besides the fresh-faced young men, there were the not-so-young men with grey beard stubble and receding hair lines with military rucksacks and plate armour who were also streaming across the border to join the *International Legion*. Regardless of age, these men marched with a fast pace and an obvious determination that indicated they couldn't wait to get into this war. *Then again, the traffic wasn't all one way...* There were security operatives from the 'other side,' stealthily functioning throughout the vast area who were creating their own dossiers on the current situation and identifying people in it. Some of these characters were casually taking photographs, their covers being as independent journalists, while other operators meandered about in the guise of an international volunteer, a taxi driver, or an aid worker. Sometimes, their edgy mannerisms and Slavic features were a giveaway as well as their positioning to areas of interest. Nevertheless, *not all were bad Soviet agents...* What Nathan didn't notice was the young, long-haired Jewish man from Brooklyn, New York, who was eagerly filming him and his colleagues from two food stalls back, using a telephoto lens on his digital camera. He was supposedly taking a wide angled shot of the larger area, 'You know, for memories and the scrapbook'. However, this man's brief was to film anyone in the vicinity who looked like they had performed military service and pass this information up the intelligence chain. This man, and other agents like him, would film Westerners, especially the young fit ones, hell bent on joining the *International Legion* and attempt to catalogue them for their records. It was really a simple job, but the primary intent was for the word to be circulated that Russian spy agencies knew *who* was in Ukraine and secondly, create a picture of *where* they were going. It was equally intended to scare and dissuade potential international recruits from joining the Ukrainian military as well as alerting the Russians to the combat backgrounds of the types of 'mercenaries,' as Putin labelled all the Western volunteers, they would likely come up against.

Amid all this chaos and suffering, the lean and gangly New Yorker with the telephoto camera sauntered back to the busy food kitchen where he normally dispensed scrumptious chilli fries and tacos. He indicated he wasn't feeling well and was convinced he needed to take a rest on his bunk. For dramatic effect, the back of his skinny hand was placed upon his forehead, and he took in some irregular deep breaths. 'I think I might have picked up a bug, *hope it's not Covid...*' he mournfully suggested to the group and then let out a sickly, pathetic cough. His colleagues, all with worriedly skewed looks on their faces, wished him well as they frantically waved him away from their stations. Once out of sight, he briskly walked the short space to the hostel, around two hundred metres or less, which was at the end of the tent avenue and on the other side of the road from the bus pickup point.

The hostel had become a *de facto* wash house for the myriad of volunteers and all the aid people coming and going. Besides its utilitarian functions, it was a perfect front for a spy. The New Yorker slowly crept the grubby stairs to the first floor, to his shared room, all the while taking in and calculating the sounds of his environment. He made his way in and locked the door, checking it was locked, twice. He stood as if he were frozen and listened, ear resting on the door's paneling in absolute silence for a minute. His erratic heartbeat was all he heard...*no other following footsteps...* 'Good,' he surmised, he was all alone... Then, after a cursory but scrutinous review of his meagre surroundings, he quickly went to his single bed and from underneath, he produced a locked, battered, stainless-steel case that was emblazoned with a variety of travel destination and rock group concert stickers. The case was opened after the steely combination lock was quickly and expertly navigated and he placed his laptop on the small, rickety table. The miniscule SD card from his camera was inserted into the computer and its contents sent on its dutiful way to Moscow. The now exuberant New Yorker took a deep swig of some cheap, nasty Polish vodka and reminisced how his Russian grandfather had introduced him to the potent spirit when he was a small, obliging boy. He smiled and thought how his 'dedushka' would be so proud of him, *serving the Motherland...* He took another long quaff and now the loathsome smelling booze was going straight to his head. Guided by the sense of inebriation, the Brooklyn man flopped down upon his bunk and messed up sleeping bag. Within minutes, the gratification of his mornings work and the effects of the budget alcohol quickly ushered him into a deep, sound siesta.

In a cold and grey Moscow, the secret information that was ferried to central intelligence was then rapidly dispatched to various civilian and military spy agencies. Somewhere in another part of the country, in a grey tiled and ugly building that had been built in Soviet

1950, and behind a cheap, wood composite table, sat a man in his fifties, fossicking over numerous documents and photographs. He meticulously took his time, as any craftsman does, annotating with his favoured *Montblanc* pen as he went, as well as making mental notes. At first glance, the man looked similar to Alec Baldwin but weighing ten kilos less, and the man's hair had greyed considerably in the last six months. He no longer wore a dark, tailored business suit, crisp white shirt, with a red *Hermes* tie, but now modelled a dour military style combat jacket in Russian camouflage, army fatigue trousers and tan, lightweight combat boots, a light greyish stubble adorned his cleft chin. The *Director* had quickly departed the *Agency,* and Australia after the murderous debacle in central Victoria and had been secreted out of the country via a network he had established more than a decade ago... He was now a senior intelligence officer with the *Wagner Group*, the Russian paramilitary organisation loyal to Putin. Unlike his well-paid job back with the Australian government, these days, his position afforded him more protection and privilege than salary.

He took his time studying the photographs. Suddenly, after cautiously scanning another group of colour and sepia images, he came to a tiny but recognizable grainy image, *which made him jolt upright in his seat!* He dropped the photo in disbelief, then lightly and delicately picked it up, leaned forward and examined it again, even more closely this time with a large, circular magnifying glass. As hard as he tried, he couldn't get any closer. 'Well, what do you know?' said the *Director*, when satisfied with his find, *'If it isn't my old, dear friend, Nathan Philips.'* The *Director* quickly reached for his mobile phone in his jacket pocket, dialled a number, and began talking, in fluent Russian. *'Da, Da,'* urged the *Director*, 'Don't do anything, just follow him and his entourage, for the moment.' And on that call, the *Director* sat up, feeling considerably more energized. He then aggressively rocked back on his chair and plonked his dirty boots on the messy table and smiled like he hadn't done so in a long, long while...

Chapter Ten

THE WAITING GAME...

No vital information was forthcoming... No news from anyone and Sascha's contacts had become mysteriously quiet... Meanwhile, the weather remained wet and unbelievably depressing. The men had quickly settled into their daily routine of security duty at the *United Sikhs* tent, observing the laborious comings and goings of despondent refugees. Aside from one late night drama, back at their tent, life had quickly become mundane and slightly irritating. The men spoke and laughed about the incident over coffee the next morning... It was around one a.m., and everyone was sleeping soundly in their tents, when suddenly, raucous music began playing in an adjacent marquee. Nathan re-countered how he lay in his sleeping bag for a minute or two, having been woken and annoyed at the 'doof doof' noise. The booming music continued to play, and Nathan lay there fuming, slowly and literally building up a head of steam! Joltingly, he bellowed *'shut the fuck up!'* ensuring it was suitably loud and aggressive, with the intent to influence the perpetrators. But the music continued... Nathan began to talk, angrily and rapidly to himself: *'Fucking refugees all over the place and some fuckhead wants to have a party, I can't believe this shit!'* The music and merrymaking didn't abate but now sounded even louder... A further minute's waiting ensued followed by a rapid surfacing from his sleeping bag, the hasty dressing of muddied boots, an even quicker unzipping of the tent and a brisk march to the 'partygoers' shelter.

Three men in their early twenties who were clearly very inebriated, babbling to each other, incoherently, as drunks always do. Nathan stood at the entrance of their flimsy tent, somewhat replicating the mighty and indefatigable *Colossus of Rhodes* and barked the following ultimatum as he judgingly gazed down, extremely irritated at the men by their selfish behavior: *'There are people trying to get some sleep around here, who have been working hard, and there are those who have a damn sight more worries than you lot, so shut the hell up and go to fucking bed!!'* Well, Nathan's short but candid sermon had its desired impact! One of the drunks fumbled for the radio and it was instantly switched off, while the two other men rummaged about for their sleeping bags. Nathan returned to his tent, still fuming, incensed but eager to glide back into his warm sleeping bag, and back into a deep sleep. Bill had only known the Australian a truly short time, but he knew

Nathan was prone to crankiness and anger, and after the first *'shut the fuck up'* with no response, he could only see the situation deteriorating. The men continued to drink their hot coffee and belly laugh over the amusing incident.

As the weather had deteriorated to light, bright, flaky snow and the refugee lines at the border had become increasingly longer, the *United Sikhs* had decided to transport and dispense dry clothing, hot food, pasta with sauce, and bottled water to the Ukrainian side of the border. Herbier was the driving force behind this initiative and she had travelled from the warmth of California to 'do her bit'. Young, in her early forties and Indian American, Herbier was the sort of woman who 'got things done' and along with the many other courageous Sikhs who had travelled from all over the UK, they were a formidable team and were responsible for numerous successful humanitarian projects on a global scale. Nathan and his colleagues all thought these people were utterly amazing and proud to be working by their side. It was Bill, Nathan, Phil and Garen who volunteered to help out, also to alleviate the increasing boredom experienced at the respite tent. Two of the men would grab a shopping trolley that had been seconded from who knows where, load it up and push it up hill to the immigration building on the Polish side. Depending on who was on duty, the customs people would call for the volunteers to come to the front of the line, quickly check passports and IDs, and usher them on. There was a brief walk through the 'no man's land' between national boundaries until the aid workers arrived at the Ukrainian customs building. Again, the men went through the vetting process and pushed their loaded trolleys into Ukraine.

Sascha was assisting Phil with his heavy trolley but once it had been positioned parallel to the line of refugees, he quickly whispered to Phil, 'Time for me to chat to our *Legion* recruiters; won't be long.' Phil acquiesced with a quick head nod and commenced, like the rest of the men, to hand out the various supplies or dish out the hot food. The lines were unbelievably long and continued out to the main road, where trucks and buses were patiently lined up down the road as far as the eye could see, trying to get into Poland. Like sad cattle, the refugees stood obediently in place, waiting to get the go ahead from officials. Besides a lack of food, water and shelter, people hadn't washed for days or changed their hygiene products, and the smell was grossly overpowering as it wafted from the massive, ragged assembly. Outside of roadkill in the powerfully hot Australian outback, or 'portaloos' baking in the intense Iraqi sun, Nathan couldn't think of anything that smelt worse... Herbier saw Sascha slide away and questioned Phil about his departure. 'Oh, he's going to check out the length of the queue,' Phil convincingly replied, 'to see if there are any refugee buses out there that require our attendance, and to identify areas where we could set up a field kitchen, if need be.' Herbier was taken back by this whimsical tale of dedication, thoroughness, and thoughtfulness, 'Ah, okay,' she said. 'Please thank Sascha when he returns for his concern and fresh ideas.' 'No problem,' said Phil, brightly. *'Will do...'*

While people were stirring, here and there, engrossed in the issues affecting their immediate and long-term survival, Sascha had walked past the *International Legion* recruiting tent to gauge the type of men who were on station and what condition they were in. Like the refugees, they too had to brave the elements and it wasn't fun for them either... He could see they looked extremely cold and miserable... The three large men, probably in their late thirties, were dressed in all their Ukrainian military camouflage and coats, and were moving about briskly, trying to warm themselves. There wasn't even a fire drum or decent seating in or near their tent, which wasn't very well sighted and open to the weather. Sascha made a quick survey of his surroundings, up and down the main street. A few people were loitering around the money change shops, trying to change their Ukrainian currency to Polish Zloty. Most were getting 'ripped off' in the process. A couple of large buses were parked, close by, with powerful diesel engines still noisily idling, waiting to get the 'go ahead' to cross into Poland. There were also a few dark and devious men, most probably of *Romani* extraction, loitering about with intent; either looking to hustle people out of their money, possessions, or lives... *Not a very safe place for the weak or uninitiated...* Sascha clamped eyes upon a general store that sold, among other things – liquor, and made a rapid bee line to it!

Within a few minutes, Sascha walked out with a heavy bag of select groceries; three bottles of cheap vodka, large chocolate bars and domestic cigarettes. That would do the trick, or so he hoped... He quickly sprang across the wet road, between two huge buses, and headed for the *Legion* recruiting tent. As he approached, he yelled in a buoyant and thunderous voice, 'Hey brothers...*Slava Ukraini, heroiam Slava!*' Without a second's hesitation, the men instantly stood erect and repeated the patriotic chorus, in much louder voices. The tone of friendship was now set... Sascha then suggested, as a comrade and patriot, 'I think you all need looking after too, don't you agree?' He quickly dispensed the goodies to the men, *who had thought all their Orthodox Christmases had come at once!!* Sascha would let the men, who were beaming with gratitude, vigorously swallow some of the coarse vodka before he started carefully and clinically asking questions and probing for answers... He added to their confidence by announcing that he had served in Ukraine's military back in Crimea in 2014, when the Russians had started this 'shooting match', and he knew what he was talking about because he really had been there. While Sascha had been playing up to the soldiers, there were some young foreign volunteers who waited outside the flimsy tent and looked as miserable and cold as their hosts. There was no mention of *them* getting any chocolate or vodka! It would be hours before their transport would arrive to secrete them to a base where their life in the *Legion* would commence.

Ah, life in the *Legion*! There were so many, many derogatory stories surrounding this dysfunctional mob. It had become extremely difficult to quash a bad news story, as reports and gossip had filtered through to the military community grapevine and the waiting and voracious global social media. It was reported that *Legion* recruits had been driven to dilapidated barracks for training, commanded by inexperienced leaders who were indecisive or incompetent and these new members had been made to sit on their packs all night instead of erecting shelters; other men had their rations and personal items stolen on day one of their service! There were also accounts of how NCOs had been selected, with no prior experience and who were off their medications. *Oh, wonderful!* How can you expect to fight a war if your junior NCOs are going berserk because they have ADHD or other mental health issues? Such was the fascination, the desire to join this unit, recruits had lied about their personal issues. Even if they had combat experience they were soon found wanting, completely out of their depth regarding basic soldiering, let alone the art of modern warfare!

As the war dragged on from month to month, and the Ukraine military had steadied itself and valiantly fought the invaders to a standstill, the selection criteria for the *Legion* had finally tightened up. An age limit had been imposed at sixty and later reduced to fifty, and potential recruits were now required to undergo a polygraph test to validate their identity and military service history. Still, instances of lies and deception were common, and Nathan had witnessed this type of insidious behavior firsthand... On one occasion, when delivering supplies to the refugees, he had ventured across a pair of young American boys in their early twenties. One 'all American' guy was from Connecticut and the other from Maine. He had casually asked the two young men about their military service, and they said it had been limited to the army reserve. They were tremendously excited and announced they had been told they were going to be given 'admin jobs' in the *Legion*. Nathan produced a half smile and said, 'Ah, admin and logistics, good luck with that, I hope it goes well for you...' trying to sound upbeat and not emphasising how he really believed the two naïve boys from the States had been unkindly played by the *Legion* recruiters. He sincerely wished them all the best as he knew they were certainly unwitting candidates for the 'meat grinder'.

By now, the volunteers had been dispensing items to the refugees for nearly two hours and their supplies were spent. Time to go back into Poland, re-stock, and do one faster trip before nightfall if they were lucky. Nathan and Phil were still becoming acclimatized to the short days and how sneakily the darkness and cold would creep upon them, little by little, before they knew it. With varying degrees of muscle and fortitude, the group pushed forward their weighty and wobbly re-stocked trolleys and made it quickly through the Polish and Ukrainian checkpoints.

Again, they were ushered to the head of the line. This time it would be a quick service and dispensing of items. They needed to get back over the border to 'Camp Medyka' before it got too late. Unfortunately, things were not so expedient at the Polish checkpoint on their return...

Apparently, the maximum limit of cigarettes allowed into Poland by an individual equates to a couple of packets. From what Nathan had seen in his short time there, most Eastern Europeans smoked vast quantities of cigarettes or were now into the addictive habit of 'vaping'. A young Ukrainian women had erroneously failed to declare a carton of cigarettes, much to the ire of the checkpoint guards. What happened next bordered on the farcical... Instead of extracting the young woman from the line and allowing the other refugees to proceed, the young guard, who was probably of junior rank such as a corporal (remember Hitler was a corporal!), had decided to make 'an example' of the young woman. As a cruel form of group punishment, the weak and elderly, and parents clutching their babies and children - *frozen, zombie like*, had to remain outside in the freezing cold, with snow falling, until this exhibition of power abuse had concluded, nearly an hour later. Nathan and the other men were seething but there wasn't anything they could do except give the Polish border security guards *long, dirty looks!* All the while, a young devious man from Brooklyn, five persons back in the queue, *only had eyes for Nathan and his compatriots...*

Chapter Eleven:

AT LAST, SOME NEWS...

It had taken nearly eighty, agonizing minutes longer for the group to emerge through the Polish border security checkpoint so there would be no more trips across the border this night! By now, all the volunteers were very tired, ravenously hungry, and penetratingly cold. Still, they talked and joked as they walked sluggishly back to the muddy car park and their waiting marquees, and sweet, merciful sleep. Outside of the mental satisfaction, this was their *only* reward for a hard day's work. Always quick with a joke, Garen remarked on the frigid weather, *'Damn, it's colder than a politician's promise out here!'*, and there was little disagreement with that. It was on their way back when Sascha pulled Nathan and Phil off to one side for a chat...

As it so happened, the wily Sascha had made particularly good friends with the Ukrainian *Legion* recruiters and earned their confidence; fuelled mostly by the cheap vodka, 'ego massaging' and hefty back slaps. He gleaned from them that they did remember an Australian fitting Steve Holland's description - he had passed their way nearly a month ago. They thought he was English, but they remember Steve making the national distinction, very loudly, that *'He was no bloody Pom!!'* They didn't get many Australians or New Zealanders enlisting at their tent, so this exception and Steve's age, had stuck in their minds. Sascha continued... 'After talking to the recruiters for some time and making sure they got their story right, they informed me that they heard your friend was killed in the rocket attack at Yavoriv in late March, in the Lviv Oblast region.' Sascha's news came hard, *as a hefty punch to Nathan's solar plexus* would, and his face become motionless as their friend took his time to utter his final, respectful words. *'He died with the other sixty-one Legion members who were brutally killed.'* Nathan knew of the unprecedented attack and how the base had been smashed by rockets. A corner of one of the buildings was described as though *King Kong* had viciously punched out the end rooms; a huge gaping hole comprising of two corner floors did not leave anyone with any doubt as to the ferocity of the attack. It could easily be imagined that *Kong* had then picked up and violently dumped the building back down, on its smashed foundations. Windows had been shattered, the structure had been irreparably damaged, and the building was permanently crooked and useless to anyone. Now, it stood as a monument to the ferocity and callous indifference of Russian air power.

During the attack, many of the shaken and scared *Legion* members had scattered into the nearby forest, where trenches had been half dug but the attack had been horrifyingly sudden. *But this was 'no fire and forget' by Russian missile batteries!* It was thought spies using GPS and precise timing were responsible for the attack. The sad news was that, after the initial assault, a great many of the legionnaires had returned to their barrack buildings to grab their few belongings and were hit by a second murderous wave of Russian rockets. Nathan turned his head away in disbelief, but then looked back at Phil, his face ashen with shock! Phil could see his dear friend was now completely stunned, motionless and unable to speak... Both men knew this could have always been the case, but they had deposited this horrific scenario firmly at the back of their minds. It was Phil who spoke next, to Sascha, in an inquisitorial tone, *'Okay, if Steve was killed, what did they do with the body?'* Sascha went on to explain that some of the mutilated bodies were buried in a mass grave, nearby in the small town adjacent to the base, while those that had asked for their remains to be returned to their homeland at the time of their enlistment, were taken to the morgue in Lviv. Unfortunately, what with the war and 'red tape', things like this moved depressingly slow in Ukraine. *Dead bodies were not a priority... Fighting the invaders by any means was...*

Sascha emphasised this point by recounting a

comment that he had heard from a tired and cynical babushka to some young, eager soldiers racing off to fight in the war and who would most probably die. Having seen this played out before, the old woman cried out to the boys as they marched off... *'Do yourself a favour and carry a packet of sunflower seeds in your pocket, at least when you get killed and buried, the sunflowers will grow, and you will end up doing something useful for your country!'* The sunflower is the Ukrainian national flower, a cultural symbol of peace, a core crop, and a financial asset but now, even a simple flower had become weaponised to be a state symbol of resistance and discord against Russian aggression.

Without an inkling of what was to come, Nathan violently emerged from his stupor! His voice was loud, and his anger flowed, catapulting irate words toward Phil and Sascha, *'No, this is bullshit. I don't believe it. This can't be right!'* He pleadingly continued, *'I have to make sure of this. I can't go back to Kathy with a "who knows," a "maybe," or "whatever" story. I can't! I just fucking can't!* I need to be completely certain this is how it ended for him. I know he would have asked to be sent home if he got "banjoed", *got the chop! I couldn't be more certain... If possible, we will bring him home.'* It was Phil who was now fired up and he wholeheartedly agreed with Nathan's blistering comments. *'Yeah... we are here, and need to confirm this bullshit before we go any further.'* Phil was becoming more excited and began speaking louder and more aggressively... *'Fuck it, let's go to the morgue in Lviv, yeah... let's go there and make damn sure! What else are we doing, besides sitting on our cold butts around here?!!'*

The continued search for their dead friend in Lviv was not an issue to Sascha and he confirmed to the men that this wouldn't be a problem. His contacts there would validate the presence of a Westerner fitting the description of Steve Holland at the morgue; this could be verified in a matter of hours. All they needed was transportation, and that could be arranged quickly enough. Sascha would pass on the sad news to Bill and Garen. It was agreed they would leave tomorrow, early in the morning. Before they departed, the men would thank the *United Sikhs* and suggest to them they were seeking other opportunities to help the Ukrainians in their war-torn homeland; no need telling them the complete story... Phil leisurely placed his right arm over the left shoulder of Nathan as they slowly ambled back to their tents in silence, their cramped but comfy abode for the last week or so. Nathan had promised Kathy too much to take the easy way out and just fly home with this unqualified information. If the story was true, Nathan owed it to Steve to pay his respects and say goodbye to a dear friend, *one last time...*

Chapter Twelve:

ON THE ROAD TO LVIV...

It had turned into an exceptionally cold and bitter night and most of the men found it difficult to sleep, for a variety of reasons. By and large, the refugee area was unusually silent as it seemed that everyone had decided to bunker down into their sleeping bags for warmth, peaceful solitude, and well-earned rest. Without a doubt, the day-to-day refugee crisis was starting to take a toll on the mental and physical state of all the volunteers, not just Nathan and his group. In the dingy carpark, the sound of exhausted men rolling noisily around in sleeping bags on crinkly thermal mats was heard on and off, all night, from dusk 'till dawn. Nathan was oblivious to the background sounds as his mind's nagging thoughts and doubts were profoundly active, racing about like a marathon runner on a subconscious plane... He was fortunate - *lucky more like it, if he managed to sleep for an hour or so during the whole night!* As a result, he had a slight headache, fostered by this nagging tension and unrelenting stress, probably compounded by a touch of dehydration as well. In his time, Nathan had witnessed a lot of death and destruction, on most continents of the world, but was now contemplating whether he could stomach the grisly sight of a dear close friend, now deceased. A part of him didn't want to believe Sascha's tale but he needed to prepare himself for the likelihood of his friend lying mangled, on a stone-cold slab, in a morgue, in a foreign country. This gruesome concept and its associated finality was difficult for Nathan to process... For the most part, he was annoyed, even livid with Steve's recklessness while a part of him just wanted to put this whole messy saga to rest and go home. He rolled onto his side mentally exhausted and began to doze...

It was just before eight in the morning when the tent flap suddenly flipped open. Sascha popped his head in, chirped a quick 'good morning' and alerted the boys to the chance they could get a ride at around ten a.m., but they would have to rise sharpish and get organised. A ride in a large transit van had been arranged and this vehicle would be leaving from a house nearby in the small village of Medyka that resided some kilometres away from the border outposts. The timing was stringent, and the van would depart without them if they were tardy. They would be driven to Lviv and stay at an inner-city hostel until they had sorted out their 'business'. The men didn't need to be told twice, and they set about packing their 'bits and bobs'. Sascha said he had already cleared their leaving with the *United Sikhs* and would dash off to order coffees and sweet rolls for breakfast. *'What a Godsend,'* thought Nathan, slightly smiling. Marcus had certainly presented Nathan with a huge favour by enlisting Sascha to their cause. Otherwise, their journey to Poland and Ukraine would have been incredibly difficult, if not impossible.

As the men quickly packed, the young New Yorker from Brooklyn, with the proud Russian heritage, kept a close watch from a safe distance, shielded by a food van and the comings and goings of hungry people. He could see that Nathan and his companions were leaving very soon... It was obvious, they were all sorting out their rucksacks and taking all their possessions out of their tents. After a few minutes, he keyed a memorised number into his black smart phone and made the call. He listened intently from the attached earpiece and repeated the instructions he had been given, 'Yes, I will follow them at a distance, find out where they are going and text it to you.' He finished by inquiring hopefully... 'Is there anything else you wish me to do?' A pause ensued... then a look of annoyance came across his face when listening to the stern communication from the other end... The New Yorker repeated his instructions... *'Yes, yes I know, my orders are to only follow them, that's all.'* After a slight hesitation, he spoke again, this time more confidently, to reassure his boss. *'You can count on me...'* He waited.... Now, silence only occupied the communication link and so he hung up, looking disappointed, like the petulant kid that has had his ball taken away. *He wanted to do more for the cause...*

The young Brooklyn boy was eager to please his superiors and was honoured to be given the chance to follow Nathan's group rather than just reporting on the daily occurrences and 'goings on' at the border. *It had become so mundane... so excruciatingly boring....* But now, he was getting excited, giddy in fact, and was experiencing a mild adrenalin rush. He knew his dedushka would be so proud of him; he had easily assimilated to his grandfather's brainwashing as an infant, suckled on 'selective' history and vibrant stories of the glory and spectacle that was the Russian Motherland! But more than anything else, he was excited and proud to be following in his grandfather's State Security Service footsteps.

He dashed back to his grubby room and quickly packed a large canvas daypack with some bits and pieces; clothing, binoculars, battery charger, umbrella, and small vials of poison, wrapped in cotton wool, in a cigarette packet that had been internally reinforced with thin sheets of plastic. He wasn't bothered to say his goodbyes to the helpers at the food van. Volunteers came and left the refugee kitchen all the time and *he had no time for those peasants*; in a day or so they wouldn't remember him, and probably wouldn't care. As he packed, he rang another memorised number and spoke to a man, this time in fluent Russian. A car and driver would be ready in ten to fifteen minutes. 'This should be plenty of time,' he thought, satisfied with himself. He collected his meagre possessions and ran downstairs to the entrance, positioning himself carefully on the avenue among the throng of wandering, disconnected people, and nearby to the cars and buses that endlessly came and went; he could observe Nathan and his cohort and be ready for when his vehicle arrived. The young man was revelling in the chase and was so excited, *he began trembling in anticipation and felt an enjoyable rush, once more.*

On the other side of the avenue, it had not taken the men long to pack; twenty minutes in fact. Besides shining shoes, washing, and ironing, packing was one of many auxiliary benefits of a 'military education' that most veterans carry with them for life. Nevertheless, a change of scenery would be a nice re-adjustment for all. The weather, the distressing sight of exhausted refugees – *day in and day out,* and the group's plebeian existence was depressing and sapped one's strength. But if nothing else, they had built on their credentials and experience by volunteering on the border and would have more than a legitimate reason to travel and assist people in other parts of Ukraine. Suddenly, Sascha arrived, gave a quick nod of the head and they were off on their jaunt that would take only ten to fifteen minutes to reach. As they briskly walked, Nathan and Phil kept a vigil on the homes they passed, people they saw in the street and the likelihood of an ambush. *No time to let their guard down now...* In the spring, the small village would be a pretty and tranquil place to live. But at this moment, it was probably as dangerous as most other Eastern European towns. Nathan's 'skinning knife' had been secreted to a place just behind his *Casio G Shock* watch and could be accessed almost instantly. Phil had come across a rugged hiking pole, which was lying abandoned next to its broken partner, and he would not hesitate to use that as a *de facto* lance.

The roads were saturated by the enduring rain, and they soon passed a small wood and plaster police station, although it looked abandoned. Within another minute or two they were at the house. An old Ukrainian man named Yuri skipped down the stairs of his brick cottage and first spoke with Sascha and then met each man, individually, shaking hands and thanking them for coming to assist during this humanitarian tragedy. Yuri didn't know the exact purpose of their visit and the reason for the ride to Lviv and there was no reason for him to. Black tea and slices of raw pork fat was offered to the group, and the men chatted under the cover of an old grey brick garage, at the rear of the bungalow, avoiding the relentless drizzle until the van arrived, thirty minutes later.

Denis was the driver of the *Ford Transit*, a balding, short, and stocky man in his fifties who wore dirty overalls, which were once grey, but now nearly black; so obvious was his grubby habit of wiping his hands down his front. *He was in no hurry to chat...* Other than a word or two, he didn't speak any English. He gestured, hurriedly, for the men to load their gear aboard, which they promptly did.

Some parcels had to be delivered to various addresses in Lviv by the end of the day and time was at a premium. A quick wave to Yuri and the men were off... They would need to pass through customs, and this would take time as the queues were so incredibly long; didn't they already know it?! It normally is at any checkpoint, but this was one of the main vehicular gateways to drive to the war. Denis rounded the corner onto the main road and saw the incredibly long line to the checkpoint office. He grunted and said something cursory in Ukrainian, as well as slapping his head lightly with his right hand. Without a second's hesitation, he overtook all the stationary vehicles in the lengthy queue, cut into a lane where a vehicle was exiting and proceeded to have a roaring argument with a police officer who thought Denis's actions were excessive! *The intense quarrel between driver and policeman went for thirty seconds.* All the while, Denis emphasized that he was carrying priority mail and cargo and he needed to be at the front of the line – *pronto!* He was not backing down... Finally, the officer grew tired of the dispute, threw his arms up in disgust and waved Denis on. *What did he care? He didn't get paid enough to put up with this sort of aggravation!*

A short twenty-metre drive to a customs waiting bay, by a small metal office, and the men exited to present their passports to the next available customs officer. Again, the stock standard question was posed, 'purpose of visit to Ukraine' and all the men indicated they were medical professionals on their way to help the war effort. Denis chipped in and fervently notified the old babushkas, also waiting in the line, that these men were foreign doctors and skilled medics on their way to assist Ukraine in the war. The women raised their voices as one and greeted the men with cheers and clapping. '*Supermen, Super Cossacks,*' they yelled in excitement! As if the adulation wasn't enough, Phil decided he would add to the theatre... He bent over as if he was a royal *courtier* and romantically kissed the pale and wrinkled hand of the closest woman, much to the enjoyment of all the ladies, who giggled like the excited schoolgirls they once were...

Somehow, the small *Lada Vesta* with the New Yorker and his Russian colleague had managed to follow the speedy van and had positioned themselves higher up in the vehicle queue. As it was, they would have no complications locating the van at any time as they had plenty of 'their' men stationed along the major roads, especially the main highway to Lviv. Since the war started, many of the secondary roads had been closed by the Ukrainian military to channel the Russian military to areas of their own choosing. Trees had been felled and military barricades erected, while guards, some not even old enough to leave high school, had been positioned on the major arterials, checking identities, and controlling the flow of traffic. The *Ford Transit* could only follow one main route. The New Yorker and his companion had been waved through a barricade by soldiers just after leaving customs and were hurriedly on their way to Lviv in pursuit of Nathan and his friends.

After passing through customs, Denis had accelerated the van as if he were being pursued by *Beelzebub*, Russian *Spetsnatz* or God knows who else! *The man was on a mission to get to Lviv as fast as he could!* All the occupants looked at each other in astonishment as the speed in and through the villages far exceeded what would be considered 'safe' and 'legal' in any built-up area! Phil *checked his seat belt* again to make sure it was secure... Garen *grabbed the handrail* above his head... Bill just looked forward, intently, *and stared, in mute disbelief!* Denis drove like this for the next two villages and then abruptly pulled over, raced around the back of the van, and returned with litre cans of lager for everyone. He spoke quickly and it was Sascha who translated, 'Denis has said sorry and apologises for his manners and for not passing on the drinks sooner.' But there were no apologies for his driving, which the men accepted was his custom. Again, *the Westerners all looked around in astonishment...* Denis jumped in, foot planted to the accelerator and soon the vehicle gathered speed. Not quite as fast this time, as he navigated the highway, which was not particularly busy with cars going to Lviv as the bulk of traffic was heading the other way to the border. Going in their direction was mostly heavy goods trucks heading along their route, while large 'Euro' coaches motored in the opposite direction, aiming to exit the war-torn country with their human cargo.

Nathan wasn't conversing all that much as the burden of Steve's death weighed heavily on his mind. He looked curiously outside the window, sipping on his can of pilsner and taking in the quaint houses and semi-rural farm scenes. He mused that life here wasn't all that different from back home, just uniquely Ukrainian, with a rustic beauty and a quaintness that only Eastern Europe can provide... The roads varied in soundness, and Nathan thought it was very much like his rural area in country Victoria. Country people get screwed with lack of funding for country roads; all the money is spent on the roads in the cities – *where all the votes are!* This was an enduring problem for as long as he could remember... Sometime, just before they had departed for Europe, Nathan had joked to Phil that the *Paris to Dakar Rally* organisation was planning to use Victoria's state roads as they would get more potholes and road hazards for their buck than the wilds of Africa! Such was the pitiful state of Victoria's roadways! Nevertheless, they drove on. After an hour or so, Sascha informed the men that it would be around twenty minutes until they would enter the outskirts of Lviv. The plan was to stay at a hostel, one that was central and not too far from both the morgue and the railway station, their next likely mode of transport.

Elsewhere, on the congested highway, the New Yorker and his skillful driver had done a rather good job in keeping up with Denis and his form of rally driving. They had remained unnoticed by any of Nathan's group, and now they made sure to edge a little closer and not lose the van in the afternoon city traffic, which was intense, especially with some light snow falling. Nathan thought the heavy traffic surprising, especially as the country was at war. After witnessing the swarm of humanity beating a retreat to the border, he imagined the beautiful city would be empty... *But it was far from it!* People were going about doing their shopping! There were joggers and people out walking every way he looked, and a multitude of roadworks were being conducted. This seemed crazy to Nathan as the road was more likely to be destroyed in the next missile attack. The indifference to the war was just how the 'feisty Scot' at Prezemsyl had described Lviv. Nathan reflected curiously over these displays of optimism and blissful ignorance and thought how it was 'probably the same for the people at Pompeii before they met their destruction.' However, all was not *hunky dory* on the streets of Lviv... On the frozen, depressing pavements, elderly women, and men, rugged up for the cold, attempted to sell a variety of wares, mostly old and hardly useable knives, tatty, worn dresses, an array of worthless utensils and tacky *knickknacks*, displayed on the damp ground on small, raggedy blankets; such was their desperation to make some money they would occupy these streets with their goods, freezing for hours.

Yet, amid all this drama, not too far away, on a spot off the main street, an Orthodox church loudly sounded its bells on the hour. Moments later, the van rounded a corner and pulled up very abruptly at a large sturdy and weather worn wooden door that must have been centuries old. Behind the massive door and up the stone stairs was the hostel, and their lodgings for the immediate future. Denis offered his hurried goodbyes, and the men bid him farewell as he sped off to continue his deliveries. Phil scanned his surroundings then looked at the men who appeared deflated at their impending accommodation. In an attempt to lighten the atmosphere, he spoke loudly, *'Cor, what a bleedin' dump'* in his best Cockney accent, to which the men responded with a slight chuckle. As they would discover, it was only costing them ten dollars per person, per night, for a bed and a warm room! It was Nathan who spoke in a more serious tone, 'Never mind the laughs, this will do until we get business sorted. I don't plan on being here too long!' And on that prickly announcement, the men grabbed or hoisted their bundles and followed Sascha upstairs to the reception area. The pretty brunette behind the reception desk didn't speak any English and used her computer to communicate via the *Google* translator. The system worked surprisingly well, and the men were given the keys to their room in no time...

Meanwhile, the diligent New Yorker and his driver had parked their vehicle on the right-hand side of the corner, by a pile of slushy snow and witnessed the arrival and unpacking. After five minutes, and when he was certain that Nathan and his friends were settling into the address, he instructed the driver to move on to their nominated 'safe house'. He would compose a detailed and thorough report for the *Director* and expected to return later that evening for surveillance duties. He felt quite chuffed with himself as he thought this 'spy' business was much easier than he was led to believe. *Or so he thought...*

Chapter Thirteen:

Chapter Thirteen:

YOU REAP WHAT YOU SOW...

The *Director* was more than just interested in the oscillating journey of Nathan and his colleagues. He knew the 'humanitarian ruse' was just a cover for some other covert operation. His mind ticked over, 'what could it be... oh, what could it be...' He wasn't overly concerned as he knew this would become apparent in time, and he had already put other plans in place if he needed to flush out the real purpose of Nathan's Ukrainian frolic. The photos that had been captured by the New Yorker at the border were now being circulated throughout Russian intelligence services and independent agents. All the identities and backgrounds of the men would be known soon enough. The *Director* quickly and expertly surmised that the men probably had *Special Forces* backgrounds or were former high-end operators in the police or military, and he mused, 'all with many years of experience behind them, no doubt.'

This was the circle in which Nathan always travelled, so they had to be up to something intriguing. He thought it wise to have the men followed for a while in case there were more opportunities to be had against the Ukrainians. That was his prime mission and what the Russians were paying him for; *having Nathan pay a debt to him would be an added bonus!!*

It was because of Nathan, his nemesis, that the *Director* had to 'disappear' and restart life somewhere else. He could never return to Australia and walk the soft, golden sands of his beloved Apollo Bay, where he played so often as a young boy, or enjoy the Boxing Day Cricket Test Match in Melbourne ever again. *Now, favoured pastimes consigned to the fleeting, fragmented pages of his sordid, secretive history.* There was no hope of him returning to the country of his birth... Too many questions would be asked, and besides, he was far too old and tired to go through a show trial, becoming a scapegoat for senior politicians and seeing his life *peter out* in prison, having to sell cheap tobacco and other currency items so he wouldn't get randomly sodomised... So, he 'cut and run' to Eastern Europe where his skills and knowledge would not only be more valuable and appreciated; prized... There, he would be impossible to track down and even harder to extradite back home. As timing would have it, the Russians invaded Ukraine and he became more than useful as an intelligence operative and recruiter for the *Wagner Group*. If it weren't this conflict, there was always somewhere else he could go to utilise his handy credentials or ply his villainous skills... As far as Nathan's friends went, they would simply be collateral damage...

The *Director* sat and thought hard, his current concern being the cocky but determined New Yorker, who was his 'eyes and ears' on the ground. He could sense the young man was 'painfully' eager to prove himself, but it wouldn't be the first time an overzealous agent tripped up on their first serious test of espionage. He deliberately made a point of advising, and then ordering the young man to just slow down and follow instructions, but, as always, some people just have to learn the hard way. If they're lucky, they survive and get a second chance...*most don't*. The *Director* was trusting this wouldn't be the case as he had other, vital missions for the bright young man from Brooklyn and he could see real potential in the 'kid.' His real baptism of fire would come later when he would stake out the hostel and maybe follow Nathan or one of his colleagues, if not that evening, then the next day. Although he felt a degree of concern for the young man, it was out of his hands now. He had telegraphed his instructions and would wait for a brief text report later that evening, early morning at the latest.

The *Director* was dead tired... He dropped the file he had been studying onto the table in front of him and rubbed his eyes forcefully. It had been a long day. He was feeling bushed and decided to take a nap on a cheap camp stretcher that was in one squalid corner of his cramped office. '*Fuck*,' he thought, 'don't these Russians ever spend money on comfort or cleaning? *Damn grubs! Bloody peasants!*' He stood in amazement as he surveyed the layers of dust, the oily grimed surfaces, and the 'fluff bunnies' that inhabited his messy workplace and he briefly reminisced... It felt like a 'light year' since he sat, discerning and potent, in his luxurious office in Melbourne's Collins Street! He looked around at his environment again and that thought quickly diminished; a few minutes of wriggling about and trying to get somewhat comfortable on the creaky bed frame ensued, but he soon 'crashed out,' with the young man from New York far from the thoughts in his fatigued and over-worked mind...

Back in Lviv, the men, tired and cold, had managed to select a bunk each in the main guest room and were organizing and re-jigging their kit. The room was spacious but plain, and offered only one shower, a table and four chairs; a modest kitchenette adjoined their room. Garen had selected the bunk on the mezzanine level above Nathan and Phil and both men wondered – in fact, hoped the constructing carpenter had reinforced the beams above their heads! The squeaking of boards and Garen's aggressive movements made the two close friends look at each other worriedly in silent trepidation. Could the boards hold, or would they find themselves with a new weighty companion in the middle of the night?! In the meantime, packing and preparation continued and gear needed to be sorted out. Former military men have a habit of doing the re-organisation routine to the point that it could be likened to a form of obsessive behaviour. Always having one's gear prepared at a moment's notice becomes more than a habit, it is second nature, a fixation.

While the men settled in, Sascha had reached out to a contact in the health department who would arrange for Nathan to view Steve's body at the morgue in Lviv tomorrow morning. *But this needed to be kept on the quiet.* The international media had been overly critical of the *International Legion* and its operation and the 'wheeling and dealing' of some of its members. Especially when it became well-known that there were nefarious types fighting for the Ukrainians to avoid deportation back to their countries of origin. A certain Greg Blande, now known notoriously as the 'butcher of Donbas', had skillfully managed to avoided deportation to the United States, mainly due to legal technicalities used by expensive lawyers. He was wanted in connection with two murders in Tennessee, so discretion was the keyword at this time. *No news about dead foreigners was good news!* Ukraine still wanted and desperately looked to recruit Westerners and the last thing they needed was another sordid story in the world's tabloids about some 'soldier of fortune' meeting a gruesome end. As far as Blande went, he was serving a purpose in the defence of the Ukraine homeland. Nothing to see here...

For Nathan, tomorrow morning felt like it was still a long time away and he needed to keep his mind off the subject; the morning and ensuing revelations would come soon enough. Now was the time for some personal administration and cheap distraction. It makes no difference where you are or what you are involved with, there are always the everyday things that require attention. Nathan needed some personal items, soap, chewing gum and so forth and thought it a prudent time to visit the local shops before they all closed. He cheerfully inquired to the lads if they wanted anything picked up, but they were all content and preferred to relax and chat on their soft bunks. The confines of living in such close quarters in the hostel had made Nathan feel claustrophobic and this was his ulterior motive for the shopping trip. He was too accustomed to his spacious one man, one cat cabin on the bush block back home, and he needed some time and space to relax and think of other things than what tomorrow would bring! He walked briskly down two flights of the wide marbled stairs of the hostel and, at the same time, noticed the walls and ceiling were in dire need of renovation, 'like most of Europe', he thought. In seconds he was facing the large, wooded front gate; a security buzzer needed to be pressed to exit and the same format repeated on his return.

The central location of their hostel was ideal for all their needs and had been an excellent choice by Sascha. Today, the market was running, and it offered an abundance of products to the canny shopper. This was a real market with inexpensive goods, and bargains to be had, *not like the over-priced, yuppy, pretend markets back home!* Nathan decided to give the Ukrainian bazaar a try and skillfully negotiated the multitude of rugged up pedestrians, the slushy snow underfoot, the street traffic and electric cable cars, and made his way to the first of many stalls in the hope of making some inexpensive purchases. Shoppers were browsing, squeezing fruit, and chatting, some animatedly, to the local vendors, all of whom were heavily dressed for the brutal weather. A seemingly pleasant afternoon of simple recreation, but Nathan was not to know danger was not that far away...

Crossing the street not long after Nathan was the New Yorker, who had successfully darted out in front of a behemoth of a cable car, only just missed being struck! He wore a large black sports jacket that was pulled up high to conceal his neck and face. It also acted as a barrier to the severe, frigid winds that were now incessant, blowing down from the Arctic north; the icy cold reminded him of many a bleak, frosty winter in his beloved 'Big Apple' and *he shivered at the thought...* As Nathan entered the markets, the boy from Brooklyn shortened his distance and adjusted his pace to stay in touch. Nathan was always on his guard but didn't have eyes in the back of his head, especially in the fading light of the day. With the abysmal weather and the darkness of the evening starting to take hold, it was effortless for the New Yorker to keep a safe but scrutinous distance from his quarry.

The Brooklyn man momentarily diverted his

thoughts from the task at hand and began to conjure fanciful imaginings, which he should have immediately discounted, or secured tightly in the upper recesses of his mind. Unfortunately for him, the cultural arrogance and disdain for the sanctity and equality of all life, skillfully embedded in him by his grandfather over the decades, rose ingloriously to the surface, like the pungent, grimy, *yellow fat from a boiling ham hock*, and it occurred to him that here was a fantastic opportunity to 'take out' one of the *Director's* nemeses! He had deduced by the interest the *Director* displayed in Nathan during their communications that Nathan was more than just someone to follow, he was a threat. *That was obvious!* Right here and now was the opportunity to elevate his status in the organisation and prove that he was worthy of more sophisticated assignments. In his delusions of grandeur, he envisaged rapidly climbing the 'greasy spy ladder,' followed by *promotion... better assignments, who knows what else?* He paused and re-gathered his thoughts... his eyes spun around the immediate area in a quick all-round surveillance.

Regardless of the vehement orders and instructions given to him by the *Director*, the New Yorker rebelled against his orders... 'Yet now,' he thought, was 'not the time to get sloppy,' .... Throughout his surveillance of Nathan, he had been cradling a small umbrella that harboured a concealed syringe needle at its tip. A small vial in his pocket carried a nerve agent... he could never pronounce its correct name and he only needed to place a solitary drop upon the barb to make the umbrella a killing machine - *Russian assassination methodology 101!!* Originally, this weapon was his backup for a multitude of situations, but he quickly decided he would terminate Nathan, now, at the markets, and this is how he would do it.

It really goes without saying, but the crucial element here would be the timing! *Walk quickly past the intended target... Feign a bump... Apologise... Doff a cap...* whatever necessary to maintain the deadly ruse. A fast jab to the target's fleshy calf or any other soft body part with the lethal umbrella tip and walk on briskly as if nothing happened... Within a minute, Nathan would collapse, abruptly, violently gasping for air; death following less than thirty seconds later. Unless a full and thorough toxicological examination was carried out postmortem, cause of death would be recorded as probably some form of seizure or cardiac arrest. *And Nathan was no 'spring chicken,' being well over the other side of fifty!* Complicit in this subterfuge was the fact there was no time for extreme diligence in Ukraine, during the war, to provide elaborate death certificates on a foreigner who had died from the number one killer in the world. *Case closed!* Move on to the next corpse! Here was a most deadly ploy that had been utilised with great effect by Russian agents on dissidents at home or foreign opposition abroad for decades.

The 'assassin' from New York rapidly made ready his device, while keeping a close watch on Nathan, who was still shuffling, unaware, from one congested stall to another. The men had been playing this 'cat and mouse' game for almost an hour and the New Yorker surmised that Nathan was probably close to completing his shopping. Cautiously he edged closer to narrow the distance to twenty metres without compromising his cover. However, it was during this movement, his desire to get strikingly close that the New Yorker's grand plan changed...

Phil had been lying on his bunk, restless and had become increasingly bored, tired of twirling his walking pole like a baton above his head. It had also become annoying to Garen who was attempting to read. 'What the hell,' he thought. 'I'll see what Nathan is up to...' Phil had made his way to the markets after texting Nathan to find out his whereabouts. By now it was nearly pitch-black outside; typical of the funereal darkness that only Europe provides. On his approach to the market, he gazed across the street and noticed in front of him, on the other side of the road, a suspicious looking young man wearing a large black jacket looking fixedly toward Nathan, and moving in sync with his old friend. A gust of wind blew open the wide lapel of the New Yorker's jacket, *and just then Phil realised he had seen this man before, back at the refugee tents at Medyka!*

Phil was a *savant* for names and faces and instinctively knew something was not kosher! He sprinted across the road and made the distance in a few seconds just as the determined New Yorker hurriedly advanced on

Nathan. Phil wasn't sure, but he could see the umbrella was slightly and suspiciously raised, *surmising that some foul purpose was intended!* The New Yorker didn't detect Phil advancing in the diminished light, as he only had 'murderous eyes' for Nathan who was still innocently browsing the market wares. The preying New Yorker was within a metre and about to strike when Phil desperately lashed out with his metallic walking pole to deflect the umbrella! The young man was completely surprised, spun around to his left and instantly recognized the Australian. Without warning, he thrust the umbrella and its deadly tip forward in the direction of his new adversary, who parried the implement, again with the sturdy pole! This exercise in 'swashbuckling' was not lost on Phil, who in the manner of some modern-day *Errol Flynn*, advanced with skill and spirit and struck the young American man fast and painfully hard on the forearm, *once... twice... thrice...* in quick succession!! The brutal and calculated strikes viciously hurt the boy from the 'Brook,' and he winced and drew his arm back – *fast!* The flashy scuffling and clamour of the fracas had been caught in the corner of Nathan's eye and he whirled completely around to witness the duelling contest.

The few people on the street also scrutinized, in astonishment, the actions of the two modern day duellists, not certain if they were serious or just being foolish... Attempting to gain an advantage, the younger, more agile New Yorker moved to a position where his back was facing the street and road traffic. Again, he ferociously lunged at Phil with the deadly umbrella, but Phil parried, expertly and adeptly, delivering a hefty jabbing blow to the centre of the man's chest! The startled New Yorker hopelessly and awkwardly stumbled backward in a flailing motion due to the potency of the jolt and found himself standing in the wet road, alone... He turned his head to the left briefly, and that was *all the time he had left*... In one more second, his short life was over, having spiralled down to this abrupt and horrific end!!

The elderly male driver of the hefty cable car made a horrified, squealing gasp as the young man was brutally thumped by the front fender, knocked down and sucked under the cast iron wheels of the weighty tram. Although he desperately fumbled, with his thick, meaty hands, the driver applied and re-applied the emergency brake, *but his actions were futile*... Finally, after dozens of exhausting attempts, the bulky cable car mercifully came to rest, twenty metres later. He quickly exited the cabin and surveyed the devastation... He now stood isolated, in the middle of the glassy, wet road, *and all he could do was embrace his drooping head with his sizeable, weathered hands and sorrowfully wail and weep into them!* The few women who were nearby screamed, piercing the cool night air as blood gushed out freely between the gaps in the sides of the wheels, while many a shocked man averted their eyes! Phil roughly grabbed a bewildered and questioning Nathan by his jacket collar and dragged him rapidly and forcefully down the wet and darkened street. *Now was not the time for lengthy questions or a serious debate but to leg it and just run!!* After two hundred metres, he quickly looked left and right, and they crossed the road as one. As they headed toward the hostel, Phil finally spoke, through his exertion and huffing and puffing in the cold night air, *'I'll tell you all about this... when we get... back to the room... Things... are not what they seem.'* Nathan was completely taken aback by what had just transpired and knew the rules of the 'game' had suddenly and irretrievably changed...

Chapter Fourteen:

THE PENNY DROPS...

'What the fuck was all that about?!' roared Nathan, as they entered their hostel room in a burst of unbridled commotion. Nathan went into a fast-pacing mode, and, as he trudged back, and forth on the worn and stained carpet, scratching his head and mumbling to himself, all the men could see he was not 'happy,' to say the least! They sat, patiently, waiting for an explanation... Nathan wasn't being critical of Phil but was trying to comprehend what had just happened! He stopped shuffling for a moment and shouted, at no-one in particular, *'Can't a man go shopping without someone trying to fucking kill him?!'* With a little angst now off his chest, he stood in the centre of the room, silent and immobile but with a questioning look on his face. He wanted answers!! It was Phil's turn to speak... and his best buddy went into great detail to explain his part in the attack on Nathan and what he thought of the

situation. Phil carefully recounted his precise movements and actions to the group and how he recognised the man who had threatened Nathan; the assassin who wasn't going to be a threat to anyone, anymore... 'I'm bloody positive of this... It was that young, skinny guy from New York who was working at the "World Central Kitchens" in Medyka, slopping out chow for the refugees.' *Well, he was a bloody long way from home and with some serious intent,'* replied Nathan. 'I'm not sure what he was attempting to do with that umbrella but based on what Phil has just said, I have no doubt he was trying to poison me.'

The men knew this was classic Russian spy agency practice and there wasn't anything more that needed to be said about that. It was obvious to all they had been 'branded' by someone higher up the 'spy chain' and each man knew they would have to be more diligent and prepared for a number of contingences. The 'holiday', the 'Ukrainian mystery tour' they had been on so far was now finished, over! As the ring of worried faces looked about the room for answers, Nathan walked the metre or so to Phil and placed his arms around him and moved his mouth to within a centimetre from his ear... He whispered, 'Thanks, brother. You saved my life today...*I won't forget this!'* Nathan squeezed Phil briefly and released his hold on his dear friend. It was Garen who next spoke, with some annoyance, 'Okay, we know we have been identified and compromised, *so what is the goddamn plan now?'* Sascha, who had been unusually quiet and pensive for the last five minutes now offered his opinion. 'Well, we know we have some people on our trail, as you can bet the New Yorker wasn't working alone. Great, that's now to our advantage. If they want to take us out, they will now have to use bigger resources, and that will take some time to arrange. We stay on our guard; we go to the morgue as a group tomorrow and then we make a new plan depending upon that outcome. Simple.'

It made perfect sense to everyone. *No point in seeing a Russian agent behind every bush...or under every bed. This wasn't 1950s America and McCarthyism!!* They all knew it was time to heighten their security measures, especially in city. Nathan suggested that from now on the team post sentries at the hostel and take two man shifts during the night; during the daytime, they will always have two men providing overwatch for the group. Wherever possible, nobody goes anywhere alone... *Period!* With all that having been agreed, it was now getting late and Bill and Garen would run the first watch. Nathan would need his rest as the trip to the morgue in the morning would be monumental, to say the least.

As it turned out, Nathan didn't get much sleep... again. He was beginning to feel more and more exhausted, much in the same way as he felt when he had suffered from *Chronic Fatigue Syndrome*, nearly twenty years ago. To be honest, he wasn't surprised... The trials and tribulations of the last few weeks, the foiled attempt on his life and the likelihood that he would soon be visiting a dead friend in Lviv was playing heavily on his mind. It was obvious that the strain was starting to get to him... His condition reminded him of the unceasing personal torment his father exhibited over the course of his life. There always seemed to be some new fuss, superseding some old drama and it seemed as if his father was always searching for some new lost cause... If it wasn't money issues, it was alcoholism, a propensity for violence and carnage, which probably originated with his strict Irish-Australian upbringing. *Without doubt, thought Nathan, his father see-sawed from one calamity to another.* It seemed, for him that drama became a natural tendency that became habitual, like an addiction. Now, he was starting to feel as though he was walking in his father's shoes. In the manner of other ancestral traits, can torment and misery be inherited? Is it a family curse? Can sorrow go beyond genetics and psychology, being more attributable to the realms of the metaphysical?

And it wasn't just happening here, in Ukraine. Nathan's life hadn't been a *Disney* fairytale, what with death, divorce and unfulfilled dreams setting a miserable, punitive tone for his life. With age and wisdom, he had made it a point to keep his life uncomplicated and simple. *'Simple is cheap, cheap is easy and easy is manageable',* or so he convinced himself, frequently repeating this trotted out line like some personal catechism, as some devout Catholic repeats *The Lord's Prayer.* Despite the duality of his reflection and depression, he was appreciative of one thing. He was so glad Phil was on this trip, 'thank God, I didn't turn him away as I initially wanted to...' *He also considered that it may be Phil who would be the one to get them home!* Although it didn't come as a surprise, Nathan was beginning to recognise that he was again developing some of the edgy and debilitating PTSD symptoms he had managed to keep control of over the last few years. Maybe the run-in with the *Agency* and the *Director's* cronies had been the catalyst for the re-emergence of wicked thoughts and dark symptoms. Or was the physical and mental tempo of these types of operations all too much? *Was he now past his 'use by date'?* Without doubt, the recent threat to his life did nothing to soothe the psychological tremors spiking within his mental health. Nathan was seriously bothered by these emerging themes and self-doubts and prayed upon prayer that he wouldn't be the cause or the one to let his friends down...

Chapter Fifteen:

A SHOCK TO THE SYSTEM...

A male body, medium shape, of a man in his late forties lay under a large white crumpled sheet that loosely covered the entirety of the coroner's stainless steel examination table. The table was robust, but rested on slightly cracked floor tiles that were in dire need of a decent sweep and a thorough mop. *So, it had come to this...* the confirmation of a deceased friend's passing in one of the grimiest rooms he had ever stood in! Nathan subdued his annoyance and slowed his thoughts... The only part of the body that was exposed on the table were the feet, which were now of a greyish hue in colour and certainly not whitish pink, like you see in the movies or on CSI! A sand-coloured cardboard tag, with scribbled penciled Ukrainian writing was tied to the left big toe. Nathan had stood motionless, reverently beholding this image for the last five minutes. His legs felt unbelievably heavy, like two cement pontoons, but the rest of his body experienced incredible lightness, as if he was in meditation and his limbs had become comatose. It was now 'crunch' time, but he was staggering and stuttering on the precipice of indecisiveness, cowering over the pulpit of indecision, not wanting to arrive at that pivotal moment when he would have to cast back the grubby, cotton sheet and view the remains of a dear, but tormented friend. The morgue attendant quietly mumbled something, and it was Sascha who relayed the message that they could have as much time as they needed. The attendant had been 'bought' so Nathan could absorb the privilege and the solemnity that went with the occasion. A very, very deep breath was needed and, in doing so, Nathan valiantly flung back the sheet as he exhaled. *What he saw nearly made his eyes bulge out of his heavy head and he blinked, twice, in cruel disbelief!!*

To say the cadaver was mutilated was an understatement! *What lay in front of him was a meaty mess that could hardly be considered a human!* The skull and most of the body was blackened, bruised, dirty, crushed, or disfigured. Rocket shrapnel had partly severed the left arm and there were deep cuts, and bloodied gouges throughout the torso, pelvis, and legs, which were severely fractured and flattened like rice pulp. Nathan was speechless and mentally deflated at the same time... He sensed his corporeal 'being' had sagged, as if his life's essence had absconded, taking with it any notion of *joie de vivre*. Overall, he experienced emotional abandonment as if the *'waves of this anguish'* had cruelly cast and battered him *'upon the rocks of despondency,'* and he rocked back, unsteadily on one foot, slightly lightheaded, but only for a moment...

Sascha had watched his response and was ready to catch or prop up his friend, if need be. In that split second, Nathan felt incredibly old and useless. An overwhelming sadness swept over him, like he had never before experienced... It took him a couple of sobering moments and a number of deep, profound breaths to compose himself and he made his feelings, especially of his uncertainty, known in a desperate plea to Sascha, *'I can't tell if this is Steve, Stephanie, or Sinatra! The body is mangled!'* He bellowed, *'How am I supposed to identify this! How is anybody supposed to identify this!!'* It was Sascha who attempted to console Nathan and lead his thoughts elsewhere. 'The attendant said your friend was recognized by garments that had his name on them. They are over here on the bench if you care to look?' Nathan was listening to Sascha but, at the same time, methodically scrutinising the marred body, the sight of which he was becoming more accustomed to with each moment that he viewed it.

Much to his own astonishment, he couldn't stop looking at the corpse...examining the human mess from head to toe. The hands were intact, and he decided to don a pair of black nitrile gloves and examine the extremities. He had a hunch and was hoping it would pay dividends... *He was now clutching at the flimsiest of straws... Nathan knew this but still had to try...* Luckily, the right hand was intact and normal. He then picked up the left hand and all the digits were complete. He studied the hand more closely, like an astute punter studies the racing form guide, especially the tips of the first three fingers. He looked at the hand, turned away and then re-examined the first three fingers again. 'Hey Sascha, could you come over here, please?' Sascha quickly moved closer to the table and looked at the hand Nathan was holding. 'Do you see anything remarkable on the first three fingers?' Nathan enquired. Sascha bent slightly forward until the fingers were three to four centimetres from his face. 'No, very ordinary, and soft looking hands, in fact.' Nathan placed the hand back down on the table and turned and faced Sascha. *'Exactly! This corpse is not Steve; I will bet my life on it!!* Steve and I played guitar for years and he should have callouses, rough edges and flat spots on the tips of the first three fingers of his left hand, like mine, *they never leave you!'* As he spoke, he thrust his left hand towards Sascha's face. The tough Ukrainian could see there were coarse, horizontal marks from years of guitar playing; it was true, they never go away.

Nathan dashed across the room to the bundle of filthy clothes on the bench and starting rummaging through the soiled garments. At once, he produced a bloodied shirt with Steve's name tag on it but also a pair of fatigue trousers with the name 'Edwards' emblazoned on the inside back of the pants. He paused and then his eyes lit up, wide and bright, in what can only be described as a 'light bulb' moment. Nathan believed the uniform had been stolen by the dead man who now lay on the table, who, unfortunately was wearing the Ukrainian uniform when the murderous rockets struck the base. There had been numerous reports of theft In the *Legion* such as rations, equipment, and personal items. This was common in most armies, but the word out was that thievery was rife in the *Legion*. There was also the story going around that the reason why so many *Legion* soldiers were killed was because people were going back into the buildings for their possessions, or in the case of this poor dead chap, to steal. Sascha seemed convinced by Nathan's hypothesis and waited for his next response. 'Well, this place isn't going to help us anymore, so I suggest we collect the boys and leave.' Nathan was reinvigorated and eager to resume the mission...

While the examination was being conducted, Bill, Garen, Mickey and Phil had sat patiently on a long wooden oak bench outside in the foyer. The morgue had been constructed at the turn-of-the-century and the marble floor tiles were worn and discoloured from where heavy framed trolleys had noisily scuffed back and forth upon them for over a century, carrying the physical remains of lives now long extinguished. One could only imagine the scenes of despair and human emotion that had transpired over the decades... Now, at this moment, there were small groups of families huddled together in the foyer, crying at the loss of a loved one. Notably there was one grieving family who had a son, a young soldier who had given his life for his beloved country. Friends and family would come and go. Above the hullabaloo, the men could hear the chant, *'Slava Ukraini, heroiam Slava!'* – *'Glory to Ukraine, Glory to the heroes!'* Phil looked at the sobbing family and said quietly to himself, 'Not much glory in getting your guts blown out, is there, or getting your fucking head blown off', and then he looked away, disgusted at the thought of the waste of a young life, discarded aspirations, and lost dreams...

What had also caught the men's attention had been one of the attendants, an elderly man, probably in his late sixties, who had been transferring bodies on trolleys from one room to another, presumably the autopsy room. Garen nudged Bill and they both looked the same way, 'Hey, will you get a look at that guy. He's the spitting image of Igor out of a Frankenstein movie'. The comparison was strikingly true... The diligent attendant had an unusually large hump on his right shoulder, which didn't prevent him from carrying out his duties. He transported the cadavers about with a degree of aplomb and diligence, as if this gruesome task had been performed over a thousand times, and it probably had... He would dutifully ferry corpses to a room where they would be washed and cleaned, like cheap vegetables, and prepped for autopsies, and later placed in storage in the large freezers. It would be easy to think he was moving watermelons about instead of bodies, such was the man's nonchalance.

Nathan suddenly appeared from a panelled glass side door with Sascha and fronted the men. 'Good news,' said Nathan, 'the body in there isn't Steve. I can guarantee that. Bad news for us is that we are back to square one with this search.' The men didn't look too perturbed as they had committed themselves to the task and would see the job through. 'Okay,' said Bill, 'what's the plan now?' Nathan suggested the group return to their lodgings and get ready to move. With nodding heads all round, the men picked themselves up and wandered outside to hustle up some transport. Nathan knew he would have to ring Kathy in a few hours when it was early morning in Australia. He didn't have the news she wanted to hear, as to the whereabouts of her husband, but at least it wouldn't be the horrific news that she had probably been expecting...

Chapter Sixteen:

TAKING A BREATHER...

By the time Nathan and Phil arose the next morning, most of the guys had already consumed their breakfast. Bill and Garen had visited a small supermarket nearby and returned with a delicious assortment of fresh pastries and mixed berries. There was also freshly brewed coffee, its aromatic scent intense and irresistible in the confines of the tiny communal kitchen space. It had snowed lightly during the night but neither Nathan nor Phil had heard the weather over the half-a-dozen air raid warnings during the night! Travel and stress are great companions for exhaustion and both men slept soundly, like the proverbial log. No-one was really sure if missiles had been fired at Lviv and intercepted or whether it was just a government ploy to condition the people for bigger things to come... Sascha was pacing around the kitchen area of the hostel, speaking to colleagues on his phone and it seemed as though the damned thing was permanently attached to his ear! '*Tak, Tak.... Dobra, dobra,*' he replied loudly, essentially confirming all was understood and good and then he hung up. 'Well, not much happening today' was his flat response to the group. 'I'm still waiting on my contacts in and out of government to see if Steve went back to the border or continued onward into Ukraine, most probably Kyiv.' Without doubt, Kyiv was where the action was and a Mecca for Westerners, especially those with military skills and other useful talents... He further added, 'There are photographs and descriptions of him circulating through the many government agencies I have influence with and my personal contacts. However, this all takes time, so we must be patient.' For Nathan, patience wasn't a virtue, and he was tired of hearing this old excuse!

True to his word, Nathan had rung Kathy late in the evening – early morning Australia time - and had presented her with an update of their travels, leaving out some of the juicier details concerning the recent violence on the streets of Lviv. He decided to be forthright and inform her of the visit to the morgue and the identifying of Steve's combat jacket. It was pointless trying to 'sugarcoat' the situation and she needed to be cognisant of the fact Steve may never be located. To nobody's surprise, there weren't any tears from Kathy as she had already braced herself for the worse, even this early in the piece... Nevertheless, she was extremely grateful to Nathan and his colleagues for their devotion to the quest for answers. The conversation turned to incidental chatting about the local weather and some other trivial matters such as food and shopping; just when Nathan thought the conversation was tapering to a conclusion, Kathy unloaded her bombshell. 'Nathan, I need to tell you young Nate has flown out to Poland, *on his way to Ukraine!* A three second pause followed... for Nathan to absorb the gravity of the message and then he responded with a ruffled tone, *'how and when did all this happen?'* Kathy began to explain... Nate had seen his mother frustrated, angry and confused all at the same time and wanted to do something to alleviate her grief and bring his father back home. He was becoming exasperated with the lack of results. 'He heard our conversations and how you travelled to Poland and into Ukraine, so he knows how to get to Kyiv! He's a smart kid, he knows how to connect the dots... His passport is gone, clothing too and customs confirmed he flew out of Brisbane three days ago. I only found out because his flat mate needed money for the rent, and it slipped out that he had flown to Europe.' Nathan could hear sniffling, then spasmodic sobbing spasmodically. Kathy then pleaded, 'please Nathan... at least bring *him* home...can you promise me that?'

Nathan was flabbergasted! Not only did he have the arduous and dangerous task of finding Steve but *now* he had to locate and rescue Nate, the errant son; a bright university student whose only life and military experience was working shifts at *McDonalds,* the odd camp out at *Mount Barney National Park* and a two-year, unremarkable stint with the *Australian Army Cadets*. Not exactly the credentials required to roam around Europe while there was a war on. The kid was so out of his depth it wasn't even funny! *'Fuck, the Ukrainians will eat him alive,'* was all Nathan could think, but he quickly returned to the pressing urgency of the call. *'Kathy, are you still there?'* 'Yes, yes,' came the response, with Kathy having dried her tears. Nathan continued... 'Okay, if Nate contacts you make sure to find out where he is and send his location to me via text, straightaway; use *WhatsApp*, it's encrypted. Our conversations will be safe. I will get my people onto this. I know it's easy to say don't worry, but things will be fine... *okay Kitten*?' Nathan uttered his old, sweet term of endearment for Kathy, an idiom he hadn't used or thought of for many years; he hoped it would make her feel better... *he knew he felt good for saying it...* Kathy's pet name for Nathan was 'Crackers', for obvious reasons, but now wasn't the time for serious reminiscing; with the obligatory 'goodbyes' having been said, the conversation was finished. Now, there was *a damn sight more work to be done* and Nathan needed more aggravation like a hole in the head!

    With the latest revelations and permutations spinning around inside his brain, Nathan decided to down a second coffee – *extra strong*, and with it washed down a chocolate croissant! He alerted Phil and the rest of his group to this latest situation. Marcus Hayden would also be notified. Despite the news, the goal for today was to have a 'personal day', some time off to do any necessary shopping in Lviv before they had to hit the road once more. Bill, Garen and Mickey were just about ready to venture off to their shopping destinations and the men would re-convene later in the afternoon and discuss any news Sascha may have gathered from his contacts. 'Okay,' said Nathan, 'better get my skates on or else it will be dark before I know it.' Nathan and Phil were heading to a local outdoors store to look at some sturdy cold weather clothing and other essential items. Although they were travelling in pairs and it was a leisure day, they knew they had to be situationally aware at all times.

Meanwhile, somewhere in the west of Russia, the *Director* had digested the report concerning the violent death of the young, idealistic but reckless man from New York. The account had included a statement, obtained from Ukraine police that mentioned how there had been an altercation between the young man and unknown person(s) immediately before his death. The report also stated that the most likely cause of death was 'misadventure', given that the young man wandered out in the direction of the on-coming tram. To the Ukrainian authorities it was case closed, but to the *Director*, the report read very differently... He knew his operative had ventured beyond his brief, which led to his gruesome and messy demise. This was profoundly unfortunate. He was fond of the 'kid' and regretful for his death, feeling partly responsible for handing him the assignment. But he now knew and was completely certain of the fact Nathan and his cohort were aware they were being investigated. He tapped lightly on to the table with the fingers of his right hand and then thought, 'time to put some other plans into action...'

The *Director* reached for the receiver of the grubby and heavy *Bakelite* telephone that took up a lot of space on his plain, old table and made a call to some reliable operatives in Lviv. He spoke in fluent Russian for around five minutes and then hung up, content in the knowledge these men had completely understood his instructions and could be relied upon. It was time to bring in the 'big boys'... His plan was to 'kill two birds with one stone' – eliminate Nathan and his friends, and in the process destroy whatever operation Nathan was working on. He reminded himself of the incredibly old maxim, 'softly, softly, catchy monkey'. There was no hurry... a chink in Nathan's armour would soon be exposed... This is how he would destroy the resourceful Australian and seek his revenge, not only for himself, but now for the agent who would never return home to Brooklyn, New York.

Chapter Seventeen:

TO KYIV AND BEYOND...

It may have seemed unlikely, if not possible, but the weather had become colder, even though it was late spring. The light snow sprinkling of the previous evening had melted quickly, depositing a glossy, wet sheen that blanketed roads and pavements but was frozen - the dreaded 'black ice'. People attempted to move quickly as they went about their business, as if they foolishly believed they could outrun the inclement weather and the grip of the late winter's icy talons. Forever the clown, Phil wrote 'fuck' in the snow... and thought it quite funny, to which Nathan shook his head and thought, *'what a guy...'* It had been a fantastic idea to check out the outdoors store and now Phil and Nathan were wearing matt black puff jackets that were helping to stave off the cold of the inclement conditions. The men were really feeling it, the downside of coming from a southern hemisphere country!

It was an otherwise uneventful day, except that Nathan received a lengthy but highly informative text message from Kathy, later that evening. It seemed a British colleague of Steve's in the *Legion* had come across her number in some of his documents on his return to England and wanted to pass on what little information he had about his *Legion* friend. 'Nobby' confirmed how they had just missed being killed in the rocket attack at Yavoriv and, fortunately they had been working on the trenches at the time. He confirmed how many of the *Legion* volunteers had quickly decided to go elsewhere; some of the men deserted, moved onto other units, or had managed to quit and decided to join other Westerners who were acting as Foreign Military Advisers throughout the country. It seemed that Steve was traumatised by the events and was preparing to fly back to Australia, but at the last minute had fallen in with some 'rough' men who were headed to Kyiv to work as tactical trainers. The Brit mentioned that he enjoyed Steve's company and was reaching out as he was concerned about his Aussie mate's mental state and safety. Where Steve was going, who he was with or who he was meeting in Kyiv was anyone's guess...

Based upon this new information, it was time to depart Lviv and head for Steve's most likely destination – Kyiv. With very little trouble, Sascha organised two vehicles that would arrive within the hour that would ferry the men to a 'safe house' in the Ukrainian capital via separate routes. This would minimise the chance of ambush and may throw any potential tracker off their tail. It would be a better option than the train. They would rendezvous at a small hotel sometime the next day where Sascha knew the proprietors and could guarantee their safety. Phil, Nathan, and Mickey would be driven by two Mi6 operatives who were posing as 'good Samaritans'. Paul and Nicky were a highly trained and deadly husband-and-wife team, not quite the stylish and 'sexed up' *'Mr. and Mrs. Smith'* couple portrayed by *Brad Pitt* and *Angelina Jolie*. They were a lot more subdued and 'British'. They donned hiking fleeces, helped anyone when they could and drank copious amounts of tea, which assisted them in their ruse. They had arrived in Ukraine not long after the start of the war and had been gathering serious intel while driving refugees back and forth from Kyiv to Medyka. They would negotiate the numerous highways and arterials in their 'rescue work' reporting on the state of the roads, potential choke points and ambush sites, Ukrainian military capabilities, evacuation routes and confirming British government satellite data.

Many such covert teams operated throughout Ukraine, from various countries, and it was common knowledge that British SAS and American Special Forces already had 'boots on the ground'. There was a lot at stake here, not just for the Ukrainians. The governments of the nations of Europe needed a *plan B* in the event the Russian military kept heading west after Ukraine. The endearing British couple drove an innocuous grey *Ford*

Transit van, normally laden with women and children refugees, and sometimes small animals. They couldn't be any more inconspicuous if they tried. Most of the time they were ushered through the vehicle checkpoints, as they were well known and friendly. They would be waiting for Nathan, Phil, and Mickey close by the majestic Lviv train station. Bill, Garen and Sascha would be picked up by an unmarked police car outside the hostel within a half hour, driven by an old colleague of Sascha. Garen remarked, 'Not the first time I have ridden in the back of a police car, not since my youth, but don't ask me about it, *you don't wanna know...*' Bill just grinned at Garen's frivolous comment and could only imagine that his buddy had been a wild young man...

So, with their plans confirmed and their gear in tow, the two groups exchanged brief goodbyes. Nathan, Phil and Mickey strode the short distance from the hostel in almost no time, and were quickly introducing themselves to the British spy couple who were waiting patiently by their light grey van, fifty metres from the train station entrance. On first impressions, the couple seemed like so many people helping out in Ukraine; Paul and Nicky were in their fifties, wore casual gear, with no flash pretences and very accommodating and non-threatening. The perfect covert agents! It seemed effortless for them to pass on that unflappable British charm that is inherently common to their countrymen and women; there wasn't anything they wouldn't do for someone in need, and everything was carried out with little fuss and a resolute, British attitude. Yet, they could kill without hesitation, if necessary, and had done so, on a few occasions...

After the brief but convivial introduction, the vehicle set off along the narrow, winding streets of Lviv. Phil, Mickey, and Nathan sat in the back; 'sat' being an overstatement as they 'parked their bums' on thickish foam and delicately balanced on the vehicle's cold wheel arches. Beside them were boxes of humanitarian supplies and a carton of fresh fruit. Nicky and Paul sat upfront and frequently argued, albeit with humour, concerning which navigation route to take and carried on just like your average married couple. It would be a protracted journey to Kyiv, with the checkpoints, condition of the roads and the war dragging everything down to a snail's pace. To begin with, the party would negotiate their way to a small town called Berdychiv, assess the situation there and probably stay the night. Although delighted to transport Nathan and his friends, the spy couple still had their clandestine work to do...

The men sat rugged up in the back of the cold, half-lit van and in talked about sport and music, until the talk dried up, and each man sought companionship and guidance in his own deep thoughts. For Nathan, he sat with his head down examining the dirty and oily metal floor, swaying to the constant rocking of the van. At the same time he wondered if they would ever locate Steve. He also contemplated whether he still had the physical fitness and mental resolve to see him through this journey. Nathan didn't want to admit it, but he knew that he was getting older and slowing down. He knew that most people go through similar 'soul-searching' periods during middle age. 'Oh, to be twenty-five again', he wished... For Phil, this adventure had opened his eyes. His staid existence in Melbourne was killing him. Sure, he had plenty of money with his nightclub and other ventures but, for him, money led to vices, vices led to corruption and corruption was the path to his ruin. Very much akin to the classic line:

Easy times create weak men, weak men create tough times, tough times create strong men, strong men create easy times...

His drug and alcohol lifestyle had become addictions he couldn't shake, until the wakeup call a few months ago. Now, he felt more alive than ever... *and was basking in this new experience!*

The van motored along for an hour or so before they drew up to a military checkpoint, made of 'ready set' concrete blocks, felled logs, and old tyres. It was resplendent in home-made camouflage nets which were fabricated from old strips of multi-coloured cotton cloth, courtesy of diligent Ukrainian babushkas and eager children. On this occasion the guard wanted to check passports and inspect what was in the back of the van. Paul, in his most friendly manner, alerted the guard to the fact he was carrying a couple of passengers, hoping they would be waved through. The guard insisted that he take a look. From the inside, the men could hear the heavy footsteps of military boots snappily making their way to the van's rear doors and the metallic noise of someone grappling with the handle. Without any warning, a burst of light flooded their compartment as the guard flung the doors wide open. He was taken aback by the three men who didn't resemble your average refugee, as they were clad in military style boots, and dark, rugged clothing – rucksacks positioned in a regimental line on the floor. It looked like they were tactically prepared for some covert mission! He quickly and nervously traversed his gaze from man to man, all the time clutching his AK 74 and then shouted in a deep, loud voice – *Passports!* All three occupants produced their documents and waited... The guard examined the passports for some time as if their meaning was incomprehensible. He inquired, 'Austrian?' to which two of the men responded simultaneously, with eyes rolling and a boisterous utterance: *'Australia!!'* He didn't even bother attempting to pronounce 'New Zealand', but nodded his head in fake understanding and handed back the documents. He took one pace backwards and slammed the heavy metal doors shut. The friends just looked at each other without saying a word. They then peered to the front of the van, through the perspex screen to the driver's compartment, where Paul was smiling and giving them a hearty thumbs up! It was Nathan who spoke first, 'Well, I suppose it is to be expected, what with the war on and all. Shit, I would be twitchy if I was in the same circumstances back home,' to which Phil and Mickey nodded in agreement. The vehicle set off on bumpier and more blown out roads. Next stop, Berdychiv!

Chapter Eighteen

'FUN AND GAMES' IN BERDYCHIV...

The demanding journey to Berdychiv carried on without any other checkpoint stops and they soon arrived but kept driving until they were somewhere near the centre of the city of around 75,000 occupants. It seemed to be very dated when compared to the other cities, towns, and villages the men had seen. Most of the public housing, which was clearly a Soviet byproduct, gave the impression of being in disrepair, and the roads and community buildings were also very neglected in their upkeep; judging by the flaking, houses appeared not to have been painted for decades, and metal gates and sidings were rusting. Many a small wire fence had been torn down, while gardens lay dirt bare or overgrown with weeds, and many streets were littered with old and worn cars. Angry looking stray dogs roamed the avenues and people, young and old, milled about, seemingly with little purpose. To Nathan it appeared as though this was Ukraine's version of a 'wild west town' or a derelict city, as portrayed in the TV series 'The Walking Dead.' It also reminded Nathan of some of the dilapidated outback Aboriginal communities he had observed on his travels back home, though here it was so much greener and more populated. Outside of the odd, artistic mural on the side of an apartment wall, the cheap, grubby stamp of Soviet utilitarianism was all over the place. On first impression, the city was totally bland, unattractive, and devoid of any real value. This was in stark contrast to the cities of Mykolaiv and Odessa, which were beautiful thriving cities by the coast, and localities you would really want to visit in happier circumstances. There wasn't much to write home about in this tired and dated looking city in the Zhitomir district of Ukraine. Apart from being the birthplace of the famed nineteenth-century author, Joseph Conrad, and being the site of a Nazi massacre of tens of thousands of Jews in the second world war, the locale was uninteresting. Not exactly a 'jewel' in the Ukrainian crown!

Still, here they were, and things had to get done. Nicky and Paul would visit the local infirmary and delve into their capacity to provide adequate medical aid to the military hospital. There had been rumours that the area was exceptionally low on competent medical staff and there was some conjecture as to whether it could adequately assist the Ukrainian military in the event that the Ukrainians were pushed out of Kyiv, or from the other eastern oblasts. This was all part of their fact-finding mission. Not only did the British government want to know if the Ukrainians could continue to fight the war but how were they faring regarding logistics and medical support, and that they had fallback positions if the war took a turn for the worse. Nathan, Mickey, and Phil stood by the van and waited for the couple's return. After twenty minutes they emerged and announced they were off to see the local Mayor. To maintain the subterfuge, Paul suggested he should consult with the local authorities and alert them to their refugee ferrying service and that they could cart medical supplies if required.

On Paul's word, everyone piled backed into the van, and they drove a few streets until they came to the Town Hall, which bore a slight resemblance to the famous 'Alamo' mission in Texas. The smallish, box-like building had been surrounded in a bevy of new and durable sandbags, blast tape and other hastily prepared fortifications, such as vehicle blockades. A security detail of four serious and determined looking soldiers stood near the entrance, behind a sturdy, chest high sandbag wall, seemingly ready to repel invaders at a moment's notice. The group moved towards the security guards, who signalled for them to halt. One senior guard walked over and spoke with Nicky, and after a minute or so, the group was invited inside. Once in the building, the guards aggressively indicated their intent to inspect documents and search the party. Shouting followed, and the obligatory waving of arms. Nathan and the group were surprised by the sudden change of attitude...

With a cover man positioned with his automatic weapon, one guard moved warily forward and gave Nathan a quick 'pat down'. Almost instantly, he froze and *took an uneasy step backwards!* He believed Nathan had secreted a pistol on his person, but it was only a utility pouch for his small blade, cigarette lighter and other essentials. These were removed and placed in a tray. Mickey was next but, before the guard had a chance to search him, Mickey reached down to his lower trousers and right boot and pulled out a threatening six-inch knife from down near his right ankle. Again, the guard stood back, uneasy, his eyes darting from person to person! Talk from the soldiers ceased, and the covering man lifted his weapon from the 'low ready' position and pointed it directly at Mickey. *The situation was tense, and nobody moved...* Paul seized the moment and began to protest that *'I'm only driving these guys to Kyiv; I don't really know them!'* He didn't want his cover blown and, worst case scenario, Mickey, Phil, and Nathan would have to get themselves out of this pickle! It was only a few seconds after the initial shock when the cover man decided to lower his weapon and the 'pat down' guard briefly looked at the knife and then threw it in the tray alongside Nathan's items. Weapons are easily accessible in Ukraine, so these items were not a big deal by their standards. Phil and Paul were then checked but had no items of concern. The guards decided not to bother with Nicky and the group was escorted upstairs to a 'meet and greet' with the mayor. Mickey would later inherit the comedic nickname 'Stabby McStabb' because of his choice of weapon.

Upon the invitation of the guard, the group, somewhat suspicious by now, entered a spacious but empty office and gestured to sit down at the large wooden meeting table. It was a standard government office with a map of the local area, plenty of large and small Ukrainian flags, a prominent desk for the 'boss', a bookcase, and credenzas for documents. After a couple of minutes of silent waiting and anticipation, an entourage of four people entered from the other room and approached the table. The mayor gave Nathan a disparaging, filthy look as it seemed he was sitting in *her* chair, which he quickly shuffled from and plonked himself down at the other end of the table!

The mayor was a strikingly beautiful women, well dressed, and with raven black hair and facial features similar to the actress, Mila Kunis, except that she was more athletically built and tall, nearly six feet! The mayor was accompanied by an interpreter; a man who kept apologising for his poor understanding of the English language, although he was managing quite well! He politely asked the group why they were there, in their city, at this time... Paul acted as the group spokesperson and courteously informed the officials they were in Ukraine to help the people and to alleviate their suffering with their refugee ferrying service and that they had also been informed, back in Lviv, that Berdychiv urgently needed medical assistance, which is why they were there.

Instantly, the Ukrainian entourage began talking excitedly and loudly with one another. Nathan could feel the mood in the office suddenly change... as if the spirit of friendship, like a refreshing gust of clean air had entered and completely whisked away the bureaucratic stuffiness and suspicion from the room! Without warning, the mayor stood up and made a rousing speech, with arms gesticulating - this way and that - *and to the effect that our small group would never be forgotten by Ukraine and what a wonderful thing we were doing!* The mayor then barked a few orders, and within moments her aides had brought in coffee and chocolates for the group. Smiles and laughter filled the room, a great deal of back slapping occurred, and they were regarded as heroes!

A further conversation between the mayor and the interpreter, and the group was informed that accommodation had been arranged at a local motel for them, as a gift from the city. With that, the guard arrived on cue and escorted all downstairs to where confiscated items and knives were returned. By now, a young man in his twenties waited outside to take the Westerners to their accommodation. The Ukrainian people frequently come across as being difficult and even belligerent but, like the magic and mystery of early electric light and overcoming a degree of fear to it, once you get to know the people and their nuances, they can be the most

charming and gracious people anyone can ever meet.
As one, the group thought, *'what a country!'*

Chapter Nineteen:

MAGNIFICENT KYIV!

Nathan, Mickey and the two Brits had woken incredibly early, around five am and it was now eight am. Phil was the only one 'dragging the chain,' again, and slowly rising from his bed. The mixed troupe had shared the two-bedroom apartment provided by the city, and though on the plain side, the lodgings had been clean and comfortable. Gear was now being re-packed into the van, and they would soon depart for the long drive to Kyiv. The hope was to get there by lunchtime if Phil would move his arse!

Along the way, they stopped a couple of times, gathering intel, re-fuelling and purchasing coffee and snacks to break the journey. They were surprised to see so many fuel stops open, many more than they had expected. It had come as a surprise to Nathan to see that most of the petrol stations stocked a large and varied supply of alcohol.

'Man,' he thought, 'this would never happen back home.' It seemed crazy to him that a driver could re-fuel and buy a bottle of *Jack Daniels* or *Grey Goose* vodka, hop back into their vehicle, and be on their merry way - literally. But really, when you thought about it, it is not so different to purchasing alcohol from a liquor barn or supermarket; it was just the proximity that was disturbing... Maybe the Ukrainians, like other Europeans have a different attitude to drinking? The situation was so different back in Australia, where drugged out and liquored up adolescents, some as young as 11, steal cars and go on some intoxicated and recalcitrant frenzy on the streets of the capital cities! Rebelling for who knows what as the average citizen has it better in Australia than just about anywhere else! Was it boredom... was it the slack judicial system... was it lazy parenting or plain old self-entitlement... But that was too big a problem for Nathan to concern himself with; that was for the 'head doctors' and social workers to figure out! He thought cynically, *'Ah, Australia, the lucky country!'*

As much as he treasured his country of birth, he was frequently saddened how the nation had irrevocably lost its way. It seemed to be a country in slow but perilous decline... Much in the same way as the majestic *Titanic* had slid gently beneath the waves and gathered overwhelming momentum on its inescapable and violent collision with the ocean floor! In Australia, too many radical ideas and ill-founded policies circulated without critically considering the obvious consequences, such as the all-out push for eliminating carbon emissions by trying to exist on solar and wind power and costly electric renewables. The irony here is that we don't even manufacture these items in Australia! *All the money goes back to China!* He knew from his own experience living off the grid how difficult it was to exist purely on solar power. The portable generator needed to be fired up to charge the batteries after only a few days of cloudy weather! A guy on his own could manage this but how was this efficient or viable in family households! Nathan could only imagine the immense frustration that families and businesses would experience trying to live off these power sources that are so inherently temperamental, expensive, and possessed with a short life span, due to their built-in redundancy. The political 'left' was hellbent on closing down coal fired power stations, without a feasible alternative such as nuclear power, but refused to explore any alternatives. Without doubt, 'nuclear' had become Australia's 'N' word, and here we have it, a country with an abundance of uranium but lacking the intellect and fortitude to utilise it wisely. Common sense would see a gradual phasing out of 'dirty power' and the construction of small, but numerous nuclear power facilities. However, as always, cowardly Australian governments, especially the political 'left' propose, and promote these types of unsound ideas, these Labour 'wet dreams', without sensibly calculated and detailed alternatives.

Power sources aren't the only bone of contention. This had also been the case when the referendum for

Australia to become a republic failed, largely due to the absence of a competent blueprint being laid out for the public. All show but no substance, never mind the confused phrasing or misleading narrative of the referendum question as touted by the 'lefties'! To any outsider, that flimsy excuse just smacked of sour grapes! The pattern was repeating itself again with the incumbent Federal government's mantra of giving the Aboriginal community a 'Voice' in the constitution and Parliament. Those with a critical eye, and half a brain, can see this loose, divisive plan will just put more elitist bureaucrats on the government payroll and never address the real confronting issues in the many and varied Aboriginal communities across the nation. Without too much of a surprise, some of the biggest critics of this sloppy, half-assed plan are, in fact, the nation's first peoples! Nevertheless, Nathan had more on his mind now than worrying about racial division, and genealogical entitlement, touted in the creation of a *de facto* 'Aboriginal House of Lords' in the Australian parliament, and the many other socio-economic problems back home. Time to steer the focus to the present...

During one of their frequent pitstops, Nathan checked his mobile phone, only to find there were several messages waiting for him... The most important one was from Marcus. Although the war hadn't been going for an exceptionally long time, it had taken Westerners no more than a 'nano second' to embed themselves in the workings of the Ukrainian military. As for the Ukrainians, the

Russian barbarian was at the gate, and they needed all the help they could get; *dire times require drastic measures...* Along with many of the ex-military who had joined the *International Legion*, there were ex-military guys who had made contacts with officers and senior officials in Ukraine's military, regular and reserves, and were starting to make a name for themselves as 'commanders' of training teams. Marcus had managed to secure several names from his contacts. These 'commanders' would most likely be the people other ex-military people would gravitate to for training gigs; military 'brotherhood' and all that. Marcus made the distinction in his messages that not all of these 'commanders' were dishonest, but a great many were, so Nathan needed to be extremely careful...

The undeniable truth was that many military formations and non-military organisations operating in Ukraine acted as 'standalone entities' as well as working side-by-side. For the serious volunteers, it was a veritable 'smorgasbord of opportunities', but it also meant military law, rules and any system of procedures was inconsistent, 'rough and loose', or downright slipshod. There were Georgian based military detachments that had aligned themselves to Ukraine. There were paramedical units, such as the *Hospitallers* who operated at the front for the wounded. There were relief groups for refugees and medical training organisations such as *Task Force Yankee*. As well, a great many Ukrainian foundations had been created to train fighters and assist the vulnerable, such as the *Serhiy Prytula Foundation* or *Ghosts of Ukraine*, to name a few...

In addition, there were dangerous individuals – 'soldiers of fortune,' gangsters and criminals operating as 'rogue' players in this war, 'cherry-picking' what they wanted to do and who they wanted to align themselves with. Based on Steve's military experience, he would have most likely affiliated himself with a military training team that taught the 'basics' and wasn't too particular with who they recruited, notably older guys like him. They would be more concerned with operating at volume rather than quality and it was easier for Westerners to come on board than to work for a Ukrainian organisation, especially as they couldn't speak the language. Nathan studied the detailed list of names and brief resumes that Marcus had supplied, and one name stood out from the rest – Cyrus Naylor. A young American, US Army airborne background and a self-styled entrepreneur who had already made a reputation in Kyiv; a reputation that was particularly dubious and built upon self-interest, but a guy more likely to know people who knew Western trainers.

Nathan found out later that Cyrus Naylor had skipped Oregon or somewhere in the Pacific Northwest as he had a petty criminal record and was wanted in relation to assault and drug running, albeit on a small scale. Nathan would also discover later that Cyrus' 'end game' was to be there at the war's conclusion, come off as a 'hero'. He expected to reap the benefits of a victory against

Russia, such as citizenship and business opportunities in the re-building of the country... the old 'time, place and opportunity' game! There would be so many prospects after the war, this was a certainty and Cyrus thought that he was smarter than the Ukrainians. *But he wasn't...* This would be the guy Nathan would contact first once they had arrived in Kyiv and found a place to stay. Of course, he wouldn't be able to just come right out and ask if Steve Holland was working there but could dance around the subject and inquire whether there were any Australian or Kiwi trainers as part of his training team. Nathan also hoped that he could pass on some of the other 'commander' names to Bill, Garen and Sascha. The men could make their choice and stay with Nathan or work independently or as pairs in a wider search.

Nathan had been engrossed in his reading and re-reading of the messages when he suddenly looked up and saw the vast outline of the majestic city of Kyiv. For so long, there had only been a landscape of forests, followed by the pretence of a road that had slowly transformed into a modern highway. Now here in front of him was this vast capital with its innate beauty and dominion that could easily rival and surpass many of the major cities of the West. Like a great many Westerners, Nathan had harboured a mental image of Ukraine as a land dotted with villages and peasants riding donkeys festooned with bales of wheat, or darkly clad crones with deep creased and weathered faces who spun wool on ancient spinning wheels, but Kyiv wasn't the seventh largest city in Europe for nothing! It had long been an important gateway from the West to the East, and vice versa, and it was evident in the diversity of its architecture, cuisine, and beauty of its people that many travellers had decided to settle in this capital from many lands.

Nathan was astounded by the enormity of the skyscrapers that seemed to be endless... but would soon come to experience the beauty of the parks, which were bountiful, and the sophisticated road and underground rail systems. He briefly thought, in genuine remorse, about the cities of his homeland and wasn't all that impressed with the Australian city landscape anymore... The Victorian and Federation era beauty of cities such as Melbourne and Sydney had been eroded over time, principally by money-grubbing developers, 'sell out' council officials and a multi-cultural doctrine that catered to the development of trashy kitsch avenues and non-English speaking suburbs; now morphing the Australian capitals into ugly and over-crowded metropolises that resembled something out of a 'Bladerunner' movie or some other dystopian tale borrowed from science fiction. But here, before him, was a mighty city, resplendent with *chic* avenues, noble monuments, plentiful parks and all the modern conveniences anyone could wish for! The contemptible Soviet stain that once enveloped the land, was now dissipating; it's evil taint swiftly eroded by a dynamism buoyed by unique Ukrainian entrepreneurialism, youthful exuberance, and proud nationalism. The only peculiar thing was how deserted the city was... only a few vehicles were present on the streets and the many military roadblocks and tank barricades, thrown together at short notice, dominated strategic points across the city. Nevertheless, Nathan would soon learn that in the majesty of Ukraine he found a spirited country and people that were quickly becoming very dear to his heart...

Nathan's 'star gazing' ended, as the van suddenly rounded a corner and parked outside a small hotel that reminded him of a hacienda he once stayed in at Guadalajara, Mexico. *But that's another story...* Clay roof tiles and white swept stucco walls lay before the visitors presenting them with a 'Tex-Mex' feel, that certainly wasn't Ukrainian! The hotel seemed so much out of place in Kyiv but looked exceptionally clean and most importantly, safe, and Nathan soon found the reception. The clerk was very polite and welcoming, except when Nathan asked about the location of a bunker, in the event of a missile attack. The clerk blew off the suggestion, as if it could never happen. The group carried their bags to the two rooms that had been allocated and opted for a brief rest before dinner. Nathan reviewed the text from Marcus, typed a quick response, and decided to call Cyrus Naylor. If they could somehow join Cyrus's training team, they could use the opportunity to, hopefully, discover the whereabouts of Steve Holland. In the process of training with this team, they would at least gain more intel and be in a better position.

He dialled the number. After three rings, a young American with a West Coast dialect answered bluntly, 'Cyrus here'. Nathan introduced himself by saying he had received Cyrus's number from a contact at Medyka and was looking for a role as a military trainer. He thought it prudent to fluff up the man's 'ego pillow' a little bit... 'Yeah, I was told your team is the best in Kyiv. We might be able to help each other out...' 'Okay,' grunted Cyrus, a fraction on the aggressive side, 'what's your background, what are your credentials?' Nathan told the truth. He outlined that he had served in the Australian SAS and had military operational service in Southeast Asia, operational service with the counter-terrorist squadron and had served as a PMC in Iraq. He was a qualified military instructor as well as having vast experience in the private security sector; bodyguard work and high-end stuff like that.

Cyrus asked him how long he planned to stay in Ukraine and whether he had any other friends that were also interested. The guy sounded eager but professional enough not to ask any silly questions or give out too much detail over the phone. However, he did go into some length about his connections with the government and how his team was providing military training to Ukrainian conscripts, reservists, and regulars. He asked Nathan about his age but wasn't perturbed that Nathan was on the wrong side of fifty. After all, they were only training and not fighting battles. They both knew that might come later...depending on the Ruskies! An arrangement was quickly made that Nathan and any interested colleagues would be picked up the next day by two of Cyrus's Ukrainian associates and they would be driven to the hotel where they were basing their operations. 'Great,' Nathan thought, feeling comfortable with his ruse. Here was the opportunity to immerse themselves with people who were closely connected with the war. He was positive this approach could snake its way to Steve or unravel the story of his friend's demise. Nathan peeked at his watch and saw it was nearly dinner time and decided to make his way to meet the group in the hotel restaurant, where he would share the details of his conversation with Cyrus.

Bill, Garen and Sascha's transport had also recently arrived at the hotel, they had been allocated to the neighbouring room of Nathan, Phil, and Mickey. When Nathan arrived at the restaurant, they were already sitting at a table with Nicky and Paul. They were laughing and chatting about everyday things, like the weather, some of their other adventures and how beautiful Kyiv was. At an adjacent table sat a group of three men, resplendent in khaki fatigues, dark coloured fleece jackets and sporting worn military style baseball caps, one with a Marine Corps logo emblazoned upon it. They looked like it had been decades since they last served, and Nathan could hear them discussing the pros and cons of setting up a range complex for one of the local Ukrainian reserve units. Within a minute or so, a female waiter appeared, took their order, and scurried away to another table. This was a good time to outline the next day's activities...

'Okay people, listen up,' was Nathan's cue to get the group's attention, but spoken in a subdued voice for only their table to hear. 'The plan for tomorrow is a pickup by two Ukrainians who work for a guy called Cyrus Naylor. He is a young American running one of the premier FMA teams in Ukraine. Our mission is to train "Ukrainian military" with these dudes and to get as much intel on Steve... you know the drill... possible locations, likely contacts, any sightings, and stuff like that... If Steve has worked with them, if anyone has seen or heard from him or if anyone knows where he may be. Please be discrete with this.' Nathan paused... 'We don't know Steve's condition at present, especially his mindset, and we don't want him to get wind of us and get spooked. Also, we don't know what relationships, good or bad, he has created in this country. So, we do not want or need any "blowback" retribution from some past grudge, etc.' Another pause... 'All in all, it has been incredibly hard and risky to get to this stage and now is not the time to lose anybody! Please, be extra careful and alert in a general sense. We know the 'wild and violent' situation in this country resembles "Tombstone" at times. With so many people coming and going and for so many different causes, not all are altruistic. Try and stay in pairs and always remain in comms. Capisce?' There were nods all round. Nothing more had to be said. They were experienced enough to know the dangers and how to handle themselves. Nathan's spiel was just a reminder, some mental notes for the group's benefit. The female waiter returned...

There was a lull while some drinks were served and it was Nicky who spoke next softly, and sincerely. 'I know we will be off tomorrow, but Paul and I will keep our eyes open and thinking caps on and let you know if we hear of anything.' Nathan looked at the two Brits and nodded his head in appreciation. The waiter soon returned with borscht and bread, followed by a meat dish which seemed to escape description. The soup and bread turned out to be delicious but nothing more could be said about the main course... After their meal, the group sat for a while chatting and exchanging new contact details. Nathan was glad they had been partnered with Nicky and Paul on the long journey to Kyiv and was feeling a little sad these two charming people were departing. Everyone was tired, so an early night was called. Better to rest up and be ready for what lies ahead. Judging by his conversation with Cyrus, Nathan could feel in his bones that tomorrow would be more than interesting....

Chapter Twenty:

THE MAN WHO WANTED TO REIGN DOWN HELL!

A hearty European breakfast was quickly consumed and thoroughly enjoyed by all. The gear was speedily being stowed in packs and duffle bags, and they were ready to go. They drank last minute brews of tea, coffee and chocolate while they sat patiently outside on the patio, waiting for a ride from Cyrus Naylor's men. The conversation was light, and it seemed as if everyone had taken a deep breath and was personally contemplating what may lay ahead... When the time came to depart, Nicky and Paul hugged the boys and bade their hearty 'cheerios' and were off before anyone had a chance to blink. Still, it was miserable to see them leave. They had all become close friends, reliable comrades who had all shared some amazing adventures. As they departed, they were wished the absolute best and for safe travels. Nathan kept looking at his phone, expecting a call for an ETA for the ride but was annoyed to see only a blank screen. Phil and Mickey chatted and joked with Bill and Garen. Sascha had departed with a Kyiv friend but would be available if needed. The weather was still very wintry, the wind was up and most of the city buildings, like the grey sky, took on a foreboding countenance; large gloomy clouds raced across the heavens ... A gust of icy wind blew, cuttingly across Nathan's face, and he coughed, deeply and painfully, three times in succession. 'Damn,' he thought, 'hope I'm not catching a freakin' cold.' He was always dismissive of any ailments or played down his health issues and immediately rejected this physical episode, concentrating on the problems at hand. In their travels and running about, it was easy to get sweaty and exhausted; the tension hadn't lent itself to restful sleep and, when coupled with a below average diet and fatigue, all of these elements promoted sickness. Nathan and Phil had been on the go since they arrived in Poland and the prolonged weariness was already starting to take its toll. Nathan knew all, this but ignored it just the same...

While they waited, Nathan checked and re-checked his watch so many times he began to wonder if he had some compulsive/obsessive disorder! He was about to check his *Casio* again, when, suddenly, two newly sprayed olive drab *Toyota Land Cruisers* appeared at the hotel's sturdy iron gates. Nathan could see the occupants checking the address and then the engines were killed. A couple of young, fit looking Ukrainian men in camouflage uniforms, carrying small pistols holstered on their belts, walked through the gate, and sauntered over to the men who decided to stay seated. A brawny, head shaved man, who could easily have passed for a cage fighter, inquired in a soft voice and in perfect English, which seemed unusual for a Ukrainian, 'Is there a Nathan Philips here?' Nathan stood up and put his hand out to shake the man's hand. He spoke again, 'I'm here to collect you and your people and take you to the hotel in the city. It will be a twenty-minute drive. Please, grab your things and place them in the back of the vehicles. We would like to get moving as soon as possible'. The men did as they were told, and the *Land Cruisers* set off. As usual, in these types of situations, Nathan was excited at the prospect of more adventures, but his excitement was also tempered by his naturally suspicious and cautious nature. As the vehicles moved at speed, he attempted to gauge north and south and notice any prominent buildings, or features that could be used as reference points, in the event he became separated from the others. Nathan was sure that Bill and Garen would be doing the same in the other vehicle. Both vehicles drove at great haste, 'is there any other way in Ukraine?' Nathan mused, and they only slightly slowed when coming to a military checkpoint. They passed through easily, as they placed on their hazard lights and fleetingly flashed their military credentials to the guards, who could see they were on a 'special' task; civilian vehicles stopped promptly in their tracks to let these vehicles speed by.

It seemed like they had been driving for an age when the lead vehicle turned left off Kreschatyk avenue, closely followed by the second vehicle. It braked for people on the expansive pavement which must have been at least ten metres wide, and it drove slowly through a small arched entrance that would have been capable of accommodating a small beer wagon or such like, pulled by horses in decades gone by. The entrance to this lane was guarded by Ukrainian military, armed with newish looking AK 74s, and carrying two-way radios. The men smoked at their posts and replaced the small rectangular plant hedge in front of the archway as it acted as a barrier and some concealment. To Nathan, it seemed as though this was a 'poor man's' *Bat Cave* entrance, with people now strolling by as if nothing had happened and life returning to normal. The vehicles slowed to a crawl on the narrow laneway and turned left around the corner of a large hotel that was adjacent to the arched entrance. Here they stopped and parked next to the building and some demolition rubble. There were other 4x4s parked, in whatever space they could find. They were also newly painted in olive drab and decked out as 'pseudo assault' vehicles. The Ukrainians who drove Nathan and his friends gestured with a curt wave for them to follow. They also signalled for the men to bring their gear. In single file, Nathan and his team followed the two strong Ukrainians through a rear door and down a long, narrow and dusty corridor. This must have been an administrative area of the hotel at one time. Now the ancillary rooms running off the corridor were being used as 'Op' centres, festooned with maps, radios and watchmen. The men were snatching quick peeks at their new surroundings, taking in a scant geographical knowledge of their new environment, *in the event they had to cut and run!*

Suddenly, the corridor ended at two large and high, black, paneled wooden doors, which opened slowly. The men stepped through the entrance into a large foyer, as if they had wandered through the proverbial 'looking glass'. They were startled to see twenty or so uniformed men, 'rough and tough' in appearance, in parade formation, listening intently to their commander issue orders. The leader appeared to be yelling at his men, even in the small confines of the foyer, but this loudness was *par-for-the-course* for most Ukrainians, especially the men!

As the men were absorbing this scene, another guy, wearing *Bates* combat boots, loose multi-cam fatigue trousers, tight black wicking T-shirt, and smoking from the side of his mouth, made a shooshing gesture with his finger and signalling hurriedly for the men to head over to his side of the large lobby. Nathan, his friends, and some other new Westerners who had been waiting, made the distance in a matter of steps and were quickly taken aback by the large knife that adorned the man's belt on his right side, and the roughly made tomahawk that hung loosely on his left hip. 'Hi, I'm Cyrus Naylor' said the man, in a deliberate half-voice, keeping purposely quiet. 'Place your gear down and follow me', and he gestured for them to follow him outside to what functioned as a small smoking area, roughly the size of a basketball key. He walked from man to man, briefly shaking their hands and urging them to smoke, if that was their preference.

Cyrus stood just under six foot in the old measurement and was athletically built, but in a lean, guileful way. It was instantly apparent that he was of Asian extraction and, coming from America's Pacific Northwest, Nathan assumed he had to be *Nikkei* - Japanese American. His thick jet-black hair was shaved at abstract angles, but he sported a tiny Samurai top knot as well as a painfully thin moustache and prickly chin stubble. His complexion was sickly, slightly jaundiced; an over-indulgence in smoking, drugs, drinking and a poor diet, most likely the cause. Notwithstanding, he stood with an air of supreme arrogance, though he frequently hopped about from one foot to another as if he were on some medication and or was 'busting' to use the men's room, had 'fire ants' in his trousers, or he harboured a desperate need to escape, as if he anticipated the arrival of the police at any moment! He spoke slowly and quietly at first, but then his sentences were blurted out, loudly, thick and fast. All the while he smoked without interruption; he lit up one of his cheap Ukrainian smokes so often *he didn't even realise he was doing it!* Cyrus proudly explained how he had managed to contact some notable Ukrainians - senior politicians and upper echelon officers in the military. He continued to blurt out his various stories of accomplishment and couldn't seem to help himself as if his inflated words and 'wild' stories were ego driven.

Of interest to the newcomers was how the hotel became their base of operations, furnished to Cyrus and his men, for free, by another 'contact'. They were allowed the use of a few floors to live in and to store their equipment and personal gear; a Ukrainian unit, commanded by an officer called 'Manis' utilised the other floors of the hotel. It was Manis and his men that Nathan encountered as they entered the crowded and dusty lobby. Cyrus told the men they were to take the rest of the day and tomorrow off, to get settled in, but they would be travelling to a camp some distance away on Sunday to conduct combat medical training to a unit that was only weeks away from deploying to the 'front'.

All during the fascinating briefing, Cyrus had been unconsciously feeling and caressing the six-to-eight-inch knife on his belt while embellishing his stories of 'glory' to the men. He certainly noticed that some of the 'new guys' were also studying the knife. Suddenly and rapidly, he extracted the blade out of its hand-made, stained leather sheath, *waving it about for all to see!!* The weapon was very unusual and was crude, around eight inches long, but irregular in width in places - two inches here and two-and-a-half there, and it appeared as if it had been unskillfully fashioned out of ivory or a similar material. The blade was certainly interesting, no doubt about that! Next came the sordid explanation... *'You see this knife,'* demanded Cyrus, as he held the blade up to the eye level of the group who faced him, *'you see this?!!* This knife was made from the spine of a dead Russian and was presented to me by the brave soldier that killed that stinking invader, *that piece of shit,* back in 2014, in Crimea!!' The men just stared in silence... It wasn't the conviction or charisma connected to Cyrus's speech but the sheer uncertainty of its author that kept each man glued, *captivated by every word...* The tempo and pitch of Cyrus's voice intensified, and he loosely speculated as to the reasons why the men were in Ukraine, but more importantly, the edgy American offered a lot more of *his* memoire. 'I don't really know why you guys are here, maybe to make some money or get a wife. Frankly, I don't care, *but I am in Ukraine to reign hell down on these Russians! I'm a "door kicker" and this was my job in Afghanistan!'* A salient reference to his role as a CQB (close quarter battle) operator, who as part of a combat team, cleared rooms and villages of the enemy. Suddenly, his voice was raised to an even higher pitch as if he were making a solemn vow before the Lord, Allah, or Buddha!! *'I intend to make all Russian dogs pay for what they have done to Ukraine, and you can believe me and my word on this!'* His voice became more strident, almost shouting, *'I am here to kill Russians, it's that fucking simple!!'*

There was a lull... The men studied Cyrus with a degree of stupefaction, but all stood in absolute silence, regardless of their inner thoughts about him, his performance, and his sincerity... Phil very slowly turned his head and gazed at Nathan with his eyes fixed and mouth wide open and a worried, troubled look. Nathan had nearly the exact expression and turned toward Phil, also in amazement! The fervour and conviction of Cyrus's sermon had reminded him of Gregory Peck's magnificent portrayal of Captain Ahab lusting for the 'white whale' in the classic film, *Moby Dick*. Like Ahab, Cyrus, too, was possessed by personal misgivings and psychological demons and *was on an unalterable course that could only result in destruction! The tension in the air was still thick... All the men waited, silent...* Cyrus, now more composed, spoke again, this time much quieter, 'Any questions...No... Okay. In the meantime, follow Earl, who is my 2IC and he will hustle up the keys to your rooms and have you settled in'. Cyrus's motivation was to be there at the end and reap the benefits of a victory against Russia. *Nathan had no doubt about that ...*

The men stood and didn't talk, still starstruck by the zealous recital. A few minutes later, another American, in his mid-thirties, walked casually over to the group. Unlike Cyrus, Earl came across as a 'normal', nice guy and certainly Cyrus's opposite. He was also ex-military. He sported a full-length beard and had served in Afghanistan, where he had lost a couple of fingers in combat. Earl taught high school history these days, but like many other men, adventure and the 'cause' had provided an irresistible lure to travel to Eastern Europe. Before he left, Cyrus added, 'There is a mess hall, which is just around the corner from where you entered, and they will be serving lunch in twenty-minutes. Great to see you all and no doubt, we'll talk later'. Cyrus turned and dashed off to talk to someone else and Earl led the men to where they could pick up the keys to their rooms. Everyone was still silent, still bemused by Cyrus's fiery performance. As Nathan moved off with the others to get a room and drop off his gear, he thought, *'what the fuck have I gotten us into ...?'*

As it turned out, the men were not disappointed with their new lodgings. The rooms were absolutely amazing! The hotel had provided luxury five-star accommodation until the war had put a halt to the major renovations that had just commenced, prior to the invasion. Deluxe beds and plush carpet, widescreen TVs and luxury bathrooms were now being provided, all for nothing! The only downside was that the elevators didn't work so access to the floors was only via the emergency stairs. All Nathan and his colleagues had to do now was to supply quality training and stay alive... What an opportunity to gather information in the hunt for Steve! At the very least, they were expanding their network of contacts and prospects. They didn't have to work every day and could use their private time to chase other leads, conveniently, as they were right in the centre of the capital. Regardless of their opulent surroundings, Nathan cherished the thought they may locate Steve sooner than later!

'Man, can you believe this place' said Phil in a chuffed voice, as he surveyed their impressive abode. 'At least we'll be comfortable while we search for Steve, and who knows what else!' 'Yeah, search for Steve', thought Nathan, but he knew this quest couldn't go on forever. For one, they didn't have the resources to stay in Ukraine for an extended visit, and, secondly, the longer they stayed in-country the more danger they encountered. As well, their visas were only valid for three months, so time was of the essence. He digressed momentarily, and thought about Cyrus Naylor, their new 'illustrious' commander... 'Commander, my arse ', reflected Nathan, slightly aggrieved. 'I'm going to have to keep an eye on this guy, that's for sure... *what a fucking lunatic!* He couldn't command shit if his life depended on it!' Nathan ended his personal rant and calmed down... 'Anyway, I suppose it takes all types to fight a war and he isn't the first madmen to spout such crap like "reigning hell" down on the enemy.' Still, he knew that for the all their sake's, they would have to stay vigilant. He would suggest to the others to have their gear packed and ready to 'scarper' at a moment's notice, and not to provide too much information about themselves or their plans. A quick look at his watch and Nathan knew it was mealtime. He grabbed his cap and nodded to Phil. They moved as one and met Bill, Mickey and Garen downstairs in the lobby.

So much for mealtime! The mess hall provided a major disappointment and a rude shock. The food was mostly borscht and crusty bread and slices of greasy pork fat. Not conducive to the liking of most Westerners, especially Nathan! The mess hall, in a former life, had been a karaoke bar. Stylized prints of young women adorned the walls as well as 'selfies' of beautiful girls, making 'duck faces,' and their pretty young friends prancing about the small, wooden dancefloor, just having fun, as young people do. Or did. What with the invasion and on-going missile attacks, how many of these girls were still alive... who knew? What had been similarly disconcerting on their arrival was that there was a Ukrainian woman cook who had been flagrantly puffing on a cigarette over milk crates housing a dozen Molotov cocktails. The cheap and deadly weapons had been fashioned in the early days of the war when Kyiv had been expected to fall to the invaders, but the enemy had been halted at the city's outskirts. Nathan vividly remembered the news footage of civilians using the Molotov's with aplomb, disabling Russian personnel carriers as they drove by hurling the incendiaries from their *Ladas*, *Skoda's* or *Zaz Taviras*. However, now unsupervised, these homemade firebombs were a deadly risk, especially when someone stood smoking over them! A rapid beeline to seek safety inside was made before a disaster was about to occur...

More was to be discussed on the subject of 'acceptable danger' as the men decided to have bread and coffee for dinner, occupying a table with two opposing bench seats. It appeared that with life being relatively cheap in this part of the world, there seemed to exist a flippant attitude to personal safety, and they would all encounter a great deal more of this before their time in Ukraine was up! Maybe, in their own way, Ukrainians shared a fatalistic view of the universe, especially regarding the war; similar in a way to Muslims and their concept of *Inshalla – Allah's will.*

Bill said what most were thinking about the '*zeitgeist*', the unique 'spirit of the age' they had discovered in Ukraine. 'Hey, we all know there is a war on, but you don't have to make it any more dangerous than it has to be. Even if some deity has a fatalistic plan for you... In my estimation, and my experience, two things get you killed – bad luck or fuck up! And you certainly want to stay clear of both those two categories! *It's that simple...*' Heads filled with comparable experience and memories of war and danger were energetically nodded in consensus as the men drank their bitter coffee to wash down the rough, crusty bread. Eating, sipping and silence followed... No one spoke as it was evident each and every man was thinking about their own brand of philosophy or religion and its role in their survival... and would they make it back home?

It was Garen that spoke next, somewhat enthusiastically about another subject. 'Most of the dudes here go down the avenue to a market that is open until late in the evening. Apparently, it is one of the only stores available around here. Anyone interested in a trip?' No-one could complain if food had to be self-purchased or a guy picked up a snack or a coffee on the run somewhere. Phil decided to wander off with Bill, Mickey and Garen to the food store to buy some rations, at least for the coming days. Nathan said he felt he needed to rack out upon his ever so comfortable bed, and make a call to Sascha, to see if anything had been discovered.

Not surprisingly, Nathan's brief rest had turned into a nap, and it was only the phone that woke him. He had drifted off to sleep with a slightly throbbing headache, which was a first. On arrival at the hotel earlier, he had had a degree of muscle soreness and felt like he had a brief bout of the shakes, but that had passed quickly. He was feeling much better now and didn't give the earlier symptoms a second thought. It was Sascha who was calling. Sascha's leads had fizzled out to nothing and no-one that he knew had come across any Australians or anyone who resembled either Steve Holland's or his son, Nate's, description. Nathan was further disappointed as he had hoped to make a quick trip to Poland and Ukraine, locate Steve, *dead or alive,* and be back home in a week or two. *Simple... Cut and dried... All over Red Rover!* Now the days had dragged into a week and the weeks were starting to accumulate. They couldn't stay in Ukraine forever and it was a big ask for Phil, Garen and Bill to continue on with this fruitless crusade. He felt like he could only offer a few more weeks before the search would need to be suspended.

Sascha re-confirmed his commitment to the cause by assuring Nathan there were still people out there trying and he wouldn't stop his efforts until Nathan decided to terminate the operation. Again, Nathan thanked Sascha for his herculean efforts, and he hung up.

Just then, Phil rushed into the room and couldn't wait to tell Nathan what had just happened; he was bursting to get his story out! As they were walking down to the market, a large security detail of around thirty men, all festooned with assault weapons, approached them from the opposite direction. The lead men waived them to move away and, before they really knew what was happening, they could see President Zelensky and Prime Minister Boris Johnson being escorted by bodyguards and various other hangers-on. 'Man,' said Phil, *'You should've seen it! They were only ten metres away from us. I yelled out, "Boris, you're doing a great job"* while Garen screamed, *"Zelensky, bro."* When we hollered out at them, they looked right at us, smiled and waved. Can you believe that, in this country, at this time, we get to talk to and wave at two of the most important heads of state?' This was probably the equal of coming face-to-face with Prime Minister Churchill and President Roosevelt at Yalta, in *World War Two*! What an occasion! Phil's face was crimson, and he was beaming as he conveyed his exciting story. Nathan felt a bit miffed that he had missed out on the opportunity but was pleased the boys had seen the leaders and their spirits were soaring. He knew it wouldn't always be this way and he was certain there would be dangerous times ahead. Nathan had a deep-seated feeling in his bones when it came to trouble, *like he always did....*

Chapter Twenty-One:

TRAINING DAZE...

'First class training is the best form of welfare for the troops...The more you sweat in training, the less you bleed in battle.'

Field Marshal Erwin Rommel

It was late in the evening, the next day. Nathan sat heavily on the edge of his bed in his 'flash' hotel room, feeling not just exhausted, but overwhelmed and speechless, and was finishing his second lukewarm *Heineken.* The sweet amber fluid had failed to touch his lips, downed in one mighty guzzle, as if his throat was on fire and needed extinguishing; he was beyond caring that the beer wasn't chilled at all! He gazed down at his bare feet, trancelike, and didn't have the strength to wiggle his toes. His head felt unusually heavy, and he summoned all his might to prevent it from propelling forward, and him, into the expensive carpet. *'What a fucking day,'* was all he could mutter, repeatedly, under his breath, and he gazed across the room and saw Phil lying flat out on his bed, still in his camouflage trousers, swallowing mouthfuls from a litre bottle of *Southern Comfort* as he lay on his back. Some of the tawny fluid ran down the sides of his mouth onto the chenille bedspread but he didn't care... *He couldn't give a toss!* This was the least of his troubles... As far as Mickey went, he hadn't been seen since they returned, and it was anybody's guess if he'd grabbed his things, 'packed his bongos', and caught the earliest train back to the border! It had been a ridiculously strenuous day, and the men were just trying to see out the hours as best as they could, even if it meant drowning their sorrows! What had started as an average day by anyone's standard had descended into chaos and only confirmed to the men that, unfortunately, in their hunt to locate a dear friend, they had aligned themselves with some seriously crazy and dangerous people!! Nightly rocket attacks, 'snatch squads' or a Russian invasion wasn't *all they had to worry about...*

The best and only way to understand this debacle is to start from the beginning.... Phil, Mickey, and Nathan had managed to rise early on the Sunday morning, around seven, and made some porridge and coffee from the rations Phil had purchased the night before. There had been three air-raid sirens around midnight but neither of the men heard the vile and insidious impact of any rockets plummeting into the city. However, they did hear a single rifle shot just before curfew at 11pm. As Nathan explained to Phil, it was most likely some dozy Ukrainian reservist, incredibly bored and frigid at his guard post, so he began to play with his weapon, in a vain attempt to relieve some of the boredom. As his sleepy mind wandered off... *BANG!!* The sound of the gunshot reverberated off the high walls of the buildings for the length of a city block and sounded much louder than it really was! There could have been other worthy explanations, however, the resulting shot that had barked out in the cold and still night was most likely a negligent discharge of a single round from a soldier's AK 74. The tell-tale indicator was that it had all gone exceedingly quiet after the gun blast... too quiet... as if someone was hoping, praying, no-one would investigate...

Still, they had managed to secure a reasonable night's sleep and had made their way downstairs to the backend of the entrance to Kreschatyk avenue, just opposite the mess entrance and the infamous crates of *Molotov Cocktails*. They were the first ones there... There had been some noisy movement late in the evening before curfew and a late model *Bentley*, with Lithuanian plates, sat impressively in the carpark, completely decked out in the Ukrainian *Galeteika*, digital camouflage pattern. Nathan commented, 'Well, that's something you don't see every day, a cammed up luxury car!' But it wasn't surprising to see expensive foreign cars in the capital. It wasn't only that Kyiv was a 'hub for action,' but numerous deals were being made between foundations, government and individuals concerning arms, munitions, first aid supplies and so forth. Equally, many arrangements were being made on the infamous 'black market', as it always does in war time...

Nobody gets rich on their own money.

The big British motor car looked imposing, like a tank, as it sat solitary and behemoth like, the backdrop of the grey hotel wall behind it. During the late evening, there had also been a change of plans so Bill and Garen wouldn't be needed this day, so for the lucky duo, another day off! But after a forty-minute wait, and well after the designated time, Cyrus, Earl, and a couple other foreign trainers sauntered down to the entrance, as if they had all the time in the world and walked casually out onto the busy avenue. Cyrus gestured for Phil and Nathan to ride with him, while Mickey and the other men jumped into an old ambulance that had been offered to Cyrus by a guy from Poland and had been driven all the way to Kyiv from Warsaw.

Waiting on the chilly avenue, in a beat-up, disheveled, and mechanically defective *Toyota Camry*, was Alex. They had been briefly introduced to Alex and Dimitri the previous night as they were sourcing their room keys but didn't think too much of it. The two men hadn't been all that friendly... Later, Earl had informed them 'on the quiet' that Alex was the President of the Kyiv chapter of the *Bandidos Motorcycle Club* and Dimitri was his dutiful Sergeant-at-Arms. They acted as interpreters and 'fetch and carry' men for Cyrus, and, in return, Cyrus pleaded with his government contacts for the men to stay with him in Kyiv, and not venture off to the 'front'. This arrangement pleased everyone, especially Dimitri and Alex. Nathan would discover later there were other incentives for Alex and Dimitri to remain close to Cyrus...

Both men were dressed in Ukrainian camouflage and were about the same age, around mid to late twenties. Dimitri was blonde and handsome while Alex was dark - like his disposition, wore a goatee and didn't look like the kind of person you'd want to cross... Dimitri was helping to get the car started and had the hood up, tinkering with the battery. *'Fucking piece of shit... start, you stinking suka* (bitch)' came a thick and aggressive Ukrainian accent, bellowing from inside the car, as Alex overplayed the ignition. Suddenly, the engine spluttered for a second, attempted to start, not once but twice, before roaring into life, still sounding like it was running rough and edgy on three, not four, cylinders. Alex gestured for the men to quickly get in. *'Quick, hurry, hurry, before this fucking pig dies!'* Nathan dove into the front seat and Phil, Cyrus and Earl sat in the back, daypacks resting on their knees. The fact is this car was designed to transport five Asians, not five heavy Caucasians with their kit, and things were very tight and noisy, and smelly with body odour...

With a split-second break in traffic, Alex took off as if it were the start of the *Le Mans* 24-hour endurance race! The car hurtled ferociously down the street like a fiery comet and weaved its way through the thick morning traffic, which, when compared to Alex's speed, appeared to be stationary! The race car skills didn't stop there... Alex employed a 'Tokyo drift' method when coming to corners and the vehicle slid awkwardly sideways on the damp cobble stones before righting and propelling itself headlong down the next street. He found great fascination in this and laughed loudly and often at this particular skill of his! Nathan looked nervously back at the rear seat passengers and all Cyrus could say, with a smirk, was 'He always drives like this...' They motored along in this maniacal fashion for nearly forty-five minutes before they met up with the ambulance at a service station, where the men were buying coffee and cigarettes. 'Fuck,' said Nathan to Phil, 'that puts a new handle on fast driving! *I nearly shit myself!*' Phil was accustomed to riding extremely fast on motorbikes but was speechless and just headed off to the station shop to purchase some cigarettes to calm his nerves...

Nathan remained outside and began talking to some of the other men he didn't know, most of whom were from the United States. He noticed a guy wearing an 'operators cap' with a small silver fern on a Velcro patch and walked over to him for a chat. The guy's name was Charlie, and he was from Wellington, New Zealand. He was middle aged, medium height but athletic and sinewy. Like everyone else, Charlie was outraged at the Russian atrocities and wanted to do his bit to assist the Ukrainians, in whatever way helped the most. He had made his way to Kyiv on the train with some other Westerners he had encountered on the border and had only been with Cyrus and his cohort for a couple of days. The team and its dysfunctional leader had come as a surprise to him. He was led to believe these ex-military types would be more professional and less criminally inclined. *But he was wrong...* Nathan subtlety enquired if Charlie had wandered across any other Aussies or Kiwis in his travels. The Kiwi replied he had only met one Aussie... a nice guy called Andy... on the border at Medyka, who was working in a soup kitchen, and he was amazed there weren't more guys from the 'antipodes' in the country. The two men had an instant liking of each other and planned to stay in touch.

Just as the men were getting accustomed to the cold wind gusts howling from the east, Cyrus aggressively signalled to everyone to get back in their respective vehicles. It was still twenty minutes from here to the camp and they were running late. *'Yeah, no kidding'* thought Nathan. The men took to their seats in the crappy *Toyota* and within an instant, the vehicle was again galloping down the highway. Within an instant, Cyrus had shifted from a happy mood to a belligerent silence and the atmosphere in the vehicle became instantly tense. Nathan decided just to look ahead and try and orientate himself to the city and its surroundings. They had ventured from the built-up area of the city to a district on the outskirts where the trees were plentiful and the fields expansive. The vehicle turned off the highway and slowly and cautiously drove two hundred metres down a side road. A military checkpoint was just in front and was manned by two old Ukrainian men who must have been in their late sixties or seventies, but they were diligent with their checking of the vehicles and occupants and kept their assault rifles at the 'ready'. Cyrus produced his credentials, a small green book that was stamped with the Ukrainian trident upon it. The men made a cursory glance at all the passengers in both vehicles and waved the procession onwards. As the vehicle followed a route that rounded the camp, Cyrus spoke, 'I have identity papers from the *Legion Obolon* in Kyiv. Once I get photos of everyone, we will go out to the unit and get ID papers like mine. If nothing else, it just makes it easier to get around Kyiv and into military bases.' Technically, the unit identity cards would place Nathan and his friends in the territorial forces of the Ukrainian military, albeit a reserve unit. It certainly was better than pulling out the passport every time, only for the checkpoint guards to view the document with a quizzical look. However, Nathan was more concerned than just being inconvenienced at a roadblock. Searching for Steve in Ukraine was one thing, *joining the Ukraine military was another!!*

Within a few minutes, the two vehicles parked at a side road and the men piled out, milling around for further instructions. Cyrus briskly walked over to a commander who was patiently waiting for the group's arrival. He went by the name of 'Ronin', and in addition to his camouflage uniform, combat boots and pistol, he carried a *Euro* 'man bag' that seemed strangely out of place with his military *ensemble*. Nathan could see an earnest conversation was being held as heads were being energetically nodded and accusing fingers pointed but, despite the lively exhibition, the two men were amicable with each other. *Just the way conversations work in Ukraine...* After five minutes, Cyrus ambled over and announced that they would be training a platoon in combat first aid, though only the basics and then they would focus on extraction drills under fire. After a lunch meal, courtesy of Ronin, they would be teaching the theory side of combat first aid in the lecture theatre. This instruction would be conducted by the combat medics who had travelled in the ambulance. The two main guys here were Tyler, a former US Navy corpsman and Baker, a Marine Corps medic who had served time in Afghanistan. The rest of the men were instructed to help as required.

It was at this point that Cyrus began to show his true, dysfunctional nature. Anyone not directly involved in the training was attempting to keep a low profile and trying hard not to disrupt the lesson. The guys stood, talking quietly, about twenty metres away from the class. Out of the blue, Cyrus stormed over to the assembly, which included Phil, Nathan, Mickey and Charlie, and started to rant. He barked at the men, ordering them to make sure they prepared detailed lesson plans for future classes and to rehearse their subject material before presentation. Among a barrage of other criticisms, he voiced, *'I don't want to look like some Jackass because you guys are lazy'*, and on that insult, he marched across the field to talk with Ronin. *'What's his fucking problem!'* was all Phil could say, and the rest of the group concurred. More cracks were beginning to appear in the man's character...

After thirty minutes, the class took a break, mainly so the soldiers could extricate their wounded in small teams as well as maintaining a firefight with the enemy. Before the new class was due to begin, a couple of the men, including Nathan, made a beeline over to the woods to take a piss, but they were quickly stopped by a Ukrainian corporal who said the area was probably mined. Apparently, a young recruit had ventured out there the previous week only to have his leg blown off; a classic case of 'bad luck and fuck up,' both at the same time! This warning certainly stopped the men in their tracks, and they carefully retraced their footprints and politely requested the whereabouts of the nearest lavatory! Anyway, it wouldn't be long before lunch and Nathan and a few other men thought it more prudent to 'hold on'.

The next part of the day's training involved combat medical extraction drills. The Ukrainian platoon of around twenty men had been broken into groups of five. The plan was that one member of each group would be the casualty, and the other men would act in pairs, one pair covering, while the other pair would grab the casualty and drag him back to suitable cover, or as far as they physically could, and apply combat first aid. The rear pair would then cover the two lead men, who would run rearwards and pick up the wounded man and continue with the extraction, away from enemy fire. This 'leap frogging' drill would be managed by grabbing the man under the arms, or his combat vest and dragging him and would be continued until they were they believed they were safe; the drill could go for hundreds of metres but, for the purpose of the exercise, the soldiers would only go about fifty metres or so.

Although a basic manoeuvre, it took some time for the Ukrainians to get the gist of the drill. Mickey, Nathan, Charlie, and Phil attempted to play 'sheep dog' and roam from group to group providing guidance, inspiration and motivation. The usual 'back slapping' and loud cries of 'GOOD, GOOD,' 'DOBRA,' 'DOBRA,' and plenty of the 'thumbs up' sign always seemed to do the trick! It wasn't long before the drills sunk in, and the men were smiling and immensely proud of their efforts. Time for lunch and that piss. The Ukrainian soldiers had struck a friendly chord with the Westerners, who had been soldiers like them, once upon a time. War stories from bygone conflicts, cigarettes, and coffees were exchanged, finishing up in a photo shoot with their newfound friends, draped in the Ukrainian flag. They all headed over to the mess hall and, at last, Nathan finally found an opportunity to learn more about Steve Holland...

In the lunch queue stood a giant of a man with a fiery red beard. He wore an Irish Celtic symbol patch on his combat shirt and Nathan could hear the man's oscillating accent, loudly above the kerfuffle of soldiers lining up for their midday meal. In typical Aussie fashion, Nathan strolled over to the big man and asked, 'How's it going mate, my name's Nathan and this is my old mate

Phil, *what in God's name is a big bastard like you doing here?'* The Irishman was a goliath... *there was no getting around that!* His head appeared twice as big as that of an average man and it would be easy to imagine him playing in the front row of the Irish rugby side. 'Gees,' Nathan thought to himself, '*...his Mum must've suffered a lot when he was born!'* He looked at Nathan and a mighty grin spread across his face. 'Ah,' he said, 'I would know that accent from anywhere... Aussies, right? How are you going cobber?' trying, but poorly attempting to emulate the Aussie slang word for 'mate'. Nathan and Phil eagerly shook the big Irishman's paw, but it was like placing a tiny baby's fist in an adult's large baseball mitt, such was the enormity of the man's palm. 'I'd hate to be hit by you,' remarked Nathan, *'I think you'd knock me into next week!'* However, the Irishmen pronounced in his soft, rolling brogue that he was more of a gentle soul and really wasn't up for fisticuffs... unless provoked!

Sean was his name (of course!), and he indicated that he had joined the *International Legion* but left, like so many others, after the debacle at Yavoriv. It had been strongly suggested to him by some Ukrainian friends that he enlist in this unit as they were trying to fashion themselves after a 'Ranger Battalion' and were going to operate in small reconnaissance teams, hitting opportune targets, as necessary. This method of 'war fighting' appealed to Sean, and he enlisted. Nathan pressed the man further as he wanted to discover more about Yavoriv and whether he had come across another Aussie, in his fifties, named Steve. Sean thought pensively for a few moments and then he remembered... It had been several months, and he hadn't had time to dwell on his time there, especially with training and the war... He then began an interesting dialogue concerning Steve and some of the other friends he had met as all the memories came racing back... He described Steve just as Nathan remembered him and said that while they weren't in the same platoon, the few Anglo-types in the unit would spend time together at the end of the day's training as they had shared interests, such as football, culture, and a common tongue. He distinctly remembered the night of the missile strike and how the whole evening could only be described as pure mayhem! He was one of the lucky few who made his way to the safety of the wooded area at the back of the barracks, which was a good three hundred metres away.

Many of the other soldiers were too slow to react or were in shock at the ferocity of the assault and its subsequent carnage. For some of the new recruits, it was the first time some of these soldiers had seen dead, mutilated people or screaming wounded. There was little or no command and control, and it took an awfully long while before even basic first aid was administered! The 'officers' were paralyzed into making any form of decision or too much of their debating and officialdom led to inaction. The missile attack was the straw that broke the camel's back for many, and soldiers left the unit in droves, some to Lviv and others to the capital. They weren't worried about the repercussions and would sooner take their chances elsewhere... As Sean stated, *'Who could blame them, or force them to stay after that calamity?'*

As far as Steve went, the 'big Paddy' hadn't spotted him after the attack but was certain he wasn't in the number of men who were killed. He had talked to a mutual friend who indicated Steve and other Westerners had left for Kyiv, possibly to join another military unit or to head home, like so many other volunteers who had chosen to. Nathan and Phil greatly thanked Sean for the useful information and hoped to catch up with him later. They swapped Aussie and Irish patches, shook hands, urged one another to 'keep safe' and went to their respective tables.

While the conversation with the big Irishman had been going on, Cyrus and the other trainers had been sitting with Ronin at a large solitary table that was to one side of the large mess hall. Cyrus gave Phil and Nathan a suspicious look as the men took their seats but continued to talk to Ronin and one of his lieutenants. The men eagerly gulped down the delicious fruit compote drink; a beverage made of local berries, which was thoroughly enjoyed by all. The meal was chicken and vegetables and, as always, was basic but pleasing. Once the men had downed their lunch, they walked to the lecture theatre where the combat first aid theory class would be held. Rough, loud soldiers wandered into the room, chatting, and laughing in small packets and took their seats. To Nathan's surprise, the odd soldier was looking at video clips on their smartphones, texting or looked like they were about to go to sleep... This would never have occurred in the Australian Army and Nathan remembered back to his younger days in the military... Any soldier attempting to sleep would be barked at and then ordered to stand at the back of the classroom! Different countries, different standards, but Nathan knew the Ukrainians would have to get their shit together in a hurry if they were to stave off the advancing Russian hordes. In a minute or so, the class was operating in earnest with a standard, 'explain, demonstrate and imitate' methodology. Nathan, Phil, and Mickey assisted when necessary and lent a physical hand to assist some of the soldiers who were struggling with the practical side of things, like applying dressings and combat tourniquets.

Surprisingly enough, it wasn't long before the class concluded, and the trainers were jumping into their respective rides. Now, Cyrus had gone from looking like 'Mr. Cranky' to laughing and cajoling with the trainers, like their best buddy. Again, Alexi took the wheel and the vehicle rushed off after engaging with the roadblock at the camp's entrance. It seemed they were back at the hotel in no time. On the drive Nathan was amazed at the number of new buildings that were still being constructed, even though the country was on a war footing and the future was uncertain. As the men exited the vehicle, Phil grabbed Nathan's arm and ushered him off to one side, using the pretence of getting a coffee at a street stall to keep Nathan at a distance from Cyrus and Earl. Nathan looked confused but followed; soon it would be clear. *'Did you see what was going on at the camp and in the back of the car?'* questioned Phil. 'Not really' answered Nathan. *'I was clutching the door handle and bracing for impact, the whole way!'* 'Well,' said a tired and jaded Phil. 'I know why Cyrus has been acting like flipping Dr. Jekyll and Mr. Hyde all day. *The guy is off his nut!'* Phil had witnessed Cyrus snorting crack cocaine in the back of the class at the camp and in the *Camry,* using the flat part of his daypack to use the drugs. *'Fuck me'* replied Nathan, *'No wonder that bastard is all over the shop... he is high one minute and coming down the next.'*

Confused, and in a quandary over the day's proceedings, Nathan sat on his plush bed and truly wondered what he had gotten himself and his best friend involved in... He certainly thought there would be issues on the way to locating 'Dutchy' Steve Holland, but he didn't expect he would have to negotiate the ravings of a psychotic crackhead and his criminal compatriots! Nathan mumbled to himself, somewhat despondently, 'No wonder he kept the biker president close as he was most likely the source of drugs, and this was just training day one! *This shit just keeps getting better and better...'*

Chapter Twenty-Two

COULD IT GET ANY WORSE?

Slowly but surely, the pent-up tension began to subside, and Nathan lay back on his large single bunk, socks off and right hand supporting the nape of his neck as he rested on a firm pillow. He briefly flexed his thoughts for a moment and wondered about Sascha. He hadn't heard from the tough little Ukrainian for a few days now and was becoming a tad worried. 'Damn' he thought, 'I hope this guy hasn't bailed on us...' Just then, a brief text message arrived from the man in question. 'Goddamn it, this guy must have ESP' Nathan murmured to himself, astonished at the sudden, eerie, connection. Sascha had been terribly busy... Since arriving back in the capital, he had been contacting many of the commanders of the various army reserve units in Kyiv and had presented himself as a go-between the foreign trainers and the Ukrainian military. This way he could prod and poke and ask all sorts of questions without raising suspicion.

So many units had been formed or re-formed it was hard to keep up; various assault brigades, SSO-Special Service Organisations (primarily Special Forces), infantry regiments, assault units, and the list went on... Ukrainian military commanders were making outrageous claims to procure foreign trainers, promising high rank, accommodation, and handsome salaries. At this stage, no FMAs were being paid money for their training and expertise, or none that Nathan knew of... Some FMAs had been reimbursed for their time in the form or rations, the odd hot meal along the way, transportation rides or basic accommodation. But there was a need to be careful. One group of FMAs had been arrested by the police as they, unknowingly, were training a Ukrainian group bent on overthrowing the government!

From the trainers' point of view, they did exercise a large degree of power over the situation as they could basically do a 'try before they buy' and move onto the next unit if they desired. Their currency was quality training to a NATO and Western military standard, and the Ukrainians were desperate in this area. There were so many Westerners in Ukraine coming and going it was difficult for commanders and the authorities to keep standards up, and the demand was always high. For the trainers, most of talk coming their way was all just speculation, lies or fairytales, and to the Ukrainians, the Westerners pretty much all looked and acted the same.

At times, the whole situation for everyone concerned was complicated and confusing, especially the language barrier and determining what the task was...

By a stroke of luck, Sascha had been contacted by a Commander Yaroslav, who had been attempting to recruit some quality foreign military advisors to his reserve unit. He had recently used the services of a small team, with one of the men being an Australian and with whom he was very impressed. However, the man had left abruptly and without any explanation. Sascha gathered Yaroslav's intent was more for Yaroslav's prestige than for the combat readiness of his unit and he believed he was just another Ukrainian officer that was more interested in his survivability and how he would be perceived after the conflict. This was a familiar theme, and it was an open secret that many of the Ukrainian officers had not attended a reputable military officer academy, such as *Sandhurst*, *West Point* or *Duntroon*. It was rumoured that Yaroslav had received his appointment due to political connections, and it was common knowledge that running a successful business or managing a profitable chain of petrol stations could also warrant an officer's commission in the Ukraine military. Not exactly the best credentials to be a competent soldier, a leader of military men, or a war strategist!

Suddenly, the name of this commander jogged a mental note in Nathan's brain. 'Yes, that's him, this was the guy Cyrus was rambling on about earlier in the day in the car, and how they were going to visit the unit the very next day', thought Nathan. It was hard for Nathan to clearly remember some of the names as, unfortunately, they all sounded the same to him! *What a coincidence and what luck!* Nathan was confident this situation would steer him to some credible information concerning Steve's whereabouts. This is what he hoped anyway... While a lot of the details had been sketchy, Sascha was able to confirm that Steve had scarpered to Kyiv looking for a training opportunity. For Nathan, the question begged... 'how many Australians could there be in this city training the Ukrainian military?' If nothing else, it would confirm or deny an avenue of investigation but, if in the negative, may lead Nathan and his friends to fresher and more rewarding trails... The information was undoubtedly hit and miss, but that was all they had. Not a lot to go on and not a lot of assistance from anywhere. There wasn't an Australian Embassy in Kyiv as all the diplomats and staff had been recalled and there certainly wasn't an 'Aussie Quarter', like London's famed Earl's Court.

Still deep in the trough of his thoughts, Nathan was surprised when the bathroom door suddenly flung open, and Phil emerged, slightly wet, wearing just a towel and whistling and singing a popular tune from the late seventies:

Lookin' for some hot stuff baby this evenin' I need some hot stuff baby tonight I want some hot stuff baby this evenin...'

'Ah,' the classic *Donna Summer* tune Nathan

hadn't heard in a millennium! Phil had freshly shaved - exceptionally close and had laid out some of his better clothes on his bed, and the singing continued... Nathan was fascinated, studying 'Merry Phil' and his chirpiness for a while, and then commented, *'What's all this in aid of?'* 'Mate, I've got a date in twenty minutes just down the avenue,' came the cheery response... 'promise I'll be back by curfew'. Well, this was all news to Nathan, and he inquired... 'How did you arrange all this?' Phil explained he had signed up on the local *Tinder* and was meeting a young girl named Alina and they were going to have coffee. All simple, harmless, and non-committal. 'Mate, you are one special dude, you'd manage to locate a cool date at the mouth of Hades, or a hot woman under a breezy date palm in the Sahara, and if I wasn't mistaken, wasn't it *Grinder* you were checking out!' Phil laughed deeply at the glib, homophobic reference to the dating app for gay men, and reminded Nathan that there wasn't much else going on, and that he didn't come to Kyiv just to lay on his bed, day in, day out! *'C'mon Nathan, don't be such a buzzkill!'* Nathan could see his point and Phil had been a good 'trooper' so a spot of R&R wouldn't hurt him. He cupped his hands tight, palms flat together, as if he were praying... 'No worries, mate, have a great time but please, and pretty please, be back before curfew at eleven or you'll be locked out, all night.' Phil finished dressing and was on his way to the door, when he quipped, *'Don't worry about me, I'm the proverbial bad penny, and I always show up!'*

For the rest of the evening, Nathan kept himself occupied by using *Google* to educate himself more about Ukraine, but now, it was ten minutes to curfew and still no sign of Phil... Nathan was annoyed and let out a loud *'Damn, fuck, bugger!!'* He had tried texting his best friend on numerous occasions in the last hour, but there had been no response, nothing. He was starting to become really worried, and began pacing the room... He knew that if Phil was caught outside during curfew hours, he would be severely beaten by street criminals, the police and military or even worse, arrested or executed, like the Czech guy that had recently been found, bound and shot. It wouldn't be the simple tap on the shoulder and a polite 'There you go my son, be on your way, be seeing you...' by a roly-poly police sergeant with the oafish charm and ineptitude of a Sergeant Schultz from *Hogan's Heroes*. More likely, he would be carted off to a dark, damp cell and interrogated for hours to ascertain if he was a Russian spy, or an agent of some other nation, for that matter; never mind what his passport declared or what plausible story he could conjure! This treatment was said to be *de rigeur* with the Ukrainian Special Police Forces, most notably the *Berkut*; a simple beatdown would the least of his troubles!

With a multitude of scenarios racing around Nathan's mind, and not totally sure what he should do next, he was completely startled when the door was thrown wide open, and Phil staggered into the room, with a trail of blood streaming down from a nasty gash on the right side of his face! He teetered forward and fell into Nathan, who transferred all this weight to his braced right leg and he lowered Phil gently onto his bed. Nathan rushed into the bathroom and clutched a small, grey fleecy towel, doused it under the cold-water tap, wrung it dry and used it as a makeshift compress on Phil's hemorrhaging wound. The towel was soon crimson red, heavy, and dripping with blood... Phil was looking groggy, and his eyes were glazed most of the time... Most probably a slight concussion and Nathan needed to keep his friend conscious until he could get expert medical help. He quickly texted Garen and told him to make his way to their room with his medical kit - *pronto*! While he nervously waited, Nathan questioned Phil about his injuries, whether he been hurt anywhere else... He couldn't rely on Phil's mutterings, so he performed a quick primary survey of Phil's injured body, running his hand over his frame to check for fractures and lumps, looking for bruises and to feel for wet spots indicating further bleeding and trauma. Despite some defensive wounds on his hands, some bruising, and some scratches to his face, it was only the deep wound to Phil's head that appeared to be of any real or immediate concern. Thankfully, Garen was responsive and arrived at Nathan and Phil's room within in a couple of minutes. He conducted his own professional and extensive medical examination. In the meantime, Nathan begged Phil to explain what had occurred... *'Had it been the military or secret police who were responsible for his bashing or was it some villain?'* Thankfully, Phil had recovered slightly after his brief rest, and was less baffled than when he first broke into the room. He was more coherent of what was going on around him.

He began to recount the incident... Although he was viciously and unmercifully set upon, he had the presence of mind to free himself from his attackers and struggle his way down the narrow back streets to the hotel. It was fortunate the route from the cobbled square was mostly downhill, down the street at *St. Michael's Cathedral*, down the icy and treacherous pavement to the Philharmonic building at the bottom of the steep gradient, and then a few hundred metres back to the hotel along the avenue. It was only a few kilometres in total, but when you're in a strange city, it's cold, and *you've been clobbered*, it probably felt like he had just run a marathon! Again, Nathan pressed him for details, growing ever more impatient. *'Mate, who did this to you, cops, military, crooks?'* 'No,' said Phil, softly, *'it was the three brothers of the girl I met at the Buena Vista Bar'*.

Having perked up slightly, it was now time for the *truth to be told...* Phil had met the young Ukrainian beauty, as arranged by *Tinder,* and had sat with her for coffee and a bite to eat. The girl spoke exceptionally good English, and they laughed and had gotten on really well, for a first date. The enchanting evening had provided Phil with a brief respite from the troubles of the last few weeks. All was going fine until it was time to leave... Just prior to the customary 'goodnight' peck on the cheek, the girl informed

Phil that he had to give her three hundred hryvnia, to pay for her company for the evening. Well, this came as a slap in the face to Phil and he flatly refused! *I don't pay for the pleasure of a woman's company, or even for sex... Forget it... I'll spring for the 'average' coffee and the over-priced meal, but no other add ons'!* The money wasn't a hefty sum, especially when it was converted to Australian dollars, but it was the 'stinking' principle that mattered to Phil, and how many wars had been fought in the name of a 'principle'. Damn, the siege of *Troy* had started over the stolen love of a beautiful woman!

Alina, equally incensed by Phil's refusal to pay for her 'charming' company, looked past him for 'muscled inspiration' from her three brothers who sat ready at the back of the room. Before Phil knew it, he had been manhandled by ruffians, picked up and thrown around like a rag doll, bouncing off wooden furniture and brick walls. His saving grace was they had dined in the upstairs floor of the bar, a tiny area, mostly for couples, and it was difficult for all three men to get at him at once... Phil vaguely saw the weighty vodka bottle that came crashing down upon his skull but had, on instinct, managed to turn slightly, in the nick-of-time, so it had only become a glancing blow... He knew he needed to get out, *tout de suite*, before it got worse. He waited for his moment, made a break, and sprinted for the door, and freedom!

The smaller of the three brothers had attempted to block his way but Phil hit him in the chest, hard, with the full force of his shoulder and the momentum of his substantial body weight, like a hefty *Manly Sea Eagles* prop forward, and the two, semi-embraced men careered backwards through the glass door, into the bitterly cold street and onto the iced pavement! By now, the bar staff were attempting to quell the *fracas* inside and the upper floor of the bar had become congested with diners, onlookers, and employees, all gawking to comprehend what had transpired... Still armed with the survival urge Phil kept moving, certain he wouldn't get a second chance at escape... *He needed to act quickly...* He hastily lifted himself off Alina's brother, who had been winded by the experience and was now vigorously gasping and searching for air, just as an asthmatic's breathing becomes frenetic when triggered severely by dust or pollutants... Phil thrust a left leg forward, then a right shoulder in the same direction and continued this metronomic process until he had developed a quickening pace and was now propelling himself with some velocity down the vacant street. Maybe it was the cold night air, the blow to the head or the winded brother who lay on the sidewalk - *who knows...* but Phil was semi certain he had forsaken the running steps, and the associated clamour of an angry pursuit; these threats were now far behind! All he knew was that he had to get back to his room before curfew and was driven by this singular purpose. He swayed and he lurched, he bumped off walls and ran breathlessly and exhaustedly back to the hotel! The guards at the entrance didn't take much of a look at the condition of the Westerner as they had seen Phil leave a few hours earlier and, frankly, they weren't all that interested.

Just as all this information was sinking in, Garen rapped on the door and entered. Nathan gave the big Texan a quick update on Phil's injuries and stood aside to let the man go to work, which the medico did with the minimum of fuss. Nathan was incensed, and if smoke could bellow from his ears, *it would have!!* 'How dare they,' he thought, simmering at the cruel irony of the situation; he was both angry and bewildered at the fact that not only did these people assault his best friend, his old army mate... Albeit as a cover for their real intent, Nathan and his colleagues were in this country trying to help the Ukrainians defeat a foe that was hell-bent on destroying them!! Garen patted Nathan on the shoulder, releasing him from the grip of his angry thoughts. 'Only a slight concussion, he's okay to come down to my room and I'll watch him through the night, he'll be fine. The gash on the head is nothing and looks worse than it is. I'll fix that too!' 'Thanks, Garen... thanks so much!' was Nathan's reply, and he accentuated his appreciation with a monkish nod of the head. Phil was lifted from the bed and was now more coherent and looking so much more alert; even the colour had returned to his face. Garen placed his big right arm around Phil to steady him and they left for Garen's room and wouldn't return for the evening. Still, Nathan was seething, *'Hurt my best mate, will you'* he kept repeating to himself, over and over! At times like this, Nathan only saw red... his anger now acting as a fiery foundry that would manufacture a nasty plan to fix the 'little red wagon' of Alina and her *three, thug brothers...*

Chapter Twenty-Three:

ALL IN DUE COURSE...

Nathan slowly roused from under his toasty warm sleeping bag, but kept his eyes tightly closed and *prayed...* and *hoped...* and *cajoled...* and *implored* all the forces in creation to ensure today was going to be damn sight better than yesterday's debacle! Already, there were some positives to be had. Firstly, all the trainers at the hotel were heading to the headquarters of a formation of the *Legion Obolon of Kyiv* to provide combat medical training as well as instruction on infantry minor tactics to the newer members who had just joined the unit. The age of the recruits ranged from enlistment age, around eighteen, right up unto those men who probably needed to stay home, as they were in their late fifties, or even older. It may be a sad, cruel thing to say but 'war' is a young man's game... With some luck, maybe some digging and questioning would lead to a fresh set of tracks to Steve 'Dutchy' Holland.

Hopefully, *something... anything...*

The Legion's headquarters and facilities were in a school. Like so many other educational buildings across Ukraine, this one had been adapted to aid the war effort. Besides having many classrooms, toilets and showers, these facilities also housed large kitchens and recreational areas and were therefore perfect for a military application. Much propaganda had been made by Ukraine and the world media when a school was bombed or rocketed, *'another murderous Russian atrocity...'* but, in this case, students cheerfully co-existed with the military attired men and women who came and went. Life would be made easier for the unit, and safer for the children, in the coming June when the students went home for the summer holidays. The important distinction to note was that not all schools were being utilised by the military, however, it was a necessity of wartime to exploit the schools as training centres and a terrible misfortune if anyone was killed in the process. The unit was a short drive from the hotel, less than thirty minutes and, after the obligatory stop for 'mornos' (morning tea) the men arrived at the unit. Vehicles were promptly parked and those with authority, on both sides, met to discuss the day's events. Nathan made a mental note of where the bunkers were, in case of a rocket strike. He noticed there were four apartment buildings adjacent to the centre. 'Damn,' he thought, 'I'd hate to be living here, right next to a 'high value' target. May as well paint a cross on your sodding roof and get it over with really quick'. Despite the danger, people went about their business casually or walked around their estate, either in blissful ignorance or steadfastly internalizing a patriotic fortitude and nationalistic commitment, which many people in the West would fail to comprehend. Anyway, where would they go and what would they do? There was nothing else for them but to 'suck it up'.

As soldiers started congregating for the training, the men were loosely assembled in a tiled, concrete inner square, within the confines of the Soviet style building. Most of the Ukrainian 'soldiers' were smoking, chatting, drinking *Red Bull*, or showing off assault weapons or sniper rifles they had acquired themselves, at great cost. One soldier had purchased his high-powered weapon for a sum of ten thousand hryvnias! Other men stood around examining a bleached human skull that demonstrated a single bullet hole in it, laying on a table, a Russian skull that was a trophy from the Crimean conflict. Another macabre surprise for Nathan and his friends and something he would never have seen back in his old army reserve unit! Finally, Yaroslav ambled out of the main office with his *aid-de-camp* and two other Ukrainian officers. To look at him you knew this 'officer' was soft, incapable of even knocking the skin off a semolina pudding! Slightly pudgy and non-athletic, he presented a greasy, *know-it-all* smile on his face; the type of look you'd expect from a gangster, like Al Capone! The word on this 'officer' was two-fold but commonplace. He was either handed his position as unit commander due to his connection to people high up in the government or was that type of 'officer' who ran three gas stations and was deemed 'officer material.' Regardless of the hearsay, the fact was he had never attended an officer training school in his life but was now in charge of an exceptionally large unit within the Ukrainian military, in the nation's capital. This would never occur anywhere in the West! And the sad reality is they would be the last line of defence if the Russians ever managed to get close again to Kyiv. He was arrogant to his own men and held a blatantly obvious degree of contempt for the foreigners who had travelled so far to support Ukraine in their fight, in their time of need. Still, he used them all the same...

Through all these goings on, Sascha was being employed as an interpreter and had managed to convince Cyrus that he was here to assist the team; what with his other connections in government and the private sector. The ruse had been carefully maintained so much so that Cyrus was completely unaware of the association between Nathan and his colleagues with Sascha. As was the case, so many people came and went it was impossible to vet anyone seriously or to thoroughly know their true allegiances. Guys trotted out the 'old boy network', or gave a brief, embellished story about one's military history and connections, all citing how they could be of immense value to the collective and the cause. There was little viewing of documentation at this level as a person's story was the usual means of acceptance. People didn't carry their personal dossiers with them, and most commanders didn't ask for them. These were serious, dangerous times and desperation doesn't gel with an over-zealous bureaucracy!

By now, Nathan knew it wasn't only the Ukrainians who had untrustworthy people to contend with. This understanding had been cemented in his psyche when he had been introduced to two men back at the hotel, both extremely middle aged; a South African named Roland and a Brit ex-paratrooper from Manchester who called himself Crooky. Nathan took an instant dislike to both men and his instincts weren't wrong very often. Roland was attempting to be a 'go-between' in Cyrus's half-assed operation and another group that was bringing in military hardware from Poland by a guy who went by the name of Piotr. Roland and Cyrus frequently argued and shouted at one another, in public. Roland would end up drinking until all hours and go missing, courtesy of his hangovers. He seemed to have a perpetual smile on his face but that was a façade, a masquerade shielding his inadequacies and severe addiction.

Crooky was forever wearing his British Army Parachute Regiment windcheater, as if it had been tattooed on! He chose to strut about, like a peacock, as if he were straight out of parachute training school, with his brand-new airborne wings! He would corral anyone he could find and play the 'old soldier', passing on his supposed expertise, as if he were the expert on everything military....

The truth was that he had been grazing on an exceptionally good paddock for decades and wasn't in any physical shape to do much at all. The pitiful reality was he was just some sad, pudgy, Manc, ex-army, *know-it-all* bastard who had packed his kit when the war commenced and arrived in-country in some misguided, delusional belief, most probably ego driven, that he could actually do something worthwhile. He had stumbled on Cyrus and pestered him to the point he had been placed in charge of admin and logistics for the team, pretty much a job here, and a job there. Essentially, he didn't do much except drink cheap lager, devour copious packets of salted pork scratchings and spin 'old soldier' stories, with a thick Northern accent that was unintelligible to most people with a grasp of the King's *patois*. Crooky indicated that he would be leaving soon as he thought he had done his bit in Ukraine, when, in fact, the formidable northern wife back home in Lancashire had, most probably, ordered him to return to their council house – or else!

Meanwhile, in a country to the east, the *Director* sat back on the wobbly two rear legs of his ancient wooden chair while reading, with great interest, the detailed report concerning the fracas at the *Buena Vista Bar* between Phil and the local thugs. The bar was a known haven for all sorts of spies, Ukrainian SBU (Secret Service) operatives, Soviet GRU military spooks, FMAs, mercenaries, gangsters, pimps, and wannabes of all types, but was particularly a hip joint at the moment. For the owners, sales had never been better! He pushed the broad collar of his lined jacket closer to his chin as the single bar heater wasn't functioning properly in his shabby office, again... Outside, the Russian winter winds had been fervently blowing and howling all morning and there was no respite, anywhere from the iced breezes... *'Fuck this country'* he declared with a modicum of bitterness for his new homeland. The Melbourne winters were nothing like this, extremely mild in fact and he was convinced the spiteful, gnawing cold would send him to an early grave! He re-gathered his thoughts... 'Ah, it appears as though this Phil, this friend of Nathan has a penchant for pretty girls. A ladies' man it seems... *This may be the way in that I've been looking for...'*

The *Director* would instruct one of his 'Kyiv men' to locate Alina with a view to enticing Phil to return to meet her at the bar. Of course, she would be handsomely compensated for her trouble. The pretence would be that she was sorry, it was all a mistake or some 'cockamamie' story like that. Even the promise of sex, anything, just to get Phil there as he was positive Nathan would be faithfully by his side. This time, another ferocious bar fight would ensue, with the usual suspects but one or two of the foreigners gets killed. The locals wouldn't be shocked and their *'Oh, dear, how sad, never mind'* attitude would soon be forgotten, just like the dead Westerners. More casualties of a brutal, dirty war... With these thoughts in mind, he instantly dropped forward onto the front legs of his chair and picked up the receiver of the ancient *Bakelite* telephone. A short conversation ensued, again, all in fluent Russian, and after five minutes he hung up, feeling a sense of smug contentment. The wheels were now in motion for a *round-the-clock* surveillance of the Kreschatyk hotel and a calculating plan to dispense with Nathan Philips and anyone else who dared to get in the road...

Chapter Twenty-Four

SAME SHIT, DIFFERENT DAY...

The day had warmed by just a couple of degrees and the craven sun had now only decided to peep and engage with the earth through the dispersing clouds. This not only elevated the local temperature, but also the spirits of those training outside on the shabby sports field at the back of the *Legion Obolon's* Headquarters. The seventy or so male recruits, of various ages, had been put into three platoon sized groups and each group occupied one third of the field. Most, but not all participants were in camouflage uniforms. As well, not all carried real AK 74 weapons as a few of the soldiers had to 'make do' with wooden facsimiles. The training now concentrated on infantry formations on the move and things weren't going quite as planned... There were a mixture of new and old recruits and, as usual, in the Ukrainian way, passionate debates frequently broke out on how to perform the manoeuvres or the rationale for the lessons.

Bill was attempting to explain the fundamentals to his group when a security guy who been watching the performance, yelled out from the sidelines without invitation or any real knowledge of what was trying to be achieved. *'You're doing it all wrong*. The men need to move to the left to make the formation work. Anyone can see that!' This interference infuriated Bill, who had been, in an earlier life, a Marine Corps Instructor of many years standing. In a pleasant and firm voice, he cooly responded, 'Okay, thank you for your opinion... but please, *now go and fuck yourself... I know what I'm doing'*. The man was confused by the tone but understood the expletive inference and decided to take a seat on a bench and refrain from future comment. Bill's size also put him in his place! He continued with the lecture, while Nathan and Phil moved to where they could be of more assistance, as there were more instructors than really needed.

Nathan walked over to the furthest group as, from the outside, it didn't seem as though they were really accomplishing anything. Their instructor was a guy called Captain Matt, who had been a logistics officer in the Marine Corps and had served in Iraq. Unfortunately, he was attempting to provide an 'officer's explanation' of how things worked and seemed to be going into great detail concerning the 'whys' and 'wherefores' of how the formation should be conducted. The soldiers looked confused... Too much information... Matt's group was lagging behind the other two platoons and time was running out for training. Nathan didn't want to steal the man's thunder but suggested that they could 'walk and talk' through the problems, emphasising the mantra of 'slow is good and good is fast' to the soldiers. This seemed to be an acceptable option and the platoon stood up from their seated lecture and commenced to produce a 'staggered' formation.

Capt. Matt appeared to be an alright guy, but his time with this team was short lived... When the day's lessons had concluded, he had cozied up to a very pretty girl, around seventeen or eighteen years of age, who had been eyeing the men, and watching them train all afternoon. We all knew she was somehow connected to the unit, but the girl turned out to be Yaroslav's daughter and he didn't take too kindly to some old guy, who looked a lot like 'Jack Black on a bad day,' whispering 'sweet nothings' into her ear. He was quickly given his marching orders by Cyrus and was gone before the day's end. However, it wouldn't be the last time Nathan saw Capt. Matt...

The ability for Nathan and Phil to freelance the troops also provided an opportunity for the men to chat with Ukrainian NCOs, some of the junior officers and the older hands. They would offer smokes, gum to the trainees, and discuss the war, their families, their hopes, and aspirations for when it was all over. Nathan carefully weaved in references to people coming and going, foreigners like themselves. When it came to any information concerning Steve Holland, he had not been seen or heard of by this group. Sascha provided the same assessment later that evening, after the day's instruction had concluded. While it seemed bleak, the training team would be visiting other units. As Sascha reminded Nathan, there was now a vast network of men in Kyiv now working to locate one Australian. 'Be patient...' Also, Garen had reached out to his connections in the paramedic fraternity, the *Hospitallers*, *Ukrainian Red Cross* and such like and he was waiting on any news from there. They were all certain it wouldn't be long before some news was forthcoming.

With the training concluded, the men offered their friendly goodbyes to the soldiers and jumped back in their vehicles for the usual wild ride home. It was a given that they would be pulled over at the checkpoints, but Yaroslav's only redeeming feature was, true to his word, he had provided identity cards to the men. The training team was now formally connected to this formation of the *Legion Obolon of Kyiv*. All the men still carried their passports, but the small, square green identity card was basically a 'hall pass' in the city. Technically, they were now members of the unit, but it was later discovered this had mostly been a ploy by Yaroslav to bolster the unit's numbers in order for him to attain more funding, and to make him look effective because the size of his unit was swelling. Although some conscription had been introduced back in 2014, the mobilisation of people into the military in 2022 was only gaining momentum as the war progressed.

To an untrained eye, this commander was doing a helluva job!

Soon, the worn ambulance and clapped-out *Camry* were hurtling down the empty freeways and vacant cold looking streets of the capital. At times, they were the only vehicles on the road and the absence of cars and human life reminded Nathan of the Will Smith apocalyptic movie *I am Legend*; basically, the last man left alive on earth. Well, things hadn't gotten that bad but the thematic association with the movie made the city appear eerie and dangerous, especially when the weather was austere and cheerless. Sure, it was a dangerous situation they lived in but as far as the immediate danger went, Nathan had said on numerous occasions that a guy probably had more chance of dying in a car crash in Ukraine than a Soviet missile landing on them! Unfortunately, Nathan's visionary comments would be realised, *a few months later...* But for the moment, the plan for the evening was to go to for dinner and a couple of drinks at an 'English Pub' called the 'Suku' which was run by a couple of thirty-something Ukrainian entrepreneurs who refused to shut down just because a war was on! It was decorated to replicate an English pub, sold an array of continental beers and cooked great burgers and fries. Conveniently, it was only a couple of backstreets away from the hotel, on the steep hill side winding back up to *St. Michael's Cathedral.*

Nathan was mystified at how a great many shops were open, considering the Russians had very nearly entered Kyiv only a few weeks before and the city was under constant rocket attack. 'God,' he thought, and somewhat inspired, *'these people are so brave'* and he admired their 'fighting spirit' against incredible odds. While they drove, he recounted a poignant incident that stuck in his mind from the other day. He had popped by a souvenir store that was in the underground passage to the train station, near the hotel, to buy a couple of military style patches, cheap souvenirs of his time in Ukraine, but the shop was closed. A vendor next door was open, so he inquired about the time the souvenir shop normally opened. The Ukrainian woman, svelte and in her forties, looked at Nathan and flatly asked, 'Where are you from?' to which Nathan replied, 'Australia.' The women then probed more, as if bemused by Nathan's response. *'What are you doing here?'* To which Nathan cheerfully answered, 'We have come to help you and Ukraine. You are not alone... You have friends across the world!' He knew this wasn't the complete story but, in a way, it was a credible half-truth. Without warning, the woman broke down and began to sob. Nathan felt awkwardly responsible for inflicting this sadness and placed his arms lightly around the woman as she cried. He started to choke up too and the pair just stood like that for a couple of minutes... Suddenly, the car hit a pothole and he was jolted back to the moment, yet the memory of the incident and the woman's vulnerability lingered...

The 'clapped out' *Camry* kept driving and Nathan

kept thinking about his experiences… A few new members of the team had arrived. Going to the pub would be a convenient way to break the ice and trawl for information. The night out would only go for a couple of hours and then a training session back at the hotel was planned with Garen, to learn the latest TCCC (tactical combat casualty care) teachings and methods. Just because one is in a war zone doesn't mean there isn't scope to continue training and swot up on the latest methods! As Nathan was studiously observing life outside of the vehicle, he heard a ping on Phil's mobile phone. He looked across and just raised his eyebrows at Phil, who darted his attention away from Nathan and was rapidly texting to the person on the other phone. When he finished, he whispered 'Alina' to Nathan, which drew a scowled look from his best friend. Phil just shook his head and quietly said, 'I'll talk to you about this later.'

In another five minutes, the car rounded the cobbled corner onto the Kreschatyk avenue and came to a skidding stop outside the large hotel, just opposite the security detail guarding the entrance. As the men exited slowly, lugging their heavy daypacks, body armour and helmets, Nathan felt relieved when he gazed across at a massive billboard of 'Dwayne-the Rock-Johnson' on the massive wall of the opposite building. The advertisement promoted the *Under Armour* product and captured 'The Rock' all sweaty and bulked up in a modern gym, glaring fixedly, *as only the 'Rock' can stare!* It may seem ludicrous, but Nathan felt like he was close to home when he saw this image of the big guy from the West. Even in this uncertain environment there is comfort in one's cultural language, simple customs, and sports identities. In less than a minute, piping hot coffee was bought from one of the street vendors outside the hotel and its warmth and familiar taste certainly cheered the morale of the men. Their routine purchase of the beverage at this time of the day had become a treat and added a pleasant finality to the day's training.

Before he knew it, Nathan was slowly jogging up the hotel's inner stairs to his room; even the stairwell was freezing, and his huffing and puffing was creating small mists of air in front of his face as he ran. He was desperate to talk to Phil in the sanctuary of their room about this 'Alina' business. As he entered the room with all his kit, he saw Phil sitting on the bed. Nathan was about to speak but Phil cut him short. In a way, this intervention was to Nathan's benefit as he was breathing hard and just put this down to a lack of fitness and the number of stairs he had climbed. 'Mate,' I know what you're going to say but Alina wants to apologise for what went down the other night and says it was all a misunderstanding. English confuses her sometimes, and her brothers took it the wrong way!' Phil continued by defending the men who had assaulted him and said he would probably do the same thing if he had such a stunning sister. *Hey, you know what guys are like, don't you?* They probably thought I was only there for one thing.' Nathan's expression was frozen in total disbelief at what he had just heard! He thought it best not to raise his voice and argue but to try and calmly reason with Phil. As quietly and as coolly as he could, he responded. 'Phil, are you out of your mind? That girl tried to hit you up for money and those guys jumped you the other night. This is your story, as you told it to me. I respect you; I trust you, *but now is not the time or place for war-time romances, especially with that whore!'*

It was then that Phil bared his soul. 'My life is a tragic mess. Failed marriages, loser bikers for friends and I am in-debt to my eyeballs! The bank is just about ready to foreclose on my beloved building in Melbourne! This is why I came with you, not just to help you out but I'm running away from all the dramas back home. *Fuck, I might even find some happiness over here.* Who knows? But, please, *at least give me a chance to try and make my life better than it is. Please?'* Nathan was shocked at this confession. He had an inkling that life hadn't been 'wonderful' for Phil for some time, but the reality is, we never fully know the truth until it arrives too late, on our doorstep. We all have many faces and Phil had managed to put on an incredibly good act. He then dropped his head and was genuine in his remorse for his soured life. He wasn't just pretending to get a night out on the town to chase some skirt! 'Okay,' replied Nathan, who was finding it hard to believe what he was saying, 'we will meet up with Alina, this 'lassie', again but can you make it tomorrow night? I will get the boys to come along as backup. They don't need to know the full story, but I would prefer if we were all there for you.' Phil nodded his head in appreciation and reached out his hand and the two men vigorously shook on the arrangement. He then went over and embraced Nathan, like a real brother would...

An instant later, the door was suddenly flung open, and it was Bill that entered the room, barely fitting through the doorway, and saw the two men in a semi-embrace. *'Well, if I am interrupting something I can come back later...* You Aussie guys, I don't know about this mateship thing and talk of 'down under', all sounds a bit suspect and queer to me.' He let out a roar of a laugh and gave both guys a friendly shove, which nearly propelled them both across the room! 'Come on then, get your shit together, we're supposed to be going to the pub, old chaps', trying to pronounce the last three words in a dandified, *la di da* English accent, but doing it really, really badly like Americans generally do... Nathan and Phil said they would reconvene down in the lobby in fifteen minutes, after a quick shower and a spruce up, then off to dinner and a few, well rewarded beers. Bill nodded happily and waved a big Texan hand as he left the room. The boys darted about, chasing up new clothes...and throwing off boots... Nathan offered Phil the shower first. He felt as though he now had a better understanding of Phil's behavior and might be better equipped to assist his old friend. He certainly hoped so... Thinking of the psychological hurdles and barriers connected to both of their situations, he pondered, 'Man, what a time and place to try and become a Jerry Springer or Dr. Phil!' He knew a few cold beers and a tasty burger tonight couldn't fix all their woes, but it wouldn't hurt their morale either, the rest they would sort out later; of equal importance to Nathan was the convenience of this uncomplicated supposition, of providing a helping hand and that's all that mattered, here and now.

Chapter Twenty-Five:

NEW COMRADES AND NEW LEADS...

Nathan, Phil, Bill, Garen, Sacha, Mickey and a couple of the other trainers walked through the mock Elizabethan doors of the *Suku* English pub. Strolling a couple of steps down to the bar, they were greeted by a pretty blonde barmaid, brandishing menus. The overpowering cosiness of their environment felt as though a toasty electric blanket had been wrapped around one and all, instantly raising the mood of the group. The men were then steered to a couple of large booths which were fashioned from Baltic pine and leather. Sporting, hunting and English village images adorned the walls in picture frames or as ornaments. Horse collars and English product signage, such as *Cadbury*, *Lipton* and *Jaguar* were also strategically placed, for added theatrical effect. Maybe for a Ukrainian, who had never visited the UK, it passed the 'cultural test' but for Nathan and Phil it just came across as a kitsch, yuppy, post-modern boutique bar that seemed a long way from another world that didn't exist in England anymore. As for the name of the pub, *well...*

Burgers, ribs, and beers were quickly ordered, and the men sat down and began chatting about their experiences over the past few days with training and the people they had encountered. The chat was bubbly and jovial, and the men were excited in anticipation of a great meal and evening.

Two trainers that had tagged along, Mitchell and Devlin, Americans who had only turned up at the hotel the day before. Both were ex US Army and had served in Afghanistan. Unfortunately, they were sporting serious cuts and bruises to their faces and Mitchell had a black eye that had been carefully examined by Garen, due to its severity and possible retinal damage. Phil was interested in the story behind the injuries, so combing his skewered diplomacy and simple honesty, he inquired, 'what's the story with you guys and what's with the eye?' Nathan could just about hear the collective groan at Phil's innate insensitivity, and while Devlin seemed hesitant to speak, Mitchell was quick to offer an explanation. It seemed that the two men had, in their haste, joined the 'wrong group' when they arrived in Ukraine. This is an easy mistake, even for an experienced operator. If you will, picture the scenario: you arrive in a foreign country, tired, homeless and with little funds. So far, your trip has been self-funded, and you don't know where your next buck or meal is coming from or where you will be living. The language and cultural norms are a complete mystery, and you don't really know where you are, geographically. You mistakenly apply the same moral and legal standards here as you would at home and get conned by friendly guys telling you they are in the business of making life hard for Russians, and your life easy. So, you take them on good faith... *but that's the catch! It's all been a con!* Like a modern-day Ukrainian *Fagin*, herding 'lost boys' to his lair to do his bidding, or a *Svengali* character who seduces and dominates the 'innocent,' you become another hapless victim to a Ukrainian tyrant and mobster... until the penny drops, and you can fashion an escape, *if you're lucky...*

With some chance on their side, the two Americans were fortunate to get beaten and not end up in a dark forest, face down with a bullet in the head, in a shallow grave on the outskirts of Kyiv. The training group they ventured into was mostly Ukrainian, Georgian and a light sprinkling of Westerners. What they didn't know was the leaders of this group were scamming relief organisations of funds and supplies and selling these goods on the Ukrainian black market. When the two Americans saw what was going on and queried the process, they received a vicious 'beat down' for their troubles, and it seemed as though Mitchell had put up more of a fight than his compatriot, such were his injuries, and probably the reticence for an explanation from Devlin. The worst thing to come out of it for these men was some temporary physical discomfort and a slight bruising of their egos! *Time to move on...* A contact gave them Cyrus's number and here they were, not exactly out of the 'frying pan and into the fire' but at least this time among men, with some honour...

The conversation continued over their meal and stories were soon abounding about the *Legion*, other FMA trainers in-country and the situation of the war. Basic questions were posed: who will win, how long will the war go for, how long can we stay without applying for residency and, more importantly, what are we going to do if this all goes to shit, very quickly? Just about everyone agreed that if the Russians made another surge and did enter Kyiv, they would go to the *Legion Obolon* and fight alongside the guys they had been training. Better to do this than to be on a refugee train that gets strafed on its way to the border or end up bleeding out in the basement of a hotel destroyed by a Russian missile. As the old adage goes: 'better to die on your feet than to live on your knees!' They all knew they wouldn't receive any special treatment from the Russians; hell, Putin had branded these men as 'mercenaries' without any special privileges! So, it was up to them to make life as hard for the Russian invaders, or *Orcs* as the Ukrainians called them, as much as possible.

The term *Orc* had been fittingly applied to the Russians. They certainly suited the classification of Tolkien's invaders; ugly, cruel, merciless trespassers, who laid waste to all the beauty and natural wonder that lay before them... Like the *Orcs* that had invaded the mythical realms of *Rohan* and *Gondor*, Sauron/Putin wouldn't be satisfied until he conquered all Middle Earth/Europe. This is what had drawn these men from the West to assist the Ukrainians. It was plain before their eyes... and only a simpleton didn't get the message. President Biden's words of non-interference had essentially been a green light for Putin to invade -- *Biden, what an idiot!*

Putin certainly knew NATO wouldn't risk a nuclear holocaust, which essentially made this highly funded, unique fighting force militarily inert. He had them bluffed! Unfortunately, this sad story has played out so many times in human history. As Edmund Burke, the Irish statesman, once announced: 'The only thing necessary for the triumph of evil is for good men to do nothing'. This is why Steve Holland had caught a plane. This is why Mitchell, Devlin, Earl and even Cyrus, to a certain degree, had put a hold on their lives and made the journey to Eastern Europe. In the most basic of terms, *this was a historic fight between good and evil!!*

In between the dining, drinking and general frivolity, Nathan had managed to chat to Mitchell on the quiet and enquired about some of the Western trainers he may have come into contact with. Mitchell did remember an Aussie who he had only briefly met a few weeks back, and who fitted Steve's description. Nathan queried more, but during the discussion he had to pardon himself on several occasions as he experienced coughing fits. 'Damn,' he thought, very annoyed at himself, while he announced apologetically, 'pardon me, I must have something caught in my throat'. He felt deep down that something was wrong, but here, in Ukraine, wasn't the time or place to see a physician. He continued with the conversation... It seemed that after his experience at Yavoriv, Steve was being more selective with who he served with, where he was and what he was expected to do. This was totally understandable. But he came across as being edgy, untrusting, and suspicious of just about everyone, Westerners and Ukrainians. He had only visited the house where Mitchell was staying once, and he left after a thirty-minute conversation and had not been heard from or seen since... But what was crucial in this account was that Steve had indicated he wasn't going to leave Kyiv anytime soon, he wanted to find a decent organisation to ply his trade with. This information was valuable news on two fronts.

Firstly, Nathan knew Steve was probably still alive and, secondly, he was still in Kyiv, somewhere... He would relay this information back to 'his team' later that evening. Nathan now believed he was close to locating his friend and he could feel it... It might sound cliché, but Phil, Steve and Nathan were like brothers, close family and could sense things like this. Why he hadn't contacted Steve and Kathy before all this began, he'll never know.... As a result of *his* failure to connect, he solemnly vowed to contact his close friends on his return to Australia, even by a simple text. Unfortunately, the pace and pressure of modern life all too often pulls us away from those we really care about, and soon we become estranged from those that really matter. Nathan, on his return, planned to rectify this...

Chapter Twenty-Six:

REST ON YOUR ARSE, REVERSE!

The changing nature of their environment was annoyingly repetitive, especially to Nathan. The roster had indicated a solid day of training, out at the camp on the outskirts where they had met Ronin. *WhatsApp* and *Signal* were now being utilised as the main means of communication within the group with alerts indicating any sudden changes. This format 'ticked off' Nathan as a simple orders group at the start and end of the day would suffice; other orders could be issued as vital and necessary. It seemed even more ludicrous that there was such a dependence upon using mobile phones, especially with rumours circulating that the Russians could easily hack telecommunications and pinpoint people's whereabouts, especially Westerners... Some of the men had raced out and purchased Ukrainian SIM cards, in an attempt to dispense with their national dialing codes, and therefore conceal their identity and location. Unless everyone used secured means, they may as well have spent their few hryvnias on a strong coffee or cheap Ukrainian cigarettes! Simple, segregated, verbally coded communication is always a better alternative, followed by computed based options using various social media accounts, known only to a select group of users. Crime syndicates and terrorist cells still operate this way. An overreliance on mobile phone technology produces discernible algorithms that could facilitate a drone strike, a vehicle ambush, or a street abduction. Ideally, just stay off the air and if that's not possible, limit communication to restricted and random bursts of information. Still, Nathan gritted his teeth and accepted the new way of doing things, even if he thought it dangerously stupid.

Not everyone received the news about the cancellation of today's training. Nathan, Phil and Mickey had risen early, as they usually did, gulped down another quick breakfast consisting of tea, porridge and dry fruit and made their way down to the bench seat just opposite the door to the mess hall. As always, they were the first to arrive. The emerging light of day was just beginning to have a slight impact on the darkness. The weather was terribly cold, and the morning was manifestly 'battleship grey'. They glanced across toward the kitchen entrance, and the crates of *Molotov Cocktails* hadn't moved. The guys turned toward each other and just smiled... It didn't feel like it was getting any warmer and, as usual, the

Ukrainian guards that came and went smoked heavily but gave the men a brief acknowledgment as they travelled to their sentry post, near the main street.

They waited... and waited some more... The departure time had come and now long gone, with their usual 'transport' nowhere to be seen. However, this was the way of things with this outfit and Nathan and Phil had to go with the flow... even if it was repetitively annoying. For a unit compromising of so many ex-military professionals, discipline and timings were extremely slack. Suddenly, both of their mobile phones pinged, and a brief text detailed that the training for today and the coming days had been cancelled. *No reason given... Rest and wait until further notice...* Local shopping and sight-seeing permitted. It was just like being in the army again with the infuriating regularity of '*hurry up and wait*' and the old cry of '*rest on your arse, reverse!*'

How odd, thought the two men who had sat in on the briefing with Ronin, Cyrus, Earl, and all of Ronin's staff. Nathan just shook his head in disbelief... They had sat 'glued' at a large table at the camp's mess hall for nearly an hour thrashing out the type of training Cyrus's team could offer and how long it would last. Could the Westerners provide tactical training, medical lessons, demolitions, and sniper instruction? As well, Ronin's staff made it a point to query the military credentials of every FMA there. When it came to Nathan, he quickly outlined his surfeit of wisdom and experience. Although he didn't speak their language, he could hear the word 'Spetsnatz' being spoken and knew they were talking about him and his *Special Forces* background. It had all sounded so promising... Nathan was certain he would be of significant use to this unit as their plan was to operate as a Recon/Ranger outfit. Essentially reconnaissance, but with a capability to strike at major Russian assets, such as tanks, artillery, and communications, if the opportunity presented itself. Now it seemed that the plan had changed. Either that, or Ronin had just been 'pulling their chain'...

Such inefficiency was common here. Nathan thought how this must be so disappointing to the many volunteers who had ventured all the way to Ukraine, at their own expense, and were constantly in a form of frustrating stasis... government red tape, bureaucracy, malfeasance, corruption, nepotism all added to the reason why the war was being fought so badly. You didn't have to be Von Clausewitz, the famed German tactician, to realise this!! Notwithstanding, the incompetence of the Russian forces lends itself to a separate and lengthy discussion, and equally long-winded dissertation. To an outsider, it didn't look like the Ukrainians knew what they were doing - plain and simple. The long-standing differences between the Russians and Ukrainians should have been the impetus to create a modern defence force in the wake of Ukraine casting aside its Soviet shackles. The real 'light bulb moment' should have been the separatist uprising in Donbas in 2014!

It had come as a rude shock and a sense of bewilderment to most of the Western ex-military men just how unprepared the Ukrainian military was when they instructed their soldiers and visited their bases. The men were dangerously unfit, the equipment was in a pitiful state and incredibly old, while tactics and training were based on ancient Soviet dogma. In a nutshell, there weren't any modern standards and discipline was sorely lacking. Officers and senior NCOs set their own agendas and the men followed, like sheep. To an outsider with the slightest military experience, this wasn't a professional army in any true sense. On one occasion, Nathan had tried to convince a senior sergeant at Ronin's unit that it was sound practice to patrol as slow or fast as the tactical situation dictated. However, the senior NCO trotted out the tired old Soviet response that patrolling had to be at a certain distance, at a certain time, based on the Soviet manual. Maybe it appeared as a lone cry in the woods, but fortunately, there were a few pioneers in government and the military with bigger ideas and a national plan to create a modern army based upon NATO and U.S. Army standards. Unfortunately, not such a great idea when the Russian Bear is attempting to crash through your gate...

'Fuck it,' said Phil, *'let's go for a bit of a sightseeing tour! Who knows when we'll get the next chance...* Anything is better than just hanging round here!' Nathan bobbed his head casually in agreement, and it was decided 'Nathan's team' would get better acquainted with Kyiv and their

immediate surroundings. *'Hell,'* thought Nathan, *'if this place turns into another Stalingrad, we'll need to know every rabbit warren and bug out route, as much as possible...'* This notion was probably at the forefront of the minds of the men he had grown accustomed to, and these men were some of the best professionals he had ever worked with. The friends gathered together around fifteen minutes later, and started walking down the avenue, on the other side of the road from *Midon Square*. They passed the major post office on the corner, just near the rail subway, and then down to where the markets operated at the end of the avenue where the main road splinters off to the left, up the hill, or down, being off to the right.

It was interesting to see so many people, male and female, wearing Ukrainian military uniforms. Of course, a war was on but wearing uniform in public was frowned upon in Australia, except on *Anzac* and *Remembrance Day*. Would it change if Australia was at war again? Nathan wasn't so sure, what with the 'woke' agenda and the 'namby-pamby' emphasis of not trying to offend someone... even an enemy? But here, in the capital, there were flags fluttering about defiantly on staffs in any given direction and proud nationalistic signage adorned buildings, and shops that was intended to spur on the masses in this fight, or to celebrate valiant struggle, like the 'Gallant defenders of Mariupol'. The proliferation of huge posters that adorned the walls of buildings reminded Nathan of the Orwellian 'speak' and social conditioning in the dystopian, fictional classic 'Nineteen Eighty-Four', but the stakes here were for keeps in this real-life, action-packed drama!

For personal protection from the challenging elements, Nathan wore his rugged black fleece from *Mountain Designs* that had accompanied him on so many adventures, while the other men wore similar warm and sturdy clothing; fleeces, dark cargo pants and hiking boots; perfect gear for their type of training. When compared to the Ukrainians, they distinctly looked like foreigners, a kind of modern day 'wild bunch' ...even without opening their mouths. The intended goal was not to make it appear too obvious, by wearing *New York Yankee* baseball caps or non-Ukrainian military fatigues. However, while the men tried to blend in, it was clear, even barring their cultural nuances, that these men looked vastly different from the standard Ukrainian. Not only did they have a physical dissimilarity, built around size and facial features, but their clothes were contemporary and up-to-date Western, unlike the 'perceived' Western fashion that so many European or Asian nations try to model their styles upon, but end up creating a cheesy facsimile of the true Western original.

In their casual and relaxed walk down the avenue, Nathan and the men marvelled at the remarkable architecture, the spaciousness of the streetscape and the sophisticated shopping that was on offer. *Chanel, Prada, Hermes* and all the stores that a serious shopper would discover in London or Paris were strategically situated on the charming avenue and many of the major stores were still open, even as the conflict raged in other parts of the country. The group walked past *Lviv Croissant*, which had become a favourite snack eatery during their stay in Lviv, and they fondly remembered the great city. As diligent as the men were, they did not detect the two operatives who were 'ghosting' them from the other side of the street. It was so much easier for these agents to blend in with a crowd as their Slavic features and garb were true to their location. They wore woven flat caps and long black woollen coats for protection from the elements and did not look out of place. Concealed were *Tokarev* Type 54 'Black Star' semi-automatics in old leather holsters, with spare magazines, large folding knives on their waist belts, and short extendable batons positioned in a special side pocket of their trousers, for added protection. The two men would frequently pause and talk, for effect, but keeping a safe and inconspicuous distance from Nathan's team. Follow and observe were their directions...*that's all*, and these orders came directly from the *Director*! *There would be no slip ups this time...*

In a short while, maybe ten minutes or so, the men arrived at the market after travelling down and around the busy streets. 'Time to buy some more porridge,' Nathan contemplated, but he deviated from his original plan, 'man, I'm just about sick of porridge,' and his inclination turned to other tasty items like chocolate and the local *Roshen* variety that was exceptional. As a chocoholic, he knew which shopping aisle he would head to first...

Although unappealing from the outside, the supermarket was as modern as anything you would find in the West and provided all the necessities the men could want. In fact, it was more sophisticated because the automatic teller machines offered various language settings so all goods and transactions could be understood in English and other languages. 'I bet there would never be a Ukrainian setting on the machines back home in Australia' Nathan reflected... The men were astonished at the low prices and the plentiful quantity of produce and quality goods, mostly because they were ahead financially due to the benevolence of an obliging currency exchange rate. Surprisingly enough, there did not appear to be the mass shortages of foodstuffs that the global media had canvassed nightly, in zealot-like-fashion, on the television. Still, some of the men were already short on funds and didn't know how long they could stay; the common phrase being touted was 'I'll leave when the money runs out...' Nathan knew that as much as they wanted to remain and locate Steve, it was impossible to remain indefinitely. Phil had been extremely generous with the funds he provided, and the other men didn't say where they received their money from, but Phil guessed they were probably funding most of the operation themselves or were on a limited stipend from a benefactor, back home.

With shopping completed and the weather becoming a tad chillier, the small group made their way back to the hotel, but decided to venture down another street that was parallel to the main avenue just a lot narrower. The two operatives in the long, dark coats followed at a respectable distance... Nathan and his crew took in the sights of the different and intriguing styles of architecture and noticed plaques on the sides of building that paid tribute to artists, doctors, and philosophers from long ago. It seemed as though all the men were impressed by Ukraine's contribution to the development of humanity, but Nathan thought of how he never heard of any of these characters in his high school history lessons; this was a shame that he would also rectify on his return home. Soon, another two hundred metres passed, and the men emerged facing a massive dome that acted as a skylight for a shopping centre that was underground and adjacent to the subway. It was the *Globus Mall*. Phil glanced to his left and noticed a closed *McDonald's*, much to his disappointment. Nathan gazed to his right and could identify the main post office on the corner and across the road, *Midon Square*. A diagonal path was taken, to lead them back to the avenue and then just a few minutes away from their hotel.

Not too far away, a news crew was filming a story about the war and as the men approached it was Phil who yelled out, *'Hey, I know that guy, that's Geof Parry from Seven News Australia'*. The men halted and loitered to one side to pay attention to the reporter putting his 'spin' on the war in the capital. The anchorman noticed the small, interesting group and signalled the camera to stop rolling. Parry looked at Nathan and Phil and inquired, 'Are you

Aussies?' *'Bloody oath!'* shouted Phil, really laying on the Australian accent. The next questions asked by Parry were painfully obvious – *'What the hell are you doing in Ukraine? You do know there is a war on?'* Nathan was more discrete than Phil when he offered the story.... they were all in Ukraine helping with the humanitarian cause, instructing on first aid courses and so forth. Well, at least part of the story was true.... The men had been teaching some combat first aid to the soldiers. *That wasn't a lie.*

A long-time journalist, Parry paused and studied the men, unconvinced. He switched to Nathan's other colleagues and took in their physicality and 'hard' demeanour. *'Yeah, right...'* he said, in a skeptical tone. 'Medics and humanitarians, *Okay... Yeah... Right...'* Upon concluding his accurate evaluation of the group, the reporter announced he had 'to dash' and finish the story in another part of the city, and he quickly bade a safe farewell to Nathan and his friends. The film crew all boarded the white *Renault* van, marked with 'News Reporters' on its front, back and sides, and headed off in the direction of the *Friendship Arch*, a few minutes past their hotel, and on a large knoll at the end of Kreschatyk avenue. 'Well, fancy that,' thought Nathan, 'the world isn't that big a place anymore, especially when you can bump into a homegrown reporter on the other side of the globe, in a war zone, in Eastern Europe.' The two tough looking men in the shady, long coats didn't know what to make of the short meeting with the 'Press'. They had positioned themselves by an enormous bank window, casually to the rear of Nathan and his men, and directly opposite the news crew. They waited for Nathan's team to set off again, which they did once they had re-gathered their ladened shopping bags.

Off again, the procession turned left at the next corner and followed the avenue down the one hundred metres or so, to the hotel entranceway. The two spy operatives knew Nathan and his team were staying there but now it was vital they keep tabs on all their movements, especially if they ventured out again. A phone call was quickly made to the *Director*, who was by now en route to Kyiv. He had some big plans for Nathan and his associates and desperately desired to be in on the 'action' at the end. More of his superior operatives were also on their way and they would base themselves at a city hotel, not too far from Nathan's. The *Director* was pleased with himself, delighted in fact... He could not help thinking about the impending opportunity, and how Nathan Philips *would be terminated...with prejudice...* a saying he suddenly and surprisingly remembered, belonging to former CIA colleagues. Nathan's 'boys club' and any other Westerners from the hotel would be collateral damage... It would also announce a clear and blatant warning from Moscow, especially to foreigners - *Fuck with us and you will die!* The day was winding up and the outside air was becoming increasingly cold. Unbeknown to Nathan and his colleagues, they were on course to a brutal confrontation later that evening...

Chapter Twenty-Seven:

MURDER ON THE DANCE FLOOR...

After another long and tiring day, Nathan and Phil were pleased to be back in their safe and salubrious hotel room. It might not be their home, but they did their best to make it feel like their own 'Anglo' patch in Ukraine. The room was rearranged to their liking, chairs were pushed aside, and gear positioned as chosen by the individuals. Mickey had draped a New Zealand flag at the head of his bed to remind him of his 'slice of heaven' on the other side of the world. Although it was cramped with three male inhabitants, there was still enough space to double as a viable exercise area for the men to workout. Yet, it was more than just a hotel room... Nathan learnt an early lesson when he was first deployed and that it was not only necessary but crucial, especially for morale's sake, to fashion one's space and to transform wherever he had lived into a tiny bubble of 'down under'.

The men were busy unpacking their shopping when Phil's phone pinged. It was Alina and she was inquiring as to when Phil would meet her again, back at the *Buena Vista Bar*. On the face of it, the text read as a genuine and heartfelt plea at reconciliation, a fresh start. *'Damn, this girl is insistent'* murmured Nathan quietly to himself. He didn't want to dampen Phil's spirits or get into a silly argument. Phil cast off his shopping and plonked down on a chair and began furiously texting, and this went on for a few minutes, until he abruptly stopped and looked up smiling. 'Fancy a night out, boys?' was Phil's question to the two men who had stayed quiet and motionless during the text messaging. It seemed that Alina desperately wanted to meet Phil that evening, around seven, and, if nothing else, patch up the various emotional wounds from the other night. Her doting and hulking brothers would be there, but they also wanted an opportunity to apologise for their vulgar behaviour towards Phil the last time they met. They still planned to chaperone their beloved sister but would remain discrete, sipping coffee or smoking from the back stalls. Mickey glanced across at Nathan and the men agreed they would be only too pleased to tag along and have a night out before the next training stint; there was a rumour the men may be going away for a few days to tutor a mortar unit in infantry minor tactics, just outside Kyiv. May as well enjoy the free time they have as the situation was so viscous that anything could happen at any moment...

It was now around five in the afternoon, so the

men had ample time to get ready. Phil looked extremely satisfied with himself and laid out the best clothes he had. He jauntily went off to the bathroom to shave extremely close, and to shower exceedingly long... He would look his best and brightest this evening... Nathan looked across at Mickey, made the 'love heart' symbol with his two hands in front of his chest and softly whispered 'amore' in the best Italian accent he could muster. Nathan's demonstration and whispered overtures of 'love', plus the sudden turnaround in the fortunes of Phil's love life was enough to give Mickey and Nathan a good chuckle. But it didn't end there... Both men turned and looked at the bathroom door, where vibrant singing could be heard, and they sniggered again as Phil was carefully and purposefully sprucing himself up to become the *Don Juan* of Ukraine! While they patiently waited for their turn at the bathroom, the two men lay easily on their beds checking their phones for messages and taking in a brief rest. Unknown to the two men, they would need all their strength and guile later that evening...

On the other side of the country, the *Director* had flown to Donbas via a commercial helicopter and had then changed his military style clothes to that of an aid worker with the *International Red Cross*. This was not only because everyone had heard of this organisation, but the fact it had been easy for him to dress the part and forge accompanying documents. His title of 'Resources Manager' partnered his own credentials and along with his uniform and captured vehicle, supplied by his *Wagner* confederates, he had fabricated the perfect ruse that would assist him execute his plan of retaliation against Nathan. The *Director* would also utilise his Australian passport and *lay on thick* the Aussie accent to further complement the deception, gaining unencumbered access through the various military checkpoints. Along with him were two treacherous Crimean separatists who had surveyed all the possible routes to enter Ukraine from occupied territory and would assist with the cunning ploy as they spoke perfect Ukrainian and expertly knew the road system they intended to travel on.

It was still pitch black in the morning when the *Director* and his accomplices set out to secretly enter Ukrainian held territory. The drive would be painfully long, but their best calculated route was to the north of Mariupol, on to Kherson and Cherkassy and then heading north-west towards the capital. Time of arrival was sixish in the evening, give or take ten or twenty minutes... Based upon this rough timing, the *Director* still had ample time to assess his Kyiv surroundings. A quick hit squad will have already been assembled. As for other matters, a compensatory reward for Alina and her brothers would be dispensed at the end of the evening for their critical, duplicitous part in the deception. For the former Australian spy, here was a window of opportunity... *Who knows when another chance would present itself*? The *Director* knew damn well he had no choice but to sashay through this gap, this fissure of luck, or *it would slam shut.*

The *Director's* Kyiv agents, who had been spying on the *Buena Vista Bar,* had witnessed the violent altercation with Phil and the brothers and had reached out to Alina and her siblings shortly after the incident. They were careful not to give themselves away as Russian spies but had purported to be Ukrainian SBU operatives whose determined task was to remove foreign troublemakers. To Alina, it seemed a plausible story and besides, *no-one ever contradicted the SBU!* The young beauty was still aggrieved at her treatment, particularly the insult upon her reputation. Alina just scammed Westerners for drinks, a meal and her company; she wasn't one of the many prostitutes heading to the 'front', and was okay with seeing Phil kicked out of her country. In her mind, this was the most logical outcome; she didn't expect any 'real' violence. She pondered for a moment... 'maybe Phil will get the punishing slap she missed delivering the other night...' Besides, she thought *he was too old for her* anyway... 'the dirty old man!' Regardless of the outcome, Alina was positive her conscience would be clear, and her honour rightfully restored after the evening. At this stage, all parties fostered a different, but calculating mindset as to why they were meeting, *but they were on a collision course...* to rendezvous at seven pm at the trendy *Buena Vista Bar.*

Back at the hotel, Phil had been grooming himself for nearly an hour and was singing loudly, drumming on the countertop and baying like a wolf cub at the moon! His expectations were high... Neither Mickey nor Nathan commented but occasionally they looked at each other, making kissy faces or smirking at Phil's bubbling anticipation. Suddenly Nathan's phone pinged, and it was Marcus. 'Well, I'll be damned', thought Nathan as he hadn't heard from him in a number of weeks. Regardless of the communication hiatus, Marcus continued to stay in the background and had provided on-going support for the operation. Nathan read and whispered the text softly to himself. By its conclusion, his eyes had become visibly enlarged as a result of the message's disturbing content! It seemed their flukish encounter with Geof Parry had captured Nathan and his friends in the camera lens and made the national news back in Australia. What was of more interest to Marcus were the two shady 'goons' who had also been captured in the camera's objective eye, *lurking, mysteriously in the background*. For someone with years of covert agency experience, it was elementary for Marcus to identify the two men as agents, not just because they looked 'dodgy' or wore long black coats!

Comprehending the danger and urgency of the matter, Marcus had swiftly made probing inquiries conce-rning the two sinister figures 'skulking in the shadows', and his European contacts had unquestionably branded them as Soviet agents but more likely to be *Wagner* operatives. *'Damn this,'* barked Nathan, angrily, making Mickey take a sudden interest in Nathan's communique and such was the outcry, he sat upright on his bed. Nathan blasted out a quick acknowledgement and thanks text to Marcus and sat on his bed mulling over options. He seriously believed they had thrown these dudes off their trail after Lviv. Only briefly did he ponder and admire the doggedness of these 'bad guys'. Just then, Phil came waltzing into the bedroom whistling merrily, with a wet towel around his waist. He perceived the concerned look on Nathan's face and the serious interest shown by Mickey. 'Hey fellas, what's up?' he asked in a bright tone, not realizing *how bad things really were...* Nathan looked at the two men without blinking an eye and announced, *'Time to do some serious planning boys...*

Thirty minutes later, empty cans of soft drink, half-drunk cups of coffee and cigarette laden ashtrays lay scattered on the side tables, after the small but resolute band of men had concluded their discussion and planning brief... It would be easy for Nathan and his crew to high-tail it out of Ukraine, but that 'chicken-heart' type of behavior would not locate Steve Holland, nor would it be the way they would want to depart the country, with the *proverbial tail tucked between their legs*! A coward's way out... *And they had all shown they possessed more substance than that!* If it wasn't in Kyiv where they might get the 'chop', it would be somewhere else, so, better a ground and time of their own choosing... On that belief, the group was unanimous! The more Nathan and his team thought about it, the pleadingly soppy and ingratiating text to Phil from Alina had sounded *too good* to be true and the *meet up, makeup* and *lovey-dovey* story just smelt rotten, like the proverbial 'Afghan drover's loin cloth' according to Mickey! Without any doubt, it had all the sinister hallmarks of a vicious, nasty trap...

'Okay then' said Nathan, looking at each man earnestly and taking time for his determined narrative and the ultra-serious effect of his words to sink in. 'We know what's likely waiting for us, but we have the element of surprise. These guys may be expecting some of us but not all of us and they don't *really* know what we are capable of. Frankly, I doubt whether they will want to make too much of a scene, they won't want to create a 'shit storm' as it will interrupt their operations in Kyiv, and you can bet 'London to a brick' there will be a whole SBU sweep to flush them out. Consequently, I believe we can only expect a couple of small teams. We are small fish... They will think they have this covered. I don't have to tell anyone what to do but just to "expect the unexpected". It's time to screw these guys over, give it to 'em really good... *like they would do to us*. To all, good luck.'

Not another word was spoken, but a few deep breaths were taken... The men just sat in silence for a moment, looking at their fellow comrades. They then departed, in ones and twos, to make their preparations and play their role. There would be two teams: Nathan and Phil, followed by Sascha, Garen and Bill. Mickey would 'hold down the fort' back at the hotel. The latter group would head out first and recon the *Buena Vista Bar* and report back to Nathan, who would arrive around twenty minutes later. There was no hurry to arrive on time. They would be fashionably late, and this would give Alina and her confidants time to get anxious, and hopefully provide more illumination and information on who they were with and what their overall plan was.

Unfortunately, not all things go to script... and it all began with a slight glitch, as it had been frustratingly difficult to converse with the Ukrainian driver to discuss and confirm the exact drop off location. However, the *Bolt* cab eventually let Sascha's crew off, up the hill on a junction, past *St. Michael's* church. This intersection was only a block away from the bar; around two hundred metres or slightly more. The metropolitan police headq-uarters was just down the road, a couple of hundred metres more, downhill, back towards the main part of the city and diagonally opposite the wide, brick square, in front of the imposing monastery. No movement, not even a peep was coming from police headquarters... one less thing to worry about. Bill and Sascha walked together quickly up the long, rising block but dispersed in different directions around fifty metres after they had left the traffic lights at the sizable intersection. Sascha kept walking past the bar, and then turned quickly into an alley. Bill stayed on the opposite side of the road facing the bar and positioned himself in a darkly lit doorway of a disused building, after quietly removing the light bulb from its mount. Garen remained close to the corner intersection and lights, sitting casually at a café, scanning 360 degrees in a subtle way. If the mission was successful or they had to abort, they would secure transport at the designated fallback position, where Garen was waiting. If the mission turned out to be a complete disaster, the men would have to disperse, escape, and evade and fend for themselves for the immediate future. All knew the risks, so *failure wasn't an option...*

As Nathan's men, watched and waited, the blurry, half-light translucency of early dusk was starting to take hold in the capital. This would significantly assist Nathan's men in their concealment and their ability to observe and attack, but more importantly, withdraw when the time came. A perusal of the area produced an interesting picture... A black *Volkswagen Golf,* with four nervy looking occupants was 'on station' a few metres down from Sascha's hiding position, on the bar side of the street, while the two men that had followed Nathan's crew earlier in the day, occupied metal *al fresco* tables out front of the bar, sipping coffee. They had not changed or modified their clothing and the image sent to Nathan from Marcus confirmed their identity, and now, their likely intent. Outside of this street vista, there didn't appear to be any snipers in the upper windows of opposing apartments. They were not discounting that there may be some...but the tight timeframe made it unlikely. There was nothing for it... Nathan and his team would have to take their chances...

When the tactical situation had been deemed satisfactory, Sascha flipped open the cover of his mobile phone and dispatched a one-word codeword text to Nathan. In an instant, a reply code was transmitted from Nathan... received and understood by the wily Ukrainian. The *time now was for waiting...* The *time now was for being alert...* The *time now was to be ready to act with ferocity when required...* Nathan and Phil were on their way and would be at the bar in less than ten minutes. Phil had received another begging text from Alina, only confirming to Nathan that the situation was highly suspicious and most certainly perilous. The two men would exit their taxi directly out the front of the bar and move quickly inside the venue and to who knows what sort of trouble...

Meanwhile, on the other side of the sprawling city, the *Director* looked impatiently and piercingly at his watch again for the umpteenth time, with pursed lips and with a degree of annoyance, as his sedan slowly picked its way through the congestion of vehicles. The road traffic was unusually heavy for this time of the evening, considering most people were eager to be home at day's end. It seemed like only the 'young' people of Ukraine were enthusiastic to venture out into the brisk evenings. On the bike lanes, some of the capital's younger citizens were jockeying scooters in evening wear, which looked slightly bizarre for a few reasons: the formality of the attire, the type of transport taken, and more importantly, that the nation was at war. Nevertheless, they motored along, seemingly without a care in the world... For everyone else on the road, things weren't moving so rapidly...

A military convoy of massive self-propelled guns on heavy Ukrainian Army transports was slowing proceedings down, but the nervous driver assured the *Director* they would be out front of the *Buena Vista* bar in precisely ten minutes. '*Damn this*,' murmured the *Director*, '*And I thought driving in Melbourne at peak hour was bad...*' While this was happening, Nathan's taxi was arriving at the bar. He and Phil exited the vehicle and were quickly inside the establishment after a dozen rapid steps. Nathan noticed the two seated operatives outside but chose not to pay too much attention, and thought, 'let them savour the belief they weren't identified'. Before Phil or Nathan had a chance to survey the premises, Alina rushed forward to greet them from a side stall and placed her arm inside of Phil's and held him tight. 'Come with me darling and let's talk, all this fighting is so unnecessary...' As if on cue, two thug brothers re-positioned themselves to form a human wall to prevent any exit at the entrance, but Nathan knew what they were up to. Play the 'straight man' and it will work to my advantage he reasoned, confidently and casually.

Drinks were soon ordered, and Phil did his best to make out that all had been forgiven and forgotten. Alina gave Phil a kiss on the cheek to seal the deal and create the impression of friendship and maybe something more... *They retreated to the intimacy of the booth...* she giggled, and they chatted animatedly, while sipping on their vodka and cranberry cocktails. *Chernigiviske* bottled Ukrainian beer was ordered, times two, while Nathan scanned the bar to confirm what Phil had briefed him of the layout. He borrowed a cigarette from Phil, lit it and let it smoulder on the weighty glass ashtray, directly in front of him on the bar. He kept the beer bottles handy, just to one side. Fortunately for Nathan, most of the seating was downstairs, and there were only two older gentlemen drinking glasses of pilsner nearby. They were picking at *Chipster* potato chips, and chewing on *shashlik,* skewers of cooked beef, pork, or lamb. No threat there... They would wait for the 'opposition' to initiate the attack, or they would counter the threat as they left. Either way, *there would be a bar fight or street battle tonight....*

Suddenly, the *Director's* sedan rounded the corner sharply from a narrow winding side street and pulled up fast in front of the black *Volkswagen*. Tyres screeched as the driver braked hard to limit the distance to the car in front. As the *Director* exited from the tiny sedan, he stared penetratingly at the *Volkswagen's* occupants, to the rear, and nodded once. They stayed, motionless, in the sedan, most probably backing up if things got too intense or if he required extra muscle. With intent, the *Director* strode forward vigorously. As he passed the two villains seated outside, the two 'heavies' stood up and blocked the entrance, in the manner of a couple of nightclub bouncers. He was in a hurry to 'deal' with Nathan and return his real work, on the other side of the border. This business was an unnecessary diversion, a hindrance, and an annoying side trip but an occasion to repay someone, *in the most meaningful and vicious way!*

As he strode arrogantly into the bar, one of Alina's brothers moved from the front exit to a table by the wall, in a flanking position on Nathan's right side. Looking ahead in a small mirror on the bar's rear wall, Nathan saw the *Director* dressed in a black trench coat and woollen flat cap, almost galloping towards him. He was in a hurry to confront the man that had caused him so much trouble and grief! Nathan repositioned himself to face the *Director* side on, with his right-hand side closest to the countertop. He had never actually set eyes on this man before, but he knew for sure that this older agent was connected to the attack on his life in Lviv!

What happened next came as a complete surprise... Nathan was startled briefly as the *Director* addressed him in an educated, private school, Australian accent. 'Well, well, well. Nathan Philips, we finally meet.' Nathan looked at the man and chose his words carefully for effect, 'And who the fuck are you', was his brash, colloquial, working-class retort! 'Judging by the accent you're from Oz and a long way from sunny home and safety pal, especially for an old fart such as yourself.' Nathan's goading was an attempt to evaluate the character of the *Director*. Would he 'crack it' and abuse his tormentor or stay calm, like a pacifist... which was more calculating and dangerous. The *Director* was about to reply but thought better of it and remained silent. He didn't want to get into a verbal stoush as this wasn't the time nor the place. No need to give anything away... *he would deal with Nathan...* and then return to his headquarters.

'Well,' said the *Director*, 'we haven't met but we do have some recent history. In fact, it is largely because of *you* that I am over here... his voiced raised slightly... in this *God forsaken part of the world!*' He continued, 'I'll jog your memory, if I may, with the name of a past colleague of mine – Madison Baker.' Nathan was not startled by this revelation. Deep down, he thought there would probably be payback one of these days...and here it was! As much of a soul-sucking, heartless bitch as Madison Baker was, Nathan was sure she did possess some friends, a colleague or two, even a companion, or maybe even a lesbian lover; someone who had their nose put out of joint when she and the government operation came crashing down...

'I suppose, judging by your age and influence, you must've been Madison's boss. Am I correct?' Nathan knew he was spot on but needed confirmation. 'How very astute of you' came the reply. The *Director* went on... voiced raised... 'It is because of you that I left Australia and have had to live *persona non grata* like some fucking peasant in this shitty part of the world! While I do have some sympathy for Ms. Baker- she exceeded her orders and paid the price... That is on her, not me... His voice lowered in pitch... My retribution is aimed at you for my inconvenience, pure and simple. You cost me my reputation, my station and most of all, a bloody healthy retirement on Queensland's Gold Coast, and for that *you will pay...'* Nathan had been toying with the cigarette in the large glass ashtray with his right hand and had kept his left hand loosely on one of the *Heinekens* he had bought, perched on his left thigh. The other bottle sat, full and heavy, ready on the bar...

The two men looked at each other, two to three metres apart, and it was Nathan who uttered the next sentence, 'Well then, there isn't any more to say, is there? You better get on with what you came here to do...' The time for talking was over! A brief pause for silence ensued, as if it were a gunfight in a John Wayne Western. The *Director* deftly went for his *Walther PPK* inside the left side of his large trench coat, with a flash of his right hand... Nathan had anticipated that such a move was imminent and was prepared for it... was the meeting going to end any other way? He sprang into action... As the *Director* fumbled for his pistol in its shoulder holster, Nathan flung the hefty glass ashtray like a transparent discus, with all his might, and it struck the man violently and accurately in the middle of his throat. He instantly doubled over, in a paroxysm of intense pain as he began gasping for air; his throat immediately began swelling from the blunt force of the perfect strike. Too many years sitting in an office, letting his skills slip... slowing down... The *Director* would now pay the price for his complacency...

While the aging Australian operative was bent over and completely disabled and out of the fight, Nathan had produced another telling move... a second after the ashtray strike, he powerfully hurled the half-filled beer bottle, with so much *gusto* and intensity that it made a cracking sound as it smacked the skull of Alina's brother, who had sat lurking to Nathan's rear. When the ruckus began, he had attempted to quickly get past the fallen *Director* and towards Nathan... he was a lot leaner and wirier than his siblings but that proved not to be an advantage... The thicker bottom of the bottle had collided forcefully with the left temple, and down he went, instantly, *poleaxed*! The second brother, who was so much stockier than his fallen, now unconscious sibling, was now attempting to negotiate the confines of the bar when Nathan took a casual swig from the second *Heineken* bottle before launching it, striking the man forcefully in the nose. Green beer glass and amber fluid sprayed across his shattered face, where bone fragments were now visible. Such was the speed and force of the blow; he was also blinded by the sneak attack. *What a mess!* The beer bottle assault was followed up by a hefty palm strike, again to his bloodied nose, *and he was laid out beside his brother!* Nathan wasn't feeling cocky, but he was delightfully surprised by the ease in which he disabled the three men. Other than to grasp their beer glasses close to their chests, the two elderly gentlemen patrons didn't make a sound or a move... not a drop was spilled over their table. *More action was about to follow...*

Outside, Sascha had taken his cue from the initial commotion from within the *Buena Vista* bar. He took three or four large paces from his darkened alleyway and raised his left arm high. His timing was spot on... None of the *Director's* men had moved yet... The house brick he had been holding shattered the back window of the *Volkswagen Golf* into a myriad of fragments when it had been flung, on the move. The occupants were stunned by the noise of the splintering glass and began clutching at their seatbelt buckles. Almost simultaneously, Sascha's right arm came down fast toward the windowless opening and a flaming *Molotov Cocktail* burst into a mighty firestorm amongst them. Instantly, both vehicle and its occupants were ignited; passengers, metal, plastic, and ammunition squealed and screamed in an all-consuming fireball. Sascha was certain a few Molotov's wouldn't be missed from the back of the hotel and he had secreted two of the fiery projectiles in his daypack.

It seemed as if the *Director's* outside bodyguards were the only ones to respond quickly when the first blow had been struck by Nathan. They had reached for their small, concealed pistols and were moving to back up their comrades inside. Bill, secreted in the shadows, had produced the shortish AK 74 SU model assault rifle, and had established a deadly bead upon the two men. Sharp barking sounds were made as the weapon bucked hard in his sizeable hands. The first agent was 'double tapped' in the skull, while Bill fired four shots at the second man, hitting him in both lungs, liver, and stomach - the old, but reliable 'sharing the love' shooting drill. Nonetheless, the two Russian operatives went *down*, *fast*, and *hard*, blood spurting from large, gurgling wounds, their 'claret' fluid now spilling over onto the entrance steps and dousing the already wet paving. Bill had easily persuaded one of the hotel guards to loan his loaded weapon and a couple of magazines for a short while, for a hefty fee of course, but anything is possible in wartime, in Ukraine!

Meanwhile, Phil had attempted to leave the booth he was sharing with Alina, with the girl's temperament changing from bubbly 'Barbie' to the malevolence of a sorceress Queen! Alina shattered a drinking glass on the side of the table and thrust it towards Phil's face... He had instinctively maintained his distance in the likelihood of an attack and took a pace forward with his left foot while striking Alina, to her nose with a closed right fist. Alina's head snapped backward, and she slumped downwards in the booth, moaning and sobbing, clutching at her damaged face... Phil made certain he didn't break her nose, but only fracture her sensibilities. Still, he felt some remorse for his actions and spoke... What Phil meant to say was 'Sorry about the bop on the nose, my dear, but, well, under the circumstances...' Instead, all Phil could actually say was '*Oh, fuck it*, you deserved it... *you lying tart!*', and on that insult he turned and sprinted from around the side of the booth to assist Nathan, as if *he* needed any help...

In the distance, sirens began to ring and wail, and it wouldn't be long before the police arrived, maybe within five minutes, depending upon the traffic... With Phil now out of the confines of the shadowy booth, he was able to survey the devastation Nathan had rained down on their opponents. Bodies lay strewn, unconscious across the bar, while amusingly, the two old men who had taken in the 'show', appeared completely unfazed, and continued with their beer and light supper. The 'gentlemen' reminded Phil of the two old condescending puppet figures on the *Muppets* television show, who were never perturbed but comically critical of all that was happening around them.

The *Director* now lay on his back and was still gasping for air as his throat continued to bloat. In much the same way as anaphylaxis can narrow the trachea, so can a massive trauma inflicted by a hurtled missile such as a hefty glass ashtray. It was an effort for him to breathe, let alone speak, but in spurts, as he glared at Nathan with frenetic, piercing hate-filled eyes that were becoming bloodshot, he managed 'I'm not... supposed to... go out like this,' followed by a bloodied gurgle. He strove to talk again, 'I was to... retire... someday... *on the fucking Gold Coast...*' As Nathan looked down upon him, the *Director* made one last feeble, pointless attempt to grab the *Walther*. Nathan kicked his clutching hand away and the *Director* lay motionless, resigned to his fate, but still grasping for cool, soothing, and life-giving air. 'You chose the wrong side, old man' announced Nathan in an unwavering, raised voice. '*And you picked the wrong people to fuck with, again!*' Slowly and ever so deliberately, Nathan spoke and dragged out his last sentence... '*This won't ever happen again...*'

As the last defiant word spilled from his lips, Nathan

raised his right knee to waist height and then maliciously propelled his combat boot and heavy heel deep into the *Director's* swollen throat!! The powerful heel strike complemented the extreme violence Nathan had inflicted earlier on the man and, this time, there was no more gurgling... The trachea and larynx were completely crushed and all hope of gathering any oxygen had now departed. The *Director* was dead... His eyes were now glassy and set, his bloodied mouth wide open, and a garishly swollen throat was bulging from the collar line of his trench coat; a look of wonderment embellishing his stubbled, timeworn face. For a second, Nathan thought of the saying his father always trotted out when dealing with repugnant people like this, 'Never give a sucker an even break', and Nathan never did.... *Not with people like this.* For the dead man, years of playing the espionage game had traversed, full circle, and it was the *Director* who now paid the ultimate price...

'Ok, let's pick up the fellas and go,' commanded Nathan, and the two men ran from the devastation at the bar and joined Sascha and Bill on the other side of the street. The men walked quickly in pairs, ten metres apart; coat collars up to brace themselves from the evening cold as the first police cars were attempting to negotiate the heavy road traffic. Nathan and his team weren't in a hurry, nor did they look suspicious. There were still many people wandering the streets before curfew, taking in a late walk, so they didn't expect to be stopped. In a matter of minutes, they made it to the corner, where Garen had hired two

Bolts and had generously paid the drivers to wait until their friends joined, completely unaware of the carnage their passengers had just created. With all on board, the two vehicles sped off. The men would drive back to Kreschatyk Avenue and the trendy *Mojo Bar* and drink a quick beer or two before heading back to the hotel later that evening. Sascha had paid off friends and associates to verify the men had been there all night, if the cops arrived...

Not a word was spoken as the men arrived at the pub, nor when they were escorted to a large booth in the back area of the establishment. Nathan ordered all the drinks for the evening and the mood was sombre... The men drank quietly and chatted about other things, like family, their interests, football, and destinations back home, wherever that may be. Nathan felt confident there wouldn't be any repercussions for their evenings work, for a few reasons... The *Director* and his cronies would be identified as *Wagner* and or Russian agents who got, pretty much, what was coming to them. That would be the official report from the Police and SBU *and no-one in Ukraine would spill a tear for them!* Alina and her brothers would keep *schtum* as they wouldn't want to be connected to enemies of the state. 'Hey, we were there to meet friends and got caught up in the violence', would be their alibi. As far as the two old men went, they would take it in their stride as most older Europeans do. In their lives they have seen dictators, famine, wars, and bloodshed, and most probably will again... For them, it is all part of the human condition in their part of the world. In an hour or so, the men would take the short, casual stroll back to their hotel and beat the dreaded curfew, but for the present, they sat and enjoyed their drinks and conversation. Although his mind was still galloping to a dozen places at once, Nathan knew in his heart and head that they didn't have anything to fear, ever again, from the *'Director.'*

Chapter Twenty-Eight:

ANOTHER MAGICAL DAY IN KYIV...

There hadn't been any blow-back from the melee at the *Buena Vista* bar. Nothing... In fact, the men had arrived back at their rooms, with the hotel and the surrounding area as quiet as a long-neglected tomb. *No police inquiries... no recriminations from any of the Director's men... no response from the Police, GRU or SBU or anyone else for that matter!* It was only Earl who approached Nathan and Phil the next morning and commented, in a friendly but slightly inquisitory tone, 'Hey, I heard you boys had a wild night last night, *anything you want to pass on?*' Nathan and Earl got on well and shared a professional regard for one another. They had run a few training sessions together and respected each other's work. '*No,*' said Nathan, 'just a few loose ends that needed clearing up. In fact, the end result helps us all, and I'd appreciate it if you kept it on the down-low?' Earl smirked and patted Nathan lightly on the shoulder, 'Not a problem, it stays with me... by the way, Cyrus wants to have a talk with a few of us and you, Phil and Mickey are included. Get a coffee and we'll meet you in Cyrus's room in thirty minutes... All good?' Nathan gave a quick thumbs up and gestured to Mickey and Phil for them to meander out to the coffee stand at the front of the hotel and get a brew. Nathan was concerned the word had drifted back to Cyrus about the previous night's 'activities' but he wasn't too worried. He would deal with it if the situation arose. If 'push came to shove', Nathan would fall on his sword...

It was another fresh morning on the avenue and there was the usual hubbub from office workers moving quickly on their way to their offices, shop girls strolling excitedly to cafes and clothing stores with their girlfriends and busy citizenry fussing about in the performance of their daily routines. As always, the Ukrainian guards sat on their rickety chairs out front, looking rough and perennially tired, cradling their AKs and puffing away contentedly. Garen, Bill and Sascha were already by the usual coffee stand, sipping their hot beverages, and taking in the spectacle of a city at war, and making comments about the poorly constructed defensive measures that had sprung up at intersections and around the streets surrounding *Midon Square*. '*Damn*,' said Phil, '*these people couldn't lay a sandbag wall to save their lives!* Geez, I haven't built one since my army days in the late seventies, *but I know I could do a damn sight better than this!'* Pausing, he thought about what he had just said and realised, that in his insensitive criticism, that's what these defensive measures were designed for, to save Ukrainian lives, no matter how poorly they had been constructed. 'I suppose you have to give them points for trying....' he said sheepishly, in an apologetic attempt to be more understanding and positive. Garen and his two cohorts were off later to visit the *Hospitallers,* who were stationed in barracks style accommodation at the rear area of *St. Michael's Cathedral.* They were going to follow up on a lead that Steve Holland had joined this group and had been deployed to Donbas or Kharkiv. Nathan spoke, and informed his friends that Mickey, Phil, and himself would be having a conference shortly with Cyrus. Nathan wasn't expecting an inquisition but reaffirmed it would be on his head if Cyrus made a big deal out of last night's deadly shenanigans. However, this 'all on my head' attitude wasn't acceptable to his colleagues. If Nathan had to go, they would all pack and leave, *so be it*!

The time flew - as it always does in good company, and it wasn't long before Nathan, Phil and Mickey were trudging up the hotel emergency stairwell to locate Cyrus's room. Their room was on the fifth floor, but Cyrus's and Earl's room was on the seventh level. They soon located the room and knocked politely. Cyrus opened the door and brashly told the men to enter, quickly. Nathan could feel the boom was about to be lowered, judging by Cyrus's demeanor. 'Okay,' he thought. 'Our actions may slightly compromise Cyrus's team mission in Ukraine, but getting a *Wagner* hit team off our backs helps everyone. Better at the *Buena Vista* bar, than being targeted on a highway or side-street or taken out in our rooms.' He had his calculated response ready and was just waiting for any accusation to be levelled at him...

As the men got comfortable and sat on the few chairs available, or on the bed, Cyrus looked at each trainer and began to speak, in his usual machine-gun fashion. 'Okay guys, I have heard back from the unit commanders of the groups we have trained, and they have been extremely impressed by your training methods and attitude. In fact, the unit commanders embedded spies into the soldier squads to try and catch us out but we have proven our worth. *Well done!*' The men were stunned by these words, as they were all expecting a vastly different narrative! After a pause, Cyrus went on to say that because of their excellence, the word had spread to many other units, particularly a heavy mortar unit that was being prepared to go to the 'front' in a matter of weeks.

More surprises followed, as Cyrus continued... 'As a result of the credit and prestige you have afforded our team, I have chosen you three, alongside Earl and two other medic trainers, to provide the necessary instruction to this mortar unit. You will depart Friday afternoon after teaching tactical drills to recruits at the *Legion Obolon* base and this mission will run for four days. *Is everyone happy with that?*' All the men nodded their heads in agreement. If nothing else, it was a real feather in their cap, and the boys could really be proud of their efforts! Cyrus finished with a feigned smile and then began handing out Polish poncho liners and Japanese ration packs to the three men. He had acquired these random items from Piotr, his Polish friend and they were distributed as an obvious reward to the men. This was another dimension of the 'Jekyll and Hyde' persona, which Cyrus nurtured. From one minute to another, he could be a complete 'psycho', a calculating 'shyster', or a rewarding benefactor! It was a surprise each day as to which personality he could or would take on... The meeting finished abruptly, and everyone went back to their rooms with their newly acquired goodies.

'Well, can you believe this', shouted an excited Mickey as he played with his Polish poncho liner, or 'combat woobie' as Nathan affectionately called his. The old army poncho liner had been around for a long time. In fact, it had been issued way back during the Vietnam War and was generally a prized possession for most soldiers. When combined with a military wet weather poncho, it made a handy, lightweight sleeping bag and was a sought-after piece of kit. As far as the Japanese ration packs went, well... no-one was in a hurry to try these. Nathan hadn't heard anything back from Sascha and his search for Steve with the *Hospitallers*, so it really didn't matter if they went on a training mission over the weekend. In fact, Nathan hadn't

heard from anyone in the last few days... Kathy hadn't responded to his texts, especially any news concerning Nate. Marcus was glib with his responses and any and all contacts in Kyiv had dried up. Since leaving the hotel, Nicky and Paul had re-confirmed that they would pass any relevant news that they came across during their travels through Ukraine. They, too, had been silent. It was as if a communications chasm had opened, and Steve, along with Nate, had spiralled down into an abyss, never to be heard from, ever again!

From Nathan's own perspective, money was starting to get really, really tight. Although the exchange rate was still generous, funding oneself in a warzone can't go on forever, with no source of income! Of more concern was the fitness of the team and they were all beginning to suffer, medically and psychologically. Nathan had developed a cough that didn't want to quit and was waiting on Garen to source the appropriate meds for his ailments. Noticeably Mickey had become slightly reclusive and was pining to leave...a few sad phone calls from home had now placed a heavy emotional burden on his shoulders. Nevertheless, a trip to the 'back blocks' of Kyiv would be a diversion from their present issues and concerns. At least it would offer more intel on the units of the Ukrainian army as well as an East European geography lesson, which may come in handy one day...

It had been a heavy mortar unit that had reached out to Cyrus through the perpetual 'contact' network, and they were hopeful of gaining some Western military expertise. This unit was exceptionally competent with firing their mortars but were lacking the skills to engage with an enemy, especially in close contact; if they were assaulted, they were incapable of employing offensive and defensive tactics against the Russians, or casualty evacuation for their troops. Their sole standard operating procedure was to scramble aboard their vehicles and drive as fast as they could to somewhere safe. To Nathan and his colleagues, it was obvious this unit could really use some military know-how as they were bereft of any real tactical knowledge. So, with all that having been thought, planned and said, it was time to pack and to prepare themselves for the upcoming training mission. Other than this, Nathan would have a workout, if his chest allowed it, and he pleadingly hoped for an good night's sleep.... he certainly needed it.

Chapter Twenty-Nine:

TRAINING MISSION

Although Nathan and his friends had only been coaching with Cyrus's group for a couple of weeks, it didn't take long before the routine took on a 'Groundhog Day' feeling. Days came and went, and most people weren't sure what day it was, half the time! What made this situation tiresome was the fact the team had an on-going commitment without even a pencilled in closure date. This made their task laborious, mundane, and seemingly never ending; much like maintaining the *Sydney Harbour Bridge*. To the painters and riggers, *the job never ends...* and it takes a special mindset to deal with a 'never ending story!' Another valid reason to go on a training mission somewhere besides Kyiv.

Breakfast had been taken at the usual time and the men were making their way to where they would usually get their ride, on the avenue. They were skirting around from the back entrance, when they were suddenly bailed up by 'mad' Manis, the commander of the Ukrainian unit that shared the building. So far, they had been fortunate to avoid this 'nutter' as he clearly had the trappings of a complete sociopath! Manis would fly off into fits of rage and a rumour circulated that he had fired his weapon at the ceiling in his hotel room while under the influence of cocaine! Judging by his mood swings and demeanour, this gossip was probably not too distant from the truth!! In an unexpected outburst, he screamed that he wanted to speak with Cyrus and kept demanding that someone contact him.

It was common knowledge Cyrus and Manis despised one another... Cyrus had contempt for the Ukrainian because he was far below his U.S. military standards; Manis was a poor commander and soldier and would openly abuse and bully his men. For Manis, he detested the situation that a 'Westerner', an 'American' like Cyrus, was assisting his country at a time of war. This feeling was further fuelled by the fact Cyrus was Japanese American and it was a prevailing belief most Ukrainians did not tolerate people from Asia, the Middle East or Africa, or anyone not of their Slavic ethnicity. It was rumoured that many people with these foreign backgrounds were given their 'marching orders' at the commencement of the war. LGBTIQ+ people were also corralled into this 'no go' category. Nathan had, however, witnessed in his travels, many non-heterosexual people as couples within the greater community.

This is not to say all Ukrainians are racist or bigoted but there are overt examples of race and identity haters, such as Manis, and the extreme right of Ukrainian politics, and enough examples of non-inclusiveness suggesting that segregation based on race, ethnicity and sexual orientation is a dominant theme; especially with the older Soviet-indoctrinated generations. Nathan picked up his phone, rang Cyrus, and informed him of Manis' demands. Cyrus was clearly annoyed and indicated he would be down in a few minutes. This was relayed to an impatient Manis. The men then turned on their heels and continued very quickly and purposefully to the front of the hotel. No-one wanted to be around when these two psychos butted heads!!

As the men kept watch for their transport, their friendly coffee vendor was waiting for them as usual, and all those who were going out to the *Legion Obolon* base bought a hot 'pick-me-up.' The weather had become very icy once more, and this would be the norm for the next few days. *Damn...* The piercing cold wasn't doing Nathan's chest any good and he would throw out a mighty rasping, bronchial cough on occasion. Before the rugged-up men knew it, their transport arrived, and they were quickly ferried to the base. As always, trainers and soldiers milled about, puffing smokes or vaping, laughing, and chatting until the officers of the unit managed to get their act together and attend the morning's parade. A general discussion was had... *and then another... and another...* before any movement occurred, and it was a constant source of amazement how even the most basic elements of military life always and without fail, turned into a philosophical debating society with the various echelons of the Ukrainian military! Finally, a decision was made! Today's training would be inside, utilising the old but large classrooms, and they would be instructing fresh recruits on the various basic firing positions, lying, kneeling, and standing. To the trained, this was a simple activity, but to those with little or no military experience, or to the uncoordinated or downright confused, it was crucial to have the ability to fire their weapon, and engage enemy targets accurately and consistently, at various ranges.

With orders having been barked, debated, and finally understood, recruits and trainers headed off to their designated classrooms. Nathan was working with Mitchell that morning and they had a sound understanding of what needed to be taught. Unfortunately for Nathan, he was starting to feel hot... more feverish than anything else, so he suggested that Mitchell conduct the lesson. Complicating Nathan's health was the fact the men trained in their heavy body armour, so they would be dressed like their Ukrainian counterparts; this was a fundamental way of gaining respect between trainer and trainee – 'do as I do, not do as I say'. For Nathan, the added weight placed a great deal more strain on him, physically. He began to sweat freely and was certain he was coming down with some nasty bug. Hopefully, it was only a slight fever, 'a twenty-four-hour job', but his mind was in dread of anything worse. His shirt, particularly the spots under his arms, were drenched... As it turned out, the training was 'on-song' for the morning, and soon, it was time for lunch. All the trainers and their squads broke for the meal. Borscht was again on the menu - *surprise, surprise...* coupled with something that looked like pork medallions in a greyish brown sauce. In the mess hall, it was the first time Nathan had seen Mickey or Phil for the entire morning.

As Nathan softly cradled his cup of black, sweet tea. Besides some crusty bread, this was the only nutrition he was capable of ingesting. He sensed Phil staring at him with. He turned his head, stared at Phil's gawk, and remarked, flatly, *'What?'* Phil didn't hold back. 'Fuck, you look like *shite*, are you taking anything, because you really should...' *'Geez,'* thanks for the diagnosis, Dr. Freud, *and no,* I'm not on any meds. Garen said he will pick some drugs up for me this arvo.' Although it didn't sound like it, Phil was really worried by Nathan's deteriorating condition. Nathan remarked again, *'And, don't worry, I'll be okay to go on the training mission later this evening.* I normally sweat these things out fast... twenty-four hours or thereabouts.' Mickey and Phil didn't say anything else, but just looked at each other with concerned expressions on their faces and serious thoughts on their minds.

Before too long, they were back in the classroom and training. This time they were focused on teaching small groups on how to react in a 'contact' situation with the enemy, whether front, flank, or rear. Again, Nathan asked Mitchell to run the lesson as he knew in no uncertain terms that he was now *feeling like shit*. Some of the senior Ukrainian members had managed to purchase small firecrackers to use as battle simulation. These tiny 'whizz bangs' would be thrown during training but to whom, when and where was anybody's guess! The recruits enjoyed the pseudo-realism and were dedicated during their military drills, so the firecrackers had the desired effect.

Being a Friday, the instruction only went for around ninety minutes as the training was shortened for an early start to the weekend. Most of the Westerners saw this as a 'cop out' as they all believed the Ukrainians needed as much quality training and time to perform it, but you can't argue with the unit commander! Nathan and Mitchell headed to the foyer of the building to catch up with the other instructors. It was obvious Nathan was in a world of hurt... He sat on a chair, leaning forward despondently with his head bowed, his shirt, and the top of his trousers around the beltline, were ringing wet with sweat. His face looked ashen though he hadn't really done anything all day! He kept telling Phil he would be okay and was certain the meds Garen would give him would quickly fix him.

Contrary to the weather reports, the day had warmed, and the sun was shining brightly, with the charming radiance and gleeful acceptance that only a perky winter sun can bring. *Bolt* cabs would usher them back to the hotel and it would be a very quick change, a grab of the kit and outside again to their transport and off to the new training mission. This time, transport was being provided by the mortar unit, so they didn't have time to waste. As Nathan picked up his bag to leave, Phil spoke again, in a most concerned tone. *'Mate, are you sure you're okay?* No big deal if you miss this gig. I'm sure there'll be others...' Again, Nathan assured Phil he would most likely sweat this cold out and be as 'right as rain' in the morning. *'Don't worry,'* he said, 'there'll be no dramas. I'll be fine tomorrow, you'll see...' Both men knew there would be no more talking or debating the issue as patience for the conversation was spent and, hopefully, Nathan would recover quickly, as he indicated. The cabs soon arrived, and the men were on their way. Not a lot of chatter ensued as Nathan was feeling poorly and the other men were weary; it had been a long and eventful week.

As the trainers arrived back at their luxury hotel, Nathan paused at the stairwell, before he made the arduous climb to the fifth floor and their room. He looked upwards with some trepidation... it was going to be a *bloody hard climb!* He was now feeling terribly ill, and every part of his body ached, even during urination. 'Damn,' he thought, *'What a fucking time to get sick. This bloody flu doesn't want to quit.'* He trudged, slowly and painfully, upstairs and to his room, where Phil and Mickey were darting about, collecting their body armour, helmets, and personal items to take with them for the next few days. The boys were not taking any chances and would carry just about everything they had as they weren't certain about the sleeping quarters awaiting them. Nathan's gear was ready to go, as always, but both the men assisted their sick friend with his gear and soon they were back downstairs on the avenue, waiting for their rides.

As luck would have it, just as their two *Toyota Landcruiser* transports pulled up, Garen appeared and rushed down the street to catch Nathan before the team departed. As he passed on the medications and instructions to his friend, his next words just about knocked Nathan off his feet! *'I've located Nate, he's fine, and he will be back at our hotel, by the time you get back. I'll text you more of the details later, take care, see ya!'* Without any time to spare, the vehicles were loaded with gear and personnel and the vehicles set off down the busy avenue, which was experiencing peak-hour traffic, *thick and fast* - Ukrainian style! Now Nathan sat tightly in the backseat with the other men, feeling dumbfounded but as delighted as he could be given the heavy cloud of illness sapping his very existence. Although his condition made it difficult for him to concentrate, he was incredibly pleased Nate had been found and he looked forward to reading Garen's texts, later that evening.

Unfortunately for Nathan, the journey was not enjoyable, not in the slightest... His body aches were increasing, he felt 'achy-precious' and the pain amplified throughout his system. He attempted to take his mind off his predicament by viewing parts of Kyiv he hadn't seen before, but it wasn't much of a relief. After thirty minutes or so, the lead vehicle pulled into a gas station and all the men piled out to buy food and drinks or have a smoke. Nathan exited the car very slowly and carefully and waited until Phil and Mickey returned with a can of *coke* for him. Nothing really had to be said as the men could see Nathan was in an awfully bad way... He kept professing, 'Don't worry, I'll be over this tomorrow', but Phil wasn't so sure... Like the proverbial 'clown car', so many large bodies loaded back into the smallish *Toyotas*, and they were away. It was another forty minutes to their final destination. The evening was beginning to set in but isolated farmhouses and vast paddocks, yet to be sowed for a crop, were still visible within three hundred metres or so from the roadway. Nathan closed his eyes in an attempt at respite from his suffering, trying to block out all the noises, bumps, and calamity from their road trip. The cabin of the car was warm, but Nathan was beginning to shiver, and he knew *this wasn't a good sign...*

To Nathan it felt like hours, but it was only a short time before the vehicles were pulling up to a set of old but sturdy iron gates, in front of a small barracks of only four buildings. A uniformed Ukrainian soldier was waiting to check identification and permit vehicle entry. Two minutes more and the cars were parked by a large tin shed and the men were directed to grab their belongings. They were to be shown their sleeping quarters and then the mess hall where they would have a late supper. Unfortunately for Nathan, every slow pace he took forward, every short step he climbed and every item he carried felt heavy, laborious, and physically distressing. He, Phil, Mickey, and Earl were taken to a four-person bedroom, and they placed their gear down. Steel spring beds, bedspreads and thick mattresses looked comfortable enough, and the room was spotlessly clean. The ablutions were ten metres down the hall, and they were part of a long-tiled corridor that was old in design but immaculately clean also. The other men had placed their kit down on their beds and were walking out of their rooms, following a Ukrainian NCO to the kitchen and for supper. Nathan followed slowly behind the rest of his friends, Earl and the two medics, to the mess hall which could probably accommodate seventy to a hundred men.

It is generally hard to tell when looking at Ukrainian men if they are happy, or if an inherent gruffness is their standard pose, but judging by the unimpressed look on the chef's face, he had been waiting some time for these men and seemed to be in a hurry to dish out the meal and be on his way. Terse words were spoken between him and the Ukrainian soldiers, but Nathan wasn't sure if there was a problem, or it was just the accent of the men that sounded aggressive. Although tired and in need of a shower and a good night's sleep, all the men grabbed large slices of bread and large bowls of a meaty soup. Nathan was struggling to get down even a few mouthfuls from the small porcelain bowl he had picked out. Instead of feeling better, he was getting worse, *if that was possible...* It seemed as though the medications were having zero impact upon his condition. When he could take it no more, he stood up, excused himself and said he had to go to his bunk. Some of the Ukrainians wondered where Nathan was going as a briefing concerning the next day's activities was planned to follow dinner, but it was clear that this man was extremely sick and needed rest.

To say Nathan was feeling ill was an understatement! It was difficult for him to place one foot in front of the other and it took him awhile to locate his room and unroll his sleeping bag; *a painful act in itself!* No time for brushing teeth... No time for laying out tomorrow's clothes... No time for anything except to sleep and hopefully, recover by the next morning! As Nathan lay gravely ill in his winter sleeping bag, on top of his wobbly bed, his mind was starting to turn off. He was aching and sweating profusely but, remarkably, still actively cognisant of all that was around him. There would be no time to check any texts, these could wait until tomorrow... He was never a man to give in, but Nathan was deeply worried at his condition, to the point he was in fear of his mortality; his last thoughts before he dropped off to sleep were that he didn't think he would make it through the night... Of all the grand adventures he had been on... Of all the supreme danger he had faced... *It had come to this...* He didn't expect it, but Ukraine was most likely *the place where he was going to die!*

Chapter Thirty

NO BUENO, THEN A REPRIEVE...

Searing, penetrable white light flashed in front, upward and outward and all-around Nathan's fluttering eyes, *oh so briefly*, and then he was semi-unconscious, again... In time, he regained a modicum of consciousness... Voices uttered incoherent words and syllables that Nathan couldn't fathom, and he was out to the world once more... *'Nathan's boiling... He's got a fever,'* was all he could make out, in a fleeting moment of lucidity, and then he was out for another deep *sleep*... As he would later discover, it was Mickey who had returned early from the briefing, only to detect Nathan unconscious and violently shaking and shuddering in his sleeping bag. Without hesitation, he ran to get one of the medics, and it was Tyler, the ex-U.S. Navy corpsman that he found first. Tyler had impressed everyone with his likeable persona and skill set. He had lived in Ukraine as a junior when his father was a diplomat with the U.S. Consul. It was Tyler who completed the initial assessment on Nathan and had identified this stricken warrior was experiencing the severest of fevers. He had examined Nathan's eyes to assess his level of consciousness and had taken his temperature. By now, Nathan was unresponsive to anyone. *It wasn't looking good...* Phil had located Nathan's meds, and these were assessed by the former Navy man. A quick nod-of-the-head suggested Tyler approved but he went fishing in his medic's bag and produced some additional drugs. 'You boys will have to keep a close eye on him, which I know you'll do... This could be touch and go as I am certain he has pneumonia *– and as bad as it gets!* Any change, such as his breathing or if the fever continues to increase, then come and grab me straightaway, and we will rush him to the nearest hospital. For the present, he stays in bed, on meds, resting and under supervision... I prefer not to move him in this state.' The men nodded in unison at the medic's comments and Mickey and Phil worked out a roster by where they could train the Ukrainians but have also have constant surveillance over Nathan who was balancing perilously on death's precipice. Time *to play the waiting game...*

For Nathan, the warmth of the thick *Dacron* bedding provided some reassuring comfort as he stirred very slowly but was soon fully awake. He usually dreamed and would share his crazy imaginings with his friends, but he felt as though he had been in a coma, *for how long he did not know?* He curiously looked about the room and found a white ceramic plate with bread and cheese on it, and a steaming mug of tea, resting on a plain white wooden chair at the bottom of his steel-framed bed. He appreciated the gesture but really had no appetite or the strength to move. Nathan was just pleased he was still in the land-of-the-living. His surroundings were quiet, as one would expect in a hospital ward or a quality hotel. Physically, he still felt very warm, clammy in fact, but at least the profuse sweating had dissipated. He was still aching with an intensity he had never experienced before... Every bone and muscle in his body throbbed, as if his anatomy was waging a personal war with him! He could feel pockets of wetness in and around his sleeping bag and was amazed that his coughing was the least of his problems. He glanced at his watch, using his fingers to separate the eyelids on one eye, and it was around ten in the morning of the next day. All he knew was that he was busting to urinate, and he made a valiant attempt to get up and go to the ablutions. Almost instantly, he fell back on his bed and took in a couple of sharp breaths as he negotiated the agonising pain and discomfort. *'Damn, that hurt,'* he thought, and he knew he would have to mentally prepare himself for the next time he tried to get up.

As Nathan was gingerly reassessing his position, Phil turned the corner and casually strolled into the room. He stopped and took a long, hard look at Nathan. 'Buddy, you're in a real bad way... I'm not going to downplay or bullshit you on this as this situation can go two ways. Tyler says you probably have pneumonia, and we all know that's a killer.' He went on to say that Cyrus had organised an ambulance for tomorrow, which was Sunday, and you will be taken back to the hotel in Kyiv, to recuperate before re-commencing any training duties; that is if you have recovered a whole lot more and don't get any worse. 'Damn,' Nathan remarked slowly, in a raspy voice, 'I thought I was crook but not as bad as this. Sorry If I've put you guys out.' Phil continued... 'The plan for you is to rest up today and be ready to head off tomorrow. Garen will be in the ambulance and is extremely anxious to see how you are. So just take it easy, keep up the meds and rest.'

Phil went on to inform Nathan how the drills with the Ukrainians had been going, and that they expected to go to the weapons range tomorrow, to perform some advanced infantry manoeuvres and weapon skills. He paused, took a serious look at Nathan and then quietly spoke... 'Just on the off chance that things get worse, who do you want me to contact, back home?' Nathan had been looking up and out to the side as Phil had been talking but now placed his head flat back on his pillow. 'Don't worry about trucking me back to Oz,' said Nathan matter-of-factly. *'If I die, throw me in a dumpster, I don't care! Ukraine is a good a place as any...'* Phil wasn't surprised by what sprang from Nathan's lips. He had heard this many times before... Nathan didn't have any next-of-kin and he didn't want his military 'family' to have to *drag his sorry carcass back home!* He didn't believe in an afterlife and openly stated that 'Once you're dead... *you're just rotting meat!*' Phil had to dash but said he would be back in a couple of hours. For Nathan, it was time to take in some fluids... It was a tough act, but he managed to slowly sip the warm tea that Phil had graciously provided him, along with an empty *Gatorade* bottle which he could use as a piss decanter, as he was still too weak to go to the bathroom. He awkwardly used the bottle, making sure he didn't wet himself or his bedding, and then lay flat and quiet in the comfy sleeping bag, which was his protective world. In exactly one minute, he was asleep.

It was the talking and clip, clopping noises on the outside hall linoleum that woke Nathan and he blinked at his watch and was surprised it was so late in the day. Apparently, the men had returned from the field training, ate dinner and were now on their way for some evening lectures, back in the mess hall. He perused the room and saw a fresh plate of food coupled with a mug of tea, resting once more, on the old wooden chair at the bed end. Phil and Mickey had taken turns on watch during the day, but Nathan had not been aware of Mickey in the two hours as he sat diligently opposite Nathan's bunk. He now tried to get up but just didn't have the strength *and collapsed back onto the bed...* In a few moments, he was asleep again....

It was around one in the morning when he stirred again. This time he desperately needed to go to the bathroom. All the other men were fast asleep, and he moved very slowly and purposefully to limit any noise and disturbance to his colleagues. As he entered the hallway, wearing only a T-shirt and underpants, he could make out the sounds of snoring emanating from the other rooms on his floor. Although he felt so much better than he was on Friday night, his bones ached viciously, and he shuffled instead of walking as if every precious movement and vibration caused him distress... He trundled along the ten metres or so, painfully and deliberately, and imagined that he was feeling as old and going as slow as the biblical figure, 'Methuselah'. Nathan flicked on a light switch and then found the toilets immediately after the washroom.

Nathan stood in silence as his eyes *couldn't believe what he saw before him*... There were four toilet cubicles, and each cubicle housed a squat toilet; many of these could be found in the old Soviet buildings they had frequented but were difficult to use, even for an able-bodied person. *'Fuck me!'* he whispered angrily to himself, in anticipation of the coming struggle... To the uninitiated, a person had to have the dexterity of 'Nadia Comaneci', the famed Romanian gymnast, to squat and negotiate the foot places and bowl of such a lavatory system!! The last time Nathan had used such a device was when he was stationed in Malaysia, during the 'Counter-Insurgency War', back in nineteen eighty-one, when he was a young, fit and agile soldier, and it was bloody difficult back then! A quick inspection of these toilets and the fact that none of the cubicles had a handrail led to Nathan taking a deep breath and breathing out, little by little, feeling as equally deflated mentally, as the stale air that was exiting his lungs. *'For fuck's sake, how am I going to use this with no handrail?'* he pondered in frustration as he attempted to gauge his next move... 'Okay,' he thought, 'need to go in, turn around, drop the pants, bend over, and try and grab the bottom underside part of the cubicle wall with my left hand, rotated backwards. Grab some paper with my right hand and 'do my business' without falling into the bowl or crapping on myself or my clothes!' It sounded easy but as his balance was shot, and he had the strength of an anorexic kitten, all made for an interesting exercise! With 'true grit', he ventured forward... The whole process took longer than normal for your average human being, and when Nathan had finished, he mentally and physically groaned.... believing this was one of the hardest things he had ever completed in his life. He thought to himself, most furiously, 'If I ever became President of this country, my first act would be to ban squat toilets!' Such was the drain upon his vitality, it took Nathan double the time to hobble back to his room, where he slid back into his sleeping bag and collapsed, exhausted!

It seemed as though he had only just fallen asleep when Phil was gently pushing Nathan's shoulder and stirring him to wake. *'Morning beautiful,* how are you feeling today?', he inquired cheerfully. After last night's ordeal it would be expected that Nathan would be worse for wear, but he was feeling so much better, 'washed out' as if the fever had broken, stealing all his energy with it.

He was still coughing slightly, and his body still ached in places, but he was at least fifty percent better. 'Mate,' said Phil, 'just a quick heads-up, Garen is on his way and will be here in 'twenty mikes' (military for minutes). Time for you to grab your gear and wait for him downstairs. I'll give you a hand.' The rest of the team would stay until Tuesday before they returned to Kyiv. At present, the Ukrainian unit was being run through 'man down' drills; what to do, who to involve and how to extract wounded if their unit suffered casualties. The soldiers were picking up the lessons quickly, much to the pleasure of the trainers.

Phil carried all the gear while Nathan tentatively walked down the old, tiled stairs to a large foyer that was complete with its own security room and guard, who was watching a small black and white television; a football game was in progress. Phil offered a hearty goodbye, shook Nathan's hand, and left. A dark haired but stout cleaning woman appeared from a side room and began sweeping the greyish tiled floor with a broom that had been fabricated out of long dry sticks. There was a longstanding joke in Eastern Europe that the worker had to provide their own wooden pole and sticks as the 'State' never provides anything... On retirement, the worker is allowed to keep their pole as a token of their long, hard years of servitude... *Some joke*... Nathan was engrossed in the routine of the peasant woman, studying her technique with the witch-like-broom and the matter-of-fact way in which she approached her duties, waddling and swirling around the floor and resembling someone who was slowly performing a waltz for one... Within a short while, the ambulance arrived, and Garen, and another American medic named 'Tex' entered the foyer. Garen smiled broadly when he saw Nathan and was extremely glad to see that he was looking much better. He happily carried his kit to the rear of the vehicle. It was this ambulance that the men used to help ferry them to their training assignments, it was this ambulance that Cyrus had conned a Polish company out of, and it was this ambulance that would end up with a seized motor because no-one had bothered to do the daily maintenance service on it. Nathan was always astonished by many ex-military men who professed to be ultra-professional but ended up being 'ultra-slack' when it came to doing the basics, like checking their vehicle's mechanics!

Having been positioned in a side seat, Garen and Tex performed a set of observations on Nathan, which included his conscious level, blood pressure, temperature, and oxygen saturation. A stethoscope was used to hear the peculiar 'goings on' inside his chest. The two medics conferred and told Nathan that they were going to place him on a saline drip. Apparently, his condition was still critical, and that he was so dehydrated he couldn't cough up the pus and phlegm, explaining why Nathan wasn't coughing all that much now. The medicos went into action and before he knew it, a catheter and saline drip was running from the back of his hand. As Garen stated to Nathan, 'You should be feeling better shortly...' and then came the philosophical rub... 'but do you know what, we should never have caught that train to Medyka in the first place, 'cause look at all the mayhem, all the death, all the sorrow that's happened since...' Nathan nodded slowly and said flatly to Garen, confirming his assessment but adding, 'Getting on the train was a great adventure, getting off the train was where it all went pear-shaped... *never get off the train, man... just never get off the train...*' and he proceeded to shut up, rest up and prevent any more exertion.

Mickey and Tyler had appeared to talk to Garen and Tex and to say their heartfelt goodbyes. It was also time to 'take the piss' out of Nathan before he departed. 'Hey,' laughed Tyler, 'you'll be okay... the word is you survived the "Korean War", so this should be child's play for you!' So much for any respect for an 'older veteran', but Nathan was deeply thankful for what his colleagues had done for him. In no uncertain terms, *they had saved his life!* It had already circulated back to Cyrus that the Ukrainians were mightily impressed with the training and there would be future opportunities though Nathan felt miserable he hadn't been an active participant but was sure his chance would come later; that is if he hadn't located Steve Holland and was homeward bound. With goodbyes and farewells completed, the ambulance set off with Garen driving, like he normally preferred to do back in Texas. It wasn't long before the small villages gave way to larger roads and highways and taller brick buildings. Nathan just took it easy, sitting comfortably in the back and reflecting upon the last few weeks...

Overall, the 'team' had been operating together for nearly a month and the leads on Steve Holland had been meagre, if not invisible. They had barely survived a host of dangerous situations, namely the deadly melee at the *Buena Vista* bar, and Nathan had nearly died of pneumonia. Kathy had been texting Nathan periodically but was unable to provide any more information on her wayward husband or son. The Australian government had little knowledge, or *truth be told*, little interest in the matter. No political mileage to be had concerning a rogue Aussie veteran, or a young man wandering abut Europe, and Kathy had given up all hope with the Ukrainian authorities. Sacha's contacts had borne little fruit; a snippet of an idea here, a murmur of a conversation somewhere, and a whisper of a lead elsewhere, and the whole situation had become frustrating for all concerned. Money and living expenses were nearly depleted and Phil couldn't bankroll this expedition forever... Nathan knew he had made a vow, a gentleman's oath to Kathy, but he also realised that their effectiveness as a unit was coming to an end. The only upside was the weather was beginning to improve and the long, drab, and bitter winter was being gradually overhauled by a buoyant spring that had been sorely missed and long overdue...

As his mind raced and he grappled with new ideas and various scenarios, the ambulance continued on its way, surely and steadily through Kyiv's streets. The ride back to the capital felt brief and soon they were pulling up outside of their hotel. Nathan was pleased to see 'home' and was delighted he would soon enjoy the solitude and comfort of his room. He eagerly looked across the street and took in a long and welcoming gaze at the 'Rock...' A few of the other trainers were waiting for his return and Nathan was surprised to spot Cyrus who was genuinely concerned about his health and insisted Nathan take it easy for the next few days. Although there had been a few men who had arrived and had left quickly for home, and people frequently clashed, there was still a degree of camaraderie amongst the men, which you only get when having served together in risky situations and environments. In the background, Nathan could make out Bill and Sascha and walked slowly over to embrace them and their cheery greetings. *'I think it is time for a sit down and a long chat...* Let's wait until Mickey and Phil are back, and we can all get together, probably on Wednesday', suggested Nathan as they strolled back into the hotel. It was clear to his friends that he was extremely serious, and it wasn't just his health that had altered his demeanour; they knew the situation was going to change. How much so, *they would soon find out...*

Chapter Thirty-One:

THE BEGINNING OF THE END...

Nathan spent the next couple of days convalescing. He went for short, relaxed walks to help break the tedium and to regain his strength, but this was only after the saline drip had been removed the day after his return. The weather had improved ever so slightly, with more sunny days than grey ones. For everyone else, the training of various Ukrainian units continued. Cyrus's 'training team' was still highly sought-after, all-over Kyiv and beyond. Why wouldn't it be? Quality training all for a bowl of borscht? A unit commander would be crazy to pass up on this opportunity. Bill, Garen and Sascha would furnish Nathan with updates at the end of the day, and it seemed as though things were going well. Still no word on Steve Holland...damn! But at least he had news on young Nate... Garen had located the young Aussie who had been working as a volunteer with the *Ukrainian Red Cross* only a few kilometres away from the hotel. He had endured a miserable time on his trip to Europe to look for his father; his money was stolen, he was beat up by Polish street kids, his health was also suffering because of the climate, and he was basically living on the 'bones of his arse'. He was blessed to have fallen in with other kind volunteers at Medyka and had been offered a small administration role with the Red Cross organisation.

Nate had managed to have a decent conversation with Garen and was advised that Nathan would be back in Kyiv on Sunday. He sounded pleased at the news and said he would visit Nathan in a few days as he had made commitments to the people who had taken him in, to assist in the delivery of humanitarian goods in and around the capital. From Garen's messages, it sounded as if Nate had just about had enough of Ukraine and realised, he'd made a huge mistake coming over on a 'one-man mission'. The news of this pleased Nathan and he would endeavour to convince the young man to return home and if need be, would fund him to make this a reality. On the face of it, that was one problem nearly solved... He wouldn't contact Kathy until all this was certain and all the ducks were in a row, with a flight booked. Nonetheless, he was feeling positive.

The three days Nathan spent on his own didn't go to waste. Besides recuperating on his bed, taking medication, and resting his body and soul, it gave him time to reminisce, review, and re-think over his life and not just what had occurred in the last four weeks. This was Nathan's problem – sometimes *he thought too bloody much!* He started to wonder if he would return to Ukraine, after he first ferried himself home to Australia. Would he be in the right physical and, more importantly, mental state to resume a search? Would it be possible for his comrades to continue with this quest? Would Steve Holland ever be found? So many questions were running through his mind that it felt like he was experiencing a mental meteor shower, with each miniscule comet a question that was now rocketing around inside his head, lighting and inflaming the crevices of his mind like a sky show from New Years Eve! Most of the time, he would rest his head on the pillow and gaze at the ceiling, cogitating, and planning. Sometimes he would do this for hours, until he was exhausted. He would perform this ritual in the morning and afternoon, and it was only meal breaks, a casual stroll, or a dive into a deep and restful sleep that interrupted his thought patterns.

A particular subject for Nathan's consternation was 'time'. Time is cruel... it slowly depletes us of our physiological glory and robs us of those we deeply love. If we live long and well enough, hopefully, we will have accumulated more joy than sorrow, but for many of us mortals, it doesn't always work out that way... For a great many people, time on this planet is heartless and unforgiving... Recuperation and its time wastage also has its penalties and thinking too hard is fraught with the unnecessary depletion of this valued commodity and the dangers of depression, sinister thoughts of self-harm and suicide and the ironic act of self-termination and the cessation of 'one's' time. For Nathan, it was the critical review of his life that caused him to endure the painful bouts of melancholia, as it always had done. Fortunately, he had never overstepped this mental boundary to other dangerous realms of thought and actualisation. Here he was, in his mid-fifties, single. He had never anticipated the agonising and sad loss of his first wife to dementia, nor had he expected the breakdown of his second marriage, ending in divorce. During his life, he had studied hard, applied himself, with determination and discipline had proved that he was a cut-above-the-rest, but now found himself living alone and unfulfilled, except for Moochie the faithful cat! As they say in the classics, 'good guys finish last'.

Again, the problems with his life dated back to his time in the military, and to the formative conditioning of his family life. The calculated and incessant brainwashing had taken its toll, like it does to so many veterans – *male and female*. Of course, it would, especially if you were seventeen years old when you enlisted and were institutionalised. You were practically still a child when raised on a diet of rank nationalism, fervent patriotism, and the glorious and 'holier than thou' scriptures of the *Anzac* legend. Not such a problem if you had a limited stint in the defence forces or were a lot older and more mature when you enlisted, or built with the sort of resilient character that can brush off the intense propaganda and authority that is repeatedly subjected upon you. Add this pervasive indoctrination to some of the life-changing situations occurring in the military, such as the crazy life or death moments experienced on deployment and training, and there will be issues, and the creation of 'Jason Bourne' clones.

Nathan's thoughts traversed to some of the poignant moments of his military career... It is really hard not to feel constant anxiety after the Troop Sergeant decides to burn C4 instead of returning the unused explosive back to storage and it blows up, sending debris and metal fragments whirling past your face. It is really difficult not to feel a sense of betrayal when your Platoon Sergeant at Corps training repeatedly bashes one of your best friends and threatens every other member with violence. It is really challenging not to feel a sense that justice isn't served by the military, the Department of Defence or the Federal government when another colleague has been sexually assaulted by a civilian and his version of events is dismissed, because he is male. Nathan could go on and on... bullying... promotions based on mateship and not merit... members bumped off deployments so 'old boys can get a gig, *etcetera, etcetera*... He was sure this script isn't part of the fabled version of the 'Anzac Legend' that C.E.W. Bean, the famed *World War One* historian skillfully composed and has been passed down from generation to generation.

Furthermore, Nathan's family life had not contributed to a serene state of mind. This is largely where the debilitating seed was planted but later nurtured by the military. His father's alcoholism and violent outbursts further contributed to Nathan's anxiety and his use of violence to sort out his own problems. Unfortunately, Nathan's younger brother bore the brunt of many of these violent exchanges and beatings, which would not be acceptable in today's world, but were commonplace in their childhood. His brother had left home at an early age and had suffered from various dependencies, which ultimately cut short his life. The family was clearly dysfunctional, and the only person Nathan got on with was his mother; he was estranged from his sister and was around fifty years old when he found out that his younger brother had passed away.

In addition, it is common for boys and young men to 'butt' heads with their fathers. This has been the case since time immemorial. Some may see it as a physical rite of passage from being a 'young bull' to a 'mature bull' by taking on the 'old bull'. In Nathan's case, he had had three physical and extremely violent exchanges with his father, and this placed a heavy psychological burden on him, which he would carry through his life. Nathan didn't believe he was a violent man, but the 'conditioning' had lent itself to 'violence' being the first port of call in any confronting situation. Nathan would see 'red', literally at the drop of a hat, to use old but precise *clichés*. His last major confrontation had been only a few years back. Nathan had been driving his beloved 1967 Mustang Fastback in the north of Victoria, just past a *McDonald's* restaurant. Some guy who hadn't been watching where he was going, stepped a bit too close to Nathan's vehicle and then decided to lash out at the car, kicking the vehicle's rear quarter. A fist fight ensued, and it was only when the paramedics arrived that Nathan ceased beating the man; the only thing that saved Nathan from prison time was that the guy happened to be carrying a concealed weapon; so, clearly not a model citizen. And there had been other situations like this... To Nathan it seemed he had inherited his father's violent streak, and it was the family curse. With such a mental burden, it is no wonder he got depressed or 'cranky' when such thoughts contributed to him feeling like his life had been wasted.

Nevertheless, despite all this historical anguish, the days wore on and Nathan was dozing on his bed, when, around four pm, abstract shadows from the fine lace curtains were being cast against the backdrop of the wall where the flat screen TV was. There was a sharp knock on the door – *rap, rap, rap...* Nathan woke from his semi-slumber and quickly sat up. *'Come in, if you're good looking...'* he shouted, in a loud, cheeky voice. The whole team was here, and Nathan climbed off the bed to go and shake the hands of Mickey and Phil, who had just returned from the training mission. 'Damn, I am glad to see you're looking much better than the last time we saw you', and on that comment Phil gave Nathan a strong hug. Mickey, Bill, Garen and Sascha offered their bright 'hellos', and everyone found a seat on a bed or a chair.

'Well, we may as have a group chat, seeing that everyone is present', remarked Nathan. He paused for a moment to arrange his mental notes, giving the men time to get themselves comfortable. He started... 'I will be blunt. As I see it, we haven't had a lot of success trying to locate my old friend, Steve. And I believe we are just about at the end of our operational capability. Money is tight, our physical and mental health is deteriorating, and the leads have dried up. For all we know, Steve is probably lying in a mass grave somewhere.' He finished with the blunt assessment, *I don't think there is much more we can do...'* He paused again, looked about the room at all the stern faces of the men who had become his close friends and said, 'It has been a grand adventure and I owe my life to everyone here, and for that, I can never repay the debt. I almost croked it the other day; I certainly don't want to see anyone lose their life in Ukraine.'

A further pause followed and then Nathan opened the discussion for the group. It was Mickey who spoke first with a degree of resignation, 'Yeah, I'm just about done... My partner and family back in Queensland are having a tough time with me being over here, and I need to go back for them.' Bill then said he had family and business commitments in Texas that couldn't be put off forever and it was time he moved on as well. Garen announced he would stay, and felt he needed to contribute more to the Ukrainian cause; he would join the *Hospitallers* and serve on their six-week deployments at the 'front', but he would continue to keep an eye out for Steve or for information pertaining to his whereabouts. 'Hell, I don't have a lot to go back to at home, and the people appreciate what I can do over here', was his final comments before Sascha indicated that he too had family issues he needed to attend to. His wife and two daughters had fled to Portugal when the war broke out and he hadn't seen them since. He couldn't leave the country as a government ban was in place preventing all men under sixty from leaving Ukraine. He was hoping he could reunite with them at the border or in Lviv. It was Phil who spoke last. 'I'm getting a divorce' was all he declared, and the words stunned the room. 'What the?!' was all Nathan could get out before Phil spoke over him, muttering, as if in a trance...'Yeah, I know that things have been shit for a while, but I didn't think it would lead to this... I have given her all she ever wanted - cars, house, money and now all she wants to do is freakin' dump me... funny thing is, there isn't even another woman involved this time, isn't that a kick in the head?' Nathan walked over to Phil, who was sitting, slumped in his chair with his head gazing at the carpeted floor. 'Don't worry old mate, things will get better. If worse comes to worse, you can always live out at the block with me.' Phil slowly raised his head and looked directly at Nathan and said, 'Thanks mate, I may have to take you up on that...'

The discussion produced a lot more curve balls than Nathan anticipated, but it was all out in the open and a group decision had been made to finish their tasks and take the long trip home. Nathan indicated to the men he would contact Cyrus on their behalf and let them know they were going their separate ways. Of course, Cyrus wouldn't be happy, but this wasn't the army, and no-one had signed their lives away to die for Ukraine, or the crazy *Nikkei* American for that matter. He would also contact a guy called 'Otis', who was loosely connected to Cyrus and his organisation. Otis drove a van from the border at Medyka to Lviv and then on to Kyiv. He ferried goods such as first aid supplies, body armour and sometimes personnel. As luck would have it, he was making a run to Kyiv tomorrow and could be there to pick them up, mid-morning.

Armed with this knowledge, he suggested to every-one to pack all their belongings and be ready to move on a moment's notice. With the meeting finished, Bill, Sascha and Garen slowly and solemnly walked out of the room, leaving only Nathan, Mickey, and Phil; or as Nathan affectionately called them, the 'A' team. Nathan returned to his bunk and suggested they all go out for one last dinner in the capital before they ventured home. Everyone agreed. Mickey and Phil started sorting their gear and showered. Nathan looked out at the window of the large advertising poster of the 'Rock', Dwayne Johnson, but his mind was miles away... The trip back wouldn't be easy, and the route was demanding... There was still a war raging and they wouldn't be relatively safe until they got over the border. Nathan was only operating at around seventy percent of his ability and would have to commit every single fibre of his strength and every ounce of guile to make sure they all made it home...

Just as Nathan was about to rise from his bed and get ready to go out, there was a loud tap on the door. Garen popped his head in and cheerfully said, *'Have a guess who I've found...'* He opened the door wide and walked in with Nate trailing sheepishly behind him. Nathan raced across the room as fast as he physically could and embraced Nate, his *Godson*, in a bearhug! The feeling was reciprocated as Nate tightly hugged the older man and they clinched, like two peas in a pod! They stayed like this until Nathan broke the grip, and then proceeded to give Nate a verbal spray! *'What in the fuck were you thinking, coming over here, on your own? Your mother is just about going nuts, completely out of her mind!'* The guilty look on Nate's lean and rugged face displayed his obvious remorse and he elaborated upon what Nathan had just said. 'Yeah, it was a pretty dumb thing to do, but I thought I could help... I couldn't just stay at home, seeing Mum falling apart... *I had to do something!'* Nate confirmed what Garen had told Nathan about the beating, and the theft of his possessions and he finished by saying, 'I'm not only physically and mentally spent, *but I'm broke as well'.*

Nate and Nathan now sat down on opposing beds, like book ends, regarding each other and the enormity of the situation they both found themselves in. 'Well don't worry too much,' said Nathan, reassuringly, 'I'll smooth things over with your mum, and as luck has it, we are all about ready to ship out tomorrow, and I expect you to be heading off with us'. Hearing this, the smile instantly returned to Nate's face, but he frowned and said, 'But I don't have any money to catch a plane and stuff like that...' Nathan just put his hand on the young man's shoulder and said he would pay for the airfare and any incidentals. 'Damn, you can work it off by visiting me down at the block and polish one or two of the Mustangs or some other bitch-work, like digging my septic system... how does that sound?' The relief upon Nate's face was priceless and he energetically shook his head in agreement. The young man stood to leave but gave Nathan another hug and a mighty handshake. He needed to get back to assist his *Red Cross* buddies but would pack straightaway and be ready to go in the morning. He turned and marched out, noticeably happier than when he entered.

All the while, Garen had been observing Nathan and Nate but hadn't said anything. With the young man out of the room, he spoke. 'He's a fine-looking boy, is that Nate... *sort of reminds me of somebody...*' Being slightly distracted with some packing, Nathan replied, 'And who might that be?' 'Well, if I had to put my money on it... *I would say you!* Same lean but muscular build... similar facial features and dark complexion...same hankering to run off and help someone in trouble... *and the same moody looks...*' Nathan hadn't visited Nate since he was a young boy, many years ago, but he had grown into a strong, good-looking young man. 'Nah, said Nathan, 'I think you're off your meds, or should get on some...*I can't see a resemblance'.* 'Oh well,' said Garen, '*just putting it out there...*' The big Texan turned and as he walked out, said that he would catch up with the fellas later, at their farewell dinner. Nathan offered a quick goodbye, but the seed had been planted... Could Nate be his son, or was Garen just joshing with him? '*He does look a bit like me,* but in some ways he doesn't... geez, I don't know, it was so long ago when I was with Kathy...' Nathan abruptly quit the self-interrogation and decided to text the fantastic news to Kathy, that at least one of the family was coming home and he knew she would be happy with that! However, the nagging thoughts now had life, actively treading just under the surface of his consciousness and wouldn't stop until he finally knew the truth. Now, more than ever, *he had a vital reason to return home...*

Chapter Thirty-Two

PUTTING YOUR LIFE IN ANOTHER MAN'S HANDS...

It wasn't surprising to the men that Cyrus wasn't impressed by the sudden 'defection', as he called it, of many quality trainers from 'his' team. But as Nathan explained it, there were pressing issues for all the men to depart Ukraine and it would be better and safer if they did it in a small group. As he pointed out, their time had been short, but their input had been considerable, and they contributed greatly to the sophistication and reputation of the outfit. The phone call was short and didn't get messy; no one reverted to name-calling or any other insinuations of betrayal. Nathan thanked Cyrus for the opportunity and that was that... 'Phew, glad that is over, that could've gotten ugly...' It was now time for their small troupe to be on their way.

The team had ventured off to have breakfast together as all the other remaining trainers had departed for their assigned duties, either back with the *Legion Obolon* or with other units who were destined for 'action'. The men had decided to eat at 'Lviv Croissant', only a few hundred metres down the road on the majestic Kreschatyk Avenue and where Nathan met up with Nate, who was travelling light, with an old duffle bag that most probably belonged to his father at one time. 'Lviv Croissant' was always popular as the coffee was great and there were so many croissant fillings to choose from. It would be a pleasant way to say farewell to the city, visiting a popular haunt for the last time. After a bit of banter and chatter, Nathan scanned his phone to read a fresh text. He informed the team that Otis was on his way from Lviv and would be arriving at the hotel within the hour, depending upon the traffic and security roadblocks. They had plenty of time as everyone was packed and ready, and all they had to do was ferry their gear downstairs to the van. Although there was a degree of frivolity, Nathan could sense the men were disappointed they had not achieved their objective. It was obvious because everyone was avoiding mentioning anything to do with the missing Australian and not just because Nate was present. Sascha reminded Nathan he would still fall back on his contacts on a regular basis in the vain hope some information surfaced. Bill, Garen and Mickey were also quick to offer their services, in any capacity if they were able... Phil looked at Nathan - he would always be his closest friend and trusted ally and would stick with him, *through thick and thin.* The breakfast ended up turning into the veritable 'last supper' as all the stout men, all the original disciples from the eventful train ride to Medyka from Warsaw, would soon be on their separate ways...

Just when you think you've seen everything... along comes the unexpected. It was Otis, arriving in spectacular fashion in his vehicle. The dark blue, hand-painted, and dilapidated van performed a sharp left-hand turn, much to the ire of the other road users, who beeped and shouted obscenities, as Otis promptly braked directly out front of the hotel. Nathan's team had been loitering about with their gear when they viewed this dynamic driving display, but neither man said a word, they were stunned. And they were all thinking the same thoughts... How were they going to get to Lviv safely and in one piece, with *this guy, and in this wreck?* As the vehicle finally came to rest, two young men exited the van with their armour plates and baggage and scurried away, as if they couldn't escape from Otis and his driving antics fast enough! A few seconds after, an American exited the heap of a vehicle, which was a very early model *Ford Transit* van. He could only be described as a 'bean pole', tall, extremely skinny, even possibly anorexic. He was chewing rapidly, on gum or something, and then spoke even faster... He introduced himself, said they had to leave in five minutes and would need to pick up a female passenger before they left the outskirts of Kyiv;

this pick up being a favour for Cyrus. None of the men argued at the news and loaded their bags smartly into the van, in what space they could, and they chose their seat for the journey. It was already obvious that everything Otis performed was at breakneck speed, but also noticeable was his body trying to play catch up with the rapidity of his mental processes...

Without another word, Otis raced inside the hotel and was back on the avenue within five minutes - just as he had announced and not a second more! The van's driver door was flung open, and he leapt in. 'Okay, boys,' he stated happily, *'time to be gone!'* and upon this cheerful declaration, he started the engine, revved it heavily, a damn sight more than it needed, as if he were a NASCAR driver, gauged a slender gap in the on-coming traffic and *then shot off!* The men held onto their safety belts or whatever was handy. A quick turn down the hill onto the cobbled roadway had everyone bouncing in the back and casting negative looks at the driver. Suddenly, the traffic became thicker, and the vehicle slowed, much to the relief of all the passengers. Ten minutes later, after much crunching of the gears, the van turned into a narrow side street where the girl would be waiting for her ride.

From the outset, it was *painfully obvious* the van was too wide to navigate its way through the narrow corridor. But this wasn't stopping Otis... *Oh no,* he crunched the gears again, complained that he didn't normally drive 'stick', especially in a 'British van', as he edged his way forward... Straightaway, the vehicle grazed its broad body alongside that of a silver-grey Volkswagen sedan, but nevertheless continued, *inch by painful inch*, which did not impress the *Passat* driver at all! Inside, the men winced as they could hear and feel the metallic bumping and grinding. For some inexplicable reason, Otis reversed, again chewing the gears, as if that was a central part of his driving ritual, and the van added more deep scratches and gouges to the greyish sedan! The driver leapt out of his car and began shouting angrily. As luck would have it, the girl they were going to pick up had witnessed this debacle and raced over to assist. Daryna spoke politely with the men in an attempt to pacify him, but he said he was going to call the cops! This was relayed to Otis and the question then became: 'How much did the driver require to cover his expenses, the damage, and his inconvenience?' With no leeway or time to haggle, a figure of a few thousand hryvnias was decided upon. Otis plucked out the compensation from his jacket, in a huge wad of notes, like some gambling high roller. He paid the driver, who instantly progressed from aggressive to passive upon receiving the large sum of money. Daryna bravely jumped into the front seat. Quick introductions were made, Otis attacked the gears, throttled the engine and they were on their way...

The route from the outer suburbs took the van past several quaint villages that had been devastated by the Russian attacks. Nathan had witnessed the brutality of these air strikes all over Kyiv, but the hits had been piecemeal, here and there, and nothing like the devastation he now witnessed. He truly felt sorry for these villagers and what they must have endured... It was obvious these hamlets weren't military targets but spitefully destroyed as some form of Russian payback! The traffic was extremely light... a car *here*... a truck *there*... Also, there were burnt out military vehicles from both sides, torn and twisted and resting in awkward positions alongside bridges and concrete bridge columns along the major highway. This is where the Russians had been halted... There was mostly silence from the rear of the vehicle, unlike the front where Otis was *running at the mouth* faster than the revolutions of the engine! He was babbling on about this and that and was an expert on everything.... In between his declarations to Daryna about his life and loves, he mentioned he was from New York and was in Ukraine by the grace of his family's money. According to him, they were stinking rich! However, the men in the back weren't convinced with his stories... or their authenticity. They had come across guys like this before... Like all the other 'lost souls' over here, he too was looking for 'something' or 'someone' to validate his existence.

The vehicle had been travelling for a number of hours, and it would still be many more before they encountered the outskirts of Lviv; probably later in the evening but hopefully before the ten pm curfews. Unfortunately, most of the gas stations were closed and those that were open were ordered by the government to sell only thirty litres of diesel to each customer: a fuel conservation method. How long this war was going to go for was anybody's guess. After driving past several closed gas stations in the last half hour, the inviting bright neon lights of an open filling station appeared further down the road. As if on cue, everyone perked up in their seats as this would be a great time to stretch cold and cramped legs and purchase coffee and a few snacks. The van turned off the road and then swung across to an empty lane to re-fuel. *Without any warning*, the van clipped the bollard that protected the fuel bowsers and came to an almighty stop! Straightaway, Otis jumped out to investigate the extent of the damage... Not a word was spoken by anyone inside the vehicle as everyone was dumbfounded... Two accidents in one day! *WTF*... Who would believe this? *Who in God's name drives like this!*

The console operator inside the gas station prese-nted a dumbstruck look on her face and instantly her companion hurried out to see what had just occurred. More loud voices, gesticulating by the Ukrainian attendant and soon more cash was being pulled out of Otis's coat pocket. Phil, sporting a slight grin, decided to state the obvious, '*Damn, this is going to be one expensive trip for Otis*'. A few moments after his second payoff, Otis opened the sliding side door and gruffly announced we would have thirty minutes break while he re-fuelled and refreshed himself. As the passengers walked quickly towards the gas station's shop and restaurant, they could hear Otis swearing to himself – '*Damn British vans...*' *Stupid seat on the other side...*' '*Fucking stick shift gears...*' Mumble, mumble, cuss, cuss, expletive and so forth and this went on and on the whole time he was pouring the limited number of litres of diesel into the vehicle's tank.

As it turned out, the group were the only people being served. Hot food was off the menu but other snacks and things like protein bars could be bought. The main thing was they could get a hot coffee into themselves and stand for a while; it was particularly frigid and cramped in the back of the van. The vehicle would have to refuel again before they reached Lviv and it was already starting to become dim in the early afternoon; the trickery of the dark foreboding clouds and faint light seemed to forever announce the end to the day's illumination but now, darkness was creeping, inch by inch, across the land. Not a lot was being said as the group was tired, particularly from the strain of the 'madcap driving' and the general resignation that their time in Ukraine was over; the prospect of an awfully long journey ahead of them seemed to sap the animation from one and all...

Nathan was still recovering from pneumonia but managed to chat to Nate about his various adventures in Europe and the 'missing years' between him and his 'old friends'. It was Phil who made light conversation with Daryna. Her story was that she was a student and English interpreter who had provided interpretive services for Cyrus and his 'eclectic' group over the last month. With a break in her studies, she had decided to visit her parents, who had relocated west to Lviv. Daryna had been beseeched by her parents to move to the relative safety of the western oblast, but defiantly she refused. Her *home* was Kyiv. Her *friends* were in Kyiv and so was *her life*. She would not be intimidated by Putin. 'A very brave young girl' Nathan thought, and all the best to her and Ukraine. This was the measure of the Ukrainian people, summed up in the *chutzpah* of a tough, young girl! For all the hyperbaric weapons, rockets, and tanks the Russians threw at them, Daryna was not prepared to give an inch. *Not a damn inch!* Ukraine was *everything...* Nathan thought about his own people and wondered if the same courage and boldness would apply in an equally threatening situation. He wasn't so sure anymore...

Just as Nathan pondered that thought, Otis sauntered over and said flatly, 'Time to go'. The vehicle was quickly re-loaded with the travellers, and they were off again, with the crunching of more gears. By now, it was an early evening's half-light, and the headlights of the vehicle trickled a beam that was barely discernible to the driver, let alone the passengers. *Dodgy headlights! Another vehicle defect!* Soon, heavy, blinding rain began to fall, to the point it bounced forcefully upwards on the black road in front of them as they sped steadily and *extremely fast* towards their destination.

Heavy haulage trucks were passing on the other side

of the road and came too close to the van too many times. Otis was drinking can after can of *Red Bull* and spending more time on his conversations than on his driving skills. After one near miss too many, Nathan yelled out, *'How about slowing the fuck down and concentrating on the road... We all want to get to Lviv in one piece!!'* Sounding more like a command than an instruction, Otis throttled back to a more manageable speed. Hell, they all wanted to get to Lviv, but not in a pine box! This was a side most people never saw of Nathan. He tried to be the 'nice guy', the 'peacemaker', but sometimes, when people pushed his buttons, *the gloves were off...*

Before they knew it, it was time to refuel again...they were only eighty kilometres from Lviv. An old balding man was the attendant who sat at a two-way comms window and the rest of the station was locked tight as a drum. Surprisingly enough, the attendant didn't care how much fuel Otis required as the day had been slow, and he was about ready to close. Then another slight problem presented itself... Otis had driven straight past the pump, only very slightly but the fuel nozzle wouldn't reach the van's tank. As much as he tried, the lanky American couldn't reverse the van without stalling. Nathan told him to get out of the vehicle, and he reversed the van or otherwise they'd be there all night. *'Fuck me,'* he thought, 'I know Americans generally drive automatics, but this guy is the worst driver I've come across in my travels...' At least they only had an hour or so to go, but the time was becoming critical as it was just after eight-thirty and curfew was close at hand. As Nathan looked around at his compatriots, he could see they were all becoming more fatigued the longer this driving saga continued. The day's adventures had become a sapping journey...

By now the roads were 'car free' and they could make out the faint lights of the city on the glowing horizon. As it happened, they didn't need to go all the way into Lviv but just to its eastern side, where an apartment 'safe house' was awaiting them. In another twenty minutes, they entered the outskirts of Lviv, only fifteen minutes before curfew! *Tik tock... tik tock... tik tock...* Tension was building in the vehicle. Daryna would be dropped off first as her apartment was en route to their lodgings. But, just as things seemed to be going smoother, the Lviv Police appeared, flashed their lights, pulling the van over to inquire as to why they were out driving so late, in a vehicle with such bad headlights. Luckily for all, *it was Daryna to the rescue!*

A story was presented that these men had been greatly assisting the Ukrainian military in the war effort and this was the only ride they could get back to Lviv; the frenetic day had galloped into the realm of night due to the bad road and weather conditions, which is why they were driving so late at this time. Luckily for the men, it wasn't so much what Daryna said, but the way she said it that convinced the police. A quick *'Hurry up and get on your way'* was indignantly ordered, and the officers sped off. A group sigh of relief was felt, and an appreciative cheer rang out for Daryna! Two minutes later, a fast turn of the corner, a slide over some wet tram tracks and another right turn and they were at the spot where Daryna would exit the van and be on her way. The tough Ukrainian girl expressed her thanks and goodbyes and was off like a shot, disappearing quickly into the shadows and forever imprinted into the memories of the men.

Time was running out, and the vehicle still had a few kilometres to go... The van turned a corner and then had to negotiate a wet cobbled road, on a steep hill that with a testing gradient, *even for a seasoned driver.* Otis made the rookie mistake of slowing to a complete stop before he changed down in gear. The van's wheels slipped and spun on the wet and oily surface – *no traction at all* – and he braked to prevent the vehicle rolling backwards any further. *Mickey leapt to the rescue before anyone else had a chance to...* He barked for Otis to get out of the driver's seat and then he took control. Mickey let the vehicle roll back slowly to a flat spot on the road and then accelerated fast enough up the hill to maintain a grip on the surface without spinning out as he selected the appropriate gear. He turned to Otis, 'I may as well keep driving, *you navigate, okay*?' Otis was relieved to hear this and said they were only two streets away from their destination. In no time, the vehicle stopped at the apartment and the men quickly grabbed their belongings, entered, and walked up to the first floor.

The building dated back to the beginning of the nineteenth century and was spacious with large rooms to accommodate ten to fifteen people. By this time, Nathan was beginning to feel really ill again, with a slight headache as well, and announced he needed to 'rack out'. A room was offered that was already housing a visitor, but Nathan was fine with this. As no other beds or couches were available, he took out his air mattress and sleeping bag and chose a corner by the far wall. Having undressed, inserted ear plugs, and positioned his 'piss bottle', Nathan shut his eyes and briefly thought, 'I'm done with today...hope tomorrow turns out better...' Some noise and talking was going on in the kitchen area as people were being introduced but Nathan didn't care. *He was on his own time now....*

Chapter Thirty-Three:

JUST ONE DAY AT A TIME...

Nathan had slept soundly through the night, aided by fatigue and illness, and only hearing the odd muffled noise of someone talking in the 'wee hours' of the morning. He hadn't really absorbed the layout of his room last evening but as he lay in his sleeping bag he gazed up and about, taking in the ornate and somewhat *baroque* figurines and other art that decorated the high walls; the room was fashioned in what would be described as an old *rococo* style that would not be found back home. 'Well,' enough of this stargazing nonsense, *time to get up!* Mickey had shared the queen-sized bed with a stranger; Phil and Nate had found space in an adjoining room. The bed was now vacant...people were up and about. As he left the room, he met a couple of Brits who were in transit to somewhere else in Ukraine, to a place that Nathan couldn't even pronounce the name. They didn't say what their task was, but he could see they were also ex-military and most probably up to something...

Otis was in the tiny kitchen area, smoking and drinking a *Kozatska Rada*, the Ukrainian version of *Red Bull*, and having a heated conversation with someone on his phone. 'Always a drama with this guy,' Nathan thought, but he would coax the American to help him with changing his flight details as he was a whiz when it came to computers. At least he would be good for something! He could hear Mickey and Nate talking quietly to Phil in the other room and decided to pour himself a freshly brewed coffee. This would keep him occupied for the next twenty minutes or so. Otis obligingly helped Nathan with his flight change and, as he stumbled out of the kitchen, trying not to get into anyone's personal space, he found himself gazing at a very athletic looking American woman wearing a singlet, probably in her early thirties, smashing out a body strength exercise routine in the large corridor. The lean and fit woman was performing pushups, lunges, burpees, and star jumps. In-between her routine, she was stretching. With sweat on her brow and a heaving chest, she stopped and introduced herself to Nathan as Cherie, with a genial smile. 'Hi, I believe you're Nathan, do you have time to talk?' The young woman quickly extended her hand to shake and gestured for Nathan to sit down on a small fabric covered chair in the hallway. 'What can you tell me about Cyrus and the training mission in Kyiv?' *'How much time have you got?'* was Nathan's sardonic reply.

Cherie was a Marine Corps logistics officer who knew some of the ex-Marine Corps guys who had been training in Kyiv. It had been strongly suggested to Cyrus that the team needed to bring in a logistics specialist to run the day-to-day operations connected with training – transport, stores, venues, contacts, and things like that. It was painfully clear to most people that Cyrus had taken on too much. His stress invariably led to issues with instructors and ancillary people connected to the program and was amplified greatly by his mood swings, especially when connected with the 'mind altering substances' he was known to ingest. Cherie had interviewed Phil and Mickey earlier, but now wanted Nathan's assessment. Nathan was never keen to talk out of school, but this was no 'junior prom', and he thought it was vital to let her know what she was getting herself in to... *So, he laid it out.... warts and all...* Nathan didn't hold back and spoke of the drug abuse, the conflicts with Cyrus and the Ukrainian leadership, his connections with outlaw motorcycle club members, the numerous and fantastic promises that had been made, the dodgy relationship with the *Legion Obolon* unit, crazy Manis, and some of the dubious trainers that had become part of Cyrus's team, or the more accurate description as a modern day 'wild bunch'! For men that had been in the military, there were those individuals who came across as nothing more than self-serving pimps and mercenaries, only out for themselves. Sure, the men weren't serving anymore, but their behaviour hardly resembled anything that was remotely regimental or honourable.

Having absorbed Nathan's straightforward comments, Cherie appeared unfazed, judging by the expression on her face. She informed Nathan that she wasn't all that surprised by his critique, as she had already heard of some of the bizarre goings on of this training team, and how the operation could only be described as 'a cluster fuck', to use an old military idiom. As far as Cyrus went, she said he sounded like a used car salesman or a sleazy politician; plenty of wild deals and insincere promises that were always too good to be true. Her trip to Ukraine was a favour to former comrades and a personal commitment to see what she could do to help the Ukrainian people. As far as the Marine Corps went, her adventure was being kept on the 'downlow'. 'Well,' there you have it, all the bare bones,' said Nathan. 'Are you still headed to Kyiv?' Undeterred by all this, Cherie said 'yes'. 'May as well, I'm over here now, right?' Nathan dipped his head in respectful agreement and looked around to see Phil coming down the hallway. 'Mate, what do you reckon, pack up and leave for the bus station in half an hour,' was all he said, and Nathan nodded again. 'Do us a favour and give Nate a heads up?' Phil gave the thumbs up gesture and wandered off to alert the young lad. It was time to get cracking, he left Cherie and went back to the room where Mickey was just sorting out his gear. Timings having been outlined; it was now time to leave.

The thirty minutes lapsed surprisingly quickly and

soon Nathan, Mickey, Phil, and Nate were standing out front of the refined old building, in the cold, dank street, their rucksacks perched against their legs, waiting for a cab to ferry them to the major bus station. Here they would board a bus to transport them to over the border to Krakow, then on to Warsaw and home. Garen, Bill and Sascha had ventured out to see the men off, as they were leaving the next day. The two Americans had a reunion with other American friends planned for tomorrow. They would go home via Poland and Germany. Sascha still had a few anxious days to wait before the arrival of his family. The men were fidgety, as if something had to be said, and someone was waiting for somebody to speak up first. There really wasn't any need for drawn out goodbyes. Each man thanked and wished each comrade a safe, pleasant, and quick trip home. They had been through some tough and wild times together but had come through them for the better. Strangers had become close friends; friends had now become brethren. In a way, a *'band of brothers'* was created by the war. *What came next was a surprise to the whole group!* A beige *Renault* cab turned the corner and pulled up in front of Nathan. Out stepped Cyrus, partnered with a large and sinister looking Ukrainian man that was unknown to all. Cyrus began by saying he was glad he caught up with everyone before they left and offered everyone a return gig with the team, should they decide to revisit Ukraine. He finished by stating that he was attempting to secure free airflights to Poland for trainers. 'Well,' Nathan thought 'what do you know, *a fucking car salesman to the end!'* As it turned out, the cab was now theirs and the four men from the 'antipodes' enthusiastically jumped in, waving goodbye to their comrades who were shivering on the sidewalk.

A tinge of sadness descended upon Nathan as their cab manoeuvred the wet and busy streets of Lviv. Here they were, making their way home and he still hadn't located Steve or had any encouraging news for Kathy. He felt like he had failed, which was a sensation not normally experienced. He looked around the cab and was proud to be sitting next to stellar men of immense integrity and resilience but could sense that they were tired and had reached the end of their emotional and physical rope. The cab was silent... In no time, the *Renault* pulled into the chaotic bus station. Buses of all description, age, colour and make were arriving and departing, yet in the middle of all this confusion and diesel fumes, an elderly Ukrainian woman, wearing a filthy old pinafore, swept the laneways and emptied bins, without being hit. It seemed like a miracle, but she was oblivious to any activity outside of her work and appeared as if she had performed the ritual over a thousand times. The men dropped their gear just under an electric sign that designated the numerous destinations and the accompanying bus. Of course, the destination language was only in Ukrainian! Mickey raced inside to the information counter to see what bus they needed and what time it would leave. A lone American, most probably a man in his late fifties and looking like a businessman or professional, came over and asked if he could wait with the men as he was on his own and felt safer being with other Westerners; he had overheard Nate speaking English. 'Sure', said Phil, and they began chatting. Mickey came out looking flustered... Apparently, the information people weren't much help but another multi-lingual passenger assisted Mickey with his questions and soon the tickets were bought.

As it turned out, the American was a highly rated physician from a prominent hospital in the 'States' and had offered his services to medical authorities in Ukraine. Again, the 'kingdom culture' raised its ugly head and he was shuffled along from one hospital to another. As he explained and then pleaded to the authorities, he would do whatever the hospital officials wanted him to do, even just assisting with surgery, but that seemed too much of an invasion for the bureaucrats and senior doctors. The fatigued looking American was disillusioned and was on his way home, like so many other dejected Westerners. He had planned to visit a few countries in Europe, and was taking the afternoon bus to somewhere else in Poland. Nathan and Nate went and bought coffees and the men chatted and shuffled about to keep warm in the 'glacial' bus station. Good company always helps to pass the time, and the lively and interesting discourse with the American had certainly achieved that. Before too long, a newish looking bus to Krakow arrived and there was a rush to board the large vehicle by eager locals. Gear was quickly stowed, tickets viewed and stamped, and everyone took their assigned seats. It looked to be a full bus; mostly occupied by desperate looking women and children. The boys wished the affable American all the best and occupied their bus seats.

With all on board, the juggernaut reversed out of its bay, faced down the road and soon it was on its way to the border. A few additional stops were made, dropping off and picking up passengers, but for the most part the metal leviathan smoothly and efficiently made its way west. In just under an hour, they were approaching the Ukraine/ Polish border, when all physical and mental momentum came to an annoying, grinding halt. Trucks, cars, vans, and buses were being funnelled into two or three queues of about a kilometre in so in length, from a vast number of arterial roads that led to the checkpoint area where passports were being verified. There would be no issue with any of this if the vehicles were moving but not a single car or bus was edging or crawling forward, as if the guards in the office had gone on a 'go-slow' or a complete strike! Drivers began to let the passengers out; especially those with nicotine cravings. In fact, most passengers alighted vehicles, standing in awe at the inaction before them. Minutes turned into an hour, and then an hour became seven hours, before Nathan and Nate's bus finally moved to the checkpoint. During that time, babies had been repeatedly pacified by parents and elderly passengers suffered heavily under the gross ineptitude of officialdom.

After the bus ground to a halt at the designated checkpoint, a blonde female Ukrainian customs officer stepped on board, proceeded down the aisle, and demanded passports as she went. Upon receiving non-Ukrainian passports, she would inquire brusquely in English, *'What was the purpose of your visit to Ukraine?'* Nathan said simply and softly, 'Humanitarian work, first aid assistance'. This satisfied the officer and she moved to the next person. A young man travelling to Germany on business produced his credentials and permits to depart Ukraine and the officer moved on again. Finally, she came to a Ukrainian couple in their fifties. The man looked like an academic or some kind of office worker... He had that 'soft' appearance... What seemed like an interrogation began, and the man and the officer traded heated words. Quite suddenly, the fiery debate ended, and the officer loudly ordered the couple off the bus and into the passport office. The passengers waited for around twenty minutes before the same female officer returned, and passports were redistributed among the passengers. The Ukrainian couple did not take up their seats... The driver was given the all clear and the bus moved forward, unhurriedly, toward the Polish checkpoint. The young girl sitting next to Nathan commented upon the absence of the couple to which Nathan replied, 'It could be worse...' With a quizzical look on her face she inquired, *'How could it be worse?'* to which Nathan flatly stated, *'It could be me...'* The girl sort of got the half-joke but struggled to understand Nathan's 'black' humour. Maybe she was tired as she still had a ten-hour journey to go to her final destination – Germany. There was no time for anyone to console themselves with the detaining of the Ukrainian couple. He knew the rules – no males to leave Ukraine who were under the age of sixty. *He took a chance and failed...* In fact, other men had been caught wearing women's clothes in a brazen attempt to flee the country! At the Polish checkpoint everyone had to collect their belongings and feed them through the security scanners. Passports were efficiently checked but at least the Polish authorities had their procedures down to an art form and within twenty minutes the bus was on its way to Krakow. Nathan didn't know how Mickey, Phil or Nate felt but he was relieved to be out of Ukraine. They were safe and only so many hours from Krakow...

It had been an excruciatingly long day. Nathan tried to nap as the evening took hold. Lights had been extinguished on the bus and only the faint hum of the bitumen road could be heard above the occasional snort and snore. The next time he opened his eyes the infinite glare of the city lay before him. He wriggled to sit up in his seat and felt hot and clammy, largely due to the bus heater pumping out buckets of hot air, and no longer a fever. The bus motored through the city for another twenty minutes, twisting and turning through the many chicanes of the metropolis after the long and tedious highways. Finally, a concrete bus station appeared, the bus slowed, navigated the lanes, and halted. The front and side doors opened and, again, like the proverbial 'clown car,' all the passengers spewed out onto the sidewalk as fast as they could. In a matter of minutes, it was only the four men who were still standing there. The station was silent and completely vacant. But they were in no hurry, they didn't have a connection to make. They negotiated the step leading up to the roadway carefully with their heavy gear, and they were on the upper level of the station and at the taxi rank within a couple of minutes. Timing couldn't get any better, as a *Peugeot* cab pulled straight up. The men loaded their luggage into the trunk and got in. Nathan spoke to the older driver brightly, 'Radisson, if you please', and the driver accelerated from the curb. Damn, what a long day it had been, but Nathan knew they were only minutes away from a quality hotel. He had decided to lash out, sparing no expense this time. A warm shower and clean, cotton sheets were waiting for them, and this promise of luxury the only thing that now occupied their tired, blank minds.

Chapter Thirty-Four:

TAKE THE LONG WAY HOME...

It was extremely late in the morning when the fatigued men rose from their deep slumber. It had been close to one a.m. when they had checked into the hotel. The sanctuary and solitude of their luxury, family size room was just what they needed before washing, and completely crashing out. The hotel breakfast sitting was only ten minutes away from closing when the men plonked heavily down at the table, much to the ire of one of the young female waiters who was in the process of cleaning up another table. Now, she wouldn't get her coffee break until this table had been served and she could tell just by looking at the men that they were going to be a while... *She knew the signs...* Eggs – fried or scrambled, crispy bacon, copious servings of heavy buttered toast and cereal, followed by liberal servings of strong coffee and sweet juice.

During breakfast, the small talk centred around how

they were all feeling, now that they were safe from the war in Ukraine. It seemed surreal to be the potential target for a Russian Kh-55SM cruise missile one day, and the next, enjoying a hearty banquet in relative peace and safety, in a tranquil country only separated from Ukraine by only thin wavy lines drawn on a map. They all agreed to stay at the hotel for another couple of days before catching the train to Warsaw, and that they would stay one more day in the capital, followed by the long flight home. This way they could wind down and relax a little before departing Europe. This was Nathan's suggestion as he desperately needed a few more days of rest to continue his recovery from pneumonia. They mapped out a few activities for their stay in the charming and ancient castled city, once the capital of Poland and an influential academic and cultural hub. The friends planned to take it slowly and enjoy their stopover and recharge their batteries...

The two days in Krakow came and went like any other fun-filled sojourn. It wasn't intentional but Nathan and his friends ended up doing a lot more than they had thought. Besides eating well, they had taken peaceful, leisurely walks around the pretty city square and its adjoining gardens, absorbing the beautiful, historic scenery and the serene impression of normality. People of all ages walked small dogs, couples jogged and sweated in sheer freedom, and young lovers kissed on old and worn park benches; life was very much like it was back home... There weren't any camouflaged block houses to contend with, or rusty girder tank entrapments to avoid, or Ukrainian military with weapons patrolling the streets, and there certainly was no evening curfew! Upon this casual reflection, Nathan was suddenly taken back to another sinister side of the war and the story of how a young girl had been murdered in one of the blockhouses; a weapon sling used to strangle her... He needed to re-connect with the present and clear his head of such sad and debilitating thoughts. He concentrated on their presence at a small, back lane tattoo parlour and Mickey's decision to get a Ukrainian trident tattoo on the back of his neck. By Australian prices, it turned out to be extremely cheap, and the finished product was very well done. The men had decided to visit *Auschwitz* and *Birkenau* concentration camps as the hotel could arrange a tour, and these sites were around ninety minutes away by small coach. This side-trip was intended to be a history lesson for Nate on 'The Holocaust', as well as paying their respects to the people who had suffered terribly at the hands of the Nazis. More than expected, the tour was very confronting, and the men were very sombre and somewhat shaken by their experience. They reflected upon the many parallels between Hitler and Putin, and how it seemed incredulous that in the new century, there were still megalomanic leaders hell bent on global domination and causing death and destruction. It was obvious to all who attended the concentration camps tour that humans will never understand the precious sanctity of life and happiness...

The brief vacation was over before they knew it, and a taxi was taken to the train station early on Monday morning. The journey to Warsaw was slow and uneventful; the exact opposite of the saga they had endured on the train to Medyka, only a month before. This time, the four or five hours it took to reach the capital was punctuated by brief naps, snacking, and pleasantly enjoying the country scenery. Before long, the train arrived at its destination and the men, like automatons, secured their belongings and walked briskly along the cool streets to the *Holiday Inn*. The sight of the grey, monolithic hotel, standing out amongst the Warsaw skyline was welcoming to Nathan as any old, charming friend, and within the hour, a beer, most probably a Czech pilsner, was being consumed in the downstairs bar area. A stroll, and another beer or two were followed by an early night... Phil, Nate, and Nathan's flight was mid-morning, with Mickey leaving after midday.

At this stage there were no feelings of childlike excitement at the prospect of returning home. It was noticeable the men were extremely tired, judging by their slowness to execute basic tasks, but somedays you just have to put one foot in front of the other... This was how it felt on the last day in Europe. Get up and wash. Go to breakfast. Pack gear and check room. Go to the lobby and get reception to book the taxi. Get in the taxi and arrive at the airport. This is how the morning played out. *That simple*... Time to check in. Mickey had been an invaluable member of the team, and it was fantastic that Nathan had caught up with him once more. They planned to stay in touch. The time came for Phil, Nathan, and Nate to go to their boarding area, and they kept it simple. Each man gave Mickey a big man-hug and a strong 'biker' handshake and left it at that. No words... No gushy sermons or cliched orations... No tears... They turned and briskly walked to gate twenty-nine and didn't look back - neither man knowing this would be the last time they would see their close friend, alive...

Having smoothly negotiated passport control and locating their boarding gates, it was time for Nathan and Phil to bid Nate farewell. Nate's flight had him travelling to Abu Dhabi where he would transfer to a connecting flight to Brisbane, and Phil and Nathan were on an *Airbus* headed to Dubai, and then onto Melbourne. Before they walked to their respective boarding areas, Nathan took Nate aside and sat him down for a man-to-man chat. 'Okay, I know you'll get some grief from your Mum on your return, but don't worry, all will be forgotten in a while, and you'll laugh on this in the years to come... trust me. *But promise me one thing, don't do anymore crazy shit like this as the biggest pain you can ever inflict upon yourself is when you disappoint your mother, and you see the hurt in her eyes... that damage lasts forever... it never leaves you... believe me, I know from first-hand experience!* Now go, catch your flight, and give your Mum a big hug for me when you see her!' Nate rose and Nathan could see the young man was tearing up... he was at odds with what he wanted to do... He didn't know whether to hug Nathan or offer a sloppy soliloquy to his 'Godfather'... Nathan made his mind up for him.... 'Hurry up, go, go, *or you'll miss your damn flight!*' Nathan saved the young man from making a 'scene' and firmly shook Nate's hand, before he promptly turned to his right and trotted down the soft-tiled walkway, disappearing into the throng of international passengers.

Not long after seeing Nate off, Phil and Nathan boarded their flight and took their allocated business class seats. As far as the two old friends were concerned, they didn't care what time they got into Melbourne...as long as they were inching their way back to Australia. Soon, the plane was creeping onto the blackened runway and the mighty engines powered up to a screaming pitch. Nathan slowly looked across at Phil and said, with obvious heartfelt intensity, '*Thanks, old friend,*' and then turned to face forward for take-off. In an instant, the mammoth airplane shuddered as it catapulted down the runway before rising to pierce into the evening darkness. Now, only a flicker of a navigational light was discernible in the heavens as the mighty plane headed southeast. They were *finally* on their way home...

End of Part One

Part Two

FINISHING THE JOB...

'The Warrior masters his realm. He does not flee from his fear, he conquers it.'

Lt. Col. Dave Grossman

Chapter Thirty-Five:

ONCE MORE, INTO THE BREECH...

The mixture of frosty Ukrainian beer and the challenging experience of *Banya* was taking its toll on Nathan... In and out of the burning sauna like a jack rabbit, being doused under a glacial shower, perspiring heavily, and becoming slightly intoxicated isn't a great recipe for one's health, especially for a *Banya* rookie! Although he thought he was doing it tough, some of his Ukrainian hosts were disappointed there wasn't 'harder' liquor on offer. As one towelled, sweating man commented, with much disdain, *'Beer without vodka is a waste of money!'* Like anyone else, Nathan liked a good drink, but was so glad that vodka wasn't on the table. Otherwise, in the company of these men, he would be soon residing under it! Aside from the physical flatness and the slight 'beer buzz' he was now experiencing, he was also sensing a degree of profound guilt that his best friend still hadn't been properly located, though he knew he was alive. Nathan had been back in Ukraine nearly a week now. It had been nine weeks since the initial call from Kathy and it had only been five weeks ago that Nathan had returned home as a worn-out figure of a man, and to a number of home truths... Without a doubt, he was still exhausted, mentally and physically, and he knew it. But what other options did he have? He was now having doubts as to whether he could or would ever succeed in rescuing Steve and this was playing heavily on his mind... This feeling was new to Nathan as he had always triumphed in whatever he had set out to do; be it was his military training, his academic studies, or whatever he set his mind to. However, this time, he had been extremely fortunate to return home at all; after his close call with an almost fatal case of pneumonia and the violent incident with the *Director* and his henchmen!

Nathan put these new-found feelings down to his age, and the decline of his confidence, which had been gathering momentum, albeit gradually, over the last year. Nathan wasn't kidding himself... Although he was just over fifty, he had a damn sight more miles on the clock than most people and the psychological scars to go with it... The regression shadowed him daily... a loss of memory here... excruciating aches and pains there... a fear to commit this way or that... Of course, he had glimpsed, *oh so briefly*, at the mental paralysis of self-doubt before, but had brushed it away aggressively, like some pesky insect. Now, the inner conviction and determination to achieve goals had diminished... *the burgeoning spectre of 'middle age' uncertainty* was slowly assuming control, wandering aimlessly but regularly in the plateaus of his mind and soul, debilitating any thought of action. What was more critical and of greater concern to Nathan was that his innate power to always project himself physically, but now the rugged, physical side of his character was, unavoidably, in decline... *He knew this...* and it irritated and frustrated him all at the same time! *'Damn it, getting old is the pits,'* he thought angrily. He was reminded by his mother's prophetic words from decades ago, that he too would know what it would be like to be 'elderly' one day. 'No-one cares about you when you get to your used-by-date and it gets harder as you get older, *not easier'*, she would say. To Nathan's way of thinking, he wasn't likely to last that long... But with death having recently tapped him on the shoulder, he was cherishing his mortality, just as the next person would.

Upon his return to Australia, he had spent nearly another week convalescing at his beloved bush block, continuing his rest and medications. The familiar native vegetation of home had been a welcome vista, a real tonic, and he felt now that it was time to slowly get back into physical shape. Maybe an improvement in his fitness would bolster his mental attitude and confidence. Nathan certainly hoped so... Small sessions on the treadmill and rowing machine had now developed into lengthier sessions as his strength and lung capacity gradually returned. In a physical comparison with nature, it was akin to the trickling of the tide before the overwhelming embrace of the ocean's force. For all the physical effort, it still takes time... The foundations of Nathan's physical well-being had taken a beating. In something that resembled a *Rocky Balboa* movie and the lengthy process it took the pugilist from 'Philly' to prepare to fight *Apollo Creed*, the same applied to Nathan. Light weight reps soon became heavy, gruelling weight reps. Cardio sessions increased, the bag punching bag workouts resumed and eventually, he was able to perform his favoured 'Spartan' routine; six sets of exercises using six muscle groups, multiplied five times. Protein drinks and bars and hard-boiled eggs were frequently consumed, along with *Red Bull* or strong coffee stimulants; anything to help him re-build muscle, physical vitality, and stamina. Some days he was reminded of the acute impact of his illness and how it had taken a profound toll upon his physicality. Without doubt, he was making good, steady progress but not as rapidly as he hoped.

Nathan had only been home for a few days when he had decided, without regret, to purchase his airline ticket back to Ukraine. His reasons were two-fold. The prime mission was to still locate Steve and return him to Kathy, preferably alive, or dead, if it came to that. It was of utmost importance for him to make good on his pledge. Also, he had enjoyed training and conversing with the robust and friendly Ukrainians and wanted to continue this experience. He had developed an affinity and admiration for these gruff, loud talking but determined men, and he

felt a sense of camaraderie he had not known in years...
The plain truth was they would need all the assistance they
could get in defeating the Russians, the *Orcs... the merciless
invaders...* and he had, with not much surprise, also found
the 'calling'.

Nathan had communicated with Kathy several times
since his return and they began to chat like the 'old days',
when they were young, carefree and without a single worry
in the world. Having Nate back home was a blessing and
Kathy couldn't express her gratitude to Nathan enough...
Of course, Nathan was repeatedly thanked for going to
such to such lengths to locate her wayward husband, but
he could sense she had given up hope of ever seeing him
alive. Her flat, uninterested tone, coupled with a select
negative word or phrase here and there gave her away...
Their love had died and was another casualty of the war.
Kathy had offered to fly down from Queensland to catch
up, but Nathan thought this to be an unbelievably bad
idea at this time. Even after many years, he still harboured
deep feelings for Kathy and could sense she felt the same,
and he didn't want these sentiments to obscure his focus.
He was unwaveringly loyal to his friend and the last thing
he needed was to create a 'love bubble' for a middle-aged
romance! He may have been misreading the cues, but
it was not the time for a reunion that could lead to who
knows what... A few credible excuses were employed to
fend off a visit, and Kathy seemed satisfied with that. As
far as his familial connection with Nate went, now was not

the time to seriously engage with that conundrum either...

Nathan had been in regular contact with Phil, who was heavily embroiled in a what would be a long and drawn-out divorce. Phil had also purchased a flight back to Ukraine as he was also committed to stay with his best friend, to locate Steve, and to help the Ukrainians as best as he could. Besides chomping at the bit to return to Europe, the major motivating factor in the last week was the brilliant information from Garen. *Some definitive news at last...* A dishevelled looking Steve Holland had been sighted by the big Texan while he was part of a foreign security team that was now protecting the *Hospitallers* in the warring Donbas region. He had only just been identified as his medic vehicle was pulling out of Kyiv for the arduous drive to the front. Steve's identity had been verified as Garen had spoken to the mission commander who confirmed the Aussie was 'riding shotgun' for the paramedics. *Finally... Thankfully...* At least they all knew Steve was alive and still in one piece! If he survived this ordeal at the front, he would be back in Kyiv in around six weeks, the usual time for the deployment. There was no getting around this timeframe as the deployments were locked in and it would be tantamount to finding a needle in a haystack should Nathan even attempt to locate him in that region. 'Damn', he thought, *'we never get a break, not even the slightest!'* As it so happened, Garen had only missed the guy by a few minutes! Again, reflected Nathan, 'at least I know my old mate is still alive, but why won't he come the hell home?!' This is what was so puzzling... Steve had assured Kathy he would only be gone for a short time... He survived the attack on the army barracks... and probably a lot more danger along the way, roaming all over Ukraine, and now he is off to the front. The pondering continued, 'why is he still in Ukraine and for God's sakes, *what's keeping him here?*' Without doubt, Nathan wouldn't know the answer to that last disturbing question until he finally met his old comrade in Kyiv, in six weeks' time. In the meantime, there was still a lot more training and opportunities to be had by Western training teams....

Chapter Thirty-Six

GORODISCHE CALLING...

Nathan and Phil's feet hadn't touched the ground since they returned to Europe... A forgettable flight and a boring layover in Helsinki was followed by a brief stop in Warsaw. There would be no time for a pleasant sojourn in the *Holiday Inn* and scenic walks in the Polish capital this time! What they didn't know was that an arduous nineteen-hour bus ride to the Ukraine capital lay in front of them! This time, they proceeded straight to the bus terminal from the airport. A *melee* of tired and grubby travellers was all they came upon when they strolled into the terminus. Being non-European travellers, the men genuinely believed they would quickly purchase a fare and be on their way, but their naïve optimism was utterly misplaced and inconsistent with the situation before them. An incredibly long, ragged line ran from the one tiny wire and glass window that was dispensing tickets, managed by a stern, elderly woman; another self-important official with 'resting bitch face' who didn't give a toss what people wanted or how long it took for worn-out passengers to be on their way! It felt like mental torture to purchase a simple ticket...there is simply no other way to describe it!

While certainly not as long or equalling the gravity of the following situations, Nathan could only imagine his circumstances and its accompanying psychological cruelty to other dire periods in time, of the rigours of standing in a long, slow food queue during the *Great Depression*, waiting to be rescued while huddled and shivering on a *Titanic* lifeboat, or trudging in knee length mud to the front in *World War One*. Sometimes the long mental blow far outweighs the physical insult... *At least a straightforward punch is over and done with!* After an extraordinarily painful wait of many hours, they purchased two one-way tickets, having to finally convince themselves that the tickets they had bought, with little help from the vendor who spoke zero English or cared, were the correct ones! Now ladened with more physical and mental exhaustion, the men wandered off to the find their bus.

It wasn't completely unexpected, but the nineteen-hour bus ride dragged on for much longer than the designated time as there were mandatory smoke breaks every two hours, which suited Phil and the various Europeans who incessantly puffed or vaped. By chance, the men had met a Canadian EOD (Explosive Ordnance Device) guy, a nice chap at the bus station who was also on their ride, and they had an enjoyable time conversing with him until they reached Kyiv. He was there to help defuse the mines the Russians had carefully and punitively left behind in their hasty retreat... *The rotten bastards!!* Nathan was anxious to reunite with Mitchell who had now become the *de facto* leader of the old training team. Contact with Mitchell in the last month had been maintained via the *Signal* app. Apparently, Cyrus had gone off peddling his wild plans and supposed abilities and had gone missing... The team had continued with its purpose to assist the Ukraine Military and had built upon an already illustrious reputation. Trainers came and went but now a small group were travelling to a base near the small northern town of Gorodishce, and Nathan wanted a piece of this action.

As their bus turned into the city bus terminal, Nathan was stirred by how the mighty capital looked so delightful and distinctively genial in the summer, compared with the unfriendly grey and unsympathetic cold of a spring season, whose promise of refreshing change was both teasing and infuriating by its lateness. The newfound summer colour of the buildings and the glistening of the bright sun upon glassy panes had resulted in the city and its avenues coming to life! Nothing like the sweltering summers back in Australia, but at least flowers bloomed in ceramic plant pots in cast iron frames on window ledges and *blithe*, summer fashion now harboured a welcoming and frivolous splash of colour than the drab winter hues. Nathan was amazed at how strikingly beautiful the girls were, parading their light summer frocks and carefree smiles, having abandoned their heavy, dark, woolen winter coats and dour, friendless expressions. Now magically spurred on by the sun's conviviality, the general attitude of the people was also transformed and infinitely friendlier.

In no time at all, the men had departed from their 'bus of misery' and found their gear. The June heat hit the men as they waited in the carpark at the dry and dusty bus station. Before long, a mid-sized *Citroen* sedan pulled up and Mitchell quickly got out to give Nathan and Phil big hugs to welcome them back. They were soon on their way to the villa that was being rented for them by the *Legion Obolon*. As they arrived, Nathan inquired, 'How much time have we got?' 'Ten minutes' came Mitchell's reply... '*Damn*', thought Nathan, *'no time for mucking about here...'* Excess gear was hurriedly dumped into a spare room and Nathan and Phil rescued only what they would require for the coming week. Minutes later, their ladened vehicle was on the highway for the ninety-minute drive north. Jet lag kicked in and soon Nathan and Phil were snoozing.... At least the unit they were to train this time had put them up in a genuinely nice hotel that was only a couple of hundred metres from the town, and the barracks where they would train the recruits. Even a small and picturesque lake was within walking distance!

In the grand scale of things, the war seemed to be ebbing and flowing since the initial Russian invasion. The battles were still in the east and southeast of the capital, mostly near the border and in oblasts that had been largely secured by Russian separatists. The Russians would take ground and then the Ukrainians would rest it from them. Thousands of lives were being lost on both sides, villages and cities ruined and tons of military hardware destroyed. The lines on the battlefield map were forever being re-drawn, but at this time, Kyiv seemed to be secure from invasion, only rocket attacks up to this point. This was the vital time that Ukraine needed to get its forces up to speed... Nations around the world had rallied and were sending arms, medical supplies, ammunition, and sophisticated missile systems to the besieged nation, while the global political voice carried its condemning narrative to Putin and the Russian nation. The French President, Emmanuel Macron, had foolishly urged the Ukrainians to consider relinquishing some of the land lost to the Russians, in a bid to broker a cease-fire, but President Zelensky defiantly shouted he would never compromise Ukrainian territorial sovereignty. *And rightly so!* It was in this critical time, 'the calm before the storm' as some observers thought, that an urgent need existed for Ukrainian military recruits to be being trained in the United Kingdom, by competent instructors and Foreign Military Advisers. This is why Nathan, and the other members of the team were heading to the north of Kyiv.

The plan for this training was simple... while Mitchell ran the unit tactics, and Nels, a young Norwegian who had been briefly introduced in the car, conducted the combat medical side of training, Nathan and Phil would be tasked to run a sniper course for the best shots in the unit. In saying this, the five or six members who were selected would be lucky if they could hit a target, consistently, over two hundred metres! Only a natural aptitude and lengthy spells of coaching at the rifle range could remedy this problem and Nathan would have no say in that, nor would they have the time. Still, it was his task to ensure these men were equipped with an array of sophisticated skills that would certainly give these men a fighting chance, such as camouflage and concealment, stalking, accurate judging distance to target and skillful infiltration and extraction from an area of operations. He had four days to teach what would normally take weeks in a Western army! Besides organizing the 'banya', Denis, the driver of the *Citroen*, would also act as their interpreter, and they would use the camp area and its surrounds for their training.

Initially, Nathan wasn't all that confident... Things hadn't gone to plan on the first morning when the whole platoon was on parade. An officer was calling the platoon roll when a private's phone began to ring in his pocket and the tone burst out long and loudly in song – '*It's the Final Countdown...*' *Dah Dah, Dit a Dah Dah Dah,* by *Europe*, the 80s Swedish rock band, and it went on and on for what seemed an eternity until the private finally got around to switching it off! Phil looked at Nathan, bemused, and they didn't know whether to laugh, or scream, or cry at the ridiculousness of the situation or the fact the offending soldier wasn't reprimanded for his conduct! This type of behaviour would have been completely unacceptable back in their regular army days and would not have been tolerated in a reserve unit, or a cadet formation, for that matter! By all accounts, the Ukrainian unit was more of a militia than regular or army reserve and, with this type of trainee, who knows what the instructors could or would achieve?

Nevertheless, the training did serve an additional purpose. It was during the following days that Nathan learnt a lot more about his colleagues and was surprised by their backgrounds and history. By chance, Nels had been at Yavoriv when the rocket attack came and Nathan would later be informed by some trainers in Kyiv that he had freaked out and wasn't of much help to any of the wounded and dying, although he was a trained combat medic and seemed to be 'full of himself' most of the time. He was originally Norwegian military, or so he said. However, Nels professed many ultra-right-wing attitudes and championed the Nazis and *Azov*. As well, he sported many offensive looking tattoos, owned way too many firearms and was a 'geardo', always after the latest kit. But already, Nathan saw him as a guy he couldn't and wouldn't trust. Besides his infantile behaviour, Nels was never on time, wouldn't share money – even for a round of drinks. He was dirty, untidy, and calculating. Everything he did was 'shifty' and to his own satisfaction, certainly not a team player. It always seemed that the guys who talked themselves up were the ones who were light on substance and had something to prove. Nels was a case in point...

Nathan knew he had his faults, that his military standards shouldn't be applied to his compatriots, that he was Australian, and that he was nearly old enough to be a father of some of the instructors, giving him a different generational and cultural standard and expectation. Still, he attempted to 'get on' with the other men and things were generally amicable. Nathan was surprised at the many phone calls and texts Mitchell took during the day; he thought it may have been Cyrus calling him or another unit inquiring as to whether a training team could be supplied to their unit. As it turned out, like Phil, Mitchell was also a devotee of *Tinder.* Apparently, Mitchell had three girls 'on the go' at one time and was arranging meetings for his return to Kyiv, at the end of the week. Talk about 'still waters running deep'. Even in wartime, perhaps especially in wartime, romance flourishes, and Nathan had seen this first-hand with Phil too. Nathan had trained with Mitchell on his first tour to Ukraine and found him to be a sound military operator and a nice guy. He did seem to be a lot moodier these days and would frequently 'crack it' if the situation wasn't going to his liking, or he would retreat into his shell. Nathan put that down to the added pressures of running the team and all its dynamics now that Cyrus was MIA. One afternoon, during one of Mitchell's moody outbursts, he surprisingly made a negative reference to 'contractors', knowing full well that Nathan had worked as one in Iraq. Nathan countered by targeting Mitchell's U.S. Army background and stating 'Australia hadn't lost a war until we hooked up with you guys in Vietnam and Afghanistan...' Nothing more was said.

Not being acclimatised to the European summer, the dry heat began to build, and the training days started to become awfully long and draining, especially with daylight savings time. The heavy combat Australian camouflage trousers and hiking boots Nathan wore didn't aid in keeping cool, but he always had a light moisture wicking vest under his lightweight 'expedition' shirt, always tan or light green in colour. He was more than comfortable; a lot more relaxed, and he thought, fashionable, than his colleagues who chose to wear the full multi-cam uniform. Still, Nathan experienced numerous bouts of sweating, but was cognisant he was still recovering from his respiratory illness. Nevertheless, he could feel his lungs clearing with the heat and was so glad he made the decision to return, leaving the cold of his home state and the dampness of his cabin, which, at times, felt like he was living in a sweating, leaking German U boat!

As usual, Phil got on famously with the Ukrainians, passing around cigarettes and making jokes, and both men were astounded at how easy these eager soldiers adapted to the training. While they didn't look the physical types, they easily assimilated to the coaching and were adept at camouflage and concealment. The men were impressed with the instruction and called Nathan 'Sensei' or 'Yoda' and gave up their chairs for him when he took a break or went to the mess! Based upon what he saw, Nathan was convinced these Eastern Europeans had 'sniping' in their blood, as if it percolated through their genes, and he was reminded of the celebrated Russian sniper Vasily Zaitsev, the deadly Stalingrad sniper of *World War Two*, made famous in the movie *Enemy at the Gates*, Nowadays, the Ukrainian military enlisted female snipers to great effect against the Russians. Overall, Ukrainian snipers were decimating Russian troops, and particularly senior Russian officers. Nathan felt proud in the knowledge that they were contributing to these successes.

At the conclusion of each long day's training, the men would return to the hotel, shower, and later walk into town for a meal. A local pizza restaurant was the most popular venue; outside of a few grocery stores the community had little to offer. In the evenings, adolescents would hang out around the park or the main square and drink beer from litre bottles and listen to music...there wasn't much else to do. Not a lot different from Australia and the smaller towns and cities, Nathan thought. Similarly in both countries, funding mostly supports the large municipalities, and the small rural centres are slowing but surely dying; the kids can't wait to 'escape' and leave the land for better opportunities, and the large farming estates are being bought up by the Chinese and other global multi-national corporations. Local and federal governments, and the media and advertising sector still promote a mythical 'Aussie' way of life, yet the influences of multiculturalism in the major cities now make them more akin to any other European city than the way of life experienced by our forebears.

As it stands today, most kids have never seen a kangaroo and wouldn't know how to ride a horse, let alone camp under the stars or navigate through the bush. Coupled with the 'nanny state' mentality that forbids doing anything remotely dangerous or 'edgy', it is no wonder most Aussie kids will never experience firing a rifle, fishing, working a tough job on minimum wage or doing anything else bordering upon creating a shadow of 'resilience.' It seems their biggest decision is whether they will be 'trans' or 'gender fluid', expecting all the community to accept, promote and fund their selfish and confused 'woke' lifestyles until they change their confused minds and latch onto the next craze... Oh yeah, Albanese's 'nation building' alright, but the creation of a 'snowflake' nation of individuals that will certainly struggle in future conflicts, major catastrophes, or the mundane vicissitudes of daily life, let alone a serious personal crisis. Nathan thought of the political 'left' that now dominated Australia and which boisterously supported this nonsense, setting the next generation up for failure, and was reminded again of the saying *weak men create tough times...*

The unit had planned to travel to the rifle range on the Thursday and Friday and this would present Nathan's sniper squad with the opportunity to test out their 'new talents' in the field. The main test is to create a 'sniper's hide' from which to fire at a target and withdraw without being observed. Some of the men had created their own sniper 'ghillie' suits and used these to perfection. With the field exercise having gone exceptionally well, it was time for Nathan's squad to fire their standard weapons at the range. All the training team were involved as safety officers during the live fire exercise. Generally, the Ukrainians are competent shots at close range. Falling plate targets were used in preference to targets that are normally patched out and scored. No one was interested in grouping shots – *you either hit the target or you don't!* Also, moving targets were not part of their capability. As there didn't appear to be any proper marksmanship coaching, the main method for the soldiers was to 'pray and spray'. However, the practice was a bit too relaxed for Nathan's liking as many of the soldiers didn't wear ear protection, they couldn't be bothered, and one of the commanders even brought his kid along for a yippee shoot!

What was even a bigger surprise was how the weapons were being cleaned before returning them to the armoury. Instead of using a dedicated military oil type product, the soldiers, under the guidance of their NCOs passed around *'Amway Oven Cleaner'* and hessian sacking to assist with the cleaning of their stripped-down AK 74s. Well, Phil and Nathan just looked at each other perplexed! They could never imagine using such a product on their weapons and heaven help them if their old Platoon Sergeant caught them using it! *The boys paused...* Well, I suppose when in Rome... They both found the cleaner did a rather good job and had a newfound respect for Ukrainian ingenuity! What they didn't accept was the practice of placing a two-inch piece of motley string in the chamber of a weapon to signify the firearm was cleared and unloaded. This was taking faith to a whole new level!

With the training completed, they planned to have a small graduation parade the next morning, on Saturday. Unfortunately, this was cancelled at short notice. When the Westerners inquired as to the reason why, they were told that one of the young recruits had decided to go AWOL, and to make matters worse, he took his rifle with him! Now, a posse of soldiers were wandering the countryside and township to locate the man before he did anything else stupid. So with nothing left for the team to do, they said their goodbyes to the remaining Ukrainian soldiers and their friends, shook hands, gave a hug or two and got in the car for the lengthy drive back to Kyiv and the apartment. It had only been a week since Nathan and Phil had been back, but they were already sore and tired; it felt like a month...

Chapter Thirty-Seven:

NOW THE FUN REALLY BEGINS...

The journey back to Kyiv was the best ride Nathan had experienced in Ukraine. Comfortable, quick, safe and without incident... Outside the usual *bonhomie* shared by his compatriots over a job, *bloody well done*, in Gorodische, the sun was pleasantly shining. It wasn't too hot, the traffic light, and they were bound for the capital, to a waiting single room and some days off before the next training gig. The recent fatigue and worries seemed to melt away... like they always seem to when you're on a roll and things are going to expectations. The apartment was on the western side of Kyiv, and the Dnipro River.

This time, the two friends had landed on their feet... The apartment was one of many that made up a huge three-level house. Nathan and his mates, and the trainers, were on the second and third floors, while the owners occupied the whole of the bottom floor. The second floor embraced two separate spaces; a kitchen and eating area, and a communal toilet and euro laundry space; with stairs leading to two rooms on the third floor. Some of the quarters were bigger than others and fitted two guests while others accommodated single guests; as luck would have it, Nathan and Phil had their own chambers while Bill, who had also returned to Ukraine was with Garen in a shared room. The communal areas normally had a long couch or fold-up bed that was slept on by housemates or visitors. *It was tight but snug.* By chance, Sascha was bunking with a friend who lived only ten minutes away... Really, there wasn't much else they needed. The apartments had been paid for by the *Legion Obolon* formation that Nathan had worked with on his first tour to Ukraine, and this was the 'trade-off' for providing quality training to their reservists. Unfortunately, time and again, threats from the unit commanders surfaced that the apartments and their tenure with the FMAs could be terminated with little to no notice. This was a manipulative ploy to encourage the men to devote their time only to the *Legion Obolon* formation and to refrain from training other units. Such was the demand and the jealousy that existed in many of the military units in Kyiv and in the other regions. The men had the freedom to pick and choose their assignments, but this didn't go down well with commander Yaroslav.

Nathan sat on a futon bed that had seen better days; the frame was broken, and it lay as a flat rectangular mass on the wooden flooring.... surprisingly very comfortable.

At least it was his own room that he could rest in, exercise in, and have some time for himself. *All the comforts...* There was even an air conditioner and a skylight to vent the day's heat. 'This will come in handy', he thought, not only as ventilation but another escape route if the need ever arose...

In true military custom, gear was placed in an orderly fashion by the wall. Nathan yanked out his sleeping gear from his rucksack to vent the items and to make the room a little more homely; the camo poncho liner even looked inviting on his rickety bed! So much for some quiet time on his own – there was a knock on the door - it was Phil coming for a visit. His best friend was delighted at the new lodgings and had already settled himself in. 'Wow, can you believe this?' he gushed, *'beats the dump we lived in at Medyka,* that's for sure...' Wasn't that an understatement! They chatted about their old crappy tents, the many rainy days, their humdrum job as tent security and all the other zany adventures they experienced when they arrived in Ukraine the first time. It seemed such a long time ago, but it really wasn't...

Abruptly and loudly a call came from downstairs; an American accent urging the men to come down and to meet some of the other FMAs that were living under the same roof. In the common area gathered a variety of men, from many nations. Bill was already seated on a couch talking to a young sociable chap from Sweden named Matts, an ex-police officer from Stockholm and who had completed a stint in Mali on a UN peacekeeping gig. Around a table sat two other Swedes, a guy called 'Ragnar', resplendent with Norse tattoos and 'Viking' style hair and beard, and Sven, a slightly older and heavyset man who was fidgeting with a *snus* container, the Swedish version of chewing tobacco, except it is a variant of dry snuff that is positioned between the upper lip and gum and slightly different from the masticatory practice of tobacco chewing. As Nathan would come to discover from the Swedes, *snus* is highly addictive and carcinogenic like most tobacco products. On the other side of the room, near the tall refrigerator stood Mitchell, and Nels, who was eyeing off the *snus* and pestering Sven into giving him some, for free. Nels rarely paid for anything, including fuel, cabs or alcohol, unless it was for his own pleasure or when he was badgered into contributing! Phil and Nathan entered the room and took a seat. Introductions were made and apologies for those not there as well as an outline by Mitchell of what was likely to occur in the coming days. There was an assault unit, some twenty minutes away, that had gotten wind of the training team and had requested their assistance via one of their English-speaking interpreters. The training would be divvied up, with some trainers continuing to work with the *Legion Obolon* formation and other instructors heading to the new unit, which was strategically positioned closer to the city.

In the meantime, there were some meetings to be had with delegates from the Special Service Units (SSO) of the Ukrainian military, and with some of the instructors.

This proposal was certainly going to take the trainers down a different road. There was some talk about joining these units, giving rank to the equivalent of sergeant, and a more physical role in fighting the war. While it sounded promising, Nathan wasn't too sure about this idea. Based upon his first observations of those in the room, he really thought some of the men there were getting themselves involved in things that were above them, physically and probably skillfully as well. Still, *that was their choice.* They were all big boys and knew the risks! All he knew was that he would hang around long enough to find his friend and then depart Europe. Besides, the Australian government had an issue with its citizens fighting for other nations, especially with extremist elements.

The meeting concluded and Phil, Nathan and Bill headed across the road with Ragnar and Sven to *Lavina Mall*, a massive shopping complex and cinema, ideally located from their apartment. There was also a large hardware complex adjacent to the mall, and just a few minutes' further walk down the road was a *Novus*, an exceedingly popular supermarket chain in the country. It wasn't far from *Lavina Mall* that three guys, a Czech, a Brit and a Moldavian were all found executed, so everyone would need to 'keep on their toes.' It would be an interesting afternoon...

Chapter Thirty-Eight

PIMPS, MERCS AND FMAS...

The moment was not lost on Nathan or Phil... How *life* can be so bizarre, all at once... constantly, whimsically, and defiantly hurling balls of unpredictability and craziness at us all from a fathomless bag of mystery? Here were two old friends, soldiers, and the best of buddies, now standing at the entrance of an extravagant shopping mall in Ukraine, with colleagues from different countries and cultures in a time of war but completely and utterly astounded by the dripping sophistication of their surroundings. *H&M, Tommy Hilfiger, Under Armour, Swatch* and nearly four hundred of the world's best brands, plus a multiplex cinema and *Galaxy* theme park including a roller coaster ride, lay before them. This certainly wasn't the Ukraine in the minds of these two old mates from Oz! Sure, they had frequented *Chadstone* in Melbourne and *Centrepoint* in Sydney, but this isn't what they expected to see or *could have ever imagined...*

In addition to the high-quality shopping, the 'amazing' mall was littered with unique coffee shops and swanky eateries, and even an 'adult' store, which you certainly wouldn't see in a shopping mall back home! They decided to have a coffee and get to know their new colleagues before they indulged in shopping. Once again, the re-occurring theme of needing to do something and to stand up to Putin resonated throughout the conversation. Both Swedes were easily likeable men and had left their families to assist their European neighbours. For both men, it was also personal. Like most of Europe, their country had been living under the umbrella of a likely Russian nuclear holocaust since the *Second World War* and now it was time to 'stick it' to the Soviets. On a personal level, it was an opportunity to put their skills to the test, and apart from UN peacekeeping missions, Sweden hadn't been involved in a major conflict for generations. Like most FMAs in Ukraine, they weren't sure how long they could remain in the country, as this depended upon their savings, the types of opportunities presented by the Ukraine military, and how the war developed. Money was always the biggest factor as they had families and child support to pay; a Swedish government 'dick tax' according to Ragnar. Ukraine wasn't the place to go to make a buck if you were a military trainer.

During the ups and downs of the conversation, Nathan casually asked if any of the men had come across any other Australians or Kiwis. They did know that an Aussie paramedic was on his way over to join the team, but they lacked any other information. As it was, the Swedes had only been 'in-country' for a month and were still learning the ropes. They were more fortunate than most travellers to Ukraine in that they could go home any time, if they wanted to. It was simple and effortless for them to travel back to Sweden...catch a train or bus back into Poland and then an *EasyJet* or *Ryanair* fare for under a few hundred dollars and they'd be home in a matter of hours. '*Ah, home*', thought Nathan. Already, he wasn't looking forward to the gruelling journey back to Australia, and was envious of the Swedes, if only for their limited travel distance and cheap fares. Hopefully, Garen would have more news when he returned from his stint with the *Hospitallers*, especially as Nathan desperately needed some more answers concerning his old army buddy. With coffees drunk, it was *time to go shopping...*

Being men, the shopping part of the expedition lasted less than two hours, and that was dragging it out! Returning to the apartment building required crossing a busy and dangerous highway. Three lanes had to be negotiated quickly and it felt like they were playing 'chicken' with the oncoming cars because the traffic lights changed amazingly fast, and the drivers appeared to 'take a bead' on any pedestrian. It reminded Nathan of how dangerous Ukrainian roads were and how 'wild' their drivers could be. An offer of a meal of exotic Scandinavian fish dishes was made as the Swedes but Nathan and Phil passed on that proposal, deciding instead to eat some of the groceries they had just bought, in Phil's room. They had stocked up on canned tuna, fruit, bread, and chocolate... they had simple palettes. Kyiv and the surrounding suburbs weren't short of quality restaurants and take-aways and all tastes were catered for... Apparently, a BBQ was being planned for Sunday afternoon; a terrific opportunity to meet other trainers, associated colleagues of the friendly locals like Denis, and to make inquiries about Steve.

Unfortunately, Sunday arrived, and the BBQ in the back garden of the apartment building turned into a real 'fizzer'. The Ukrainian family who owned all the apartments sat by their BBQ cooker, essentially wire grills over hot coals in a rectangular tray, manufacturing kebabs and mostly keeping to themselves. The trainers sat in cliques, chatting, drinking cheap lager, and snacking on the buffet of chips, fruit, cakes, and cooked meat that adorned a large white plastic table. All the men lounged on plastic chairs, talking quietly, and looking visibly tired. It wasn't much of a get together, more of a courtesy to Commander Andre, one of the *Legion Obolon* officers who knew the owner of the apartments and had arranged for the men to stay there. It was more of an effort to keep everyone semi-friendly and for people to identify faces, as there were so many people coming and going. A lot of the conversation centered around funds, and what the Ukrainian military might be able to arrange for the foreigners, such as honorary positions in their military, rank and even pay. This talk was already vexing for Nathan as he was getting tired of this dumb narrative of false promises, innuendo, and plain BS! Even sadder, for Nathan, there would be no news on Steve from anyone there.

After an hour or so, the BBQ finished, and the men sauntered back to their rooms or the communal area that was permanently occupied by the Swedes. Phil indicated he would go and listen to some music before taking a light nap. Nathan was planning an exercise routine in his room. He didn't need a lot of space and the aerobic exercises on *YouTube* were a pleasant contrast from the simple walking he did to keep his fitness up, and his weight down. His exercise routine would be supplemented by pushups, arm curls with a powerband, sit-ups, boxing punches and squats. A short but strenuous regimen that kept Nathan in respectable physical shape.

Later, Nathan was resting on his bunk when the call came from Mitchell for a briefing at the communal area in the Swedes' apartment. Nathan woke Phil and they went downstairs and found themselves a seat. The meeting was two-fold. Firstly, it outlined the training for the next couple of days – *who was going where* and *what they would be doing*; a white board detailed names and areas where training would take place. Secondly, there was a chance that a smaller training team, comprising of three to four men, would be deployed to Kherson in a week or so to provide training assistance to Ukrainian soldiers at or near the front. This information would need to be kept on the *hush, hush!* Most likely a meeting would take place in a day or so at the *Legion Obolon* headquarters of their formation with the officer responsible for formulating this plan. In the meantime, Phil and Nathan were heading off to Africa Beach for the next couple of days to tutor *Legion Obolon* members as well as soldiers from a second unit that was deemed to be an 'assault force'. The Swedes would be joining Nathan and Phil, starting with a *Bolt* cab to the training area at 8 am. The meeting was brief as there weren't many questions. Phil returned to his room to make some calls back to Australia as he was still dealing with his divorce. Nathan opted for watching a movie on his laptop, using an external hard drive housing over a thousand movies and television series. He had picked this up during his time in Iraq and it been a source of entertainment and relaxation since. Nathan knew there another big day was ahead of them tomorrow...

Chapter Thirty-Nine:

ANOTHER SUNNY DAY IN UKRAINE...

Dry, strength sapping heat had slowly built up during the course of the morning... Nathan and Phil were just having a short break under an enormous oak tree, before they continued with the tactical training. There were no lunch breaks or extended time off as the units demanded as much time as possible for instruction. Unlike the Iraqis recruits that Nathan had trained and who had demanded a rest after every fifteen minutes, and who would lay about falling asleep, the Ukrainians were far more resilient and committed to their instruction with only required short rest periods. Nathan thought this was the quintessential difference between total commitment and fighting to rid an enemy from your home soil as opposed to letting Americans, Australians, British and whoever, *fight a war for you!* The 'Africa Beach' training area was a sandy strip bordering onto the Dnipro River and was on the west side of Kyiv, twenty minutes or so from the centre of the city. It was primarily a sandy, shrubby, wooded area and was sizeable enough to conduct platoon and company size training. Sven had utilised the area for instructing the Ukrainians on how to dig defensive positions and gun pits and it was a perfect site for this. As well, there were dirt tracks that could be used to instruct troops on roadblock procedures, ambushing and counter-ambushing drills. There was an old wooden mockup village that was used to train troops in basic CQB (close quarter battle), and even an old overgrown and dilapidated football pitch, perfect for exercising in the open before the troops entered the thicker, wooded area.

Upon seeing the football pitch, Nathan remarked, *'Ah, Old Trafford,'* jokingly and derisively to Phil about Liverpool Football Club's arch enemy, Manchester United and their famed home ground. In the cooler part of early morning, the troops would normally arrive in a multitude of private vehicles and the occasional bus and would park in an open area, near the big oak tree, where they proceeded to smoke and chat for a while, then gradually form up and move off under the guidance of their foreign instructors. English speaking, volunteer interpreters from colleges across Kyiv had been assigned to assist and were a great asset. On one occasion, Nathan, Phil, and some other trainers had been ferried to the area in the back of a removal van driven by a couple of German paramedics, who had linked up with the group and who thought it was clever to drive fast and give the trainers a cheap thrill... Such was the terror of that journey; men grabbed any railing they could and those who didn't were vigorously bashed about or slid around the metal floor. Matts was terribly frightened and began shouting, shaking, and pleading for the driver to stop... A laughing response came through the cab compartment with the driver informing Matts that he was traveling on the 'Auschwitz Express.' Needless to say, the attempt at Nazi humour didn't go down well with everyone... This wasn't the only time the behaviour of these lads was called into question. They were later seen courting girls known to be Azov supporters as well as smoking dope. Nathan wondered why these two bothered coming to Ukraine, especially as one of the young men had forgotten to bring his combat boots!

As the instructing began, most of the Ukrainian military hierarchy, such as the junior officers and platoon sergeants would either stand idly to one side, disappear, argue with the instructors, or vigorously take part in the exercise! There was no standard commitment or motivation as to be expected of anyone with senior rank. This was a common 'leadership' flaw which Nathan had witnessed up close with most of the Ukrainian military units he had encountered. Moreover, there were those who thought they 'knew it all'. As dangerous as the Russians were there was also the peril of having two minutes' worth of military experience and believing that one knows all there is to know about tactics, strategy, and soldiering!

The frustration of this frequently fell upon the foreign instructors, as had been the case during this morning's training.

Nathan had inquired about the platoon he was to work with and their level of combat training. He was reassuringly informed they could move in patrol formations, perform contact drills, and employ small unit tactics. 'Well,' thought Nathan, 'that sounds promising, let's see how they go...' From the outset, the platoon was inept and frankly, *an out and out shambles!* During the many field drills, field signals weren't passed on, individual arcs of fire and areas of responsibility were not adhered to, and the platoon stomped across the overly grassy football field like a herd of noisy, rogue elephants! Through Yuri, his interpreter, Nathan made it known that he wasn't impressed with the drills and the slack attitude of the soldiers, many of whom were just going through the motions...

All of a sudden, one of the lead soldiers, who was acting as a scout, took it upon himself to interject, and started arguing with the interpreter, flailing his arms about, and talking loudly. Nathan looked at the man and then turned to the interpreter, 'Okay, Yuri, what is this guy on about, *what's his problem?'* Yuri explained how the young man, who was around seventeen years of age, was informing him of how the training should be conducted and how the drills needed to be performed. *Well, if this didn't get the ire of Nathan, then nothing would!*

Nathan continued communicating with Yuri, but seriously 'eyeballed' the young man, who was still wet from puberty. '*Listen*,' said Nathan, in a loud and aggressive voice, '*tell him to shut the bloody hell up and to do what he is fucking told!* I think I know what I am doing when it comes to this shit... *This is the third war I have been involved in...* If he doesn't like the way things are being run, *then tell him to bloody-well sod off!*' Yuri paused, only for a second and carefully translated the message. The young Ukrainian could easily sense by Nathan's tone that he wasn't happy, but the delivery of the words *hit him like a sledgehammer!* The young man ceased talking immediately and retreated into his shell, like a petulant schoolboy that had just been rebuked by the school master! The rest of the platoon had been patiently waiting, and party to the conversation between Nathan and his antagonist. Phil, who had been roving around giving pointers, stood silent and thought this wasn't the time for anyone to say anything, unless they would further invite Nathan's wrath. As it turned out, and not to the surprise of the instructors, the platoon performed a whole lot better by the end of the day and were a vast improvement on the morning's dismal showing. Notwithstanding, it would be a day or so before Nathan was certain they could transition to the thicker wooded area and try out their new skills.

This was generally the format for the teaching. Most of it would be conducted at Africa Beach or sometimes a team would be ferried to a unit, not too far out of Kyiv.

On another day, Nathan, Phil and Nielsen, a Danish paramedic, were invited to a range practice, which was being conducted by their Legion *Obolon* formation. Nathan and Phil thought this would be interesting... The 'range' had been cut out of the forest by a huge front-end loader; the excess dirt and scrub being used to create the 'stop butt' for the rounds that would be fired down range. Nathan was under the impression that they were there to assist when necessary, but when they arrived at the firing point, they were informed that they would be conducting the range practice. Well, *Nathan went into a fit!* As he told the unit officer, very much annoyed, 'If you want me to conduct a range practice, then tell me what sort of range shoot you want me to run, how many people firing and what sort of weapons will be used. *Don't fucking ambush me!* This is how bad shit happens, *this is how people get killed!*' As this conversation transformed into a debate, soldiers were milling about the firing point, drinking slushies, smoking, offering advice to the firers, and disregarding any and all safety protocols. Another Ukrainian soldier, wearing an old Russian Sniper camouflage suit, was mouthing off in Nathan's direction, so Nathan told the man to shut up while he was talking to the range officer. To Nathan's surprise, it was Yaroslav, the unit commander! Not blinking an eyelid, and seething, Nathan did an about turn and stormed off, not wanting to be part of this farce.

Nathan knew that these soldiers weren't of the ilk of his former regiments in the Australian Army, but surely, even a child knows how dangerous weapons can be and there are no second chances if it all goes to shit... Nathan recounted how some of the *Special Forces* range practices in the past had been 'inventive', but safety was always paramount in their minds.... *Always!* In a short while, Nathan had cooled down and this is when he was approached by the unit second-in-command, Grygoriy. The man was sheepish in his approach to Nathan and certainly didn't want to stir up the Australian anymore... He respectfully approached, apologised for the misunderstanding, and asked if Nathan would conduct a unit range practice later in the week. This wasn't a problem for Nathan, and he welcomed the opportunity to put things right – *but on one condition...* The unit would need to attend a practice range session out at Africa Beach on Thursday, the next day. This would guarantee that everyone would understand the range practice that would be conducted and all relevant safety aspects. The soldiers would need to demonstrate their weapon handling proficiency and understanding of the practice, and for Nathan and his team, they would be able to identify any potential risks during the 'dry run'. Grygoriy shook Nathan's hand, and the range practice would be on Friday, in two days' time.

Having spent some time of an evening writing the orders for the range practice, Nathan was certain all would go to plan. The success of the range shoot would depend upon the range rehearsal and the soldiers following the format and instructions on the day. Again, Nathan and Phil were bright and early out at Africa Beach for the rehearsal day. The Ukrainian group consisted of around forty soldiers, all who would be shooting the next day, were surprisingly early and Nathan was pleased for such a good start. The training would be conducted at the run-down football pitch (Old Trafford) because all attendees would be able to view the instruction, and they assembled there, after a quick walk from the car park area. From the outset, Nathan had the group formed into their ten details of four soldiers per detail. He knew this would probably change tomorrow but it gave the troops an idea of how it would be organised from the beginning of the range practice. Next came the safety brief. The entirety of the brief was outlined and communicated via the Ukrainian interpreters. Just as the interpreter was finished giving Nathan's instructions, a mobile phone began to merrily play a tune, drawing attention to the owner, who looked bashful before requesting to make a brief call. None of the ex-military were impressed with this display and Nathan made it crystal clear that *'If it wasn't President Zelensky on the phone, it was to be switched off'* and this was a great opportunity for anyone else who had a phone to silence them.

At times, some of the Ukrainians soldiers, male and female, would make lame excuses to get out of training: 'I must catch my bus', or 'my kids need picking up'. This wasn't all the time or the majority of the soldiers, but, on occasion the importance and relevance of the training and its connection with the war effort went temporarily missing in the minds of some of the would-be combatants. So, with excuses and phones now sorted, the first firing party was directed to move to the ammo bay, just to the rear of the football pitch where the soldiers simulated receiving their thirty rounds and filling them into their one magazine. Next, they were called to the firing mound, ten metres away, on the pitch and covering off a simulated target. Nathan then issued the orders and had five members of the detail simulate loading and actioning their weapons. Then, as instructed in sequence, they adopted the lying, kneeling, and standing positions. Each member went through weapon handling drills and pretend fired their ten rounds in each position. They were then ordered to unload, had their weapons inspected and then dismissed from the firing point and scurried back to the designated waiting area. This process was continued until the entire group had gone through the various stages of the practice; around forty firers carried out the drills.

At the conclusion of the day's range training, Nathan reiterated the most important thing for the next day, and that was for every soldier to just do what they were told. *That is all they had to remember, just one thing, just do what you are told!* A few soldiers raised their hands and asked obscure questions, which had little or nothing to do with what was going to occur the next day. So, in an attempt to quash any 'red herrings' and other trivial nonsense,

Nathan singled out one of the trainees who was asking one of the random questions and explained again, slowly and carefully, for the man to do what he was simply told, and this was done by providing a memorable example. *'Okay, if you do exactly as I say, you will follow my orders. Based on these rules, I can even order you to cluck like a chicken and you will cluck like a chicken. Isn't that so?'* The man seemed confused. 'Right', said Nathan, addressing the man once again. *'Remember, all you need to do is follow instructions, any, and all. Is this correct?'* The man shook his head in agreement this time, with more understanding and a measure of confidence. *'So, if I command you to cluck like a chicken tomorrow, you will obey, right?'* The man sheepishly nodded his head in consensus. Again, Nathan made the point to all present, *'Just do what you are told. It's that simple...'* Commander Grygoriy was extremely pleased with the day's training and so too were the other instructors and commanders.

To nobody's surprise, the range practice was a triumph because of the detailed rehearsal the previous day. Nathan presented the safety brief once more and then found his confused friend from yesterday. 'Okay,' he said calmly to the young soldier, while addressing the whole group. 'If I give you any command you will follow it, is that true?' To which the man proudly said 'Yes' in an enthusiastic tone. *'Okay then, I want you to cluck like a chicken'*, announced Nathan and, without the slightest hesitation, the man began clucking, somewhat quietly but then much louder and a lot more flamboyant, and then he started manipulating his arms like wings, much to the amusement of the group and instructors! Without a hitch, the firing details were formed and, one by one, on command, they passed by the ammunition bay, moved to the firing point, listened to Nathan via an interpreter, fired their weapons at falling plate targets, as instructed, had their weapons deemed 'safe' and moved to the rear on completion. For an introductory practice, the shooting wasn't too bad, and Nathan awarded a small prize to the 'best shot', a young man who hit seventeen out of twenty targets. This sentiment went down well, and the Ukrainians moved off to their transport and home in high spirits. Commander Grygoriy congratulated Nathan and his team for doing such a fantastic job and headed off with his men with a big smile. Nathan would later discover that the commander had been in the Ukrainian military since the early 2000s and had even served in Iraq, yet he was incapable of running a basic range practice! This astounded Nathan as this type of training is in the realm of even the most basic of NCOs from his army. Again, the question begged... *what had their military been doing for so long,* besides prancing about in uniform?

Although it had been a very satisfying range practice, it had been another blistering hot day, and all the trainers were feeling exhausted. Some of the men had managed to have a shoot in the afternoon but Nathan preferred to give his rounds to a Ukrainian who needed the practice more than he. Sascha had been one of the interpreters during the day and had managed to bring his vehicle to truck Nathan, Phil, and anyone else they could fit into the small, compact vehicle. He also informed the guys that Mitchell was asking them to hurry as they had been invited to speak with the commander of all the military forces in Kyiv, later that evening, somewhere in the city. This had been arranged by another interpreter from the assault brigade unit they had been training on the other side of town. Well, this would make for an interesting evening and who knows what might come of it... For Nathan, the more people and contacts he met could only assist him in his mission to locate Steve.

Chapter Forty

RUBBING SHOULDERS WITH THE BRASS...

The men stood rigid, as dignified as anyone could be, in front of the large Ukrainian flag mounted on a polished wood staff, in a shiny office that belonged to the commander of all Ukrainian forces in Kyiv. Their faces beamed with pride as they clutched the tiny bronze medals in their large worn hands. Americans, Swedes, Norwegians and an Australian stood alongside their Ukrainian friends, who were equally proud in dispensing the awards. This was a magnificent moment for all to savour... As it happened, Nathan, Phil, Sascha and the other members involved in the range practice had returned around thirty minutes before they were due to travel to the commander's office. It was around 5:30 and it had been an exhausting, drawn out day. Range practices are especially tiring and even more so when the day is warm, and they had just experienced a ridiculously hot day... Upon their hasty return to the apartment, guys rushed about kicking off boots, showering, changing clothes, combing wet hair, and generally making themselves presentable. What they had invited to, they didn't know... All were soon aboard the people mover van that had been arranged by Mitchell and were off for a twenty-minute ride. It was all such a mystery and the men started speculating, with the talk ranging from being offered more units to train, to the hope, for some, of a position in the Ukrainian army; a thought crossed their minds as to whether they would be questioned or even interrogated about their on-going presence in the country and their future intentions... *No-one knew for certain what the evening would bring...*

As they alighted from the van, they were greeted cordially by Andriy, who had been the translator for the assault brigade that they had been working with, on the east side of the river and city. Andriy was a tall and thinnish man, and not your usual robust Ukrainian. He was very affable, but also highly intelligent, quiet, and sensitive and had become good friends with the foreign instructors. He was the perfect conduit between the Ukrainian unit commanders and the training team. Here he was now, ushering the men into the formidable headquarters building. Nathan was sure that he wasn't the only 'foreigner' who felt apprehensive. Andriy requested that the men sit patiently in the large office as they were waiting on someone who due to arrive in the next fifteen to twenty minutes. Ragnar and Sven took a chair while Mitchell and Nels looked with interest at the Ukrainian military photos on the wall. There was even a picture of 'Mikhail Kalashnikov', the famed inventor of the venerable AK 47 assault rifle. Nathan and Phil sat with their backs to the wall, facing the only door and waited, occasionally looking at their watches. Chit chat passed the time. Very soon, speculation ceased and impatience set in; for most, there was an eagerness *to get the bloody show on the road...*

Although in truth, the anticipation had been short, it seemed like an age. Nathan was impatient *for whatever was about to happen*, to just happen. According to Nathan's mother, Nathan was born 'early and eager', and it had been impatience that had dogged Nathan all his life, much to his detriment. Unexpectedly, there was some kerfuffle downstairs, with soldiers saluting and getting out of the way of someone with extremely high rank. Moments later, a balding man, thickset, of medium height and wearing Ukrainian camouflage trousers and an olive T-shirt, marched into the office, and promptly stopped, weighing up all the Western men in front of him. The man possessed a broad, friendly smile on his roundish face and was able to speak basic English. Colonel Maxim was the chief of all forces in Kyiv; although officially a Colonel, he held the substantive rank of General for his position. He cordially gestured for all to sit at the large polished wooden table and would occasionally speak via Andriy, when the translation was more complex. The 'General' thanked everyone for attending, saying that he had been alerted to the great work the 'foreign' men were doing in training Ukrainian recruits. He was also certain the men in front of him had travelled 'far and wide' and politely asked each man where his home was, to which all the men responded. He paused and solemnly nodded his head, acknowledging the commitment and sacrifices of the men who sat before him. He was astounded at the various countries and their distances to Ukraine! Like most other Ukrainians, he eagerly and respectfully thanked the men for coming to his country and announced proudly how *Ukraine would never forget this commitment* by these men. He then smiled and declared that he had something to give to each man for their devotion...

At this point, he stood up and Andriy stood beside him with what looked suspiciously like an ice bucket. Individually, he called out the names of the training team in alphabetical order and, one by one, the men moved forward coyishly and were offered a hardy handshake and presented with a medal and an official Ukraine military certification document. To say *the men were flabbergasted was an understatement!! Nathan certainly was!* Most of the Australian medals he ever received had come via the mail and he had never been officially presented with an Australian award in such a fashion, not even in the military!

After all the awards had been presented, a group photo was captured in front of the large Ukrainian flag, with Andriy and the acting 'General.' As if this wasn't enough, he informed them that *he had some other 'special' things for them!* Andriy and one of the staffers had produced three or four large boxes, all about the size of twenty-four can beer cooler, all containing food, which ranged from chocolate, butter, and cans of meat. As they were preparing to leave, the 'General' remarked that he had another gift that he couldn't present himself, but this task would be performed by Andriy... Colonel Maxim now had to dash, but he strongly shook the hand of every man, generously thanked each for their service and again stated that Ukraine would never forget them. Lastly, he said to all, *'It would be an honour to assist us if our countries were ever in the same situation'.* On his departure, all the men leapt back into the van, strapped in and sped off. Andriy, who was sitting up front, produced a bottle of the finest Ukrainian vodka, 'Here is the personal thanks from the Colonel'.

The drive back to the apartment was silent as the men were still in awe of the thoughtful gestures showered upon them by the 'General'. Nathan knew such a presentation would never happen in Australia as there is way too much bureaucratic red tape and penny pinching. It is more difficult for our own military personnel to receive awards than for an appreciative Colonel from another country to take it upon himself to award foreigners!! *He knew this from first-hand experience.* As an incredibly young soldier, he had served with the 'Rifle Company', at Butterworth in Malaysia. He was painfully aware how veterans had been fighting for appropriate recognition veteran benefits for over four decades! He quickly surveyed the van and could see all the men gazing proudly at their newly acquired medals and certificates. As the men would discover later, the medal was a 'tier one' award for *'Victory, Glory and Honour'* and was part of the complex Ukrainian medals system for defence of the homeland. Sure, it wasn't the Victoria Cross, or the Medal of Honour, just a heartfelt 'thank you' from a respectful and grateful nation. There was no way the pride and honour of these men was going to be diminished or sullied in the immediate future. A great twist to an evening that had them all nervous in anticipation....

Chapter Forty-One

PARTY TIME...

Unfortunately, not all the men had been able to be present at the 'surprise' awards ceremony. Carlos, who had been involved in many of the training missions with Mitchell and the others, had also offered his time and service to offer units of the Ukrainian military and was off on some stint elsewhere... *He came and went as he pleased...* A veritable training 'Maverick'. He had been in Kyiv for some time prior to the outset of the war, had found himself a girlfriend and was considering making this country his home. Although he was ex-U.S. Army, the 'States' had little or no appetite for him anymore and he preferred to reside in Eastern Europe. As the proud, bemedaled men floated into the apartment, buoyed by an incredible sense of lightness and euphoria that only the triumphant can ever experience, Carlos was resting on a broken-down couch in the apartment common area occupied by Mitchell, Phil, and Nathan. As he came and went very often, the wreck of a couch and the common room became his *de facto* bed and *abode* for the time being. Without doubt, the busted sofa looked extremely uncomfortable, but Carlos was the sort of guy *who could sleep anywhere and at any time*; like he was used to bunking down *on wooden park benches* or in *uncomfortable jail cells...*

Mitchell passed on the glitzy medal and its certification card to Carlos, but he nonchalantly and somewhat dismissively threw it on the couch and feigned that he wasn't all that interested. Or that's what he wanted people to think... A nice enough fellow, but Nathan thought he displayed a sense of 'aloofness' that masked other issues. He was lean and wiry, festooned with tattoos and of a Cuban/Mexican extraction, and he also wore a thin, drooping 'Pancho Villa' type moustache. Carlos was one of those guys who had the 'gift of the gab' and seemed to have a response for anything and everything. Nathan wouldn't describe him as a 'hustler' but rather just a young man, like many, who had to prove himself... to himself, very often.... Irrespective of all this, Nathan liked the man as he had a great sense of humour and they got on well.

The trainers were on a roll... Spirits were high after receiving their medals, being part of a great day's training at the range and now, it was Friday, and *the night was still young...* Carlos was heading off to some bars before the curfew and asked if anyone wanted to join in. Phil looked at Nathan and said, most energetically, '*Well, I think we deserve a night off, don't you?*' Reluctantly, Nathan nodded his head in agreement, and they quickly changed clothes and met with Carlos, Ragnar, and Mitchell downstairs.

They soon found themselves in a trendy wine bar that was once an incredibly old beer cellar. Nathan was keen to talk to Ragnar about a few things, but Phil was surveying the young and beautiful female patrons, *like a kid in the proverbial candy store...* A few more drinks were had, *the laughter was up*, and the group was up for just about anything... The discussion soon centered on going to the 'Men's 007 Gentleman's Club', which was within walking distance. If they wanted to go, they would have to hurry as the establishment was renowned for being overcrowded and they certainly didn't want to stand in a queue. The men walked briskly up the street to the nightclub district of Kyiv. Carlos certainly knew where he was going, and Nathan was assured the crafty American could probably find the 'seedy' location in his sleep!

All the talking and walking led to a thirst, so they stopped to partake of a quick drink at another venue along the way, at another subterranean tavern that sported a mock tropical theme. The last place was a tacky bar poorly festooned to be a bad facsimile of a Caribbean paradise! Not surprisingly, the venue was mostly empty except for a small group of girls drinking at a table. These drinks were quickly downed, and the march continued to the 'gentleman's' club. Three or four minutes later, the tipsy and animated men arrived at their destination. They were met at the door by a middle-aged showman, sporting a ruffled white shirt inside his crimson jacket and looking very camp, although he probably wasn't gay. Just his idea of how an impresario should look! He excitedly invited the boys to enter, and an exorbitant entry fee was paid. They were led downstairs, which sported a soiled red shag pile carpet, to a seated area of green velour covered bench seats that ran all the way around one wall. A couple of other men, probably in their fifties, were present, sitting individually, in the shadowy darkness on the far side of the room, studying the alluring girl onstage. The plush velour seating faced a small oblong dance floor with two chrome poles situated a few metres near either end; the seating was less than a metre from the stage, *close enough to view but not close enough to touch...* A strikingly beautiful blonde, in her early twenties, topless but wearing a miniscule bikini bottom, was cavorting with one of the poles and acrobatically performed backflips and slow leg splits, much to the interest and appreciation of the group. The girl worked her athletic moves and seductive glances, oblivious to the stares of the men and performed her energetic routine to some loud Euro disco tune that was completely unknown to Nathan or Phil.

Within seconds of Nathan and his friends sitting down, a waitress appeared on cue and inquired if the men wanted drinks, to whom they ordered a various number of beers and spirits. *The price was astronomical,* nearly three times the cost anywhere else, but still cheap when converted to any currency outside of Ukraine! Again, as if on key, two pretty and scantily clothed girls appeared and sat down, *snugly,* between the men and asked a variety of standard questions, such as names and where they hailed from and what they did for a living. But more importantly for them, they asked if the men would buy them drinks; a ploy to make more money for the owner – they weren't just sitting there for their looks! The two *femme fatales* hinted they could perform a variety of 'favours' in a backroom and a menu for these 'incidentals' was swiftly produced that included, private striptease lap dances, or a plain old 'oligarch tit show'. This wasn't a brothel, but Phil and Nathan knew for sure that sexual favours were on offer if the price was right! The man in the gawdy jacket re-appeared and suggested to the men to hurry up and make their choices as they were closing within the hour; another pressure tactic to manipulate guys into a hasty and, for the most part, regrettable decision. In the half light of the seated area, Nathan could identify a man sitting on the other side of the room studying one of the 'menus'. He made his selection and 'moseyed off' with the blonde girl who had just finished her erotic romp.

Suddenly, one of the 'lasses' that had been talking to Mithcell stood up and strode onto the stage. She began gyrating and attempting to 'make love' to one of the poles while the Euro disco beat continued thunderously in the background, and penetrating strobe and multi-coloured lights flashed in sync with the music. For some bizarre reason, Nathan thought about the *Kinks*' song 'Lola' and how this cesspit of a nightclub reminded him of the tawdry discotheque in that jingle:

'I met her in a club down in old Soho, where you drink champagne, and it tastes just like coca cola, C-O-L-A, Cola.'

Nathan wasn't expecting or wishing to meet any attractive looking transvestites, but sure as hell he wasn't confident that he wasn't going to bump into some either! The *tackiness* of the club, the expensive watered-down drinks, and the *hard sell* by the 'strumpets' soon had its impact and the men polished off their drinks and decided to vacate the premises. *Where to next...* A popular *point-of-interest* was just down by the Ferris wheel, a few minutes away. This was a trendy space for street performers - musicians, acrobats and mime artists and people of all persuasion. For a country at war, the *nightlife of Kyiv was amazing...*

The warm night air had coaxed people out of their home fortresses and people of all ages and sizes were drifting merrily down the street which had been closed off to traffic. As the men arrived they could see a small bar dispensing beer through a side window *doing a roaring trade*, while street artists were dancing and executing incredible athletic stunts for money. Phil and Nathan were now feeling slightly 'heady', what with the drinks, balmy night air and the nightclub exotica. This exhilaration was further enhanced by the small fat Honduran cigars that Carlos, in the manner of Houdini or David Copperfield, had magically produced! The night was now late, and the men were sated of their wanderlust desire for alcohol, for women and for frivolous adventure... Time to grab a fast cab and get back to the apartment before the dreaded evening curfew. All the men were feeling intoxicated, in a variety of ways and by many means, but joyous to be alive and enjoying each other's company in the current circumstances they found themselves in. Without doubt, this had been an extraordinary day, *one which they will long remember...*

Chapter Forty-Two:

WHAT DO YA KNOW... MORE TRAINING

There had been a trifling, annoying touch of rain over the weekend, the type that cools down the area momentarily, but viciously contributes to the sting of the day's emerging heat, and its draining and exhausting grip upon the concrete city and the sorry individual. Since receiving their medals, a spring in the step of the foreigners had been evident; the sense of team spirit was at its highest ebb and as far as the 'morale clock' went, *they were at twelve on the dial...* There was much joking and teasing among the men; always a positive sign that the group's general feeling was on the up. Nevertheless, hard work still had to be done... The training was now divided into two parties – one group continued to go to Africa Beach, while the other team worked with the assault brigade on the city's east side. The relationship of the group with the *Legion Obolon* had continued to sour, most probably due to their commander and his intransigence and insensitivity to the needs of others. They were still training elements of this unit, but not as often. The chance of a near 'front line' training mission to Kherson was still in the offing and it was a small, four-man cohort that would go. As always, information seemed to circulate either rapidly or at a snail's pace and Nathan only discovered he was due to attend a briefing for the Kherson mission not long after he had returned from the day's training. The meeting was to be held at the *Legion Obolon's* headquarters in thirty minutes.

After much haste changing clothes and gathering required items, the small band of foreigners arrived at the headquarters with five minutes to spare and were warmly welcomed by several Ukrainian recruits who they had previously trained - they were happy to see their old instructors. Denis, the principal translator since they had been working with the unit, ushered the men to a training room that looked like it had been used to teach motor vehicle servicing and engineering. Illustrations of Soviet trucks and engines plus cutaway models adorned the room's walls. Unfortunately, the 'squat' toilets were only metres away from their briefing room and the entire area stank like cattle had been slaughtered next door or someone had died! In a minute or so, a smart and well attired Ukrainian senior officer briskly entered the space and sat down casually in front of the men, who sat at the back of the room on spare chairs that were found behind the student desks. Straightaway, Nathan could see this man was a professional, judging by his crisp attire, his preparedness for the briefing and his no-nonsense demeanor. *'Finally, someone in this army who looks and acts like a bloody officer!'*

In a no-nonsense fashion, he quickly outlined his plan... There was a serious and pressing desire to train Ukrainian soldiers to a much higher standard than the Russians, so the military hierarchy was devoted to implementing on-going training, even with soldiers engaged in combat operations at the 'front'. The general plan would be to identify the best soldiers and NCOs and have them briefly removed from their units and situated at a training area not too far from the 'fighting'. *There would be three groups:* one group for medical training and the other two groups for specific combat lessons, such as infantry minor tactics and trench construction, etc. The training would go for a day for each group and the Ukrainian soldiers would rotate over the three days to complete all facets of instruction. These skilled and enhanced soldiers would then return to their units and pass on their newly acquired knowledge to the rest of their compatriots. Essentially, the task was to 'train the trainer'.

The Ukrainian officer paused and then announced, 'This is where you men come in'. He outlined that each of the trainers would be taken to a secure area not too far from the front lines, where they would live in the vicinity for the next three to four days. All up, with travelling, the training mission would take nearly a week, give or take any hiccups. Given the proximity to the front, it was preferable for the team to be armed this time, in the event of a Russian push and should they need to defend themselves alongside their Ukrainian counterparts. The 'polished' officer was wanting to know whether this idea was plausible and if the foreign trainers could produce a training plan that would instruct as many soldiers as possible in such a short amount of time. There wasn't a need for any lengthy deliberation, the men immediately looked at one other and then nodded in agreeance, signalling their ability and desire to to produce a 'workable' plan and capably enact the officer's overall proposal. The officer smiled and was satisfied with their positivity. He urged the men to keep this meeting secret and indicated that he would get back to them in a few days; his 'superiors' were the ones that would give the go ahead for a further briefing and then the mission.

Everyone seemed satisfied with what had occurred, but it was Nielsen, the medic, who had real concerns for his safety mostly due to the 'fluidity' and instability of the war. He didn't seem keen to be going anywhere near the front but at the same time, didn't want to make out he was afraid. On a number of occasions, he took Nathan aside to air his apprehension. He kept offering up excuses and highlighting the likelihood that of the area they would be travelling could be soon overrun by Russian forces. As Nathan put it bluntly, 'Mate, no-one is forcing you to go anywhere or do anything you don't want to go. *The choice is yours....*' For a big, well-built man who looked like he tackled the weights with regular ferocity, his heart wasn't in the mission; and not for the first time had Nathan identified a 'chicken heart' in a brash and cocky rooster! It had been the same on his Special Forces selection course - many of the 'bulked up' and 'talked up' candidates were lacking, physically and mentally *when it got hard... and when it really counted.* Of the few guys that passed selection, most were supremely fit and deter-mined like Nathan, but moreover were the quiet, 'slow and steady' types.

Nielsen departed the group a week or so later and found an apartment in Kyiv. The next time Nathan saw him was weeks later when he viewed the 'big man' walking down Kreschatyk Avenue with a pretty girl on his arm, and he wondered what stories the large Dane had been selling her... For Nathan, this was the last time he ever saw or thought about him... Also, as it turned out, no-one ever spotted the smartly dressed Ukrainian officer again, nor was the chance of a training mission to Kherson ever mentioned. Was a training mission really ear-marked for Kherson, or were the men being vetted by the Ukrainian military hierarchy for other tasks? *They would never know...*

Regardless of the meeting and what might or may not take place, training continued... It was Nathan and Phil's turn to go out to another assault unit and this made an enjoyable change from Africa Beach. They had a sprinkling of veterans who had seen active service in their group, but the majority were recruits. It is hard to expect people to understand and master the 'art of soldiering' who have had only little experience of it. To seasoned trainers like Nathan and his cohort, the actions of the recruits sometimes bordered on the farcical. To the practiced soldier, it is common sense to manipulate whatever terrain is at his disposal, even the camber on the side of a road or the tiniest bit of vegetation. Yet, when training the uninitiated, sources of cover from weapons fire, or concealment from attack are not obvious. These life-saving skills and the common sense to use all available elements, especially under duress, do not come quickly to the novice.

But, for a change, training had been going well before lunch. Nathan and Phil had managed to convince the guards at the gate to let them out so they could go to the service station next to the base. The two men had a hankering for something sweet, after their standard borsht and bread lunch provisions. Their mission was to procure ice cream. Security was always tight and fact the base was full of soldiers meant it was difficult to exit. Without argument, Ukraine boasts some of the best confectionary and iced treats anywhere in the world and *nothing beats ice cream on a hot, summer's day!* On their return, Nathan presented ice creams to the guards, and to Matts and Ragnar; everyone appreciated the gesture.

While they enjoyed their frozen indulgencies they waited patiently for the squads and platoons to form up again for the afternoon's instruction.

Suddenly, a deafening alarm sounded on the public address system and, as the men found out later, this was the activation for the unit to be placed on immediate alert. *If orders arrived, the unit would be off to the front, immediately...* What occurred next made Nathan shake his head in disbelief. Instead of the officers and NCOs quickly assembling their men on parade while awaiting instructions from their commanding officer, the whole scene was a complete debacle, and more akin *to the German Sixth Army's retreat from Stalingrad!* Soldiers didn't know where to form up and moved from one spot to another and then return to the first spot. An overweight sergeant, instead of taking charge, opened the trunk of his car and threw a pile of gear in it, so he wouldn't have to cart it around on parade, including his rifle! Soldiers casually ambled out of the multi-tiered barrack block and wandered over to the main ground as if they were off to a picnic. Other soldiers who thought this proposition looked 'promising', slowly wandered over there and joined them. Gradually, platoon and company sized formations developed, but all the while people were darting away and then hurriedly return with a 'forgotten' rifle or a rucksack or a sleeping mat...

This was a sight to behold for the foreign trainers who just stood by and watched in awe and disbelief! Even more incredulous was when the commander of the unit *finally* did turn up, he stood as a solitary figure twenty metres in front of the gaggle that represented his troops! He then called for the company commanders to come out to his spot and receive orders. Those men equivalent to 'Major' rank marched forward to their leader. Somehow, the platoon commanders, who were Lieutenant rank, thought that they were part of this instruction and wandered out to the centre with the other officers. Now, the platoon sergeants thought they were in on this too and also casually wandered out to the centre. Somehow, junior NCOs believed that they were also involved in the orders group and sauntered out also. *Now there were too large groups.* Soldiers in their formations on the left side of the field and an almighty mob in the centre that resembled a drone of worker bees, moving around the central 'queen'. In a way, the scene was reminiscent of the Islamic Hajj in Mecca, and the swarm of moving humans... all that was missing here *was the Kaaba monument!*

In spite of this mass congregation out in the middle, soldiers were still wandering about trying to find their platoon or squad. Phil remarked to Nathan, 'How long do you think *this rock show will go on for?*' Without a moment's hesitation, Nathan replied, '*Too long for this little black duck... Fuck it,* let's get a *Bolt* back, *I think we're done for the day.*' All the other trainers nodded in agreement. *This was a unit that was expecting to be deployed within the next couple of weeks!* The best thing that happened that day was news on their return to the apartment. Apparently, Cherie and Tyler, who they had last seen in Lviv, were now in Kyiv and popping in for a visit. They had been helping out near the front and had been to some of the more dangerous areas of the war, such as Donetsk. This would be their last meeting before going home.

Chapter Forty-Three:

OLD FRIENDS, STORIES, AND THINGS TO COME...

It had been a fantastic evening. A night to remember for some time... Cherie, Tyler, and a couple of other lost faces from the past had arrived. They had a 'BBQ' but all the food had been cooked on the stove as the relationship between the owners of the house and the fragile connection with the *Obolon* unit was beginning to unravel. Cooking outside was now *verboten*! A few drinks, notably the potent 'Riga Black Balsam' from Latvia had been gulped downed, a banquet enjoyed, paired with a lot of banter and an opportunity for Nathan to play some music on the worn semi-acoustic guitar he had found in the apartment. Of greater importance and interest were some of the tales originating from their guests. Apparently, Cyrus, like the celebrity he thought he was, had been touring the country, 'touting' his wares, but was now spending time with a Ukrainian rock star and was last seen in Lviv at a benefit concert! This was the very last news that anyone had heard about him. Everyone agreed that it wasn't a good idea to be connected with the man as his reputation in the wider sphere of Ukrainian life had taken a mighty hit. Cherie and her compatriots were only in Kyiv for a day or so and would rendezvous with other contacts in country before making the journey back to the U.S. Before they left, Nathan took the opportunity to say thanks once more to Tyler, for his assistance in saving his life earlier in the year. *It was the very least he good do...* Tyler appreciated the sentiment and the robust shake of hands.

Overall, it had been a few great days. Some really 'cracking' training opportunities, recognition, and a catch up with old comrades. It was now Tuesday and time to get back to work. This time, Nathan and Phil were to conduct another sniper's course with a unit not far from the centre of Kyiv. The introductory sniper course would be like the one that had been so successful at Gorodische, many weeks before. For the other trainers, the 'schooling' followed the usual format of infantry minor tactics. It was a big unit, comprising of a few hundred soldiers and they were jam-packed into their headquarters, with most of the men sleeping on the floor in the unit indoor basketball court. During one of the breaks on the course, Nathan had been watching a young boy no older than nine or ten, practicing boxing training with his father. Their gear was rudimentary, and they used a portion of the park as a boxing ring; obviously, they didn't have access to a proper gym. Nevertheless, the boy was sharp, fast and his drills were impeccable, and he gobbled up the training as voraciously as a lion consumes a freshly killed wildebeest. Whether he could emulate the famed Klitschko brothers and become another world boxing champion that would be another matter, but witnessing the 'fight' in the boy further inspired Nathan's confidence in the combative spirit of the Ukrainian nation.

As far as the sniping went, one of the young snipers on their course really stood out... Nathan would later work solo with this man relaying to him all the things he had experienced with regards to sniping and marksmanship training, especially in an urban environment. The enthusiastic young man had even bought his own sniper rifle, at very great expense. He had studied as much as he could from online sources and from those he knew in the military and was semi-proficient regarding theory. More importantly, he was cunningly smart and quite able to work independently of others; two of the essential prerequisites for a highly competent sniper!

All Nathan was really doing was assisting to 'finetune' the man's skills, especially concerning camouflage and concealment, hide selection, egress routes, mission planning and, hopefully open the sniper's mind to other concepts and practices. Unfortunately, there wasn't an opportunity to see the man shoot 'down range' as there had been a communication issue with the unit hierarchy and only so many people were allotted to the designated range practice. This was a shame, but Nathan was certain this man would be successful and get his fair share of Russian kills...

Once more, the training week went to plan, and this was another unit trained and ready go to the front in the next couple of weeks. The upcoming weekend was an opportunity to see their loved ones, hopefully not for the last time... In most other armies, military training is composed of recruit training, which goes for several months, followed by respective corps training, such as infantry, armour, logistics and so on. The arduous training usually continues for more months before a soldier is considered competent and is posted to his or her unit. This was not the case in Ukraine. Such were the dire circumstances that a great number of the soldiers destined for the front were armed with only a minimal amount of training – a mere few weeks in fact! This is why the training team had been so busy for such a long time but now, to the surprise of many, it seemed as if the training, for them, was starting to wind down. The timing was fortuitous as Nathan had heard from Garen that Steve's time at the front was coming to an end, and he would soon be taking a few weeks rest in Kyiv before contemplating his next move.

Aside from running some CQB drills for the *Legion Obolon* unit, not much was on the horizon... The Swedes, Mitchell and Nels all appeared to be getting itchy feet, *again*, and constantly discussing their options and the opportunity to get involved in something different and somewhere else. Many a evening, there had been talks to do this and that.... 'Hey, why don't we join the *International Legion*, at least we will get paid there,' said one. Another one would chime in... 'Hey, why don't we join one of the SSO (Special Forces) units, like the *Omega Group* or the *Kraken Regiment*. I believe commander Andriy, Yuroslav, Gregory or whomever is interested in us... There is talk of status, money, and accommodation.' The conversation went back and forth, back and forth, and back and forth...

Nathan shrugged this off as nonsense, as the trainers had more to offer than what the units could deliver, especially their mortality. *'Shit, I value my life more than for a few, stinking hryvnias,'* Nathan thought to himself. The reality was that most of the units they trained couldn't even afford new weapons or decent equipment and soldiers were having to purchase a lot of their own gear. The 'leaders' of these units were just yanking the chains of the younger, desperate Western guys to keep them interested; there may be a war on, and they may be in command of a military unit, *but they could only promise so much...* Someone in the group reminded the others about Nielsen and how he had left the team and was living in a self-fund apartment in Kyiv. He was now sourcing his own contacts and the group only saw him here and there. The Aussie paramedic from Brisbane had also come and gone that 'bloody fast' that nobody could remember his name or his face or if he was still in country. He too had located an apartment, and no-one had seen or heard of him since. Was that another option for the team...go their separate ways... and maybe, someone might land a better opportunity for all! A variation of the classic theme 'divide and conquer'. Nathan could feel the angst and uncertainty and believed that after all their successes, the team may have reached their zenith and was ready to disband.

The real 'kicker' came when the exhausted men returned from training late on Tuesday afternoon only to discover an eviction notice placed on their door! Mention was made of money not being paid and the group were to be out of their apartments by Sunday, and the rooms had to be spotlessly cleaned. Talk about *kicking a man when he's down!* Apparently, the *Legion Obolon* formation had decided to forgo further payment to the landlord, and the services of the team were no longer required. To be honest, this had been coming for some time. Later that evening, Nathan discovered a *Facebook* page of the unit members receiving service commendations for getting their unit up to speed. All this had been achieved through the hard graft and sweat of Nathan and his associates. Long hours, unbelievably searing hot days and battling through communication and financial issues. Well, 'where to live now' became *the thought that pervaded everyone's minds...*

Chapter Forty-Four

SOLDIERS OF MISFORTUNE – 'DOWN AND OUT' IN KYIV

To say that morale had taken a hit was an understatement! To use an old Australian parlance – *'It was lower than a snake's guts!'* Fortunately, it was at this critical time that Sascha pulled out one of his amazing contacts that was, of all things, a blessing in disguise, even if the guy was a Russian Orthodox priest! Although the 'man of the cloth' was of the 'other' major church in Ukraine, the cleric was very pro-Ukrainian at a time when there was unbridled suspicion and antagonism against anything or anyone remotely Russian. He had been alerted to the plight of the foreigners and advocated a 'gathering' at his church, which also housed rooms for refugees, orphans and women who were victims of violence. The priest suggested that the men come over to discuss accommodation and partake of a light supper. It was best for all concerned to assemble to see if this arrangement would work. Luckily, it was still early in the week and while it had been easy for Nathan and Phil to pack their meagre belongings, some of the other men had accumulated a few items along the way. Ragnar and Matts had returned to their homeland the week before, taking the train from Kyiv to Prezemsyl and then onto Krakow followed by a short flight to Sweden. Matts had run off the rails slightly as he hadn't been taking his meds and had been drinking heavily, acting like a 'silly boy' but with depression thrown in; it was a good time for him to go home with Ragnar's guidance. On their travels, Matts had made a scene with the Polish police and was lucky Ragnar was there to smooth things over or else they both could have ended up in a Krakow jail cell!

Back in Kyiv, it was mostly Nels who was going to be the one the guys would have to watch… He was notorious for being dirty and unkempt, a 'grub' by any other name, and keeping his room and its surrounds as filthy as a pigsty. *The group certainly didn't need any more dramas from the landlord or the Legion Obolon!* What had really killed the relationship with the Ukrainian unit was the arrival of Mitchell's old companion, Devlin, the guy also involved in the 'beatdown', months earlier. He had reached out to Mitchell hoping for a night's accommodation for himself and for two colleagues. All perfectly honest and not too much trouble for Mitchell, or anyone else for that matter. But what eventuated was unforeseen... *Three guys and a large dog turned up...* they stayed more than the one night and *made a lot of drunken noise...*the uninvited dog then *crapped on the grass and the owner walked into it...* and you could *imagine how appreciated that was!* And, as if that wasn't enough, having finally departed after outstaying his welcome, Devlin slithered *back into the apartmen*t, when it was deserted, *like the snake he is*, and stole body armour and other pieces of valuable equipment. You can just picture the *outrage* from the men! *The group was seething!* The gear was only returned after promises of another beatdown to Devlin! Much to his credit, it was Matts, the ex-copper, who had acted as the go between Mitchell and Devlin, *who was way too scared* and *way too crafty* not to drop the gear off in person; his unflinching cowardice saved himself from a group flogging!

Sascha ferried the men, in a car he had borrowed, to the meeting with the priest. The church which was only ten minutes or so from their present dwelling. They were soon lingering in the small gift shop of the church, which sold holy icons, bibles, prayer books and religious mosaics of all types. It was typical of most Orthodox churches that the men had seen during their stay – old, quaint, and partly Byzantine in design, resplendent with a gold domed roof. An addition to the original design was a small hall which was used for choir and Sunday school activities. Above the hall was a small quarters being used for those needing immediate housing. A small rectangular room on the ground floor adjacent to the hall was used as a meeting and eating area and had a tiny but quaint kitchen flowing off it. Unlike many of the churches that were traditionally white, this house of worship was painted a light green colour and there was a small vegetable garden on the side of the basilica that faced the hall. Almost immediately upon arrival, the men were offered light refreshments of crisp black tea and fruit cake by the devout female shop attendant and, before long, the priest had arrived.

It is probably safe to say that the image most of the men visualized in their mind of the priest was that of a clone of 'Rasputin', the crazed monk, with fiery eyes, a heavy cross swinging from his neck and wearing a long jet-black cassock. But this holy man was far removed from that wrathful, dangerous Russian. Peter was wearing a light woolen jacket in beige and dark green trousers but was sporting the traditional long beard, but with shortish hair. He was trim, probably in his fifties, and overjoyed to meet the resilient men. His eyes lit up when he greeted each foreigner with a firm handshake. He guided the group from the foyer to the small dining room at the back. To everyone's surprise, a bottle of expensive and highly potent cognac was produced, and the men vigorously and wholeheartedly toasted Ukraine, the church and each other - *even more so as they consumed the strong liquor!* They were joined by two of Peter's friends, a young effeminate man, who was a theatre performer; obviously so, judging by his dress and affectations, and an older artistic and bohemian looking woman, probably in her early sixties, who was a dear friend of both men.

More drinks were consumed... *raucous laughter and stories flowed...* and before long a tasty soup was offered, followed by more delicious cake, strong coffee, and sweet, dark chocolate. Nathan was heralded before the woman as being a former *Special Forces* soldier, who had studied at university and spent most of his time playing guitar or writing adventure stories. *The woman was intrigued... she kept eying off Nathan...* Peter starting conversing with the woman in Ukrainian...they both began to giggle, then laugh, and then bellow and it was not lost on Nathan that something was afoot! Suddenly, it dawned on him, a marriage was being arranged! Although he had downed a few drinks, *he hadn't drunk that much to get hitched to a Ukrainian war bride!* Nathan quickly raised his left hand to the priest and his female friend and proudly showed off his wedding ring, which he had never taken off, despite the fact he had been alone for quite some years. The women's beaming smile slowly dipped into a frown, and talk returned to the immediate predicament of the men. Peter was dismayed at the shoddy treatment of the adventurous and courageous men by the *Legion Obolon but* was extremely delighted that he was in a position to assist them with some temporary lodgings. Before they bid each other goodnight, they had agreed to return with their belongings on Sunday, to stay in the church hall, at least for a couple of weeks until the summer holidays ended, and the hall would need to return to its previous uses.

Apart from Nels having to be pressured, by everyone, *into cleaning his room, the bathroom, and the kitchen area of his apartment,* the move went without a hitch. Many vehicle runs were made using Nels' *Suzuki* 4x4, although it was barely roadworthy. To the delight of the group, the hall was big enough to accommodate all, now been whittled down to five... Each man grabbed a padded mat or two, one that was mostly likely used for kids' gymnastics and found a clear area of floor to set up their living space. As luck would have it, the church was well located to the city as well as being close to a small shopping area with food outlets. *It would certainly suffice until something else turned up...* In the meantime, the men would scour their contacts and all worthy sources to see what was available and, hopefully, find a more benevolent unit to work with. In the meantime, they would chill out; go for walks, eat pizzas, watch movies on the hall's data projector and keep themselves occupied until the next gig. It seemed bizarre to be watching war movies while living in a war zone but that was the popular choice. For Phil and Nathan, this accommodation would certainly be adequate for the meantime. However, they must not forget that their prime focus would be on the errant Steve Holland's return Kyiv, which was now only weeks away...

Chapter Forty-Five

THINGS CAN ONLY GET BETTER...

The move to the church hall came as a bit of a holiday from the loveless apartment environment, and a welcome respite from the eternal diet of 'rank bullshit' the *Legion Obolon* had been serving them. They stayed connected with the friendlier and more decent members of the unit, but as far as the commander and most of the officers went, nobody would shed a tear *if the Russians sent them to hell...* Nathan generally left these retaliatory matters to the religious powers of *Karma*; he believed that people have a way of getting their 'comeuppance' when they least expect it. As it happened, Nathan had reached out to an ally, an ex-military chap in Australia, another guy called Steve who headed a group called the *Lazarus Union*, a humanitarian organisation that was mostly recognized and respected throughout Europe, but little known in 'downunder'.

Some welcome funds were promptly dispatched from this saviour and *was very appreciated by all!* Rapture, the men could continue to eat and survive! In the capriciousness of life, sometimes you must hit rock-bottom before the opportunities begin to avail themselves and this was one of those moments. Now to get some work to cover their real reason for being in Ukraine. Fortunately, a call was put out from a unit in the west of Kyiv, nearly two hours away – they desperately required competent FMAs. They asked for a lunch meeting with the group to meet the commanders of this unit, and their interpreters, this coming Sunday. 'Ah, here we go again,' thought Nathan, annoyed and tired of being on this 'FMA merry-go-round', *'another bloody meeting, geez, I've lost count of how many damn meetings and get togethers we've had in the last couple of months...'*

Sometimes, when doing nothing... *absolutely, goddamn nothing...* the time inexplicably races by and before the group knew it, Sunday was upon them. They had, however, managed to have a couple of drinks with Carlos at a nearby bar. He casually informed his old flat mates that, in between his own training stints, he had been arrested by the Kyiv Police. While laughing off the event, Carlos recounted how he had decided to fly a drone at night in the capital, which for obvious security reasons was a big no-no! It was hard to imagine what he was thinking as he could have easy been shot as a Russian spy by overzealous cops! Nathan was sure that he wasn't the only one who thought, *'what in the hell did you think you were doing?!'*

but in that stupid, careless, and selfish action, the measure of the man lay in the simple fact that he couldn't be trusted when no-one was watching.

Back to Sunday... Soon, the remaining members of the team were seated at an upmarket restaurant to the north of the city. They had crossed the Dnipro river by car and were somewhere in the Darnytskyi District of the city, their trip taking them well over an hour. As always, interpreters were present and it wasn't long before the commanders of the unit took their seats, self-importantly at the head of the table. The commanding officer was a thin and unremarkable man, other than he was in his late twenties! In charge of a battalion sized group, this would be unheard of in most other armies! The last time Nathan had known of an individual being so young and in charge of a unit that size was when George Custer commanded the U.S. 7th Cavalry, and *we all know how that turned out!* The battalion sergeant major was a shorter and stockier man, who sported an old-fashioned handlebar moustache and apparently, his claim to fame was his ability to do repetitive heaves on a beam!

The unit had been formed around these two 'starlets,' as both of these men were extremely popular with the younger folk; apparently one was a blogger and they acted very independently of other units, as did a lot of formations within the Ukrainian military. However, some of their ideas were *really* out there... They were planning to purchase a great number of 4x4 light skinned vehicles from somewhere in the Middle East...costing millions of dollars, paint them in camouflage and use them in their operations as 'gun vehicles'. They were also looking at replacing their tried and tested AK 74s with the newer Polish MSBS *Grot* assault rifle – for no apparent valid reason that Nathan could think of. This meant changing calibre to a NATO 5.56 and leaving a weapons landscape where spare parts and ammunition were plentiful... *'What the fuck are these guys thinking.'*

Moreover, it seemed the unit had recently been in close combat with Russian forces and had apparently taken a severe beating, with many lives lost. The only success they had was luring some stupid Russians out of a house with crude insults, such as *'Your mother fucks gorillas from Georgia'* and shooting them as they angrily emerged. It was hard to know which side was the more stupid when hearing stories such as this. The only lesson they had really learned was not to eat pork near the front as the swine feed on dead Russians. Hence this is why they were eager to meet quality trainers. They had been using other FMAs, mostly Americans, but these guys hadn't worked out. The 'quiet' word was there had been in-fighting, alcohol abuse and subsequent 'punch-ons', and they were given their marching orders. This didn't seem like a hard act to follow but now was not the time to ask prying questions... Their 'go-to' guy was a young American from California who had made great friends with the commanders and who was informing everyone at the table of the sort of training the unit required. Nevertheless, he possessed zero military experience, ran rifle shooting back in *Cali*, but seemed to be the unit *'go to guy'* calling the shots. Their scope of training would involve most of the basics: infantry tactical training; combat medicine; range shoots and recon lessons.

The trouble with these types of meetings is that there are always the few guys who want to dominate and ask the questions, mostly in an attempt to 'big note' themselves. Nathan loathed this practice when he was back in the army and always preferred to speak to people one-to-one and get the real story, *no matter who he worked with* - cadets, Iraqis, or Ukrainians. The dinner was concluded before they knew it and it seemed as if both sides were happy with the arrangement. The training team would travel to the west of Kyiv in a few days and there would be a 'try before you buy' plan, exercised by both parties. On the face of it, it sounded like a sweet deal... The unit would provide accommodation and meals, and there may even be some funds for the trainers. Hands were shaken, practiced smiles were performed, and the parties went their separate ways. For Nathan and Phil, they would have preferred to stay in Kyiv but Garen's message concerning Steve meant he was nearly a month away and they had to find something to do in the meantime. They both really enjoyed the role of 'mentor' and were still eager to lend a hand to the Ukrainians, even if some of their units were 'dodgy'.

As their numbers were greatly reduced, Mitchell was enthusiastic about recruiting a few more trainers, and they had a few days to do so before they left to go west. He arranged a get together for several 'soldiers of fortune', mostly British and Americans, some of whom had been in the *International Legion,* at the *Suku* mock English pub later that evening for a meal and some drinks. After chatting for many hours, the reputation of the *Legion* was not enhanced and, quite frankly, if the organisation were a car, house, or boat, *it would be nearly impossible to sell!* As Lewis, an ex-Royal Marine Commando told Nathan, '*Fuck me, yeah... we didn't know what happened, it was so quick... we were patrolling this grazing paddock when the drone hit us... we took cover in an old farm building... my mate was badly hit and I took some shrapnel in my calf going out to get him... damn, we were in hospital for three days and if our mates didn't arrive and give us water or change our dressings, we'd be dead now.*' It was prudent that Nathan had returned home after his bout of pneumonia as he knew for certain that a Ukrainian hospital wasn't the place for a foreigner, who didn't speak the language in a country going through a war. Without a doubt, Lewis's tale confirmed Nathan's decision to return home as the right one!

More 'horror' stories like this followed and, as it turned out, Lewis and his mate, Stan, who resembled a heavily tattooed and muscled David Batista, were heading back to the UK. They were done with the war and had only minimal funds to see them home; the 'cost' to them had been great. On the other side of the table, a young, lean American and former paratrooper with the 82nd Airborne was talking to Mitchell, but it seemed as if he had little interest in going west to train recruits; his plans were to remain in Kyiv for the meantime. An Argentinian guy sat in the corner, brandishing tattooed airborne wings but said little; he was an ex-counter terrorist expert who was made redundant and was now travelling the world's hot spots. He possessed the '1000-yard stare' of a survivor who had witnessed so much horror... If his thoughts and history could be woven into a manuscript, he'd have a bestseller. Meals were finished and beers were drunk, and the night was soon over. There were no contenders in this lot. The other 'soldiers of fortune' went on their way... not all paid for their meals.... much to the ire of Mitchell who then had to haggle with the bar staff over the funds owed! In the general haste to return 'home' and avoid the curfew, no one had noticed the absence of Sven. Now, the curfew was in place, and it would be a long, tough night for the missing Swede.

Chapter Forty-Six

FAREWELL KYIV... ADIEU

The sun was shining brightly across a clear Kyiv sky, and it was around nine the next morning when a slightly raggedy looking Sven walked into the church hall and absorbed the stunned looks of Mitchell, Nels, Phil and Nathan. He had separated from the group outside the *Suku* bar to meet a 'friend' who was sourcing cancer medication for another Ukrainian compatriot who had a family member battling the disease. The Ukrainian needed some convincing. Sven confirmed that the life-saving drugs were en-route from Sweden, as they spoke... Before he knew it, everyone had disappeared, the streets were vacant, *and a cab couldn't be found for love nor money!* Police cars had started to patrol the lanes, roads and motorways, so Sven hid in the shady confines of a passageway for a few nervy minutes before rushing toward a nearby park during a lull... The night was fresh but not overly cold, and in the small grassed common he discovered a hiding place behind a considerable, dense rhododendron shrub that was planted half-a-metre or so in front of a brick fence. It was dry and eerily dark at the rear of the massive plant, but Sven had uncovered a comfortable and secure spot for the night. Further concealing his presence was the dark hoodie he wore, and he decided to tug the jacket's sloppy cowl over his head and try for some light sleep. In his dozing moments, he frequently heard the wail of sirens, the commotion of young men's loud voices, the *phap, phap, phap* of running feet on pavement or the flashing of red and blue lights as police and emergency services vehicle darted by. *This would have to do for the night...* It was better hiding behind a bush and sleeping rough than being mistaken for a Russian spy or troublemaker, resulting in a severe beating or worse!

Prior to his arrival, the men had been methodically packing their gear in anticipation for the drive to Ukraine's western oblasts and sorting out any last-minute details and personal administration that required attention. As it happened, the ride to the western town didn't eventuate until the Thursday, not the Tuesday as had been promised... So, on *Thursday,* the newly nominated moving day, all gear was loaded, and it was only Nels who was lagging behind, *as always,* causing tension in the group. Nathan couldn't help himself this time and berated the Norwegian, *'For fuck's sake Nels, will you get your shit together. We've had days' notice on this... and you're still fucking around!'*

Nathan was old enough to be Nels' father and the young man wasn't used to being spoken to in that way, like most people in their twenties and early thirties. He didn't like it; his generation weren't accustomed to being told 'no' and weren't happy when scolded by others, especially their seniors. The woke generation talks up a good game but constantly fails to deliver... As Nathan would say, 'These kids get their heads filled with BS from day one at school, told they can do this and that and be whatever they want to be... trust their feelings... trust their emotions... never hearing the word 'no', especially from their slack parents and, when they do, they go to pieces!! Too much individual choice and too much over reliance on a selfish 'head in the clouds' mentality. John Wayne once famously penned the quote: *Life is hard, but it's a whole lot harder if you're stupid'*. Nathan's citation for the modern era was similar but with a slight difference... *'Life is hard and even more so if you're a fucking snowflake!'* Anyway, the problem with today's young people is for the psychologists and health system to deal with and make money from, or so thought Nathan... Needless to say, Nels ultimately sorted out his gear and was the last man in the second vehicle that had been assigned to drive the men to the new unit location.

Another major surprise was in store... *not everyone was travelling to the new unit*. Phil used this moment to blurt out that he had decided to return to Australia in the hope he could reconcile all the marital issues with his wife. *'I've got to do this, even if it fails,'* he stated, pleadingly to

Nathan. 'Time for me to step up and make things right. I've been thinking long, hard, and about why I married in the first place... *I just have to give it one more try...*' Nathan didn't have any issue with this, not at all, and was in fact, delighted and pleased that his long-time friend had decided to focus on what was more important in life and not just himself or his bevy of girlfriends! But ultimately, *this was for him to decide and no one else...* Phil would stay at a hotel in Kyiv until he could catch a train back to the border and book the next available flight from Krakow. He repeatedly apologised and was sad to be leaving Nathan behind but realised his time to galivanting all around Kyiv was up. For Nathan, there was no bad blood...in fact, it was the decision of a man who had come to realise that all the improvements, the joy and reward in his life was his sole responsibility and no-one else's. Like Nathan, Phil too had sacrificed many a dream in pursuit of another vision and the consequences had rebounded on him. Common with most of the ex-military men Nathan knew, they were not fabricated from dainty crystal or porcelain, all had their numerous flaws and blemishes and were far from perfect... But now, it was *time to go...* 'Hey, you'll miss the training and the compote drink!' said Nathan, jokingly, to which Phil replied, *'How many times do you need to get kicked in the balls to know what it feels like?'* These were the last words spoken between the two friends in Ukraine. They hugged tightly, only momentarily of course, and soon Nathan was driving off, wondering if he would ever see his dear friend again.

The city of 'Novohrad Volynskyi' is a smallish city, certainly a lot more attractive than Berdychiv, and is a military garrison town that harbours many regular army units. After winding around many streets, the vehicles pulled up to the residence that the group would now occupy for the foreseeable future. To say that this accommodation was shabby and a real 'crap shack' was a gross understatement! A mangy, underfed, 'broke down' dog on a long chain inhabited the yard, and the single-storey house gave the impression it hadn't been occupied for some time. Cobwebs, rubbish, plastic bottles, weeds, and additional rubble lay all over the place. The main grassed area was worn from the dog's pacing on the chain. It was Nathan who repeated his familiar phrase, out aloud, again in his *faux* Cockney accent, *'Cor, what a bleeding dump!'* This negative sentiment wasn't popular with Mitchell, judging by the 'dark' look on his face, and it puzzled the Ukrainians, but Nathan was always about the honesty and this time, he couldn't be any more candid or direct! *The accommodation that they were presented with was a dump, plain and simple!* The front door was opened, and the group looked about the two rooms, kitchen, and bathroom. How would this place accommodate everyone? Camp stretchers stood against the wall and the assumption was that everyone would eke out a space and that would be their environment for the foreseeable future. Their guides encouraged them to quickly stow their gear as the next segment of the trip would be a visit to the barracks.

The drive to the base was short, and the unit had established their operations in what looked like a former private school facility. There were many large brick buildings, but what took Nathan by surprise was the main headquarters structure which resembled a southern plantation you would find in the sweeping Civil War saga, *Gone with the Wind*. Unfortunately, the building resembled the 'Tara' of old, especially after the Yankee soldiers had plundered, looted, and removed all the gloss from a fine Southern homestead. Here, pigeons and rats infested many of the buildings while at least twenty wild dogs wandered and scratched about the grounds. For kicks, the soldiers fed the few goats cigarettes. The headquarters building was dirty and dilapidated and was not even worthy of a renovation. Again, it was evident that a deal had been done on the cheap, but it satisfied the unit and its commanders. Some of the buildings that were designated for training had rotting floorboards and the 'kitchen' looked as if it had been closed and derelict for decades.

A short wander found the group and their guides at the base of a small hill that overlooked the river that flowed through the town. This is where most of the military instruction would occur, along the trails or upon the open grasslands. The group found most of the officers sitting by a picnic station and a short chat ensued, concerning training and expectations... Nathan was already getting a negative vibe about the situation, but didn't want to voice his concerns, just yet... The men were invited to lunch and partook of the stale bread and watery soup. During the meal, a small explosion went off, less than fifty metres away. *No-one flinched, seemed to care, or made an inquiry!* Heads remained down, tucking into lunch, all of which was very perplexing and unprofessional and not a great reflection on the unit or its commanders. Already, it seemed as though the new FMAs were getting the rough end of the stick, in relation to the quality of the unit they were to train. Nathan wanted very much for the next day to be better, when they would be taken on a tour of the weapons ranges and the town nearby. Soon, the day was at its end and Nathan went to bed early; he was fatigued and needed the comfort and solitude of his poncho liner and redoubtable air mattress. Time to focus his thoughts on his current predicament and an 'exit strategy' should the situation deteriorate further...

Breakfast was especially early the next morning as it was impossible to sleep, what with people noisily 'fluffing about' in the confines of the small house. Nathan had briefly looked around the building the previous evening, in the vein hope of locating another area where he could set up his own space but, outside of a dirty old chicken coop, nothing was available. Some goodies had been procured from a large supermarket on the way home and Nathan was chowing down on some cereal and yoghurt. *Nathan's mood hadn't improved...* He certainly was not pleased with the accommodation. *The place was truly a dump...* and they deserved better considering they were giving everything they had in terms of knowledge and experience for free. It appeared as if the unit commanders had either got their wires crossed or deliberately set the men up in second-rate housing. To make matters worse was the deteriorating relationship between Nathan and some of his colleagues... without his best mate, Phil, as a buffer for his mood swings. What made him even madder than their insipid lodgings was the perpetual and inane commentary from Sven and Nels about the fanciful training they could do. This became more evident later in the day when they went to the ranges, on the outskirts of town. There is nothing more annoying than listening to a supposed expert, boasting about how they would do this or that, without an understanding of the logistics or planning needed to put these hairbrained ideas into reality. *It all came to a head later that evening...*

Nathan was much older than his compatriots, and it seemed as if his peers thought his ideas and skills were outdated, old fashioned and not relevant in this current war. But, to use a cricketing term, Nathan 'had runs on the board', when compared to the other men. He was soldiering, as the Scots would condescendingly say, *'When you were sucking on yer Ma's teet!* He knew how to live for weeks on end in meagre surroundings; he knew how to create training out of nothing; he knew how to communicate with people outside his socio-intellectual sphere. What 'broke the camel's back' was when Nathan was trying to offer an opinion to a training discussion and was completely talked over by Sven, for the umpteenth, *and the last time...* Nathan ripped into the Swede and the man was taken back by the ferocity of Nathan's vitriol and statement that he was 'sick of being spoken over', especially by this man. Sven took the criticism but like most bullies, reverting to his standard practice of talking over Nathan once more. Outraged, Nathan got up and walked away, informing the men that *'They can do whatever they wanted with the training!'* He had had enough. It was at this point Nathan decided he would go back to Kyiv and work with another group that had been suggested to him by Garen, *Team Mission: Liberty (TML).*

The commanders of this unit had provided an interpreter to stay with the men and to assist them, however, this ruse was obvious, he was there to keep tabs on everyone, and the presence of the man was more for their own intel gathering than really assisting the foreigners. The towering man was a likeable character and Nathan spoke with him to arrange transport back to Kyiv the next morning. Mitchell came and asked if he was okay, but Nathan said he would be leaving and that was the end of it. It may have seemed strange that the former SAS guy 'cracked it', but there is a global misconception concerning *Special Forces* soldiers, perpetuated by myth, the media and SF tough guys portrayed in cinema. Sure, men who have served in elite units are generally tougher, mentally robust, and physically stronger than those in the rest of the army, however, what is frequently missed is the fact that these men are smarter when it comes to how they live, eat, rest, and relax. They wear the best gear; they buy the best equipment and they set themselves up for the long haul. Nathan could have lived in that 'broke down house' with the feral dog barking and scratching fleas outside, and trained with the 'suspect' unit, but as he informed Mitchell, 'any grunt can live in a hole'. Nathan made the choice not to compromise his standards and abilities; besides, his gut feeling was that it was time to get out while the going was good, and he always relied on his intuition. Moreover, he wasn't being taken seriously and Nathan knew that he could be more valuable and appreciated elsewhere. In simple terms, at his age he didn't need the 'BS' or aggravation... Garen would be back soon with *TML*, in a couple of weeks, and he preferred to work with him! When the time came for him to go the next morning, he wished everyone all the best, shook hands, and *didn't look back...* His time with this training team was up and he was mercifully satisfied to be on his way back to the capital.

Chapter Forty-Seven:

TEAM MISSION: LIBERTY & DR. SHEMAGHO...

A large beaming American greeted Nathan as he exited the SUV. The man was in his late sixties and well over six foot and weighing over ninety kilos, Nathan estimated. His hair was a lot thinner than in the days he served in the U.S. Army, but he was in rather good physical shape, and could get away with the 'sporty look', wearing shorts and a polo shirt. Judging by his fair complexion, it was easy to see his family were from European stock, and he picked up one of Nathan's weighty bags as if it were a teddy bear... *'Glad to meet you... mate,'* shouted Henry, in an attempt to add a bit of Aussie flavour to the meeting, but coming off sounding distinctly 'Cockney', as Americans do when they attempt an Australian accent.

Nonetheless, Nathan was surprised by the intimacy of such a warm greeting and made sure to thank the two young Ukrainian soldiers who had chauffeured him all the way from Ukraine's western regions.

Nathan grabbed his backpack and followed Henry along the stone path to the entrance, which was security coded and through a second door, also security coded, that took them inside. *Team Mission: Liberty* (TML) Kyiv operated out of a hostel that was only a few kilometres from the city centre. A sweet deal had been made with the owners, largely because of cancellations due to *Covid* and the war, and the rent was paid up until the end of the year. Garen had volunteered with this organisation in the time Nathan had returned to Australia to convalesce. With Garen's verbal reference and a quick natter between Henry and Nathan, he was quickly welcomed with open arms.

Volunteers came and went, and the current emphasis was upon providing advanced combat medical training to units. In the early months of the war, *TML* had aided volunteers who were joining the legion. They provided travel information, accommodation, and assistance to young men on their perilous journey and would greet the volunteers at the train station. Their scope had changed and expanded, and they were now providing supplies to organisations that assisted refugees near the front, carried out by their own drivers and vehicles. *TML* operated with several local 'foundations' assisting them to provide equipment and in particular, medical expertise to the soldiers. Considerable money had been sourced in the United States via fund raising initiatives there and were being passed on to those serving in Ukraine.

Once inside the hostel, they wandered through the 'rabbit warren' stopping just outside a heavy, white door that was adjacent to Henry's room. 'This will be your room', he announced. 'Garen stayed here and will move back in once he finishes up with the *Hospitallers*, in a couple of weeks.' 'Good, thought Nathan, hopefully there would be some news of Steve Holland on Garen's return. The room housed four double bunks and a couple of lockable wardrobes. There were old dark wooden floorboards and corniced ceilings that were well over twelve feet high; thick walls and double-glazed windows made for warmth and sound reduction. Hopefully, they would provide some protection in the event of a missile strike nearby. Nathan was pleased with his new abode, *'this will do'*, and he dropped his rucksack by one of the bunk beds.

As well as showing Nathan to his quarters, Henry gave the 'grand tour' of the hostel and soon Nathan could locate the showers and toilets, wash his clothes, make a meal, or just relax; such was the hospitality. Some time ago, a budding artist had decorated the walls with coloured chalk drawings of *Marilyn Monroe*, a classic New York 1920s building scene of workmen taking lunch on a girder, and even *Heath Ledger's* chilling 'Joker' face, all adding to the 'bohemian flavour' of the premises. Nathan met a few people were leaving in the next day or so, but he offered his bright hellos and went back to his room to unpack some of his things. There really was no need to make their acquaintance... To make things even better, there were cafes and a supermarket close by. This was the only expense he would have, as everything else was *gratis* for the volunteers. As he unpacked, his mind roamed...he really hadn't given much thought to the men he left behind but there was no lingering regret or malice on Nathan's part. As a former colleague, he truly hoped they would be safe and weren't in such a hurry to die for Ukraine.

Although very conventional due to his military background, Henry was an extremely easy man to talk to. He had worked his way up from the private ranks of the U.S. military to lieutenant colonel and understood how to effectively communicate with people from all walks of life. He was a highly intelligent man who knew what policies and procedures were required to make *TML* in Ukraine an effective organisation. Nathan would find out later how frustrating Henry's position really was, as he had to function with people in Ukraine who weren't up to his knowledge or expectations as well as trying to make those board members back in America understand the 'viscosity' of the situation on the ground in Kyiv and the other oblasts. Nathan remembered an old saying that fitted the man's delicate situation perfectly: *'It is hard to soar like an eagle when you're working with turkeys.'* The big American also had a great sense of humour and was a man you could easily warm to. Henry had been married several times and, like many of the foreigners who journeyed to Europe, thought his skillset would be valuable to the Ukrainians. As for Nathan, his immediate task was to assist an American nurse from Louisiana called Katy who was instructing a Ukrainian medical training team at a training centre five minutes' walk from the apartments he inhabited near the *Lavina Mall*. The usual *Bolt* cab took them there the next day. 'Wow,' thought Nathan, 'how things go the full circle, especially when you don't expect them to.'

In the coming days and weeks, more volunteers arrived. Nigel, a 'Geordie' from Newcastle, England, soon shared a spare bunk in Nathan's room and a couple of guys from France and Switzerland arrived and took up residence in other rooms. There was even a fellow countryman of Nathan; a guy called Troy, who was ex-military, an Afghan vet, and a highly skilled medico. Most of the new arrivals had completed TCCC, Total Combat Casualty Care courses in their home countries and thought this is how they would be of most help to keep the wounded Ukrainians alive; most of these volunteers had been in the military. Garen was certain Nathan's previous experience as a military patrol medic and long-time *St. John* volunteer would hold him in good stead with the current training. Nathan had many strings to his bow; besides being an accomplished instructor and educator, he had a 'practical' knowledge of medicine. Some of the others had completed an intensive three-day course and could regurgitate it 'parrot fashion', but it's another matter when you don't have the experience to connect the dots with the other medical conditions that may arise from hemorrhage, shock, and combat inflicted wounds.

By and large, the new team that was being put together were getting on famously well, and frequently joked with each other; about their complex family situations back home, or their nationalities, especially when they were eating and relaxing in the common room. *The banter was all in good jest.* Jacques would frequently poke fun at the staid *cuisine* of his Anglo-comrades, or the preoccupation with *Fosters* beer, while his counterparts would lightheartedly remark about the supposed valiant nature of the French military. *'French rifles for sale...'* they would joke – *'Never fired and only dropped once!'* Troy chipped in and had a dig at Jacques stating that the most popular film in France was *Broke Back Mountain*. The jokes weren't meant to offend but drew great laughter and amusement from everyone. Henry would drop in from the mountain of paperwork in his room, pull up a chair, open a beer and crack jokes with all the volunteers. Nathan had been given the title of 'the Golden Shemagh' or 'Dr. Shemagho' by Henry, not because of the fact he held a doctorate, but also because he was tireless in his endless promotion of the venerable shemagh scarf. Whenever Nathan taught a group, he would delve into the unending and universal benefits of carrying a shemagh and how it could be used further as a wound dressing, tourniquet, lightweight blanket, camouflage net, lightweight towel and the list went on... The group laughter made for a remarkable environment and team ethic; the reason why so many people go on deployments is because you can't find this kind of merriment and camaraderie anywhere else! *What a heterogeneous team they were* – a Brit, two Aussies, a Frenchman, a Swiss guy named Danny, and a Louisiana nurse, all being led by a former U.S. Army colonel.

Training with *TML* didn't happen every day, so instead it was planned to meet one of the delegates from the *Foundation* that operated various TCCC training missions around the various oblasts. Henry welcomed anyone who wasn't busy to partake of coffee with the contact and learn about the upcoming missions. The meeting was held at a pleasant and upmarket café that was just across the street from the *Foundation's* city headquarters. A small, balding but cheerful Ukrainian called Dymytro crossed the road, shook Henry's hand, firmly, in the manner of an old friend, and then introduced himself to everyone else. As the men spoke, newly painted olive drab transit vans were arriving and parking all the way along the street. *There must have been twenty or more camped out on the road!* These would be used or donated by the *Foundation* to the military or any other organisation that required them. The *Foundation* was headed by a very wealthy young Ukrainian entrepreneur who had a knack for securing funding for this type of project, or the sponsoring of medical training or the acquisition of large drones from other European nations, notably the acquisition of a long-range *Bayraktar* unmanned combat aerial vehicle. As the talk turned back to the upcoming training mission, it sounded like Nigel, Jacques and Nathan would be on the next trip in a few days, and this would probably go to a military training facility, or 'polygon' as they called it, near Lviv. The men were excited by this news and couldn't wait to get back and pack their gear.

Prior to the mission, they would conduct some medical training to be vetted by a contact of the *Foundation* who had some experience as a medical doctor. The men trained a group of news reporters the next day. This was a great success, and after which they were driven to a secret location around forty minutes to the west of Kyiv. It was here that they came across a unit that was being more robustly trained than any other Nathan had previously seen, and this is where he first met one of the chief trainers, who pompously went by the name 'Comandante'. This Ukrainian very closely resembled the facial features of the actor, Karl Urban, but swaggered about the grass training area as if he wrote the manual on military and medical training. Funnily enough, he carried a replica pistol for 'show'. Like most tyrants and intimidators, they get away with it because they are large men in stature but diminutive morally and for most part, technically. Nathan had seen this tired theme, *time, and time before...* Yelling at people doesn't get the results... No one likes to be screamed at, full stop! Sure, it may work in boot camp, but most people act out of fear and Nathan didn't believe that to be the basis for quality learning, memorisation, and actualisation. Hollering only has impact when it's the last quarter of the 'AFL Grand Final' and your team is down fifteen points... You've pleasantly coached, requested, or coaxed your players for their best all year but now is the time to rant and rave to scare your players into decisive action! *To give all they've got! The trophy is on the line!!* They would learn soon enough that Comandante was the lazy type of leader that will 'tell you nothing, take you nowhere and drop you off halfway'!

The unit was exercising on the edge of a grassed airstrip. Nearby, lay the crumpled remains of a Russian jet fighter that had been brought down, earlier in the war. The pilot had ejected and was still missing, *and that was the official story...* It was rumoured that captured Russians were worth high bounties if caught alive and handed over to the officials. To the surprise of no-one, this scheme had been touted by Cyrus, who suggested to all: 'If you're training down near the front and a Russian presents himself......' Another one of Cyrus's fanciful moments! As the men went through their drills, Comandante would 'screech like a banshee' at the anxious soldiers, while the foreign trainers kept an eye out for any serious breaches of non-assimilation or safety during the training. A couple of scenarios would be run later in the evening that would include Nathan, Nigel, and Jacques and this was as much for the foreigners as for the men vetting the Ukrainians.

Being on daylight savings time, the men trained well into the twilight hours and didn't get ferried back to the hostel until late that evening. Much was the hubris from the training, the men were buoyed and enjoyed a light snack and small talk before retiring. Nathan was extremely pleased with the ways things were going with his new colleagues and looked forward to Garen returning and working together again, as a solid team. It was at this point Nathan thought his move from 'Mitchell and Company' a beneficial one, but he wasn't to know and could not have imagined that disappointment wasn't all that far away...

Chapter Forty-Eight

HUSTLER'S PARADISE – HELPLESS PUPPIES AND LOST SOULS

'What goes on around you...compares little with what goes on inside you.'

Ralph Waldo Emerson

Without doubt, Ukraine is a remarkably beautiful country! There is so much natural diversity in the country-ryside, with vast sweeping wheat fields, major rivers, plentiful forests, and majestic mountain ranges, such as the striking *Carpathians* in the country's southwest. There are key cities dotted across the landscape which boast a rich tapestry of historical buildings, fascinating monuments, parks, and culture; many of these cities are now married to modern facades boasting incredible zest and vigour. *Kyiv, the capital, is simply amazing!* For the most part, Ukraine's traditions and customs are diverse, the people charming and inviting. However, when it comes to 'deceit', and the tabling of nations on the 'Corruption Perceptions Index', Ukraine is only surpassed by Russia in terms of dishonesty. Sadly, this is a fact. *Irrefutable, contemporary, and consistent...* Unfortunately, this is the one enduring memory Nathan thought would linger with him of his varied travels in Ukraine; the impression of criminality and shifty dealings perpetrated by individuals at most levels of society. Based on what he had seen and most of the people he met, he found it difficult not to consider Ukraine to be a 'hustler's paradise', and a haven for lost puppies or lost souls.

As it turned out, Nathan had not been selected for the next *TML* training mission, which irritated him to no end. *Story of his life*! How many times had he been bumped off deployments because his face didn't fit, or he was too outspoken, or someone used the 'old boy's' network and got ahead in the line? On these occasions, he would frequently hum to himself the Kasey Chambers song: *'Am I not pretty enough?'* in a sarcastic attempt to console his mental well-being and self-worth as well as reminding himself he never 'kissed ass' or compromised his core beliefs, *not for anyone!* He smiled when he remembered what an American had said to him in these situations, 'Semper Gumby' my friend – 'always flexible'. But for Nathan, old habits were hard to shake. For the meantime, he would use this downtime to work on his fitness, revise himself on TCCC protocols and take a well-earned rest.

He now lay on his bunk and ruminated upon what he had witnessed and heard over the last four months; for one, it hadn't been that long ago that he had suffered from pneumonia and its accompanying health issues. 'Still getting over it but feeling a damn sight better now...' he pondered. *Back to his central thoughts...* The dubious characters, the mediocre leadership, the corrupt officials, the deceitful foundations... the image of wealthy diners chowing down their *pate de foie gras,* in swanky Kyiv restaurants, while ageing and overweight patriots, or young boys with asthma toiled in the sun at Africa Beach! Many a time Nathan seriously considered the recruits being trained and made a frank, mental note of their chances of survival. Studying an overweight guy in his fifties, a chain smoker of the last thirty years, Nathan would shake his head in resignation, *'Yep, he's got zero chance,'* or the twenty-year-old kid who wanted to be somewhere else and who wasn't really 'getting with the training program,' *'Nope, he ain't gonna make it either.'* It all came flooding back and he deliberated... 'is this the fault of the Ukrainian political and military hierarchy, or is it the downside to being in a war, and a battle for survival, as a nation and as individuals?'

The memories continued to resurrect themselves... He recalled Carlos and his hustling persona and the drone incident in the city of Kyiv. *What the hell was he thinking?* Or was it the arrogance and bravura of being a 'Westerner', an American who was 'bailing out' Ukraine in their desperate hour, and he should be granted some slack... Did Carlos really expect to get away with nonsense like that? *He wouldn't back home...* Nathan next recalled the '007 Club' and he certainly wasn't naïve enough to think that these types of clubs weren't run by gangsters in Australia or anywhere in the West. Sure they were, but the sad part was that the club, with its stereotypical hoods and harlots looked so natural and so at home in Kyiv.

Nathan fluffed up his pillow and lowered his head back down, his thoughts turning to some of the Ukrainian military commanders he had met. Mad Commander Manis, back at the Kreschatyk hotel, always ranting, terrorising his troops and anyone else within range and, all the time appearing to be coming down off some illicit drug or hallucinogen! The latest gossip was that he had been sacked from the military and jailed – *no surprise there!* Then there were some of the officers of the *Legion Obolon*, that is if you could call them officers in the true sense. People who had received their appointments as a direct result of nepotism or dishonesty and worse still, the type of people who take credit for the hard work of others. Could these men really lead soldiers into the 'crucible of battle', honestly inspire them, care for them, and win a war against a cunning and formidable enemy? Nathan paused and thought over these ideas for a few seconds more and knew the answer was weighed heavily in the negative. He had encountered some effective leaders, particularly at the junior level, and a couple at the senior level, but he could sense that the crucial aspect of 'team' in all this was missing. Then there were the other officers who had been promoted due to their social influence or financial strength. Other commanders had made wild promises, especially to foreign trainers, who in their desperation believed the lies they villainously peddled. Their lies knew no bounds: rank, privilege, accommodation, wages, and the list went on and on...

The smarter option for a foreigner, particularly if he wanted to join in the 'physical' fight, was to enlist in one of the newly formed international units, such as the Norse unit if they were Scandinavian, or the Canadian-Ukrainian Brigade, or one of the many others, like the 'Norman' brigade. Nonetheless, the awarding of a medal for their service to the Ukraine homeland did exhibit thanks from some of those on high for what the men had achieved but like a house that is plagued with termites, the structure may look sound but the foundations and supporting structures have been compromised, corrupted and are wretched to the core. In the case of the Ukraine military, their 'house of cards' resides on the unfit, the incompetent, the 'cowboy' element, the corrupt, the criminal, and the divisiveness of individuals wanting to 'row their own boat'. So, it comes as no surprise that there is a pressing need to join the ranks of NATO...

Adding to this socio-political mayhem are the lost puppies or lost souls; essentially a great many of the foreigners and Westerners who trudged to Eastern Europe. Of course, the standout figure here is Cyrus, wheeling and dealing, *up one moment and down the next*...snorting crank off his daypack and consorting with the criminal biker element of Kyiv... throwing around pleading and powerful speeches like a thespian from *Hamlet*, who carefully articulates their prose, but nowhere near as genuine or profound but just as theatrical and manipulative, all the same. The war for people like Cyrus was a godsend as it rescued him from the humdrum, tedious existence of a boring life, *somewhere back in 'Jerkwater', U.S.A.* If he wasn't skiving about in Ukraine, he would most probably be incarcerated back home or hustling somewhere in Asia.

Nathan kept reminiscing and another dubious character came to mind... *There were so many...* This time it was good ole' Captain Matt. Nathan's first impressions of Capt. Matt was of a conscientious ex-Marine who would be a great asset to the training, but he couldn't be more wrong! After being sent packing due to his penchant for incredibly young, pretty girls, Nathan wouldn't see this rogue until he returned to Ukraine on his second tour.

It seems Capt. Matt was now in charge of a battalion of a mixture of Ukrainian and foreign volunteers. How this came about was anyone's guess! Mitchell, like most other foreign trainers, was hedging his bets both ways and had kept in loose contact with the 'Captain'. A meeting was to be held at a café on Kreschatyk. Nathan had offered to accompany Mitchell to the meeting; if nothing else it would be an opportunity to get out of the apartment. The day was warming up slowly and Nathan and Mitchell had already acquired a table under a giant umbrella and were patiently waiting. After ten minutes, they could see Capt. Matt and an offsider wander down the avenue towards the restaurant. Straight away, something wasn't right, especially with Capt. Matt's colleague... The man, who appeared to be of Spanish or Italian origin, was walking by his colleague's side, like an obedient puppy, but he was twitchy, looking all over the place and would frequently stop and attempt to take in his surroundings, *as a dog would*... As this curious 'creature' approached it was plain to see he was on some substance as he possessed a zombified look and seemed 'out of it' to all who now sat at the table, as well as the waitress. With a name like Miguel, he had to be Spanish, and the only thing Nathan gleaned from his presence was that he had visited Sydney once upon a time.

As far as Capt. Matt went, he too looked like he had been on 'a bender' or was *coming down from something*. His face was sweating heavily, and he fidgeted, looking all around, as if he was about to be nabbed, for something he shouldn't have done... As the conversation progressed, he tried to convince Mitchell and by association his team, to join his battalion and promised a try before you buy option, but was very vague on the details, such as accommodation, meals, and things like that. He flashed about some of the training photos on his camera and the one that really stood out was the senior officer attempting to fire a rocket launcher, but having the launching end, where the rocket would exit, facing the man's rear. 'See,' said Matt, angered by the image, *This is the sort of shit I have to put up with.* Mitchell and Nathan sat quietly and didn't say a word.

On the periphery of the main conversation, Miguel studied his phone incessantly, either expecting a call or checking the internet, but curiously he did so at about one centimetre from the glass face, as if he couldn't make out what was going on. It was like watching a man trying to find an electronic needle in the proverbial technological haystack! *The man was fixated*, and Nathan could only imagine what was going through his mind... When the 'three cheese' pizza arrived, and placed directly in front of him, Miguel wasn't sure where the food was! He looked and searched about, intently. A minute or two later he managed to locate the pizza, again, directly in front of him on the table. He then turned to Nathan and randomly inquired, 'Can you get MG3 machine guns?' Nathan didn't reply but just gave the man a quizzical look as if to say *WTF*! As soon as the meal was finished, goodbyes and flimsy promises of staying connected were made and Capt. Matt and his unsavoury sidekick wandered back down the avenue until invisible among the crowd; like some surreal, Ukrainian thematic version of 'Midnight Cowboy', with Capt. Matt as the tall hustler and smaller Miguel as the crippled and ailing 'Ratso Rizzo' clone. Nathan and Mitchell just looked at each other for a moment, speechless...there really wasn't anything that needed to be said. *Capt. Matt was never seen again...*

Once again, Nathan wriggled on his bunk and thought hard about some of the great international people he had encountered and worked with in Ukraine, such as Tyler, Cherie, Earl, Sascha, Bill, Henry and Garen, and most of the people at *TML*. But as decent as they were, *there were those that were just bad.* Take Devlin for instance... The guy and his mate get into a 'punch on' with hoods, but like a whipped dog he cowers to ward off a beating, probably because thugs pity the coward, but this allows his friend to suffer a walloping. Moreover, the guy takes money from a Ukrainian unit to go and fight Russians but chickens out and then photo shops a large hole, complete with helmet and military gear strewn about the place and attempting to sell this as his time at the front! Moreover, he is provided with a roof over his head by friends but reciprocates this generosity by breaking into their borrowed residence and stealing their gear, especially the body armour which is for their own survival. *What a guy! What a complete louse!* And the story just gets better and better… It was later discovered that Devlin had never received the *Purple Heart* that he claimed he had been awarded for being wounded in Afghanistan. Nathan wondered what other lies this man had peddled in his time in Ukraine. At any other period in history, he would most probably be shot for his selfish actions. It sure as hell sounded like a lot of these men were running away from something or didn't want to go back. For them, it certainly wasn't the noble cause of assisting the Ukrainians in their fight for survival.

Outside of the altruistic varieties and 'soldiers of fortune' there were other 'lost' people, individuals who had been in the military but nothing outstanding, who had travelled to Ukraine. Most of these were nice enough guys, like Boden, who was from the American South, who didn't have any substantial credentials, except for some logistics service in the Army Reserve but who was enjoying being somewhere else besides the United States. Was it either a crappy, unfulfilling job or a failed marriage or relationship? Was it mid-life crisis, like it had been for Steve Holland and were these men attempting to recapture an exciting element of their younger lives, when they were in the military, fit, had purpose and life was more rewarding and simpler? Someone once said that 'war is a reboot' and for many men the war in Ukraine was a viable opportunity to *restart, reprieve or resurrect* their sad and sorry existence.

Nathan looked deep into his soul and pondered on these existential thoughts for a few minutes… He certainly wasn't in Ukraine to reap the rewards at the end of the war. *Hell, no!* He had travelled to locate an old comrade, and in the process had assisted the Ukrainians to the best of his ability. Like many, he too felt obliged to assist and with his various skills, why shouldn't he? But frankly, he couldn't wait to get home again and had said, openly to anyone listening, *'I didn't come here to die for Ukraine*, it's not my country, but I will try to help those who choose to do the fighting.' Again, he wriggled on the bed to get comfortable... He thought on.... he knew it was always the eternal balancing act between good and evil for the human species, between the *ying* and the *yang*. After a great deal of deliberation, he decided he was determined not to let the thoughts and actions of certain people sully his experiences *nor his deep and unwavering respect or love for Ukraine.*

Chapter Forty-Nine

MISSION: MYKOLAIV

Nathan had little time to dwell on his first missed opportunity with *TML*; two further training missions materialised in rapid succession. The first training mission would involve Jacques, Nathan and Nigel and they would trek down to Mykolaiv, which was being targeted by Russian forces, to spend three days training units in and around the area in TCCC. A rendezvous was arranged at the *Foundation* HQ and then they would be ferried by Comandante in his vehicle and his crew to the training areas. It was obvious Comandante thought this arrangement a hinderance to his operation, what with the 'eye rolling' and snide comments but it was the deal that had been brokered between the *Foundation* and *TML*. *They were going, like it or not!* The use of foreign trainers was important to the military as the senior commanders valued the foreign expertise and input, as did the troops on the ground, and their presence was used to provide such training programs with credibility. But, for the most part, they were just *'window dressing'* to some people within the *Foundation*.

Heading south towards Odessa on the Black Sea coast, and then turning right as you survey the map, the men didn't arrive at the first small village town until well in the afternoon. They were billeted in a sports stadium that was built primarily for basketball, housed on the wooden court floor and sleeping on a collection of wobbly steel framed beds, which Nathan thought must've been resurrected from a rubbish dump. Nathan quickly set up his bed space and laid out his gear, as if he was back at bootcamp, *ready to go at a moment's notice*. The night was balmy and there was little ventilation, which made it difficult to sleep, but the men were tired from the long journey and soon crashed out.

After breakfast the next day, training commenced at the local soccer field, which was adjacent to the basketball stadium. The men ran the soldiers through drills that emphasised the need to apply the combat tourniquet quickly, in the right place – *'high and tight'* was the catchphrase and this was followed by timing the soldiers putting on their personal tourniquet. The soldiers tried it on themselves a few times and then repeated the drill upon their comrades. In the next scenario, wounded men had to be fitted with a tourniquet and then extracted from the fire fight by their colleagues; this invariably involved dragging the wounded from the battle. The instructors screamed, at times in the faces and ears of the soldiers, '*Hurry up...*,' '*Your mate is dying...*,' '*What are you going to do...*,' '*It needs to be "high and tight" and not slack or loose.*' The shouting and haranguing rang out over the playing field as well as utilising the popular Ukrainian term of '*Bistra Bladt*,' which could mean all of the above phrases, especially if it was yelled piercingly, with venom and the two words singularly and slowly emphasised – '*BIIIISSSTRAAA... BLLAAADDDTT.*' Essentially, this universal 'motivator' expression loosely translated as '*GET YOUR ARSE MOVING*', '*KEEP RUNNING YOU SLUG*' or '*HURRY THE FUCK UP*' and always had the desired effect. The Ukrainian soldiers relished the chaotic drills, as they always did. It may save their life or a friend one day... The same tuition was supposed to take place for another unit the next day, but this was cancelled, so the men made their way to Mykolaiv and an *Airbnb* that would be their home for the next two days.

Soon the vehicle entered the outskirts of the city, which was eerily quiet; the ninety-minute drive having passed quickly. The city had been recently hit by rockets and shelled, and the damage was obvious... They passed a large department store that had been recently obliterated, and Nathan hoped that it had been vacant at the time when the attack came, *but it probably wasn't...* During their limited drive around Mykolaiv, Nathan noticed this was another beautiful Ukrainian city that broke the mould in architectural design with many provincial style terraced apartments adorning the inner city. Mykolaiv went a long way back in historical terms, with ancient settlements and later 'Cossacks' having been situated near the *Southern Bug* River that twisted its way south to the Black Sea. The Russian influence here had been suffocating, as it had been headquarters for the Imperial Russian Navy for over a hundred years until the fleet relocated to Sevastopol. Now it was under assault and the push was on from the Russian forces. As the men neared their lodgings, they could make out thick black smoke in and around the city outskirts where shells had rained down, and they could hear the telltale *'crump, crump, crump'* of explosions as new, heavy shells landed on fresh targets. All the while, Comandante and his colleagues were not fazed by these proceedings; for them it was another opportunity to showcase their Ukrainian bravado... As far Nathan and his fellow Westerners were concerned, they kept their helmets and body armour handy, regardless of Comandante's disparaging comments. As a British Marine Commando once remarked to Nathan back in his days in the SAS, *'You're dead a long time...'*

The evening meal of pizza, salad and dessert had been ordered. Not bad for a city on the verge of being overrun! No matter what you could say about Comandante, he wasn't cheap when it came to dining. However, there was to be no going out in the evening and all the men had to change into civilian attire before they appeared in the street to grab anything out of the vehicles...no overt displays of military gear. Except to the *blind* or a *raving idiot*, it was obvious these men were in town for a military purpose; *a nice try at camouflage and deception but failed!* Nathan and his colleagues settled in for the night, in their spacious bunk room, either listening to music, reading, checking out their phones or cracking jokes at each other. It was around eleven, just about time the men were falling asleep when a multitude of sirens sounded in the distance and the first rocket exploded, *only a couple of hundred metres away...* Jacques and Nigel leapt off their beds, grabbing their helmets and body armour and raced into the bathroom area, which was central inside the building and thought to provide the best protection, unless a rocket landed directly on top of them! *Being a newly built house, it had no cellar.* Nathan heard the next explosive blast; it was further away, and he decided not to bother with making the trip to the safety of the bathroom. A third strike landed somewhere in the distance and Nathan rolled over and fell sleep. He thought it pointless going anywhere unless the strikes were 'close' and by then, any protection would most probably be futile.

A great many of the Westerners had brought their body armour with them to Ukraine, the type worn in Afghanistan and considered to be Grade Four which is judged to be the best protection from military small arms fire and some heavy calibre firearms. Nathan had grabbed a 'soft armour' vest that had been discarded at

TML by someone who had ventured back to America. He didn't see the need to wear heavy body armour as he was not planning to be involved in CQB or fighting from the frontlines. If that situation arose, *he would grab the armour from someone who didn't need it anymore!* This armour would mostly protect him from handguns, any 'friendly on friendly' situations, a random stabbing attack and some light shrapnel hits but, more importantly, it did not hinder his movement, which he deemed to be more crucial; he also had to consider his fitness and age. His intention wasn't to be a sitting target! No matter what the war or situation, *it was always so much harder to hit a moving target*, and this logic guided his resolve not to be caught stationary in the first place! He didn't subscribe to the 'sheep herd mentality' of doing what everyone else did based on someone else's *handle-of-the-situation*. As far as artillery and heavier calibre weapons went, *no body armour was going to protect anyone from that!!*

The next training day was conducted in a wooded area, off the main highway out of town, but the system of instruction was still the same: teach the troops how to place on a combat tourniquet and other lifesaving principles, such as hemorrhage and resuscitation, conduct speed training, supervise group training and then confirm the training by running scenarios as the assessment. Each of the FMAs would provide their part of the training and provide 'overwatch' to make sure the soldiers understood. Many of the soldiers in this unit had been around since the start of the war and had defended local installations, such as airfields from the very first Russian invaders. What amazed Nathan was the pitiful state of their kit and the lack of modern equipment. Some of the soldiers were wearing old and worn business shoes and thinly padded jackets that looked like they had been stolen off a work site! Many of the soldiers were so very unfit. Nathan came across a guy who was wearing the 'Punisher' patch on his sleeve but, to look at the man, you could only assume he regularly punished a box or two of donuts! So much for the triumphant posters in Kyiv of steely eyed and supremely fitted out men and women displaying appropriate and professional military combat gear! That was just *wartime propaganda...* Nevertheless, these guys were certainly committed, but Nathan could only make a comparison of them to a 'Dad's Army' outfit or some backwoods militia, by their looks and attire.

Again, the training went exceptionally well, and it was time for the men to head back to the *Airbnb*. A scrumptious dinner of chicken, salad and tiramisu was served, and the men retired to their room, showered, and rested; Nathan had grabbed a double bunk for himself early on in their stay and had plenty of space to relax on. This form of training is extremely demanding as there is the element of driving to the local training area, putting on the 'game face' no matter how one is feeling and attempting to train people in a language you hope the interpreter is accurately conveying. Never mind the adrenaline rushes of living in a war environment. As far as the evening went, fatigue made the choice easy, and the men opted for an early night. It was around midnight this time when the sirens blared and the first missile landed somewhere, just down the road. Again, Jacques and Nigel sprung out of bed, grabbed their protective equipment, and ran to the safety of the bathroom 'bunker'. Nathan waited... *BOOM!!* The next strike was closer; windows shook violently, and the walls reverberated with the sound, and then another closer, cataclysmic *BOOM!! 'These Russian bastards are walking these babies on to us,'* reflected Nathan, somewhat more concerned this time. He speedily gripped his Kevlar helmet and body armour and made for the safety of the bathroom area, which by now was completely occupied by people, *all nursing their solitary fears, thoughts, and apprehension...* Comandante and a few of the other Ukrainians weren't bothered with the close missile strikes and stayed in their rooms. *Then there was nothing...silence... inside and out...* Everyone waited for the 'all clear' to sound and then wandered back to their bunks and a few more hours of sleep; two more air raids sounded that night. Nathan had been true to his word and had said to his friends, 'I'm not going to the bathroom unless it is close...' *This time, the projectiles had nearly landed on top of them!*

At least the training on their last day would be out at a local weapons firing range, not far from the city. It was being exploited by many of the local units; no doubt, to get in some firing practice before their turn came to go and engage the enemy. Comandante and his Ukrainian buddies, one of which looked remarkably like the actor, Paul Giamatti, chatted with the commanders of the next training unit. A brief exchange took place by the city's roadside, and the plan was they would all travel in convoy to the range twenty minutes away, break into groups and complete the various TCCC drills and range practices. Minutes later, the convoy set off and was travelling steadily down the main road when, without warning, there was an almighty squeal of tyres, followed by a second's pause and then a loud thump, then sounds of screeching and shearing metal. Almost instantaneously, the military camouflaged *4x4* vehicle was flung, aggressively over on to its side, near the curb, *just averting electricity power poles!* A moment later, the convoy came to one almighty screeching halt, which threw all the other traffic into chaos...

Without hesitation, soldiers began running from their vehicles with their weapons, some men grabbed stretchers, while others made phone calls. Initially, it was thought the 'end vehicle' had been struck by a wayward shell, or a rocket propelled grenade, but the carnage created was due to the vehicle being T-boned at the intersection. *A plain, old-fashioned car accident!* While other soldiers rushed about, like 'chickens with their heads removed', Nathan slowly surveyed all around him from the other side of the road. His *St. John First Aid* training had taught him to resist the temptation from hurrying in, but to assess the situation first for any danger. He knew for certain that no matter what happened he was most useful staying out of the way, especially as he couldn't speak Ukrainian. The unit doctor and medics had galloped over to the crushed vehicle, but the one major casualty was a young twenty-year-old soldier, whose head was crushed, *and he was beyond saving...* He wasn't wearing a seat belt like his fellow passengers, who only suffered cuts and bruises. Nathan had always joked to the other men that he probably 'had more chance of dying in Ukraine in a motor vehicle accident' and here was the proof... A young man had bravely enlisted to defend his country during wartime but had died because of an unfastened safety device. So sad, so ironic, *and such a waste of life!*

After nearly an hour at the site, the long convoy resumed its trek to the range, leaving behind it broken glass, spilt fuel, wreckage, and *a tragedy...* The large military entourage parked their vehicles just beside the rear road on the range. Nearby, an imbedded rocket, which had hit the range during the evening but had been quickly defused, provided a source of inquiry and entertainment, and a 'selfie' photo opportunity. The first unit soon arrived, and they assembled in a loose formation, awaiting orders. Above the talking and racket, Nathan heard a man speaking English in a distinctive accent and walked briskly over to the guy, smiling and inquiring, *'Hey mate, whereabouts in Australia are you from?'* It is always comforting to hear the voice of a countryman, especially so far from home and in a country that doesn't readily converse in English. The young man was around thirty, had a shaved head and looked like he could do with a bath. He grinned at Nathan and responded, *'I'm from Adelaide, what about you?'* Nathan replied, *'I'm from Melbourne and what the fuck are you doing over here?'* The 'South Aussie' went on... 'Well, I was bored back home and came over and joined the *Legion*. That turned out to be a big mistake so a few of us fell in with this lot and it has been good ever since.' As they traded stories, another guy close by began to speak English also and Nathan asked him what part of England he was from... 'I'm from Cheshire.' he replied. Taking a chance on sporting teams, Nathan asked what club the guy followed in the English Premier League. *'Liverpool,'* came the reply and all the men smiled and found a warm and satisfying connection with country and football club! They continued chatting briefly until the unit was broken up into three platoon sized groups, some for TCCC training and the others for range practice. The South Australian and the Liverpool supporter trudged off and Nathan never saw them again...

The day happened to be surprisingly warm, even though there was a considerable degree of cloud cover; also, a tad on the humid side. Lunch had been brought out in an old Russian *Grad* truck and the men lined up to take their pick of pasta, salad, and small rock cakes. What had been noticeable in the lull over lunchtime was the sound of the repeated and multiple strikes that were blasting targets in Mykolaiv. A greater amount of black smoke billowed across the horizon over the town. The traffic on the highway was already building to a congestive level as people refused to be left behind if the Russian Army succeeded in their advance.

Jacques and Nigel suggested to Comandante that maybe it wouldn't be a bad idea to cut the training short, go back to their accommodation, pack up and be on their way. No point in getting caught out, having to try, and 'cut and run for it' among the refugees, if it did descend to that... Their legitimate concerns were laughed away as the gloating, *dumbass of a Ukrainian* who cheerfully said they would have plenty of time and there was nothing to worry about. *'Fucking alright for him,'* said Nigel angrily, 'He can ditch his uniform and blend in with the locals. *We can't!'* Nathan had spoken with Nigel about the potential for this very situation back at *TML* HQ. Both men had quickly decided if their vehicle had been hijacked and they had been hauled out by 'Russian Separatists', they would sooner go out fighting than end up in a Russian cell like some other Westerners, or worse, paraded as 'mercenaries' on television or in a 'show court'. *Now, the chance of being left behind to fend for themselves was a distinct possibility!!*

For the rest of the afternoon, the foreigners kept scanning their watches, sweating on the conclusion of the day's training. At around five, the last group had been put through its paces and it was time to go.... They took a speedy drive down a deserted road back to the city – while the other side of the road out was 'chockablock' full.

They were soon at the Airbnb. Nathan and his roommates packed and were ready to go in five minutes. They walked out to the foyer, only to find Comandante and his team, sitting around the kitchen table small talking, casually eating, and sipping coffee. They looked across to Nathan and his friends and could see they were ready to depart that instant, *but wild horses couldn't budge them from their impromptu soirée*. They also saw that the three Westerners weren't too pleased about the situation, but they were annoyingly ambivalent, they simply didn't care... After about thirty minutes of this display, the Ukrainians decided to get up, pack up and make a move to begin the long drive back to Kyiv. When the vehicle was loaded and it was time to go, they found themselves lined up on the highway with the throng of refugees, *immovable and going nowhere... fast!* The Westerners who sat patiently in the back of the vehicle looked at each other but now was not the time to say, '*I fucking told you so!*' They were hoping, like the Ukrainians, *that an escape route would avail itself!*

The ladened vehicle did an about turn and sped down a narrow street, only to discover a primary route bogged down with a plethora of cars, honking, beeping, and as immobile as set concrete... Another about turn, and the *4x4* propelled itself down another narrow street. Still, more blocked arterials... *no escape routes here...* However, *now was not the time to give up or succumb to panic!* A frantic drive down a one-way street could have ended in disaster as the *4x4* nearly collided with a vehicle ladened with passengers, also intent upon leaving, hurriedly. When it seemed as though all was lost, and all escape routes exhausted, a narrow secondary road by the river led the men to an 'on ramp' by the bridge that led out of town. A procession of cars was running the gauntlet, across the congested bridge, at around sixty kilometres per hour but surprisingly, everyone was moving, running away from Mykolaiv and its troubles. If the dramas and adventures of the day was anything to go by, *it would be a long, tense night...*

Around two in the morning the *4x4* pulled up in the laneway, just outside the *TML* hostel. The curfew was in force, but paperwork, bluff, the wearing of Ukrainian camouflage uniforms and some 'slack' roadblock security had allowed the men to return to the capital in record time. Comandante lazily got out and shook the men's hands in a most unconvincing fashion, and then hastily sped off, as if he had *finally washed his hands of their company...* They didn't care about Comandante's attitude, they were just glad to be back, safe at their Kyiv 'home'. The Ukrainians had taken turns to drive and had been speeding all the way back to the capital. At times, the speedometer displayed one hundred and fifty plus kilometres per hour. On those bad roads, and at night, that speed was dangerously excessive. Obviously, the road fatality the previous day hadn't sunken in yet... Not all the Ukrainians had been bad to work with and it was sad to leave some of the better operators as they had all trained hard and contributed to helping many soldiers survive. Nathan later discovered that around four hundred 'traitors' had been rounded up by the SBU in Mykolaiv, many who had been 'marking targets' for the Russian gunners.

They punched the code to enter the hostel. Garen was up, eating a bowl of steaming Chinese noodles in the common room and warmly welcomed the *'Return of the conquering heroes'* as he put it. Henry also put his head in and greeted everyone as he had heard the men walk past his window on their return. He went back to his room and said he would appreciate a de-brief in the morning... Funnily enough, no one wanted to sleep, the adrenaline was still high after the drive and the adventures of the last few days. Nathan that went to the refrigerator and grabbed one of his Czech beers that was surprisingly still there. He passed one to Garen, who casually remarked, 'How did it go?' Nathan just gave him one of those long, silent looks and said, 'I'll tell you about it later'. Garen stopped, paused, and dropped the genial smile from his normally cheerful face and flatly announced, *'Nathan, I've got some news about Steve, that I don't think you're gonna like.'* This didn't come as a shock, judging by Steve's reluctance to go back home, the 'shady' people he had been living with, the rocket attack at Yavoriv and his work near the 'front.' Nathan wouldn't be surprised at what Steve had gotten up to or what he was fiendishly cultivating in his tortured mind. 'Before I start, said Garen, 'Most of this crazy shit comes from paramedics who worked with Steve in Donbas and comes from reliable sources, so you need to believe me...' Garen went on to say how Steve had been spouting he wasn't going to return to Australia and was planning to stay in Ukraine at the war's end. He had already managed to string along a couple of women and had sourced an apartment in Kyiv, his 'love shack' on the south side of the river. But he also had a main girlfriend with whom he shacked up, on the westside. 'Prepare yourself... *the worst is yet to come*,' pronounced Garen, in an attempt by a *good comrade* to warn Nathan of *some really bad news*. 'Your old friend has made a lot of buddies in 'Red Sector' (a far-right, nationalist organisation) and tends to hang out with them most of the time.' This came as a complete and utter shock to Nathan, as he had never entertained the idea his best friend *was a card-carrying fascist!* Garen continued with his troublesome story... 'The problem with all this is the people he has been hanging around with. They have brainwashed him, like so many other disillusioned critters, they think this is the way ahead.'

Well, wasn't this a 'kick in the head...' Fascism was at odds with the vibrant entrepreneurial spirit of most of Ukraine's youth, but war fosters nationalism and other alternate ideologies, and for some, nationalism nurtures unbridled hate and extremist far right politics, like fascism. It seemed to Nathan this hatred of the communists had gone the full 360 degrees! Russians and other communist forces had been the principal enemies of the Western democratic forces, including the Australian Army, since the *Second World War* and from back in the late seventies when Nathan, Steve and Phil had enlisted. Now, both men were assisting Ukraine to defeat the Russians, but Steve was taking his involvement and commitment to a whole new level! 'Okay,' said Nathan, 'I get it,' very much annoyed… 'This is worse than I thought it would be, but let's arrange a meeting when there's an alignment in schedules so that I can try and talk some sense into this old mate of mine, who has obviously lost his mind and *who now appears to be as dumb as dog shit!'*

While he mulled over everything that Garen had just told him, Nathan picked up the semi-acoustic guitar that Garen had been playing earlier in the evening and began to strum Neil Young's 'Heart of Gold'. Garen started to sing, and the process of winding down began… 'Hey,' said Garen, 'That sounds damn good, we should develop this, keep it going…' 'Sure, it will give us something to do' replied Nathan. They had spoken about 'gigging' together just before Nathan went home with pneumonia. Here they were, in the wee hours of the morning, drinking beer, talking about old mates that had gone off the rails, playing guitar and talking about gig plans. The things that happen in wartime…

Chapter Fifty

MISSION: LVIV

Overall, the training mission to Mykolaiv had been extremely successful, enhancing the *TML* reputation. So much so that another team was now required to train units, at, of all infamous places, Yavoriv. *TML* had established a centre in Lviv during the early part of the war and they had been given free rent on an old factory building for the next two years; all *TML* had to do was repair windows and frames on three floors, all of which were broken. Sounded like a good deal at the time but the place would be like an 'ice box' to live in during winter and the project was a huge undertaking! A fiery and argumentative Belgian called Pierre ran the Lviv operation, but the venture in the west seemed to have developed a reputation as being a 'hippy commune', the eclectic and alternative lifestyle volunteer types that congregated there wouldn't be out of place from *Woodstock* or the *Burning Man* festivals. When requests had arrived from Henry in Kyiv, most of the Lviv branch came across as being very reluctant to get involved. People there had developed their own living space and way of doing things and didn't want to change. While Kyiv was reasonably far from the fighting, Lviv was a 'backwater', and you wouldn't even think a war was on judging by the daily life of in the beautiful city.

It took Nathan and Garen the best part of the day to drive to *TML* HQ in Lviv in a 'shit box' *Toyota Corolla* that was the newly acquired 'company' car in Kyiv... There was no welcoming committee, so they trudged up the three flights of stairs with all their kit and found newly constructed pine double bunk beds that from one end of the large rectangle room to the end, probably around fifty metres. There were a few single rooms, but these had been snavelled for the Lviv hierarchy and 'select' personnel. There was a small conference room was at the far end, and a kitchen with a large table and chairs at the other end of the long room. A bathroom and toilet were located on the same side as the single rooms, but on the opposite side of the doorway and stairs. The double bunk bed set up reminded Nathan of the barrack sleeping arrangement in the Steve McQueen war movie, *'The Great Escape'* and he was forced to utter his standard saying when confronted by such basic dwellings: *'Cor, what a bleeding dump!'*

Soon, Pierre, and an American girl appeared with and a few female Ukrainian translators and introduced themselves. In addition, there were a couple of senior American ex-military who had been residing there for a couple of days in the single rooms, with one guy being a former full colonel in the U.S. Army and the other volunteer a warrant officer. For some reason, Nathan had a gut feeling about this 'crowd' and didn't work hard to make their friendship; he was cordial and that was all that was necessary. As they would later discover, the former warrant officer turned out to be a control freak and wanted to micro-manage everything, like most people of that rank. The 'bird' colonel appeared interested but for both Americans, this was a temporary stop before they went onto other locations and operations. In the meantime, they offered to assist with the TCCC training over the next few days. As it was late, they each selected a bunk, which had a sheer cotton drape-like screen at the front for some privacy, and they prepared themselves for the night.

As always, Nathan was ahead of the pack and had already eaten and was enjoying a coffee when Garen joined him, very tired. A chained-up dog next door had been barking all night, but Nathan wore quality earplugs and hadn't heard a thing. The dog would be 'sorted out' later in the day as one of the men planned to serve the animal a large quantity of Benadryl later that night.

Soon they were on the road, heading to the base at Yavoriv, over an hour away. There was an initial confused scramble out of the city during peak hour traffic and then plenty of beautiful countryside. As they were ahead of time, they decided to stop for coffee and a snack at the adjacent small village. Garen and Nathan looked at buying some ready-made rolls at a small bakery, but the girl behind the counter wasn't sure what Nathan was selecting. To prevent further frustration, he began to cluck and wave his arms up and down, much to the amusement of the other customers. Garen just looked at Nathan and commented, 'Seriously?' Immediately, he could see the girl's face light up and she dashed off and returned with a fresh chicken roll. 'Hey,' laughed Nathan, 'It got results, didn't it?' This time it was Nathan's turn to 'cluck like a chicken' and the irony wasn't lost on him.

At the barracks, they were met by a stern looking soldier and a high-ranking officer, of colonel rank, who would escort them to the training area. They drove slowly past the building that had received multiple hits in the rocket attack, and it was then that Nathan fully understood why there were so many casualties... As they entered a secured area, platoon sized groups were already lined up for the training, and the Westerners broke themselves into teams to cover the task; Garen and Nathan stayed together. They received a brief that if they heard sirens, everyone was to head into the forest area, less than two hundred metres away. Inside the woods, deep trenches had been dug since the initial attack earlier in the year.

No sooner had the men begun their medical training with this formation when the air raid siren began wailing across the barracks. To Nathan's surprise, there wasn't a calamitous rush to the forest, nor were people pushing, shoving, screaming or any nonsense like that. It was an orderly procession that the Westerners followed into the woods. A couple of the young Ukrainian soldiers gestured for Nathan and Garen to follow them and they did so, to the safety of an exceptionally large trench. Nathan offered the men some chewing gum and the young soldiers, probably around twenty years old or so, reciprocated by offering cigarettes. Soon, they were chatting in broken English, telling the Westerners how they had just returned from training in the United Kingdom. They didn't know exactly where they were, over there, as this had been kept a secret, but they had been well looked after by their British Army hosts and had enjoyed a few ales with their trainers. They were also proud to show off some of the military gear they had been presented with. As they were chatting away, Nathan noticed several soldiers walking about, seemingly oblivious to the present threat level. He asked one of the Ukrainian lads why these men were out in the open and was surprised when he was told these guys belong to 'the suicide squad'. It seemed that when it came to safety, most of the soldiers did what they pleased and had an infantile appreciation of what modern military armaments can do. On the second day when the sirens wailed again, they all headed into the woods once more. This time, singing could be heard echoing through the forest; an incredibly talented soldier sang folk songs beautifully and played guitar while a group of his friends sat around an unlit campfire and joined in, totally disregarding the warning of imminent danger... *Nathan just shook his head in wonder...* but it didn't prevent him or Garen wandering down and sitting beside their Ukrainian friends.

And this was the procession for the next four days... a little bit of training.... go to the forest for the air raid... train a little bit more, and then travel back to Lviv. The same successful format was followed: train, time the soldiers and run scenarios as a test. As the groups were working in platoon sized formations of thirty soldiers or more, it also gave the platoon commanders an opportunity to practice how to issue orders, discuss tactics and exercise command and control over their troops. The quality and level varied... After the first platoon had demonstrated they were rudderless in a command sense and hopeless at all the basic elements, Nathan took the next platoon commander aside and suggested to him to select his three best soldiers and make them squad commanders, knowing full well this move would make a greater contribution to the group success. The platoon commander would then devise a plan based upon Nathan's sound proposals and verbal coaching, and the officer would command and control the operation. The key here was everyone knowing what the blueprint was, following the plan and being inspired by capable leadership. The scenario went like a dream, so much so that during the de-briefing, Nathan vigorously praised one and all before giving the soldiers a rousing *Slava Ukraini, heroiam Slava,'* to which they responded with a mighty yell!

All this was achieved despite the fact they were using two female translators who had taken a real disliking to one another. Zlata, a forceful older woman, suggested that the other younger and prettier woman, Anastasia, wasn't translating as accurately as she should. Arguments between these two raged like grassfire and it was evident both women detested one another... Everyone else was tired of the pettiness of this 'cat fighting' and suggested that so long as the crux of the message gets through, no one was worried.

Probably one of the best things at the TML location in Lviv was its closeness to a beer shop, where Nathan and Garen would buy one-litre bottles of sweet lager which they enjoyed while playing guitar at the conclusion of each day's training, much to the enjoyment of their hosts. By the week's end, they were exhausted, and glad to travel back to Kyiv. They had a couple of extra passengers on the journey as the Warrant Officer and Colonel asked for a ride. They didn't have a problem with this, but Henry would not have them stay at the hostel; Nathan put this down to 'politics' and left it at that. Pierre had been extremely impressed with Garen, Nathan and the other two members, Jaques and Danny, who joined the team a day or so later and graciously informed Henry of their wonderful contribution and sound commitment. When you're not getting paid, spending money out of your own pocket and living like a vagabond, sentiments like these are deeply appreciated!

Chapter Fifty-One:

ONE LAST ROLL OF THE DICE...

After the last training mission in Lviv, there was plenty of time to kill... Although the training teams were always in demand, the 'politics' within foundations, the military, and *TML* were stifling. Volunteers came and went, and opportunities ground to a halt. Plenty of talk and speculation but no action... At least the guitar playing, singing and harmonica had progressed to the point that Nathan and Garen went to a subway in Kyiv and busked around a dozen songs for the commuters to keep themselves busy. They had seen other artists, young and old, sing, dance, play the harp and cavort about and thought, 'why not?' At the first train station where they started to play, they were told to leave *in-no-uncertain-terms* by the transit police, but they found another area to perform, just by the *Globus Shopping Centre*, but still in the underground area. 'Neil Young's 'Heart of Gold' rang out, along with Neil Diamond's classic 'Sweet Caroline,' John Denver's immortal 'Country Roads,' Leonard Cohen's haunting 'Hallelujah' and U2's gripping 'With or Without You.' The music sounded pretty good, and the men were thrown a few hundred hryvnias for their efforts. *Paid musicians, at last!* The *ad hoc* concert was repeated in a local park, just for the fun of it. After their huge day of performance, the two friends visited a local pizza restaurant to satiate their hunger. On the stairs, leading up to their dining table, sat a tiny side table that presented a black and white photograph of Vladimir Putin in a frame but with a black ribbon diagonally at the bottom corner; this normally signifies the passing of someone. As well, a shot glass of vodka, usually a toast to the departed sat next to the frame. However, residing next to the frame was also a voodoo doll, a Putin doll that was festooned with pins; a pin cushion sat on the table for anyone to help themselves to putting the 'mocker', the death knell on the President of Russia. Ah, the people of Ukraine and their unique sense of humour!

Nathan wanted to keep active, physically and mentally, while he waited to finally confront Steve Holland, who would be back in Kyiv very soon, in a matter of days... Besides, it was fun and exhilarating being a 'mission junkie'. Although still committed to *TML*, he had decided to go solo, and do one last training gig. Garen had a lot more contacts in Kyiv than Nathan, and he put him onto a 'guy who knew a guy' and so forth and so on... A team of

Ukrainian journalists that had reported on the atrocities in Bucha in the early days of the war, were now documenting the conflict and the everyday lives of the gallant soldiers who were in the fight. This meant, sometimes, the crew would be embedded with combat units. This team had extraordinarily little knowledge of tactics and survival skills in a 'war fighting' environment and were desperate to locate anyone who could assist, especially someone with an extensive military skill set. Nathan and Garen met with the group's leader over coffee and discussed a plan to assist them. Their commander, Aleksey, sheepishly asked how much this was going to cost and Nathan simply said, 'Nothing.' The Ukrainians were astounded but Nathan said he was pleased to do all he could to assist Ukraine defeat Russia.

It was Sunday morning, round seven when two black SUVs pulled up, not too far away from the hostel. The driver gestured for him to get in. As Nathan entered the vehicle, he was alarmed to find a massive husky dog staring right at him, *penetratingly, with its blue eyes*. The animal had previously been invisible as it had been resting low behind the front seats. Again, he was gestured to enter, this time by Khrystyna, who grabbed the dog's collar. She was the slim, blonde wife of the driver, Nykolai, and would also be attending the training. Nathan was taken aback when shaking hands with Nykolai...his face was scarred and displayed the effects of many fractures. Early in the war, Nykolai had been captured by the Russians, beaten, starved, and then returned to Ukraine as part of a prisoner exchange. Nykolai had attempted to put this experience behind him with frivolity and generosity toward others, but Nathan would spy out the man when no-one was looking at him and could see the man's 'broken' smile illustrated the severity of the experience that was still haunting him. Nathan had heard the rumours that Ukrainians had been castrated by their captors and hoped beyond hope that Nykolai had avoided such barbaric treatment.

Aleksey was the driver of the second vehicle and was ferrying two other men who were to be trained, Oleksandr and Dragan. They were with the *Foundation* and Nathan had trained them before, with his colleagues at Mykolaiv. 'Well,' thought Nathan, 'this is a turn up. Are they here to train or to keep tabs on me?' Nathan didn't have a problem with extras coming along, especially these two as they were alright guys. As far as he was concerned, he was handing out 'pearls of wisdom' and didn't really care who latched onto them.

Besides the odd teenager on an electric scooter, or a dilapidated 'Marshrutka' bus (it was alleged these vehicles were run by crime syndicates) the roads were bare... they headed to a forest area on the outskirts of Kyiv, on the way out west. He had been waiting and observing his surrounds... *like he always did*. Nathan kept his eye on easily identifiable landmarks, such as the *Antonov* plane factory, the supermarket that had been hit by missiles and was now destroyed mock 'western cowboy' motel along the highway. As he peered through the dark window tint, he could identify people, mostly the elderly, selling a variety of fruit, kindling and other wares alongside the highway, desperate for a few hryvnias. Nathan didn't know these people and needed to keep his bearings in case it all went sour, and he had to bail out, literally, finding a route back to the city, the hostel and safety...

After an event free drive, they arrived at the designated military training area, guarded by two alert soldiers at a large front gate. Aleksey conversed with the men and within a minute, indicated it was time to grab all the gear and proceed on foot. A small 'stomp' through the wooded training area found them at a suitable site for Nathan to instruct as well as keeping the group comfortable. Intense training was planned for these men in the coming days: infantry minor tactics, patrolling and patrol formations, individual movement, arcs of fire, field signals, ambush, and counter ambush drills - on foot and vehicle, marrying up techniques, LUPs (lying up positions), CQB, camouflage and concealment, 'why things are seen', overwatch and the list went on... Most people would think this was too much for the group to handle over three days, and it certainly was a 'crash course' but from the very first discussion with Aleksey at the café, Nathan knew these men could handle it; they were incredibly smart and committed to driving the Russian invader, the dreaded 'Orc' from their lands. Let us not forget, these are the same people who 'weaponized' E-bikes and used the subtle stealth of these machines to creep up on Russian soldiers and obliterate them with anti-armour weapons. Nathan thought it was better to flood their minds with crucial knowledge, each man in turn would remember so many elements but as a collective they were a *walking and talking military library!*

To get his message across, Nathan employed his usual 'explain, demonstrate, imitate training method that was 'tried and tested.' In addition, he utilised a small set of plastic soldiers, tiny cars, mud models, and even small firecrackers to simulate training and to further connect with the multiple senses of the trainees. He walked and talked the group through each drill until they could act faster, each time, while ensuring their leader was confident with the drills and the strategic mindset connected with the tactics. 'Always employ the "one foot on the ground" principle,' Nathan would repeatedly drill into them and 'if all else fails listen to your head and your gut feeling. *Always* have a plan A, B and C and makes sure *everyone knows the plans.'*

For the most part, the group valued Nathan's teaching techniques, his sound knowledge base and sense of humour, but there is always 'one' in the group *who thinks they know more...* Vyktor was a member of the film crew, but Nathan wasn't all that sure what his role there was...'gopher', 'dogs' body', whatever... but he turned out to be a bloody nuisance. He seemed to query every method or added an alternative scheme to the training but wasn't much good when it came to carrying out the most basic of drills. As Nathan diplomatically pointed out to the entire group, without singling out Vyktor, he was giving them a 'toolbox' of tactics and 'milskills' and it was up to them which tool or skill they needed to utilise to deal with a situation.... the men had to be flexible, not rigid in mindset, like their Soviet counterparts. Pick the appropriate tool to do the job.... *simple*!

The 'spec ops' training was built up slowly over the three days to illustrate to the men what they were capable of, either on foot or fighting from vehicles. When the last drills had been completed with perfection and Aleksey was running his team like a seasoned battlefield commander, Nathan knew he had achieved what he set out to do - *he even had goosebumps* during the final drills because the guys were so good, and he was ecstatic that he could impart his knowledge in lifesaving skills, 'battlefield survivability'. He congratulated them all with a morale patch with the 'Punisher Skull' motif as a symbol of their completion of the course and their identification as a team! They took the obligatory selfie travelled back to a renowned Kyiv restaurant for pizza and beer and to thank Nathan for the valuable instruction. *Two days later, the film crew were deployed to the 'front'...*

Later that night, Nathan called his old mate Phil to see how he was going since leaving Ukraine. It sounded as though all was not lost with his marriage and they were giving reconciliation a go; lawyers had been put on hold, he'd had moved back in with his wife and made lots of other positive changes in his life. Nathan was buoyed that his best mate sounded so happy and was improving his circumstances. That was such a pleasant and heart-warming surprise and Nathan was relieved that he wasn't still in Ukraine.

Chapter Fifty-Two:

DEUS EX MACHINA

Arranging a meeting was difficult as Steve wasn't trusting of his old friend and was suspicious as to why he had been pursuing him all over Europe. Garen had passed on brief details and reassured Steve that was just a catch up between two mates and said Nathan only wanted to talk, but Nathan's presence in Ukraine outraged Steve and he went off on a rant, '*What the fuck does he think he's doing following me over here, he's not my goddamn mother!! I bet that bitch Kathy is behind this! Those two were always thick as thieves...*' It had taken all Garen's charm and serious persuasion to cajole a resentful Steve into a friendly meeting.

Nathan wondered what he would be like when they met, what his state of mind be like... Many years had passed since the old friends had seen each other face to face, and Steve had clearly been going through a lot to leave his marriage, and he would have gone through a great deal more since being in Ukraine.

As a departure from character, Nathan was running

late for a quick catch up with Garen before for the 'old mates' meeting. He needed to move fast and the brisk walk along Khreshchatyk Avenue to the 'Friendship Arch' was extremely pleasant in the early evening of an exceptionally sunny Kyiv day. Visitors were either eyeing the city views, experiencing the 'sky deck' or partaking of the ambiance of the surrounding greenery. A week had just passed since Ukraine's Independence Day when the whole road past Midon Square had been blocked off with charred and rusted Soviet tanks, armoured carriers, like BMPs and BTRs and some recovery vehicles. There had been loud folk and modern music playing, flag waving and gaiety, and the streets were crammed with onlookers, young and old, examining the ruins of Russian military power. Would or could such a display of victory over an enemy ever happen at Federation Square, Melbourne, on Australia Day - *certainly not!* Nathan would never forget this unusual sight or the seven air raids that occurred on Independence night.

Garen was casually lounging on the concrete seating at the sizable amphitheater facing the arched bridge, savouring a lime gelato he had purchased from one of the nearby food and beverage stalls, which dotted the picturesque botanical precinct. He noticed Nathan approaching and threw out a quick 'Forest Gump' wave. As he arrived, Garen stood, and trying not to spill his gelato over Nathan, they greeted each other with a hand grasp, a slight embrace and solid pat of the back. 'Good to see ya, Nathan,' Garen cheerfully said. Although it had been less than a week, Nathan had forgotten how he had missed his friend's Texas drawl and positive demeanor, he smiled and replied, 'Yeah, great to see you, old friend, how're you keeping?' The two men concentrated on some small talk for a while, about home and some of the other guys they knew, like Bill and Sascha, until Garen brought the conversation back to the matter at hand, wanting to make sure Nathan was ready for what was about to happen.

The meeting place was in a text that had been sent to Garen and he fumbled through the various messages he had received until he found it. 'Steve stipulated he wanted to meet in an open area, and we know that's all for safety reasons and to negate giving you the opportunity to drag him into a car and take him home by force.' Nathan nodded his head in understanding as both men knew this would be true if the situation arose, but it was frustrating as hell to be in circumstances where he finally located his old friend but was now, seemingly powerless to rescue him, *from himself.* How Nathan was going to explain all this to Kathy, *he wasn't sure what he would say...*

The *Bolt* driver opted for the route that took them close to the central train station in Kyiv and then headed down south to the *Ocean Mall.* The traffic was particularly heavy this morning and the route seemed to meander all over the place. The monumental Red *Star column* that acknowledged those who valiantly died during *World War Two* was passed by, down along the congested thoroughfare. The driver decided to traverse off the highway and soon they passed the *Protasiv Yar* indoor snow centre, which took the men by surprise. 'Fuck! Is this the *Beatles Magical Mystery Tour* or what?' commented Nathan, boisterously and angrily as he looked at Garen, who was also showing concern at the curious route they were on. Suddenly, the driver spoke as best he could and sensed his passengers weren't all that happy. 'Don't vorry', in heavy, broken English, 'I take back streets, save you plenty time, plenty money, okay?' and he gestured to the men with a big thumbs up and cheesy smile while spying them nervously via his dash mirror. In another ten minutes the car arrived at the mall and dropped the two annoyed men off. Needless to say, the driver didn't receive a tip or a rewarding comment on the *Bolt* app... They would rendezvous at the food court. Although most of the malls and shopping centres were open during the conflict, patronage was drastically down. Garen and Nathan walked toward the entrance as a slow stream of people came and went from the main doors; soon they were facing the food court which housed all the major food brands; *Kentucky Fried Chicken* was open, but *McDonalds* had closed all their stores in Ukraine early in the war, and were still shut, much to the annoyance of many a Westerner.

Nathan quickly scanned the massive food eating court and sitting area and spotted Steve positioned on the far side of the hall. He had adopted the 'gunfighter' seat position, having no doors or entrances behind or near him, except a towering concrete wall. Anyone that approached, friend or foe, had to confront him head on. Nathan put on a warm smile when he saw his old mate, but the gesture wasn't reciprocated. He ignored this snub and sauntered over to the table where Steve was sitting with two, exceptionally large Ukrainian lads. One of the men was dressed in jeans and a tight-fitting T-shirt, wore various tattoos, some of which displayed the *Azov* motif, swastikas, *Totenkopf* death heads and other anti-social brands. He had a chiselled face and scarred bald head that *only a mother could love...* Both men were around six feet in height, muscled up, 'tough' looking and frightfully ready in their dark, three-quarter length leather jackets, jeans, steel toed work boots and unshaven faces. As a pair, their features looked like they had taken some 'serious hits' over the years but were still around and handsome enough to suggest they could dish out the punishment without taking too many blows in return. Minders, bodyguards, whatever you want to call them... They were there for Steve's protection. *That was obvious...*

Within seconds, Nathan and Garen were standing at the table. Steve slowly rose from his seat and offered a limp-wristed handshake to Nathan. No hugs, 'hi, glad to see ya' or anything demonstrating any affection or exuberance at seeing a dear, old friend. Picking up on the serious discord, Garen chose to utter a flat 'hello' to Steve. All he received in return was a cursory nod. By anyone's estimation, *this was not a great start to the meeting!* The newcomers sat across from Steve, and Nathan spoke first, in a positive tone. 'Mate, I am so glad you're alive. We have so much to chinwag about... I'm only over here because Kathy was so worried, she hadn't heard from you in ages. It has been such a long trip trying to locate you... When do you think you'll be making the trip home?' What came next astonished both Nathan and Garen. Steve let forth a tirade of abuse upon the two men... '*Well, nobody asked you travel all over Ukraine... I'm not a fucking five-year-old, I can do what I like...* Kathy doesn't care, *it's all a fucking act.* It has been for years, *especially when I found out...*' Before the last barbed comment leapt from his tongue, he cut short his raving instantly and abruptly mid-sentence, choosing, instead to furnish his 'old cobber' with a cold, steely gaze... as if there was an underlying issue or hatred between the two, lurking and seething under the surface... Judging by his attitude and dogged resistance, Steve had been affected by something, and not just the war...he had drastically changed from the Steve of old...

Nathan was of the opinion Steve *did* sound '*like a fucking five-year-old*' by the way he was acting but thought best not to argue. No need to inflame the delicate situation any further... Let the 'cranky old man' vent and he would be more open to discussion once the gripe was off his chest. Nonetheless, the atmosphere was incredibly tense, so *Nathan gave it thirty seconds or so before it was his turn...* He inquired, with a measure of sarcasm, 'So, you're not coming home, is that it... you're gonna live out your days in happy, sunny, magical Ukraine, with cheap harlots and these gangsters?' The 'gangster' jibe did not fall on deaf Ukrainian ears and the two aggressive men sat bolt upright and looked like they were just about to leap across the table! Well, that was overstepping the mark, but *the truth had to be told!* Steve raised an open palmed hand, in a 'stop' motion and the two 'hard' lads relaxed, but they certainly weren't smiling.

Despite the obvious friction, Nathan continued to question Steve's motives. 'So, you're gonna throw your lot in with this bunch? I know we're both to the right politically but, seriously, fascists? *How do you think this is all gonna end up?'* Steve waited for Nathan's words to sink in and then shouted, defiantly, *'I'd rather be a fascist than a communist any day!* At least the fascists have an entrepreneurial, national, and cultural spirit, unlike the commies who want to change, convert, control and manipulate every facet of your life! Don't you understand what's going on here? If we don't halt communist expansionism right now, *where will it end?* It's the Darwinian model, the strongest survive and the weak perish! You and the rest of the West need to get your heads out of your arses and see that the commies are on the move. It's Putin now and before long the Chinese Reds will be marching through Taiwan and down into South Korea and onto Australia. *Remember the Domino Principle?* Tell me, Nathan, you haven't forgotten that history lesson so soon?' The saga continued... 'The political left, their gangs and their human filth will rise through the shitholes of this world, like South America, Asia, and Africa and before you know it, *there will be pitched battles...* in Sydney's George Street or running gun fights down Melbourne's Flinders Lane.'

Steve paused to take a couple of deep breaths then resumed the hateful diatribe. 'The leaders of the West have been corrupt, and pathetically impotent for decades, all tarred with the same cowardly brush. They bang on incessantly about green energy and indigenous social rights, but it is all a smoke screen, a means of destroying the past and the history of the people who built the country that is now inhabited by the self-interested, the disaffected, or race traitors, all filling their grubby pockets and setting them and their families up for generational wealth at everyone else's expense!' His gaze was fixed at Nathan as he quietly spoke, 'Is that who you are now, Nathan, *a fucking race traitor too?* Another "whitey" that has sold out?' He continued his verbal barrage... 'Our useless government and supposed leaders are no different than the Bolsheviks, Taliban, or Isis. Just look at Australia, it is totally unrecognizable to the country we grew up in. You let peasants like this in and it is tantamount to a greedy fox in the chicken coup, *they take all and destroy everything...*' Nathan took in a depth breath and knew Steve was at least right with this national assessment. 'Man, had the country changed...' Steve went on... 'To think all those Diggers died for Australia, and for what? A country that has sold itself out to the highest bidder – *fucking China!!* At least these boys in Ukraine aren't going to let anyone roll over them without a fight. His voice went up another notch... If *World War Three* is to start here, this is where I want to be. Remember, we did sign up to fight the scourge of communism, to fight for democracy and freedom!! Bloody hell, *I'm only thirty years late...*'

While all this heated rhetoric came as a surprise, Nathan knew no amount of arguing would change Steve's conviction to remain in Ukraine and he was dismayed by his old friend's hedonistic outrage. His association with this ultra-right crowd had been his 'come to Jesus' moment and there was now little hope he could be saved... Steve was swimming hard against the 'tide of common sense' and decency. Up until now, Garen hadn't said anything, but it was obvious to Nathan he wasn't impressed with Steve's decision or his wacky, far right extremism. Garen was a Jewish convert and had no time for fascists and their Nazi-like methods. He spoke in his familiar, likeable drawl, but was losing patience and unloaded his frustration upon Steve, *'Hey man, where do you get off being so high and mighty? And where did you get these stupid ideas from, out of your ass?* Your buddy has risked his life, multiple times, and along with a group of us, we have suffered bucketloads to get you on a goddamn plane back home. *Don't be such an asshole!'* Garen's voice rose, and he could be heard above the din of the customers in the packed food court. *'If we have to drag you home, then so be it...'*

For a big man, Garen could move surprisingly quick,

and he reached around the side of the table and clutched Steve's arm. Probably not the smartest thing Garen had ever done, as the two Ukrainian 'heavies' leapt forward in defence, as if they had been sitting on coiled, tensioned springs. 'Mr. Baldy', who had massive hands, *like big, knurled knots from a tree*, threw a flurry of heavy punches at the equally large Texan, who took most of the hits on his upper arms and retaliated with a couple of telling shots to the side of the man's head. He stumbled back, slightly groggy, shook himself afresh and renewed the attack, much to Garen's disbelief! Surmising that Nathan was in on this ambitious move, the second man rose to his feet and threw a series of martial arts kicks and punches at Nathan, who parried the weighty blows and kept moving about, to make himself a harder target. *These weren't 'fairy taps' that were being thrown at Garen or Nathan!* All the while, Steve was attempting to restore the peace by yelling at his escort to stand down, but this fell on deaf ears. Customers in the food court took off, startled, while other patrons looked on in bewilderment, surprised at how abruptly the commotion began, not unlike large, powerful dogs who, with seemingly little or no provocation, are quick to attack.

Meanwhile... a small, rusting container ship in the Black Sea came to 'full stop' on the engine order telegraph on the ship's bridge, yet its throbbing engines and edgy crew were military alert, ready to leap into immediate action. 'No moon tonight... good, very good' thought the seasoned Captain, as he nervously paced the bridge, staring outwards into the obscure night from every possible window. As the ship lolled and rolled with the slapping waves, 'twitchy' lookouts kept a close vigil with worn binoculars and night vision devices as they didn't want to be set upon by swift Ukrainian patrol boats or the murderous, deadly drone watercraft. At the same time, on the wet and greasy deck, three 3M-14T Russian cruise missiles were being hastily readied, to be launched from three mock shipping containers, where they had been skillfully and deceptively hidden. Soon, the firing preparations were complete and less than thirty seconds later, the Captain barked a series of curt orders and the ear-splitting *'WHOOSH,' 'WHOOSH,' 'WHOOSH* sound of powerful rocket engines engulfed the ship and the temperate night air as a trio of deadly missiles were launched; smoke billowed from the firing cannisters while lengthy plumes of yellow flame trailed behind as the missiles blasted upward and then gradually realigned their course to pulverize an unsuspecting target, somewhere in Kyiv... Without further delay or hesitation, the captain yelled, *'Three quarter speed!!'* and for the helmsman to come about, and he did so... *hard and fast!!*

In less than a minute, twenty seconds in fact, the smallish, corroding vessel rapidly picked up speed and soon propelled itself through a light swell and into the assumed safety of a thickening, rolling fog and the night's unyielding blackness; a nocturnal gloom, impenetrably dark and unforgiving as the sin just perpetrated against

Ukrainian humanity, by the nervous Russian Captain and his dutiful crew...

A mighty siren began to wail, and then a second, ear splitting siren erupted, causing screaming diners and patrons to discard their meals and shopping, and frantically scramble for the exits, with their loved ones in tow... *The sirens grew louder and shrieked*, and *the public kept running and running*... but the early attack warning notification didn't discourage the two aggressive Ukrainians in their sustained attack upon the Westerners. While he bobbed and weaved from an eruption of fierce blows, Nathan heard the first thundering impact of the Russian cruise missile, around three hundred metres away, a break of two to four seconds followed and then the second strike plummeted into the shopping mall, at its outer building perimeter. *'Oh... shit and disaster...'* he worriedly thought to himself, seriously anticipating the worst! *The noise was deafening*, like nothing he had ever heard or could imagine, the floor trembled, tiles cracked and heaved, windows shattered, and he was unable to hear himself think... Nathan *never heard the third strike...*

The last deadly missile nearly landed upon them, but hit the other side of the shopping mall, two hundred metres away, but still the men were blown off their feet from their upright fighting stances and a wave of intense heat surged through the once packed food court; the sort of instant feeling of searing temperature when a hand is immersed into a very, very hot oven to remove a pie! Those customers too slow to escape or unable to seek adequate cover were thrust against the windows of shops - either cut to shreds, decapitated, or mangled as the numerous shop front windows made from huge plate glass. Almost immediately thereafter, the sounds of moaning and then shrills of screaming began but for many of the casualties, who now lay bleeding and dying on the floor, their days of communication were at an end...

The two Ukrainian heavies lay motionless on the floor, with blood oozing and streaming from a myriad of deep lacerations and wounds; 'Mr. Baldy' was missing a left leg, cleanly severed, up high past his knee... his femoral artery dynamically squirted, unabated, until he quickly bled out and died, without regaining consciousness. His cohort lay motionless, stoney pale, and unconscious, bleeding from a maze of shrapnel wounds and his breathing was deathly shallow ... *He was not long for this world, either...* Garen was swathed in 'crap and corruption,' but on the face of it, he was coming to and attempting to ascertain what had happened and was slowly righting himself; he had only been knocked out for an instant and had avoided the flying splinters and metal fragments. For him, the luck of the draw was on his side, and *he would not die this night... But not everyone was so lucky...* Nathan had been violently upended, spun about and cartwheeled across the food court and lay, on the mucky, debris strewn floor, with a sizeable part of the shopping mall roof resting upon him. He was cognisant but couldn't move and wasn't sure if he was injured...

Of all the combatants, it was Steve who was minus any injuries and had appeared to right himself quickly after the attack. It always seems to be the way for the troublemakers... He shook a load of heavy dust off, and rushed over and gave Garen a vigorous jiggle to see if he was alert and then proceeded to help pick the man up, bruised and slightly battered by the explosion. In the process of assisting the Texan, he glanced across at his two former Ukrainian friends and knew they were beyond help... *Notwithstanding the likelihood of another missile attack,* Steve and Garen noticed the wall that had shielded Steve's back was now severely damaged, teetering and shimmying and looking like it would rain down at any time... *They needed to move fast, remove the debris, and drag Nathan to safety.*

Small fires now erupted around the shattered food court as gas cookers had been compromised, further adding to the danger. Black pungent smoke began to slowly fill the area while the wounded walked, hobbled, or crawled toward the entrances; sirens wailed in the distance. For Steve, he could see the wall was starting to creak and to sway, and he raced over to lift debris off Nathan, who by now was starting to regain his senses. Steve joked, *'I'm always getting you out of the shit. Getting a bit tired of this, you know?'* 'Yeah,' said Nathan, *'it never ends.'* The men worked fast, like seasoned emergency service veterans... By now Garen had moved to a half-kneeling position from where he could pull Nathan's jacket from under his arms and was waiting for Steve to give him the go ahead when all was clear. *'One more beam should do it...'* A weighty steel frame and some plaster rubble was raised... *All clear!!* Garen gave an almighty yank under the armpits of his friend and Nathan slid across the floor like he was a bedside rug; *such was the strength of the big man!*

Steve knew he had no time left, he could hear the bricks and mortar cracking and shearing behind him but was now tangled in some of the debris he had just released Nathan from. He spoke quickly, in a rush of words... *'Take care of our son, you silly bastard, you better....'* And before he could voice his last utterance, the heaving wall collapsed in one fell swoop, as if it had been technically detonated. The tonnes of rubble and a section of the roof it was supporting came cascading down upon Steve, who was now engulfed by whitish, grey dust and acrid smoke. Both Garen and Nathan, who were only five metres from the destruction could only stare in mute disbelief, as Steve had been there one second and now irretrievably lost... His old friend had saved Nathan, *had bailed him out,* and was his 'true' self in his final moments, but had also left him with a cryptic message he was already attempting to comprehend... But now, Steve 'Dutchy' Holland, his old army mate, was no more and would remain forever in Ukraine, his new beloved home, *just as he had wished...*

Chapter Fifty-Three:

ELVIS HAS LEFT THE BUILDING

It had been four months, thousands of kilometres, a bout of pneumonia and so many near brushes with death... Nathan had only succumbed to a few bumps, grazes and bruises from the rocket attack and was nursing some minor cuts. He was lucky... unlike others, *he would get over this...* Now, it was time to go home. A late-night phone call had been made to Kathy and while it wasn't what Nathan had promised her, there was unmitigated relief in her trembling voice that this whole saga could now, like Steve, be laid to rest. *She cried... and cried...* but these were the tears of finality, of a closure to a sadness that recognized Steve's 'fractured soul' had been lost, many years before and now the loss was final. Kathy could now begin to plan a future and move on... For Nathan, he almost couldn't believe he was travelling home, and alone! It had been a protracted and arduous journey over many months and now he was feeling dead tired, and distinctly older. The lustre of Ukraine, especially Kyiv, was not diminished by the recent circumstances with Steve Holland. Nathan took one last look at Kyiv's magnificence and mentally prepared himself for the lengthy journey home. Although not religious, but more a spiritual man, Nathan made the walk to St. Michael's monastery, lit a prayer candle and prayed to St. Michael, the Archangel and Protector of Kyiv to keep the people safe; his wish also was to return some day.

After saying his goodbyes to many good friends, he was now waiting at Kyiv's central railway station with Garen. The station's splendor and beauty was in keeping with the best of any European railway structure. People came and went, hurriedly, as most do, and there was a security screening process, remarkably like the type you would find at any major airport. People examined books and magazines and children played as their parents chatted or sipped coffee. Fifty minutes later he was departing the station, *having hugged his dear friend, his old Texan mate, goodbye...* It would be a lengthy overnight trip, with the usual passing through small towns and villages, and most people attempting to sleep. Nathan also closed his eyes... Many hours later, near the border, Ukrainian police and military officials bordered and checked documents. It seemed Nathan's passport hadn't been properly stamped on his way into the country but after displaying his numerous documents and commendations from the Ukraine military and explaining he had been providing combat and TCCC training, the officer was satisfied and left him alone. *No time to sleep, anymore...*

The train sluggishly pulled into the station at Prezemsyl at around five in the morning, just under an hour later. Nathan passed through customs quickly and inquired with a few taxi drivers about the price to Krakow by cab. However, these drivers bandied about ridiculous fares in outrageous sums of Euros. 'Forget that' thought Nathan and he shuffled his way along the damp pedestrian tunnels, beneath the railway line, to the ticket office. *Well, no surprise here*, the place was flooded with potential travellers and the line to the ticket windows meandered out the door...as it had been doing for months! Nathan looked about and identified a Westerner and asked the young man what he knew about the train schedules, if the next train was going to Krakow and when he could get a ticket. *The news wasn't good...* The ticket window wouldn't be open for some time and the train to Krakow wasn't leaving for a long time either, and it would take three or more hours to get there. *'Screw that'* Nathan thought, and he immediately walked out to the front of the station, remembering where he, Bill, Phil, Garen, the British father and daughter and Sascha had stood so many months ago. Now, that image felt surreal; new friends huddled together, at night, in the wet car park. He shook himself from his thoughts... and looked around... surprisingly, the area was devoid of all travellers and vehicles, *except one.* A silver BMW five series was waiting at the head of the taxi rank, on its own, with the driver reading the local paper. Nathan stuck his head into the window and inquired how much it would cost to travel to Krakow. The startled driver responded: '260 Euro', to which Nathan replied, '200 Euro'. The driver tried again, '220 Euro'. *'Done,'* snapped Nathan and the driver got out and placed Nathan's rucksack in the trunk of his car. Nathan was exhausted and didn't need the BS of waiting for a train and he planned to sleep in the cab and arrive in Krakow early so he could check in and freshen up. Fatigue was hounding him now and no matter how much he slept he woke up tired; drained in the way he felt years ago when he was diagnosed with *chronic fatigue syndrome. He sure as hell didn't want to get that debilitating condition again...* Before he set off on his journey home, he had contacted Marcus who furnished him with contact details of operatives along the way, especially in Helsinki and Singapore, the two main stops on the long flight. He knew he would be fine.

Now, his pressing thoughts were with Krakow. He always broke things down into manageable segments and his focus of attention needed to deal with his present situation. Soon, he had his comfortable room, situated in the old 'Jewish Quarter' of the city and made for easy walking to the centre square and nearby shopping; he also decided to visit the *Oskar Schindler Museum* as he had two days to kill before his flight. Nathan appreciated the history of the old castle city and enjoyed walking around its environs. The time flew by so quickly... Before he knew it, he was sitting in the departure lounge at the Krakow international airport, waiting for his boarding call. Soon he ambled aboard the sleek and exceptionally clean airliner and was bound for Helsinki. The flight was pleasant enough and he was able to view the various waterways that surround Finland on his approach to the airport. His stay here was only a few hours, and soon enough he was on his way to Singapore.

Nathan managed to get quite a deal of sleep on the next leg of his flight and his stay there was only for an hour or so. *But transiting always feels longer...* On his final leg home, a young French girl sat in the seat by the window next to him. The cabin crew started their dull spiel on several 'touchy-feely' themes, such as the perfunctory 'welcome to country' message and the need to respect all those aboard the flight. Nathan turned the young French girl, who was travelling to Australia on a working visa, looked deeply into her eyes and sincerely said, but jokingly, 'My name is Nathan, I respect you, do you respect me?' The young pretty girl had a competent grasp of English but was not sure about Nathan's cynicism and eye rolling at the banal announcements. For Nathan, he respected people as he found them and by the quality of their actions and character and not by their haughty proclamations or inflated egos and didn't believe in mock, enforced respect. *By his estimation, you have to earn respect, we all do!* Not just because of who you think you are or where you may have come from or whether you happened to be here before someone else. Otherwise, the concept becomes fake, tokenistic, and you may as well include it in a cereal box, for mundane consumption along with the bran! Anyway, the French girl thought the display 'amusing' and settled herself in for the eight-hour journey.

They were on their approach to Melbourne. Nathan had managed to doze a little for most of the trip and didn't bother with a meal as his choice of beef had been the number one pick by the other passengers and he had missed out; all he was offered was a stale, *petit* bun, and a second-rate cup of tea. Wow, how had flying changed from the days when you could fly *Trans Australian Airlines* (TAA), or *Ansett Airlines* and the experience was special. Real cutlery, delicious food, and prompt service. 'Shit,' thought Nathan, *'And you want me to respect people for this, a crappy bun, and an overpriced fare?* Before he knew it, the airliner was descending through the grey, menacing clouds that perpetually exist above Melbourne.

In another forty minutes Nathan was strolling through customs with his luggage and about to head outside, into the bleak Victorian weather, to hail a cab. Out of the corner of his eye, he caught sight of Kathy, who in turn smiled gleefully at Nathan and waved frenetically. *This was a surprise!* Nathan had alerted Kathy of his flight plans but didn't expect anyone to meet him on his return as he always preferred to keep a low profile, *the veritable 'grey man'*... and this is how he liked it – no fuss or fanfare. Nathan was wearing his civvy rucksack and loosely carried a daypack in his left hand, he wheeled snappishly around the barrier that separated the incoming passengers and their family and friends, dodged a few people, and headed straight toward Kathy. His 'lover' from long ago hadn't changed all that much since the last time he saw her and was still as naturally beautiful as ever, never a need for makeup with this girl! She rushed over and gave Nathan a solid kiss on the lips and grabbed his empty right hand, tightly. He could see she had been crying but her semi-bloodshot eyes now displayed a playful twinkle and vivaciousness that he hadn't been privy to for many years. Kathy pleaded, 'let's go somewhere and have a chat?'

Nathan nodded his weary head, and together, they walked over to one of the over-priced *cafes* that flood *Tullamarine Airport*. They sat down and she swiftly put a solitary finger to his lips. 'Please, don't say anything, I have so much to confess, and I need *you to listen, for a change.* She *knew him so well...* Kathy went on to say how she could not thank Nathan enough for his efforts in attempting to drag Steve back to Australia. The rigours that Nathan and his friends must have endured had been *mind-blowing,* and their efforts were *simply amazing!* She would never forget their commitment *to such a lost cause*. Kathy continued... 'Our marriage was well over before Steve went on his crazy crusade to Ukraine. For him, it was a 'get out' clause as he didn't have the courage to seek help or be helped. I know he was your friend, but you didn't pick him for the coward he was.' Those heated, cutting words wounded Nathan so much that it felt like a slap! He attempted to respond... 'But...' --NO Nathan, YOU LISTEN TO ME... Kathy insisted but lowered her voice. 'Besides a failed marriage, it was also a sham... Young Nate is *our* son, not Steve's. It was all *my* fault, I was seeing Steve, before I left you, but you didn't know... You thought you introduced us but he we were both doing the 'dirty' on you before we split up, and I know young Nate is your son. As you had just left for your sniper's course when I found out I was pregnant, I didn't know what to do and I didn't want it all to come out and hurt you and it was not the time to be a single mother! Steve found out the truth about Nate only a year or so ago... he overheard me confessing to my sister. *To be honest, I'm a coward as well.'*

Kathy now felt emotionally empty but felt cleansed from discharging a litany of dreadful sins.... she had nothing else to say... and drooped her head in sad resignation of what she had just painfully declared. It was so obvious the 'torch' that she had burned for her husband had been extinguished long ago and judging by Steve's zest for self-destructive behaviour, he was never going to change or *'make old bones'*. Now, it was time for Nathan to speak, to announce *his* declarations... 'I know all about *our* young Nate,' he replied. 'This was the last thing Steve told me... *before...* and Garen could see the resemblance, but I couldn't... *I just didn't want to believe... but I accept it all now...completely!'* Nathan's humble testimony was more than a revelation, in fact it acted as a thunderclap to

Kathy... her head snapped to attention, and she just stared lovingly at her old *beau* in complete awe... Nathan was surprised when they broke up, unexpectedly, but now the facts were bare and incontrovertible.

'So,' said Kathy 'Is there anything else I can tell you, can you ever forgive me... *what else do I need to do to make this right?*' A sustained, silent break ensued after all that had been discussed and the couple just stared at one another across the table. Now was not the time for recriminations...There had been a great deal of soul searching in Ukraine over the last months and Nathan wanted to move forward; from the trappings of his childhood, the military and the life that didn't turn out the way he thought it should... As Nathan had always repeatedly stated, *'Life is all about having curve balls thrown at you...'* and here was his proof, yet again. He saw, constantly, the crippling damage that festered in many of his old army mates and didn't want to live, die, or be remembered like that, *like them...*

Fortunately, the passage of time had softened the numerous physical and psychological hits he had endured over the years. *Time to move on... Time to be different... Time for something new and a phase for forgiveness...* Kathy wasn't expecting any latitude from Nathan. She couldn't blame him if he stood up *and flatly walked out!* He looked down from their mutual gaze, at the table's black laminex top for a moment, and his half-drunk coffee, which was still, slightly steaming... *His mind was racing... he attempted to slow his thoughts...* Nathan didn't feel the need to utter a syllable but nonchalantly swept some spilt sugar off the countertop, with the back of his right hand. *Seconds ticked by...* and he could sense the tension building in Kathy... He then raised his head so very purposefully and announced, *'I'd like to be your good friend again,* for a start, *if that's okay with you?* That's about all this tired, old 'boomer' can think of right now, but I'll have plenty to say later... *you can count on that.'* Kathy grinned broadly, respectfully chose not to comment but reached out and grabbed his old tanned, scarred, and wrinkly right hand. They just sat, incredibly quiet, and very still, with Nathan now softly caressing Kathy's hands. He occasionally sipped the cooled milky remnants of his 'overpriced' coffee for a while and this routine lasted... maybe *five... ten...* or *fifteen minutes,* while the annoying clamour of 'airport life' descended over them, but with negligible or perceptible impact. *Kathy and Nathan were off, somewhere else...* Now, this former couple had decided to cast aside their pained mutual trinity of guilt, suffering and loneliness; their meagre, slip of an embrace now bonded them physically, and mentally, and as they sat together.... they both pondered on lives that could have been... and now, wishfully speculating, *if not dreaming of a future together* and what this unexpected re-union, this exciting *genesis* in their relationship might bring...

The End

EPILOGUE

Imagine there's no countries
It isn't hard to do
Nothing to kill or die for
And no religion, too
Imagine all the people
Living life in peace...

John Lennon

At the completion of the writing of this novel, the war in Ukraine continues... It is now December 2023. Some of the characters vividly portrayed have returned home, many disillusioned with their experiences, while other individuals have found new roles in the Ukrainian military or in other humanitarian ways, all striving to contribute to a Ukrainian victory. Some characters have ventured back to the besieged nation, still eager to assist.

However, I personally know of a small group of men and women who would eagerly travel back to Eastern Europe, but it is only the lack of funds that prevent them from doing so. With much sadness, some of the men I met are now the casualties of war, destined to remain in

Ukraine or maimed forever... In my case, I believe there is nothing else I can contribute to the cause, and I feel it is now time to hang up my boots. Age has caught up with me and, as the classic 'Dirty Harry' line goes: *'A man's gotta know his limitations...'*

Still, I look back with fond memories of the tough training and crazy times, and the wonderful people I worked with and feel a sense of pride that we *did* make a difference by passing on our military knowledge and experiences and, more importantly, alerting the Ukrainians to the undeniable fact they were not alone in this fight. *The world had not abandoned them!* The importance of this global solidarity with the Ukrainian people has been repeated to me time and time again by dear Ukrainian friends. *They will never forget!*

From a military point of view, my association with various training teams was a resounding success and a remains a continual source of satisfaction. We trained because we decided to make a stand with Ukraine and sincerely believed that if only one Ukrainian soldier survived as a result of our instruction, *it was worth it!* Without doubt, I know we achieved this. On a personal level, I walk away from this massive conflict with formal commendations and medallic recognition from the higher echelons of the Ukraine military. For this, *I am deeply thankful and proud...* If nothing else, it is a profound statement of thanks from honest people who certainly appreciated our commitment, what we had to offer and our various contributions. I can only pray this conflict will end very soon and the daily suffering to so many lives, and I hope that I may be able to visit beautiful Ukraine, a country dear to my heart, blessed by amazing, resolute people in the unfettered tranquility of peacetime...

'Slava Ukraini, heroiam Slava!!'

'Glory to Ukraine, Glory to the Heroes!!'

Also by Vince Craig:

TRUTH
BE TOLD

'Truth be Told' is a work of fiction set in the Central Goldfields of Victoria and involves a major government conspiracy. A 'secret' is discovered by a gold prospector that entangles friends and foes in a battle of wits and dangerous encounters that take place in cities, country areas and the Australian outback.

A highly secretive government intelligence agency is tasked with burying the secret, which, if unearthed, could transform the socio-political climate of a nation, not to mention its strategic position in the world!

'Truth be Told' also focuses upon important underlying messages connected to temporary Australia, such as the significance of modern journalism in the construction and maintenance of the nation state, gender politics, and the highly secretive role government agencies take in maintaining the status quo.

Out now! Available at all major bookstores!